YVAIN
THE KNIGHT
OF THE LION

M. T. ANDERSON
BASED ON THE TWELFTH-CENTURY EPIC
BY CHRÉTIEN DE TROYES

◆

ILLUSTRATED BY
ANDREA OFFERMANN

CANDLEWICK PRESS

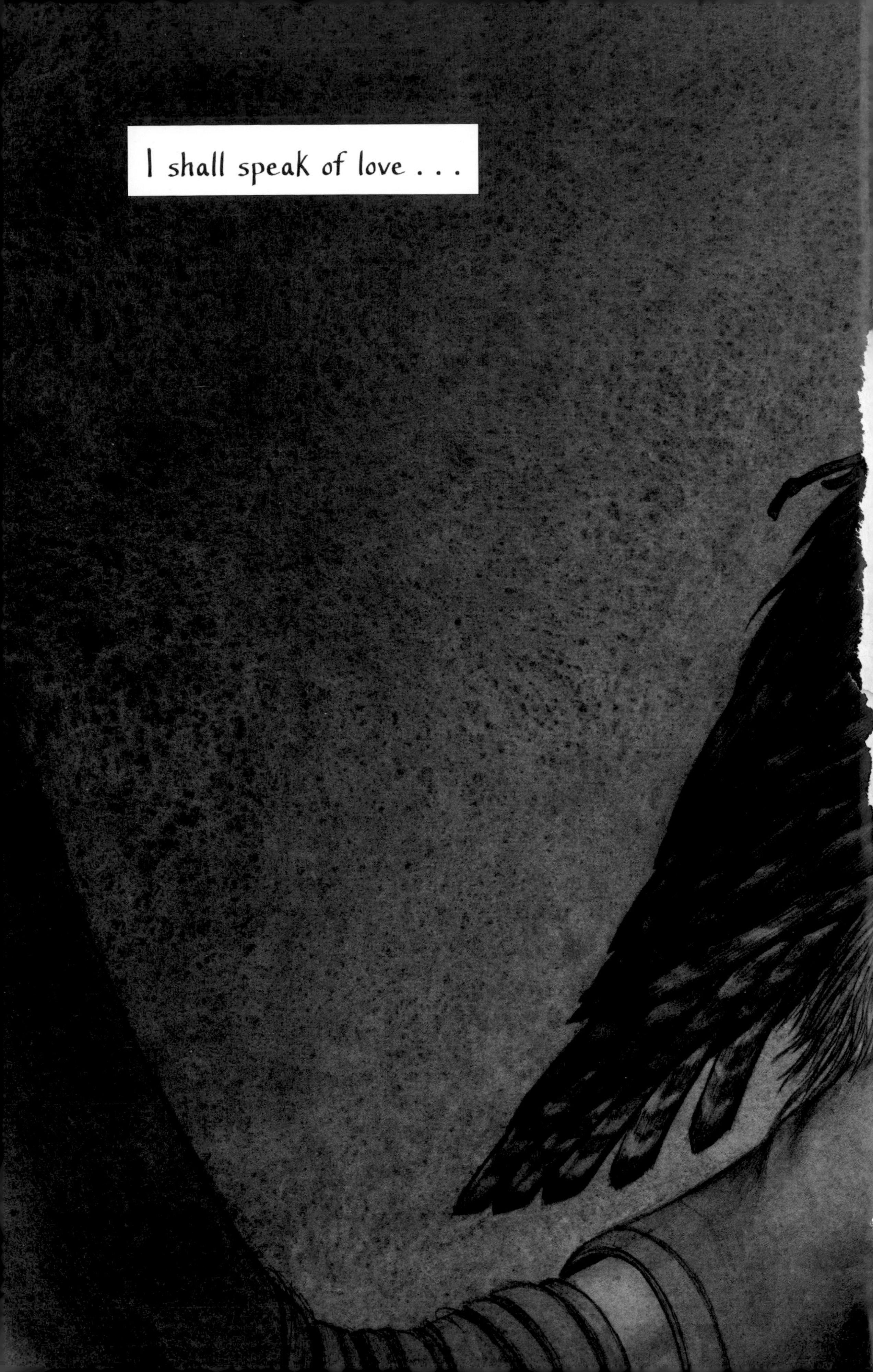
I shall speak of love . . .

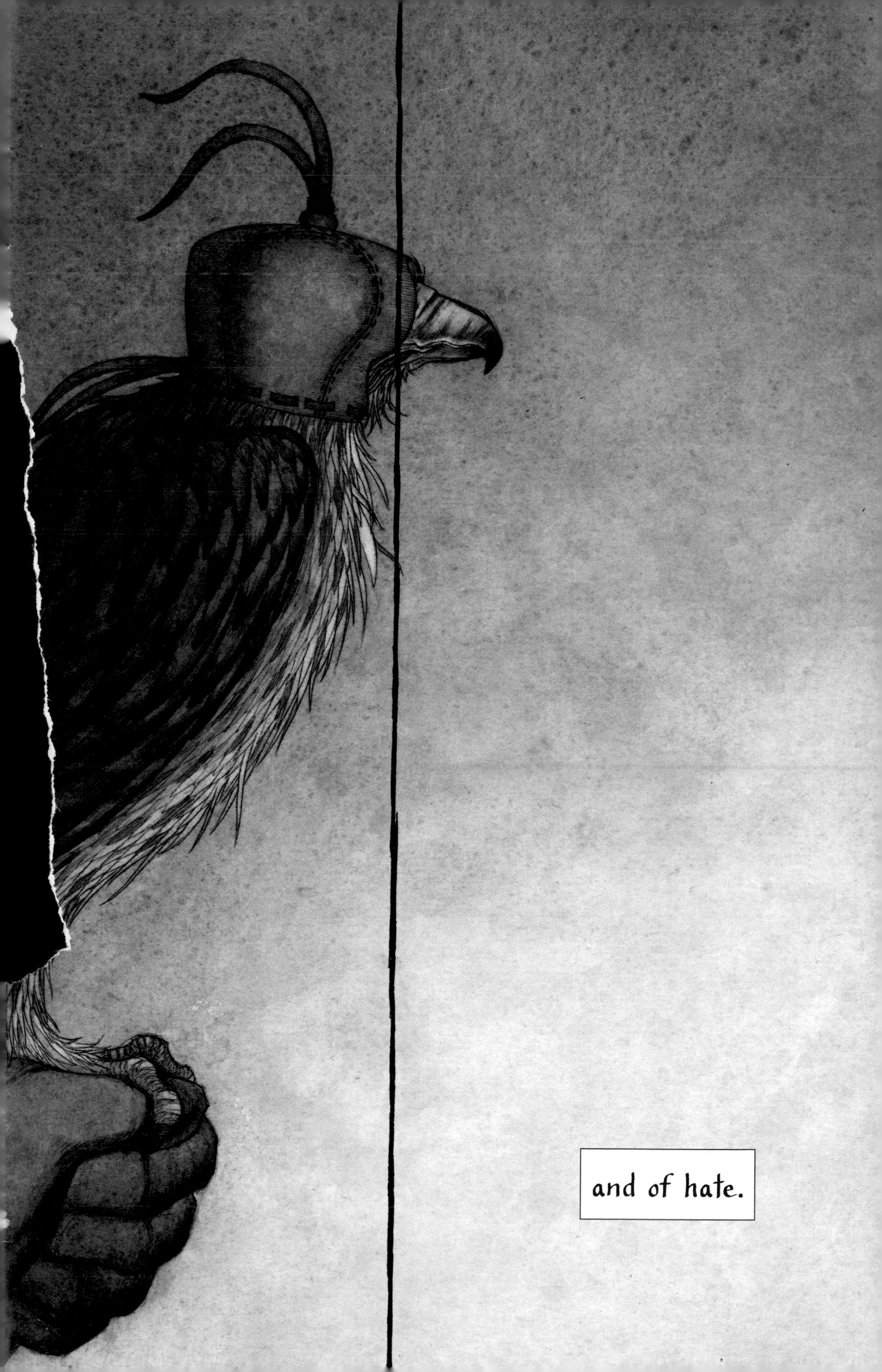
and of hate.

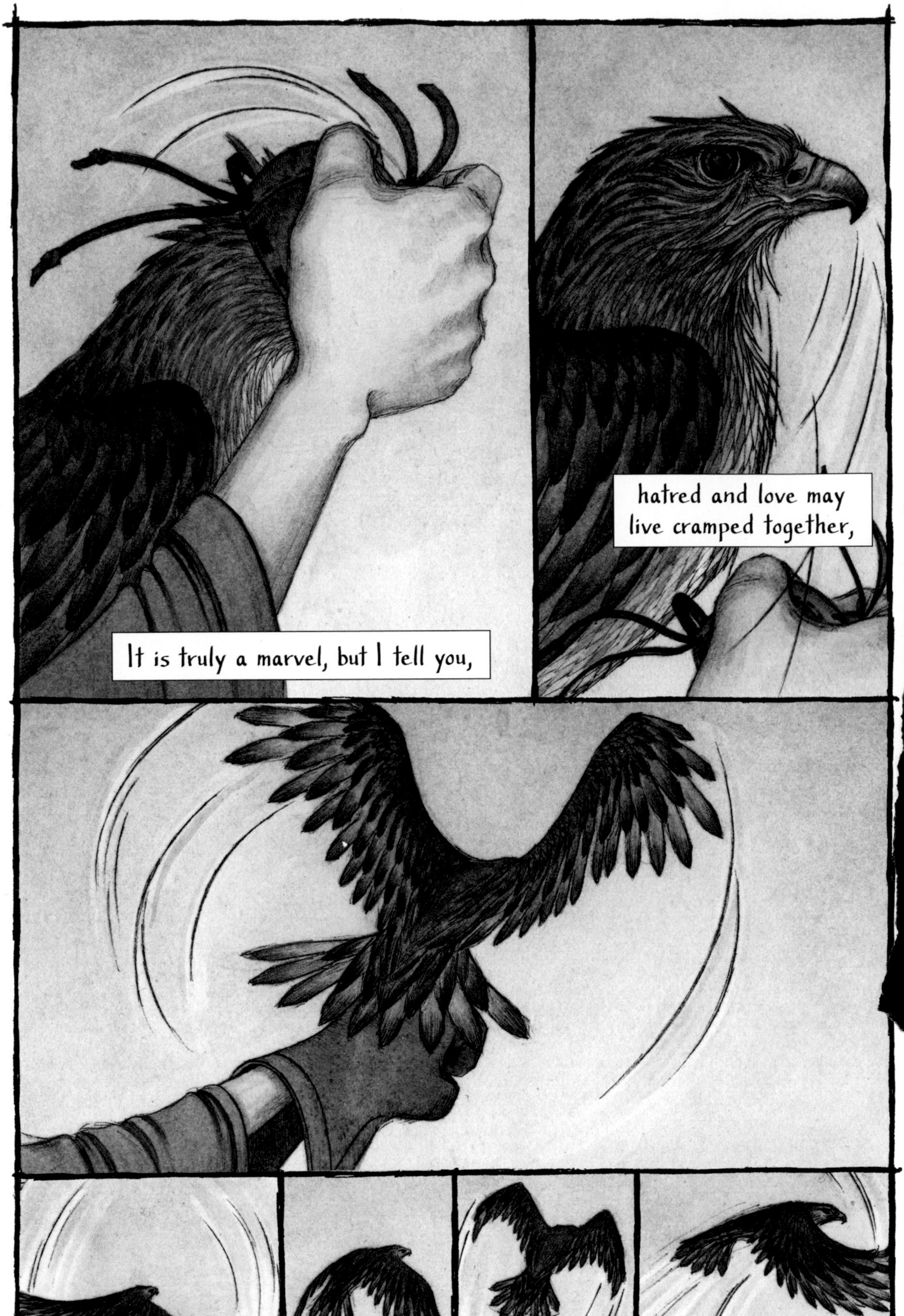
It is truly a marvel, but I tell you,
hatred and love may live cramped together,

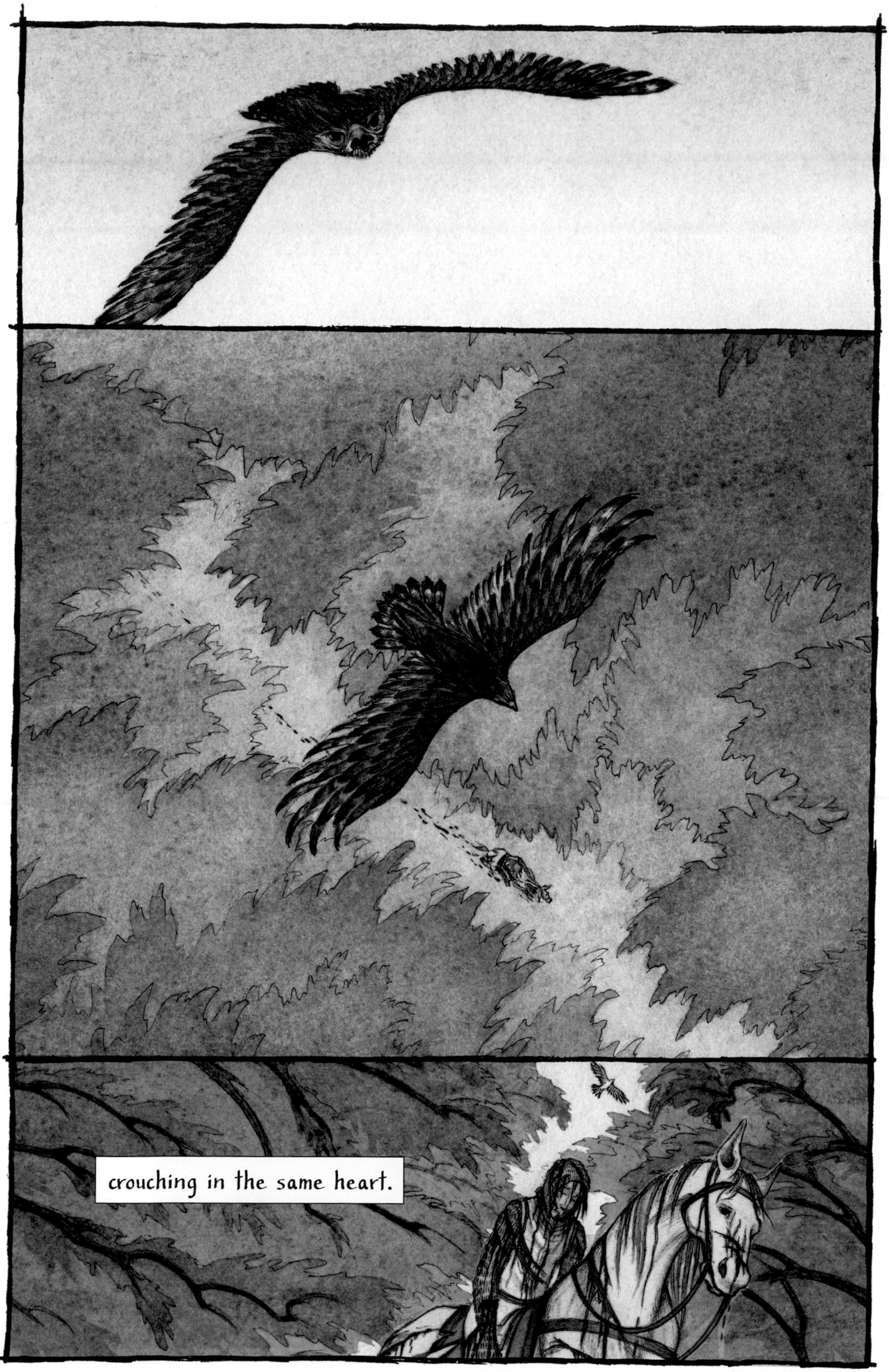
crouching in the same heart.

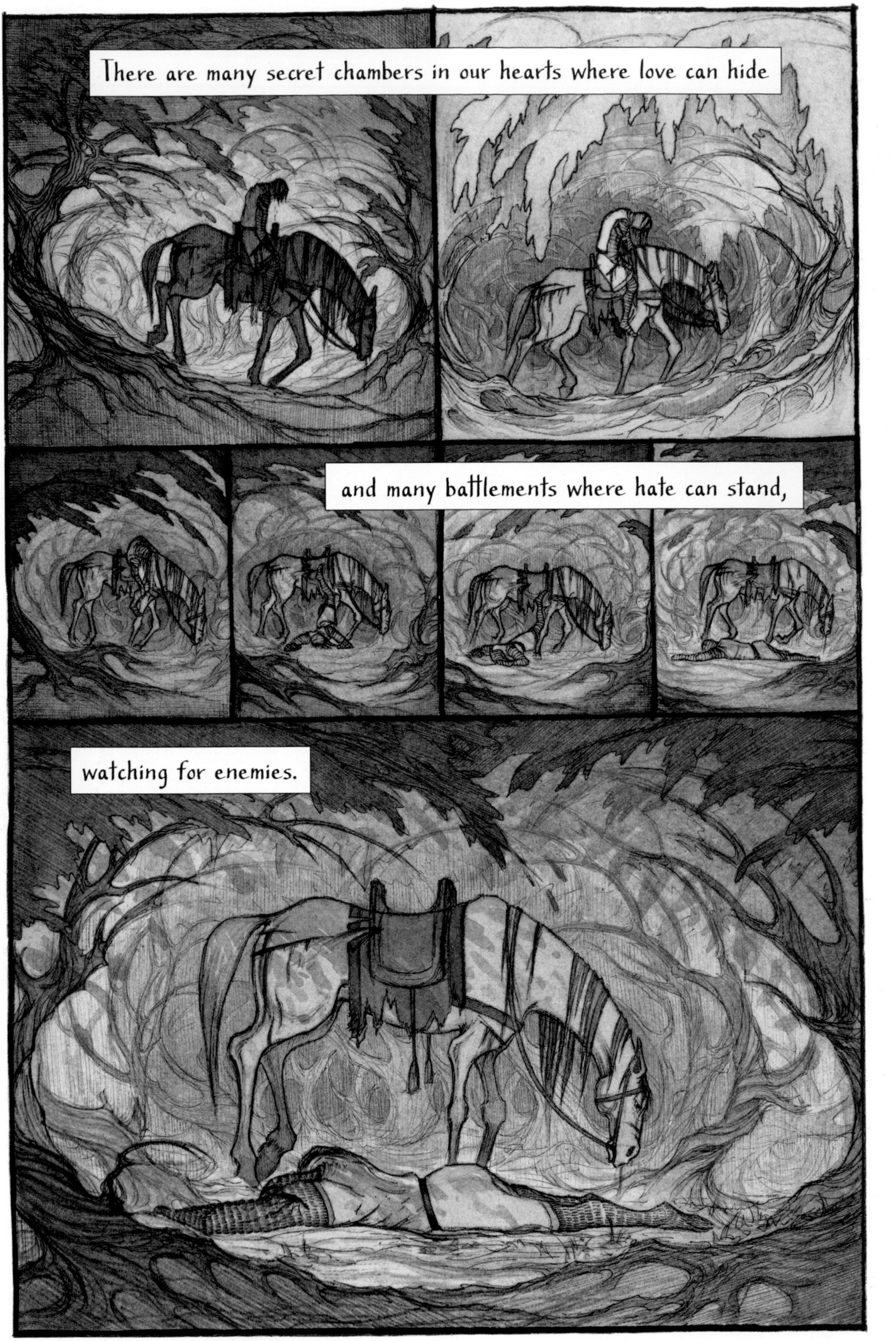
There are many secret chambers in our hearts where love can hide
and many battlements where hate can stand,
watching for enemies.

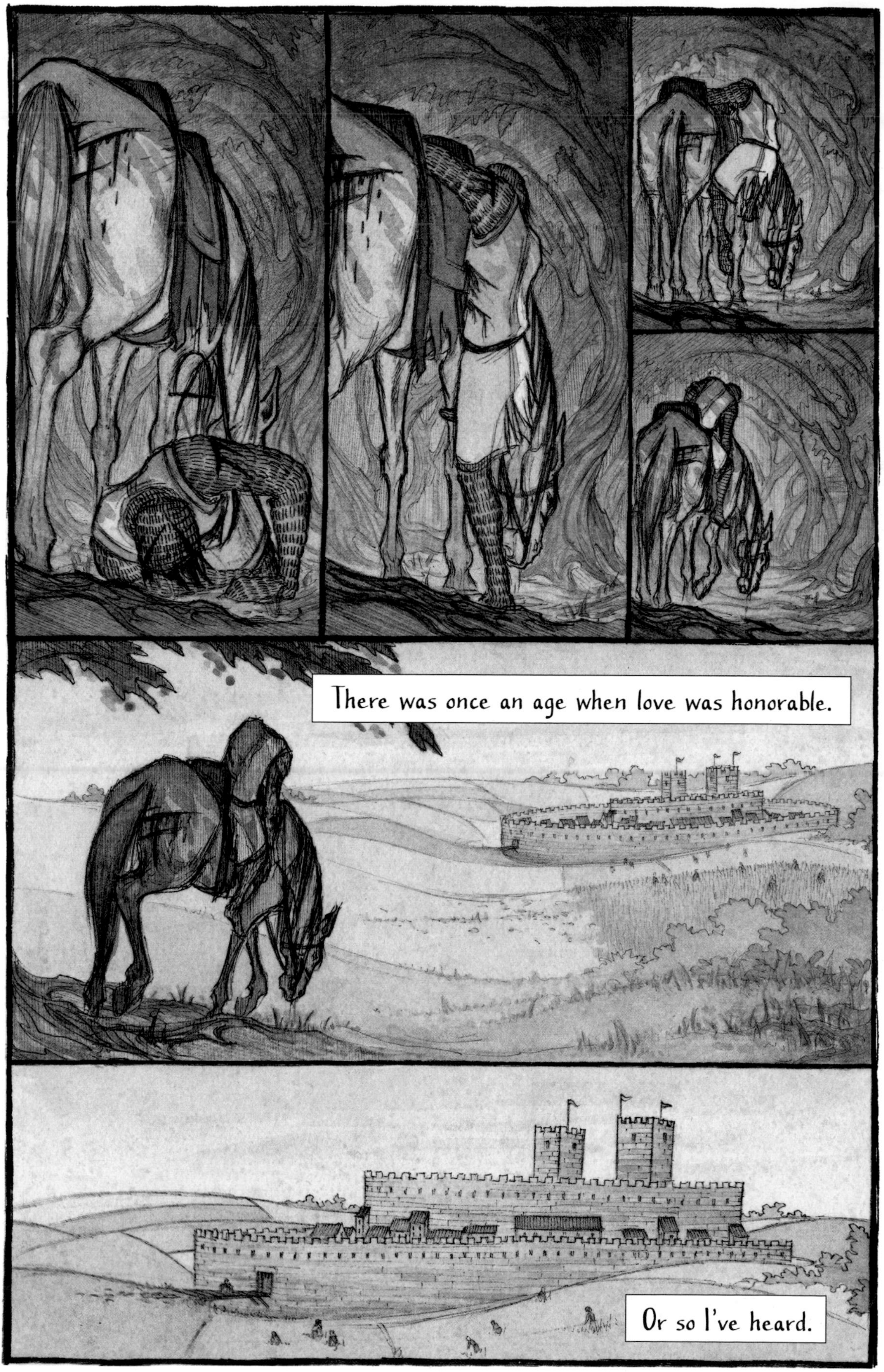
There was once an age when love was honorable.
Or so I've heard.

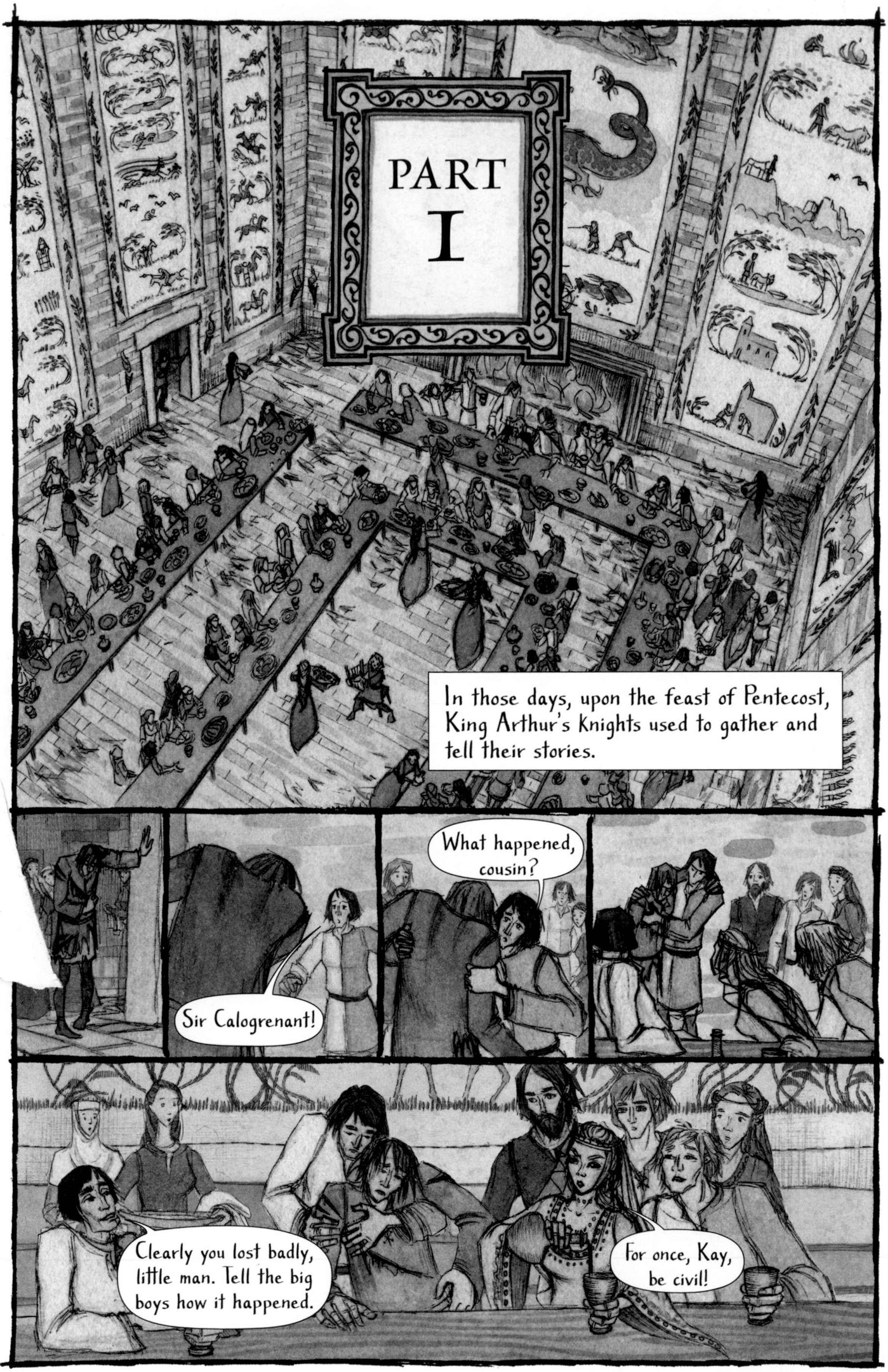
PART I
In those days, upon the feast of Pentecost, King Arthur's knights used to gather and tell their stories.
Sir Calogrenant!
What happened, cousin?
Clearly you lost badly, little man. Tell the big boys how it happened.
For once, Kay, be civil!

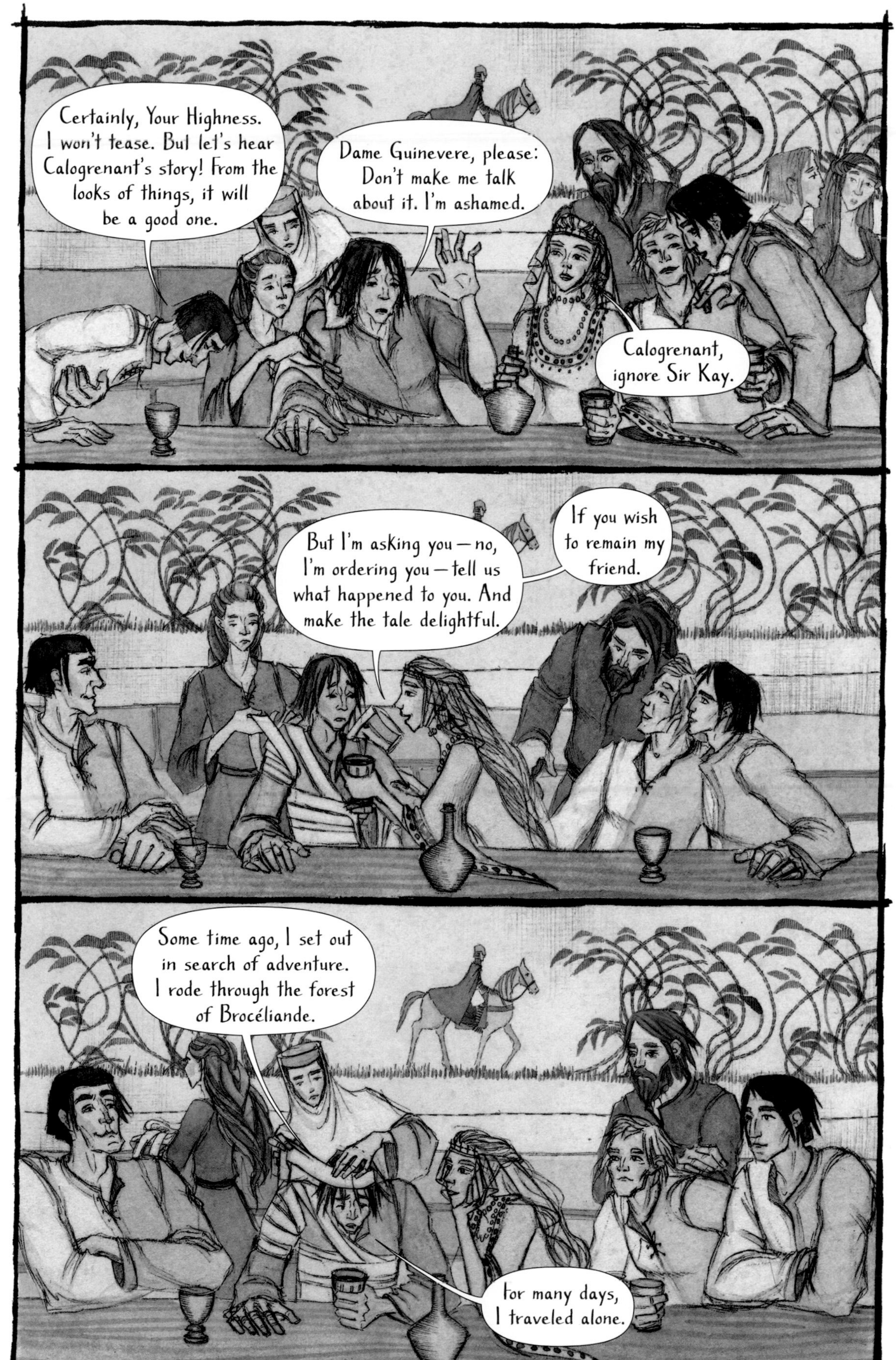
Certainly, Your Highness. I won't tease. But let's hear Calogrenant's story! From the looks of things, it will be a good one.
Dame Guinevere, please: Don't make me talk about it. I'm ashamed.
Calogrenant, ignore Sir Kay.
But I'm asking you — no, I'm ordering you — tell us what happened to you. And make the tale delightful.
If you wish to remain my friend.
Some time ago, I set out in search of adventure. I rode through the forest of Brocéliande.
For many days, I traveled alone.

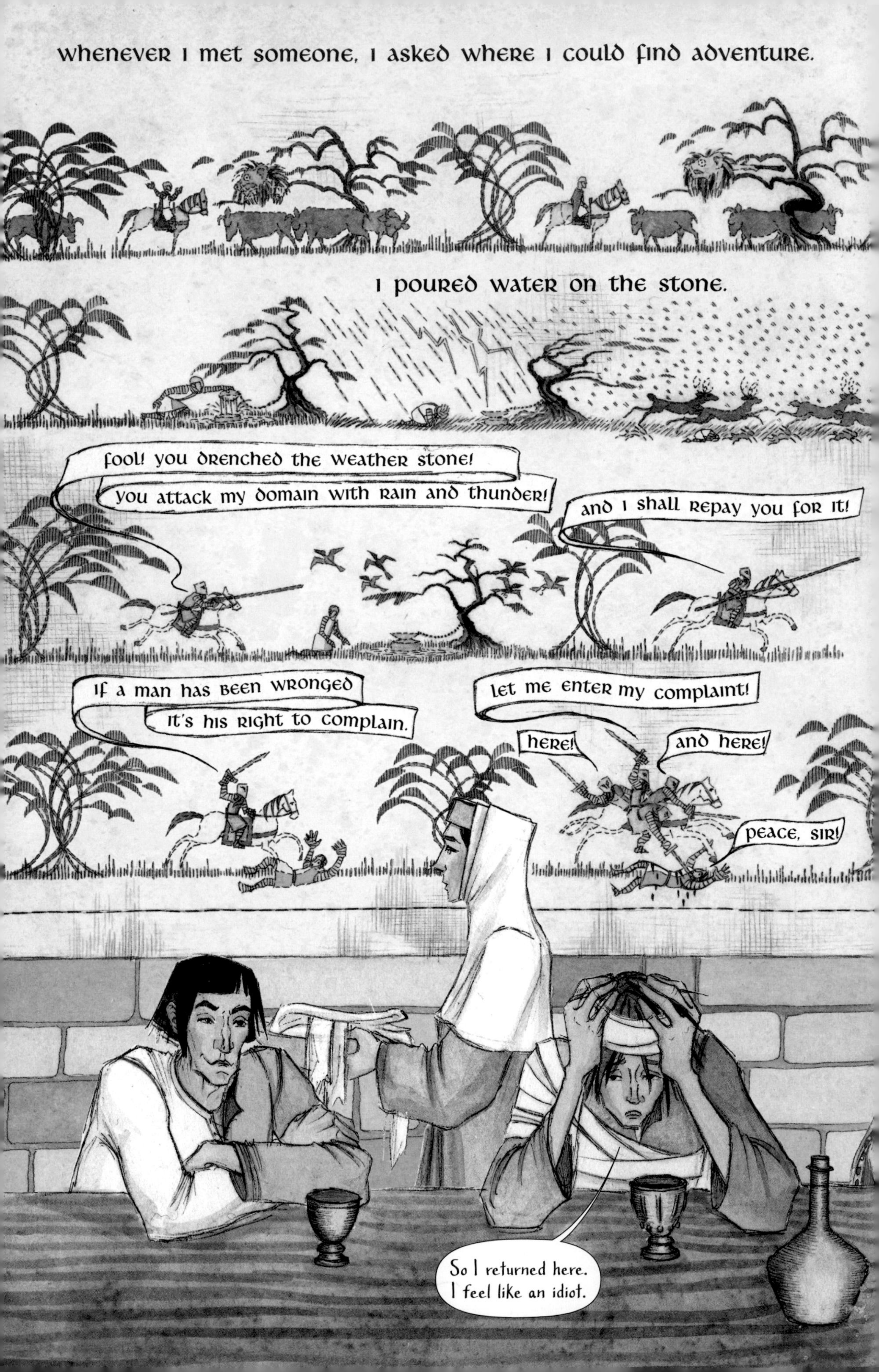
whenever I met someone, I asked where I could find adventure.
I poured water on the stone.
fool! you drenched the weather stone!
you attack my domain with rain and thunder!
and I shall repay you for it!
If a man has been wronged
it's his right to complain.
let me enter my complaint!
here!
and here!
peace, sir!
So I returned here.
I feel like an idiot.

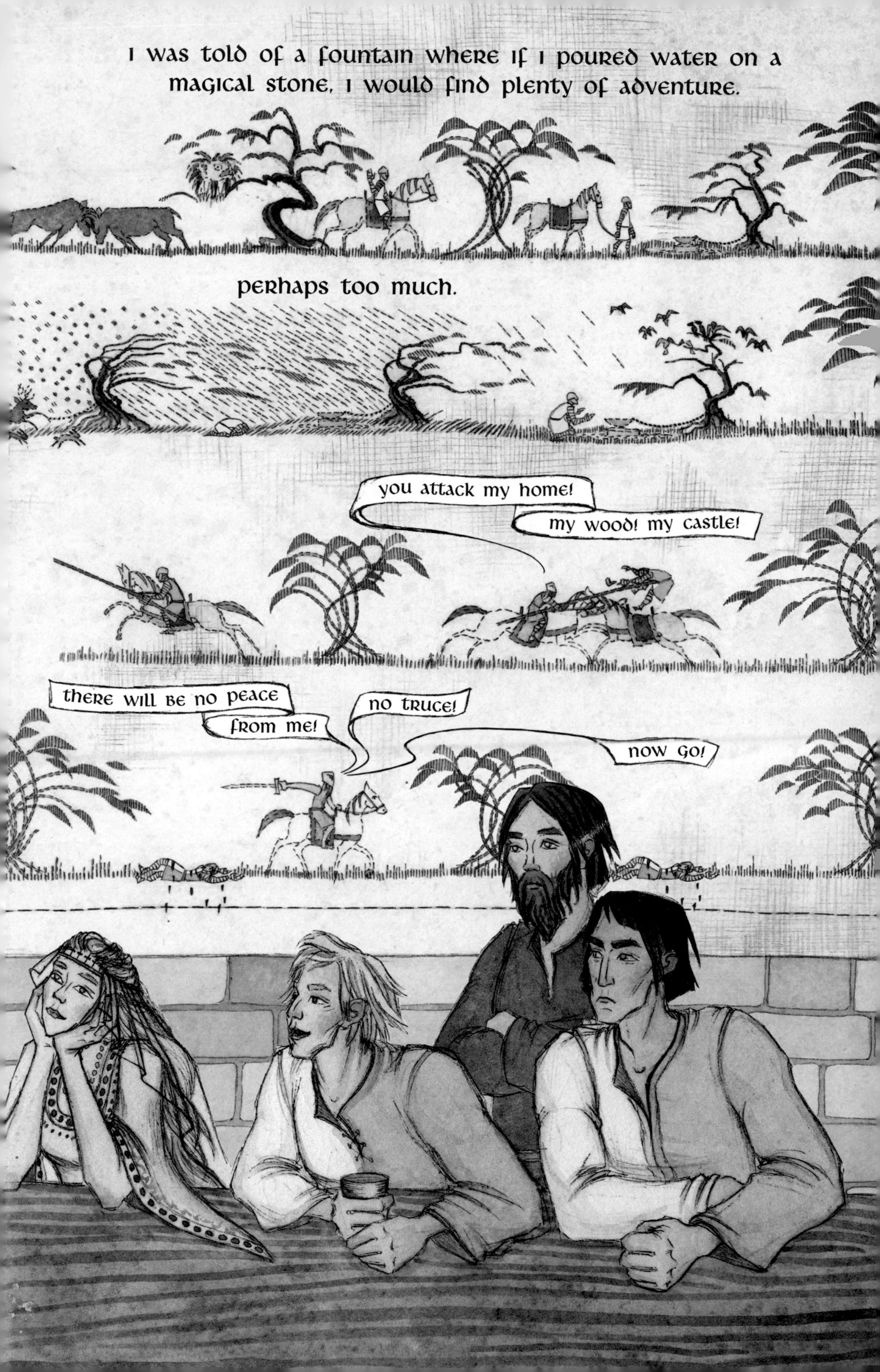
I was told of a fountain where if I poured water on a magical stone, I would find plenty of adventure.
perhaps too much.
you attack my home!
my wood! my castle!
there will be no peace
from me!
no truce!
now go!

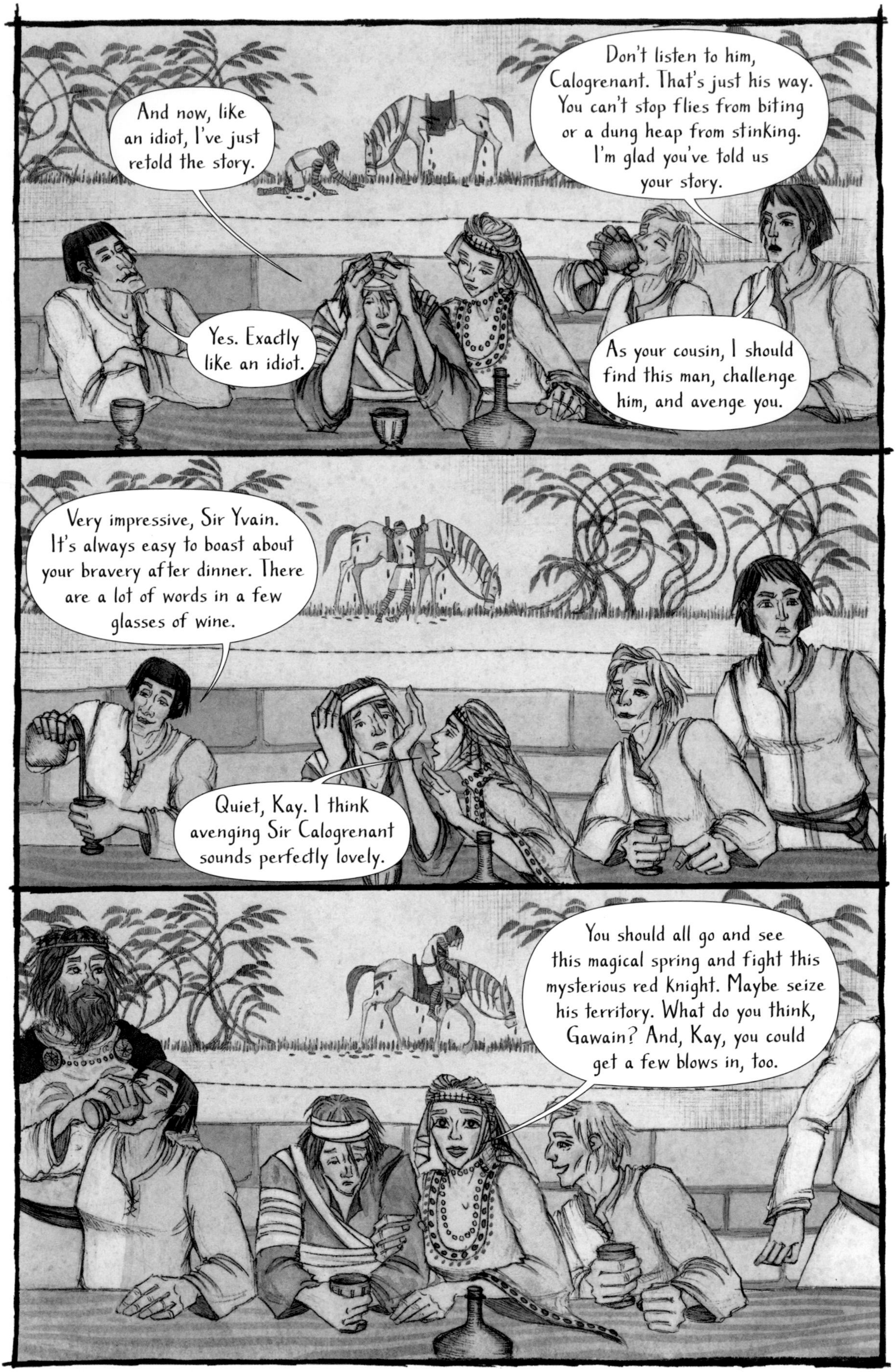
And now, like an idiot, I've just retold the story.
Don't listen to him, Calogrenant. That's just his way. You can't stop flies from biting or a dung heap from stinking. I'm glad you've told us your story.
Yes. Exactly like an idiot.
As your cousin, I should find this man, challenge him, and avenge you.
Very impressive, Sir Yvain. It's always easy to boast about your bravery after dinner. There are a lot of words in a few glasses of wine.
Quiet, Kay. I think avenging Sir Calogrenant sounds perfectly lovely.
You should all go and see this magical spring and fight this mysterious red knight. Maybe seize his territory. What do you think, Gawain? And, Kay, you could get a few blows in, too.

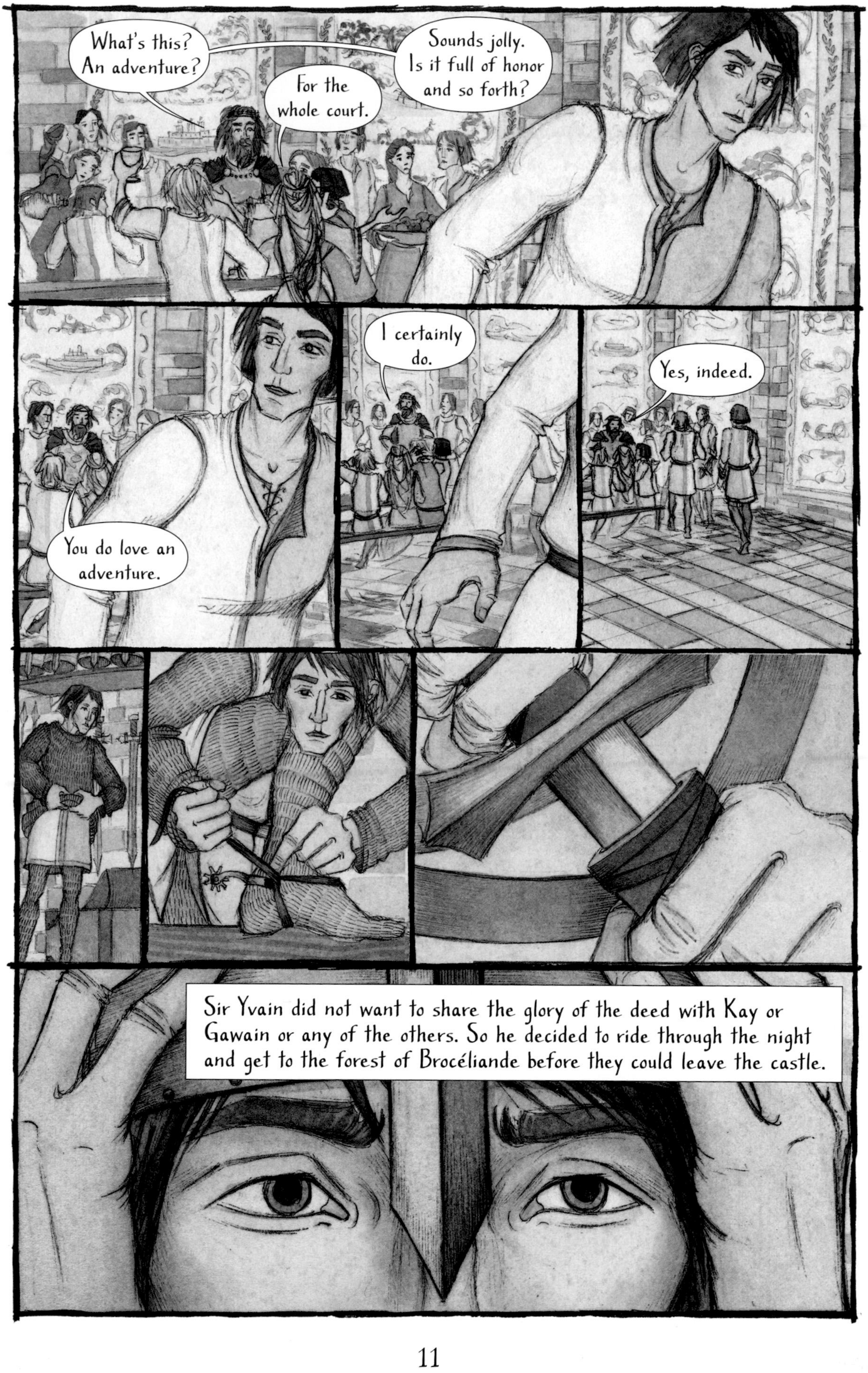
What's this? An adventure?
For the whole court.
Sounds jolly. Is it full of honor and so forth?
You do love an adventure.
I certainly do.
Yes, indeed.
Sir Yvain did not want to share the glory of the deed with Kay or Gawain or any of the others. So he decided to ride through the night and get to the forest of Brocéliande before they could leave the castle.

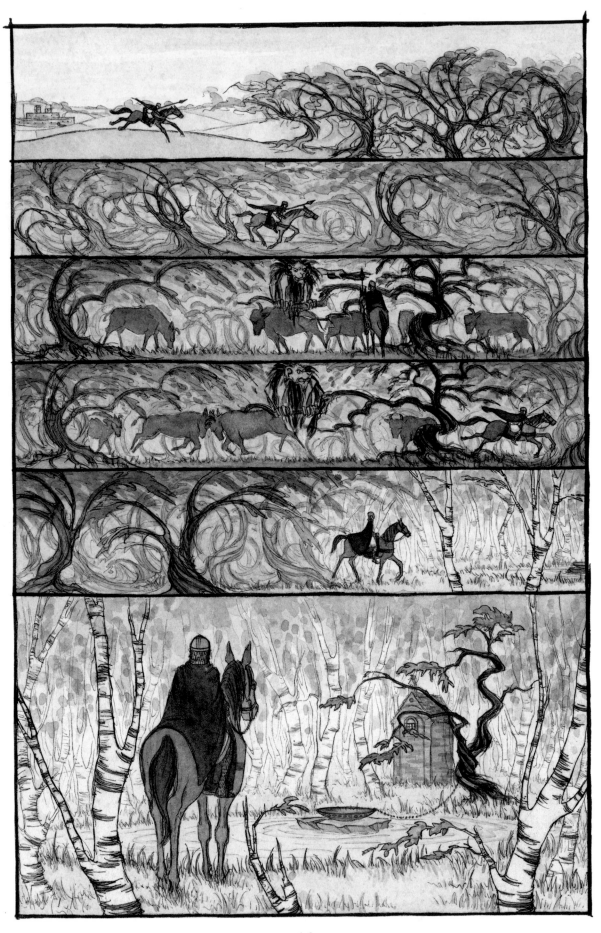

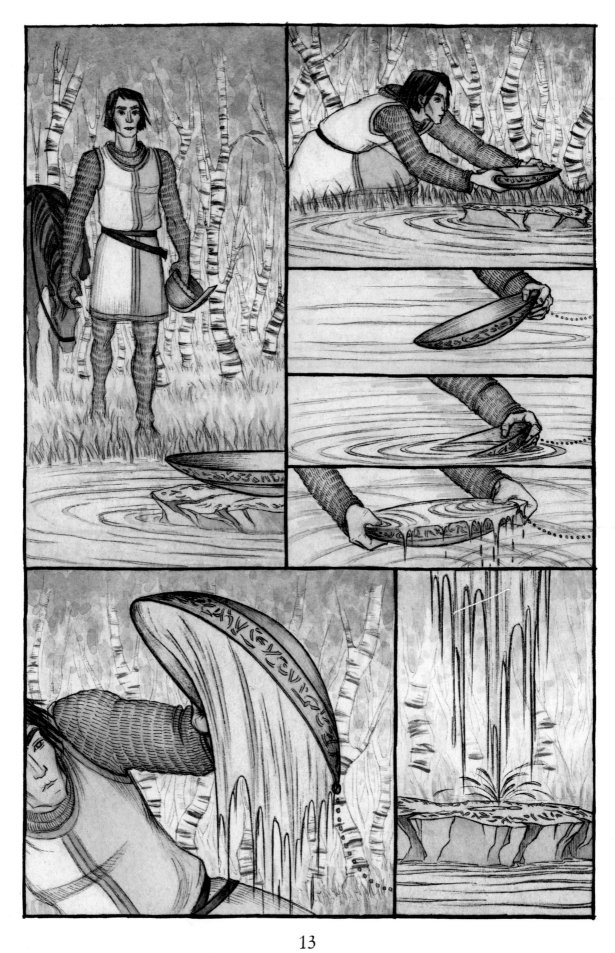

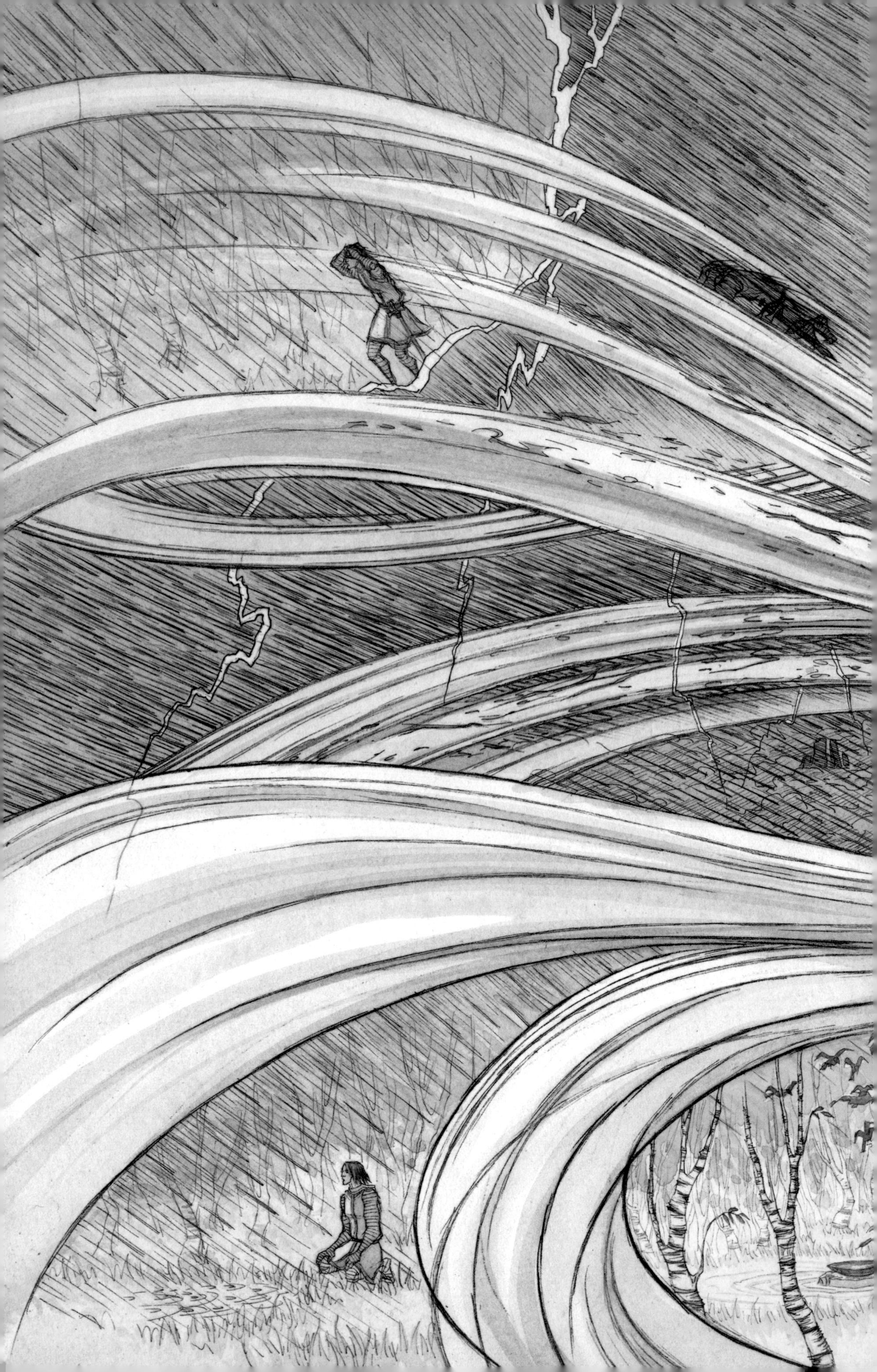

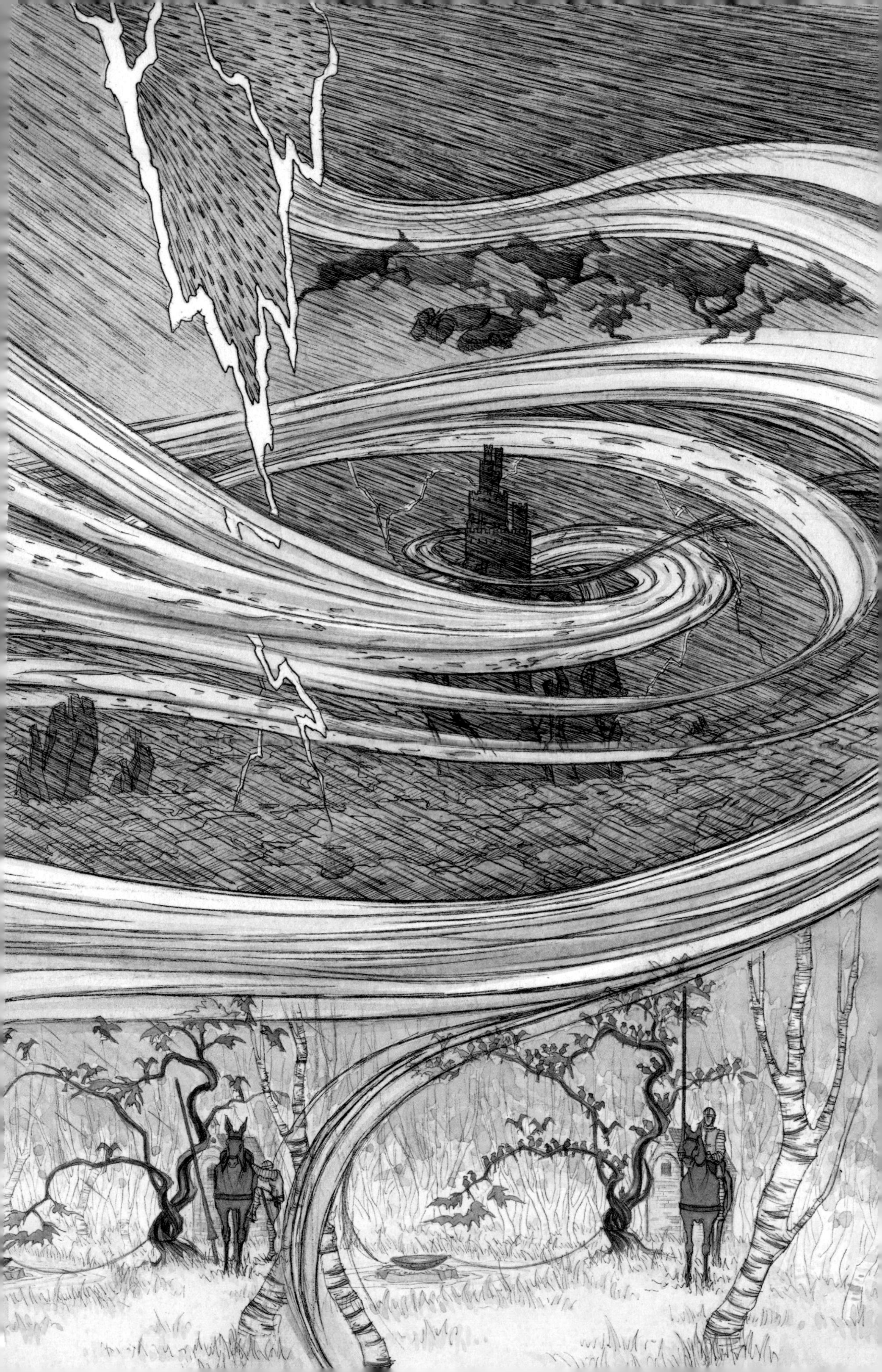

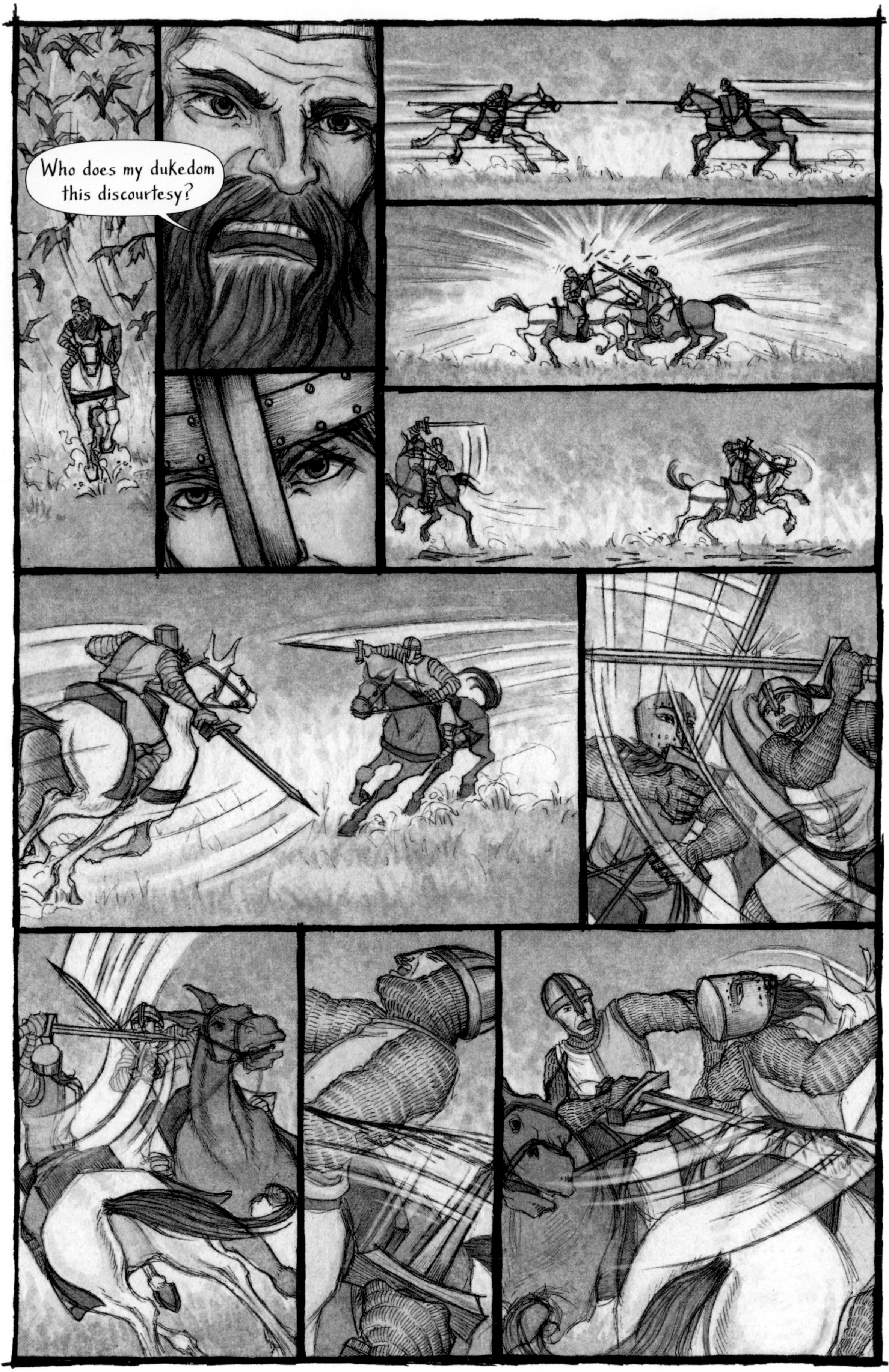
Who does my dukedom this discourtesy?

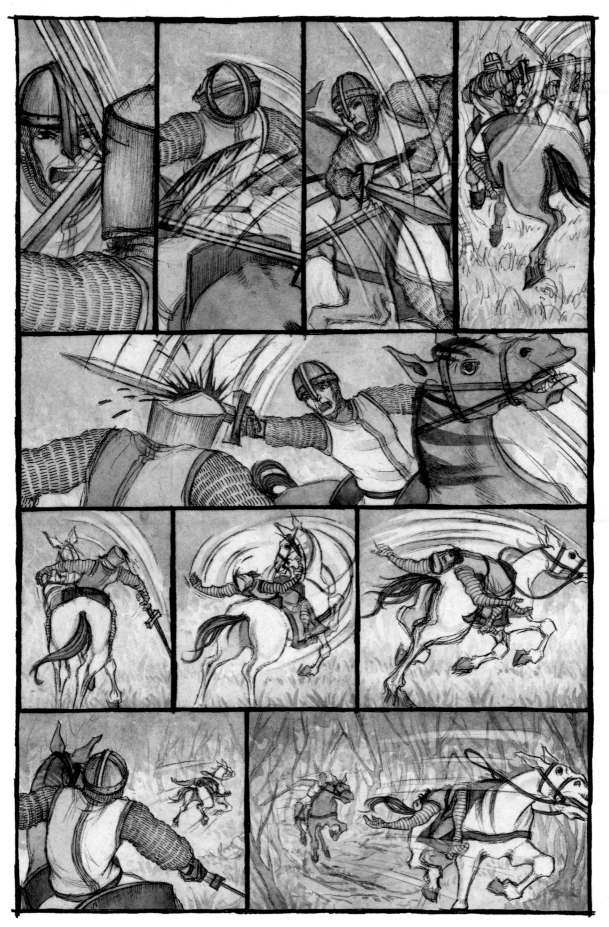

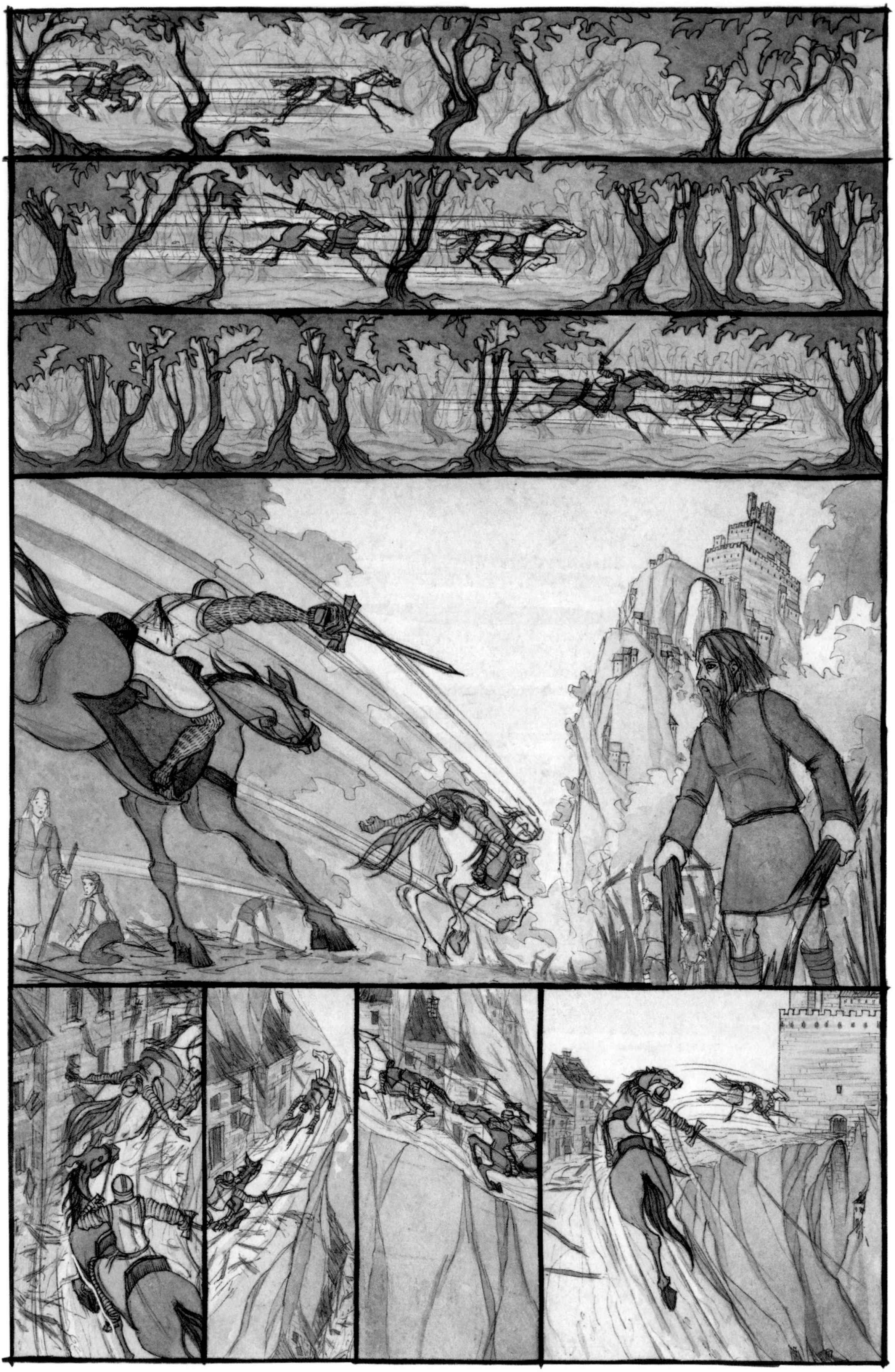

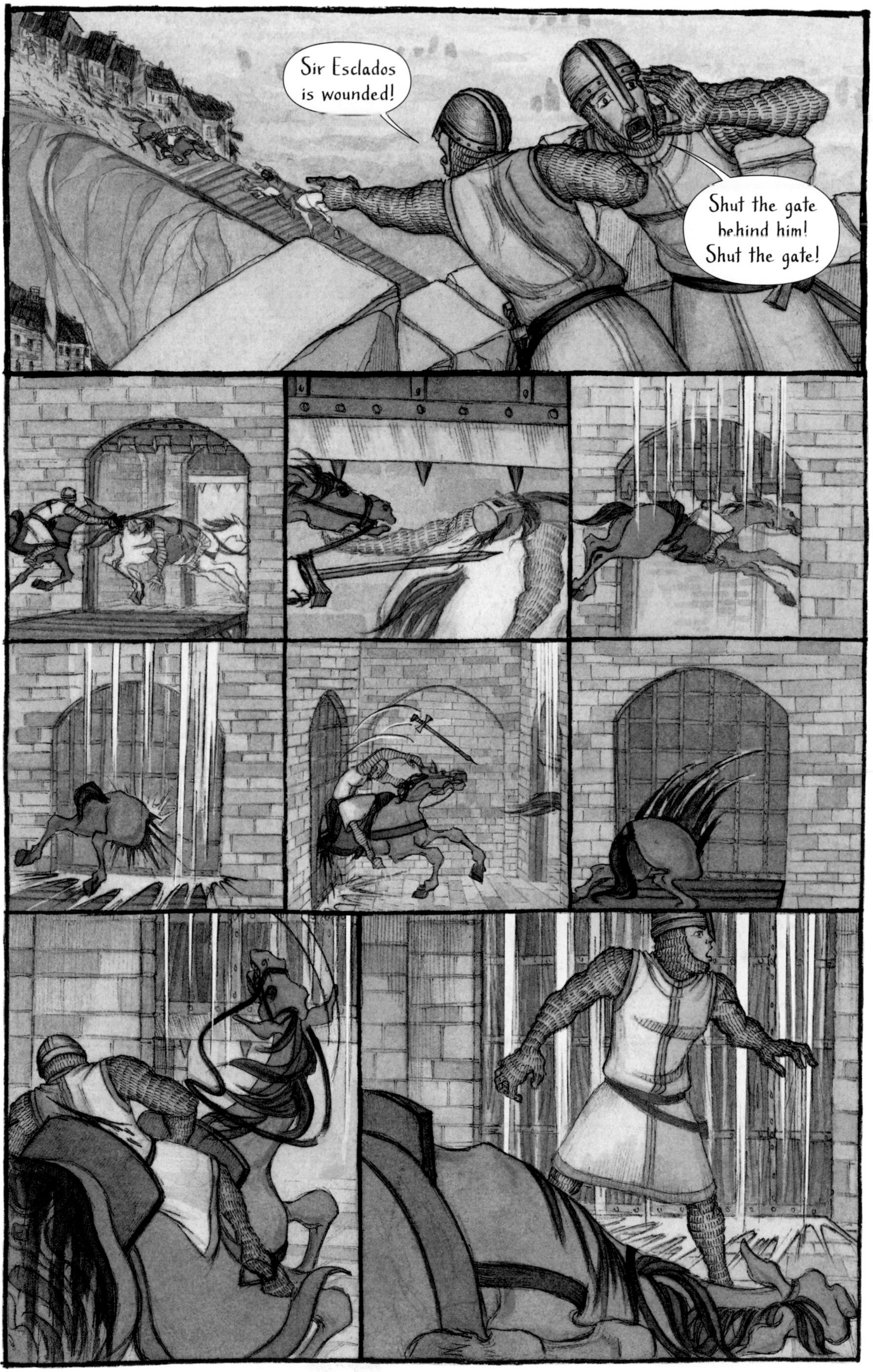
Sir Esclados is wounded!
Shut the gate behind him! Shut the gate!

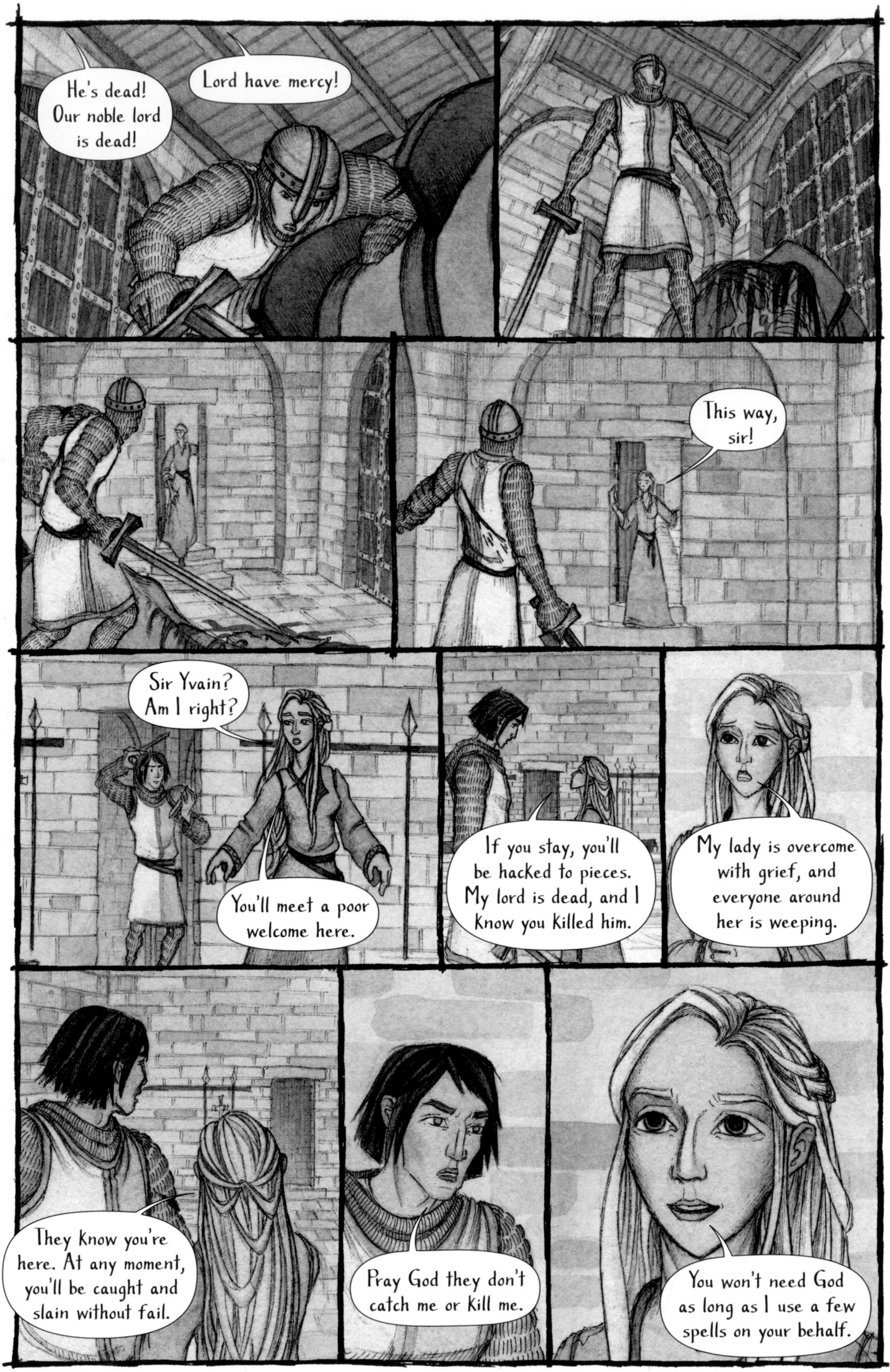
He's dead! Our noble lord is dead!
Lord have mercy!
This way, sir!
Sir Yvain? Am I right?
You'll meet a poor welcome here.
If you stay, you'll be hacked to pieces. My lord is dead, and I know you killed him.
My lady is overcome with grief, and everyone around her is weeping.
They know you're here. At any moment, you'll be caught and slain without fail.
Pray God they don't catch me or kill me.
You won't need God as long as I use a few spells on your behalf.

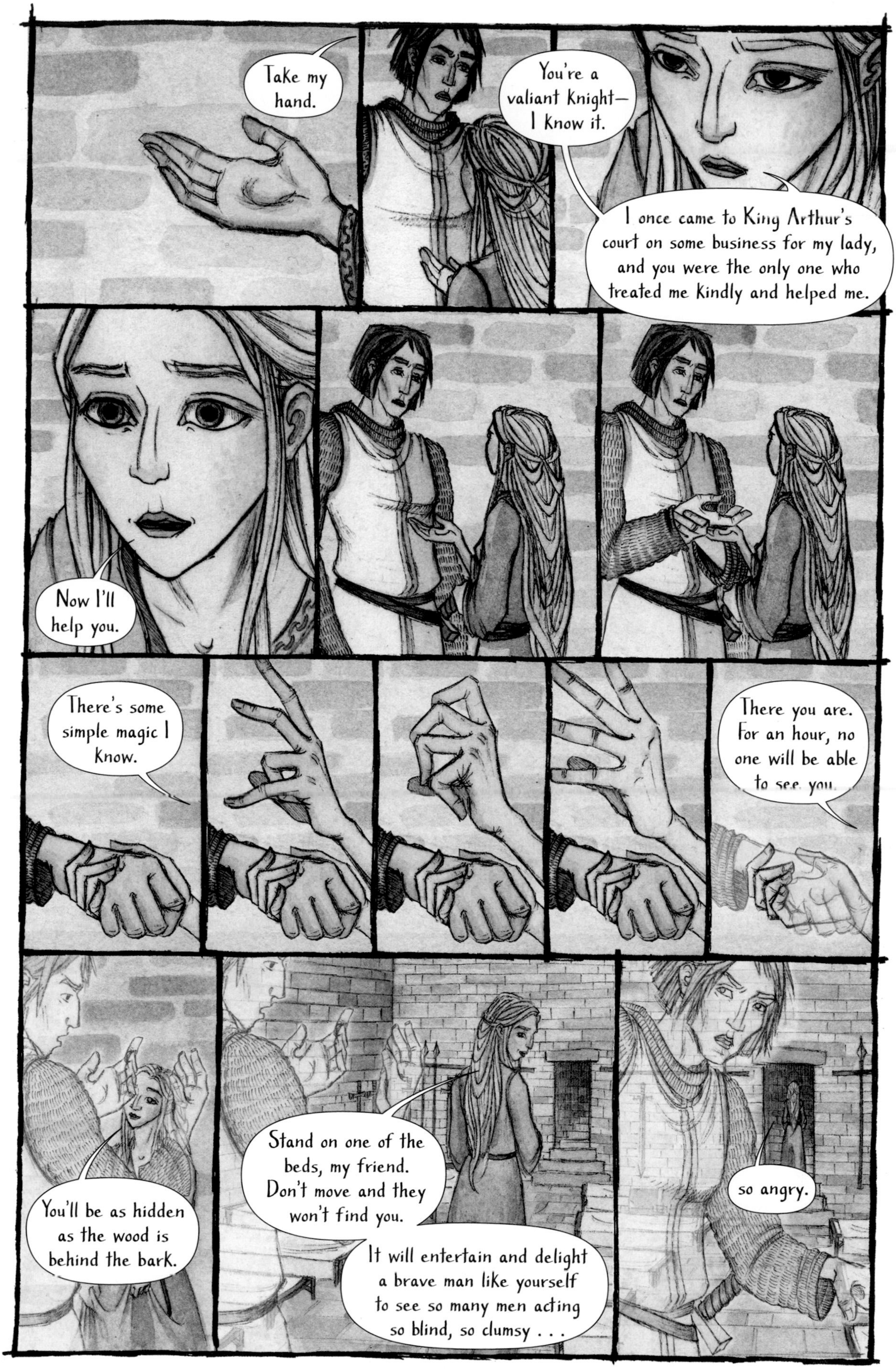
Take my hand.
You're a valiant Knight— I know it.
I once came to King Arthur's court on some business for my lady, and you were the only one who treated me kindly and helped me.
Now I'll help you.
There's some simple magic I know.
There you are. For an hour, no one will be able to see you.
You'll be as hidden as the wood is behind the bark.
Stand on one of the beds, my friend. Don't move and they won't find you.
It will entertain and delight a brave man like yourself to see so many men acting so blind, so clumsy . . .
so angry.

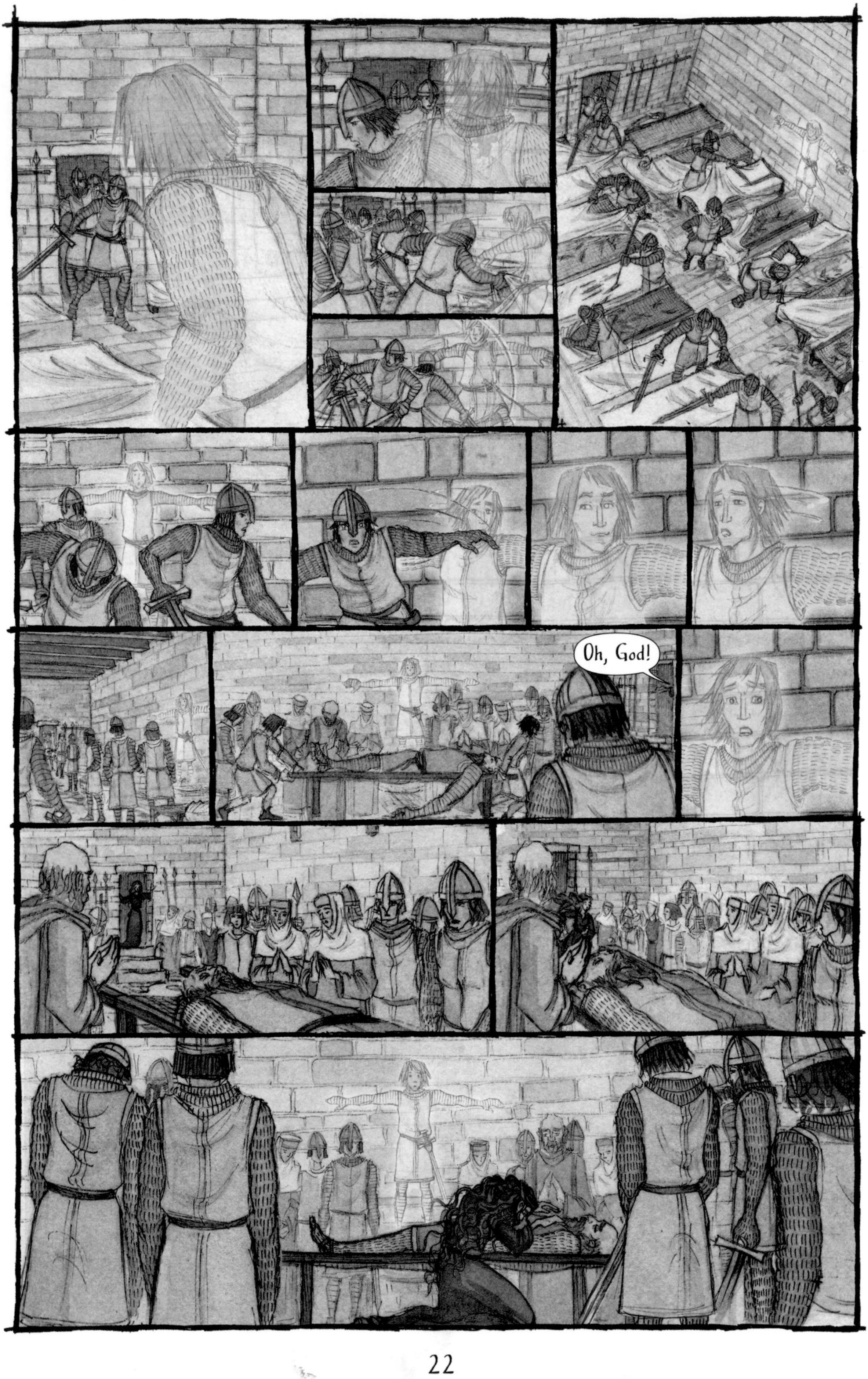
Oh, God!

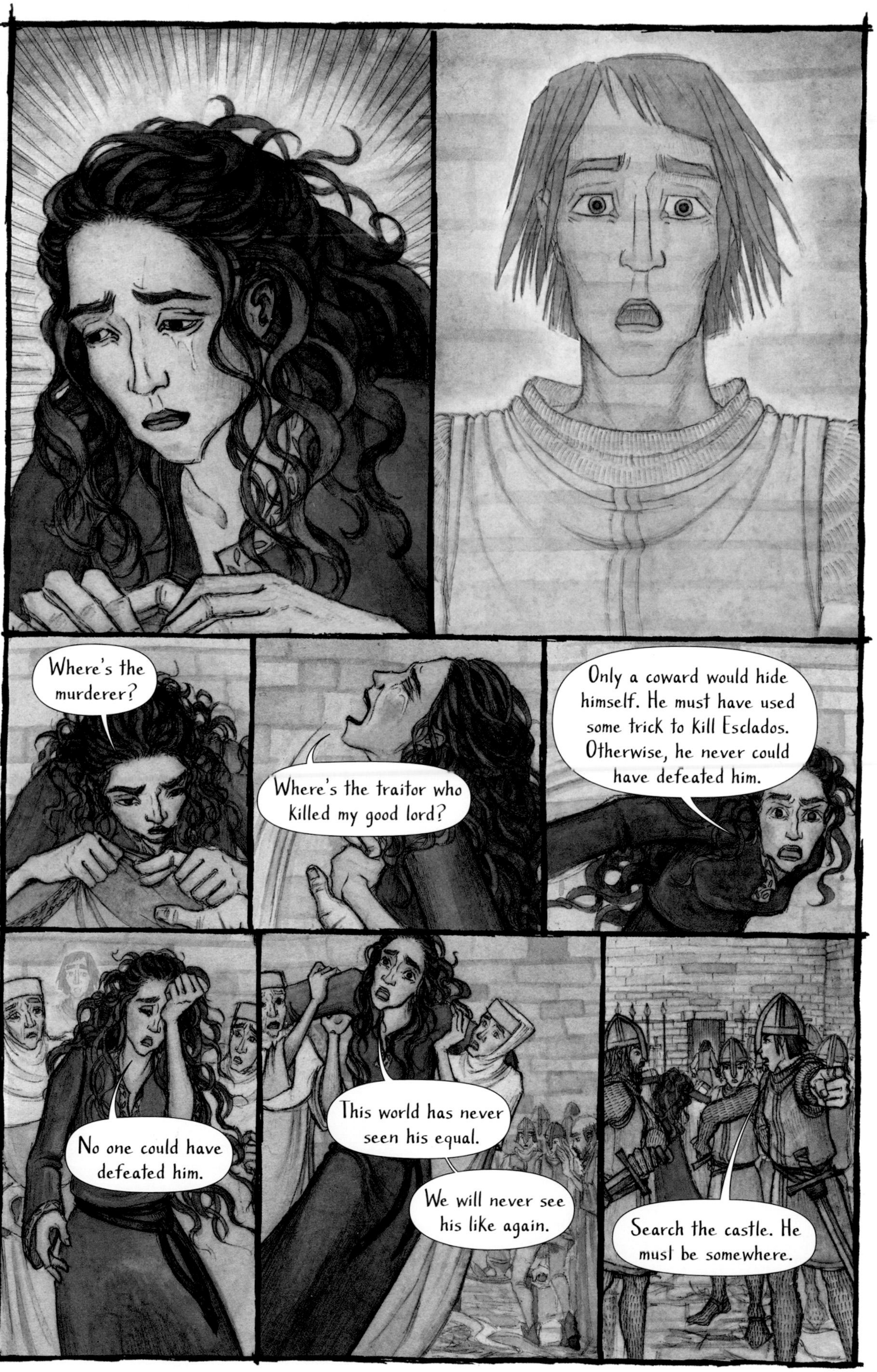

Where's the murderer?
Where's the traitor who killed my good lord?
Only a coward would hide himself. He must have used some trick to kill Esclados. Otherwise, he never could have defeated him.
No one could have defeated him.
This world has never seen his equal.
We will never see his like again.
Search the castle. He must be somewhere.

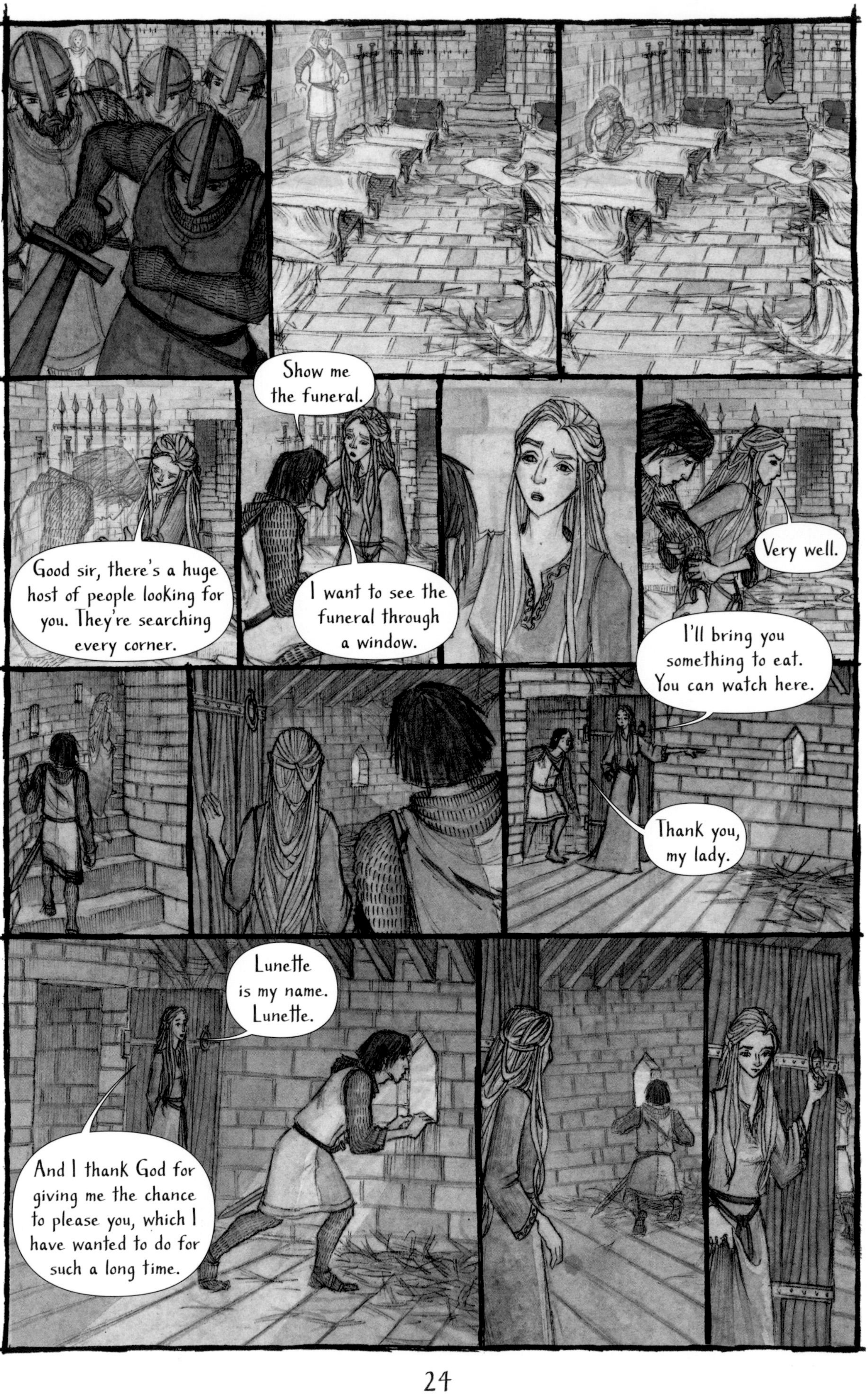
Good sir, there's a huge host of people looking for you. They're searching every corner.
Show me the funeral.
I want to see the funeral through a window.
Very well.
I'll bring you something to eat. You can watch here.
Thank you, my lady.
Lunette is my name. Lunette.
And I thank God for giving me the chance to please you, which I have wanted to do for such a long time.

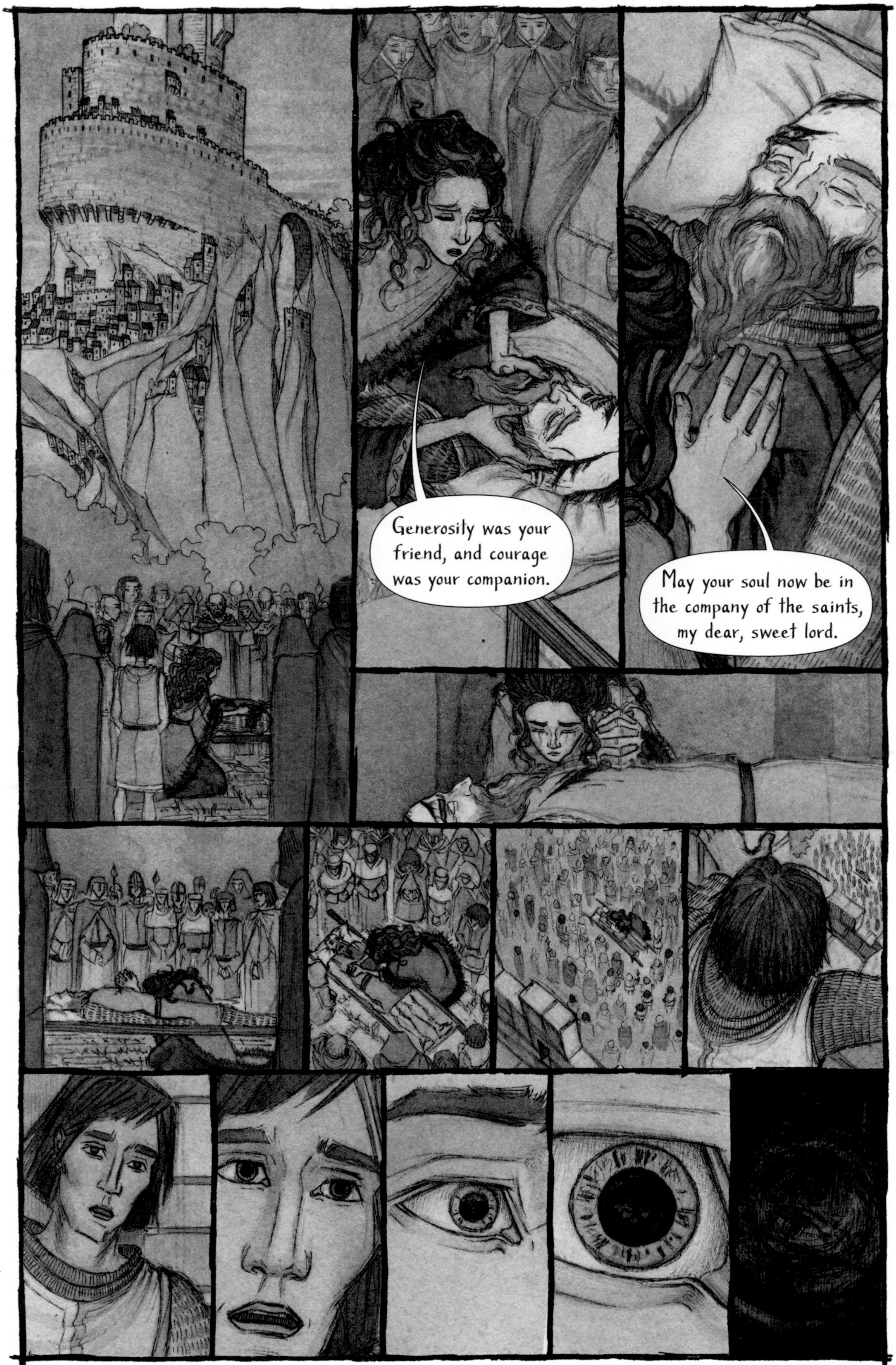
Generosity was your friend, and courage was your companion.
May your soul now be in the company of the saints, my dear, sweet lord.

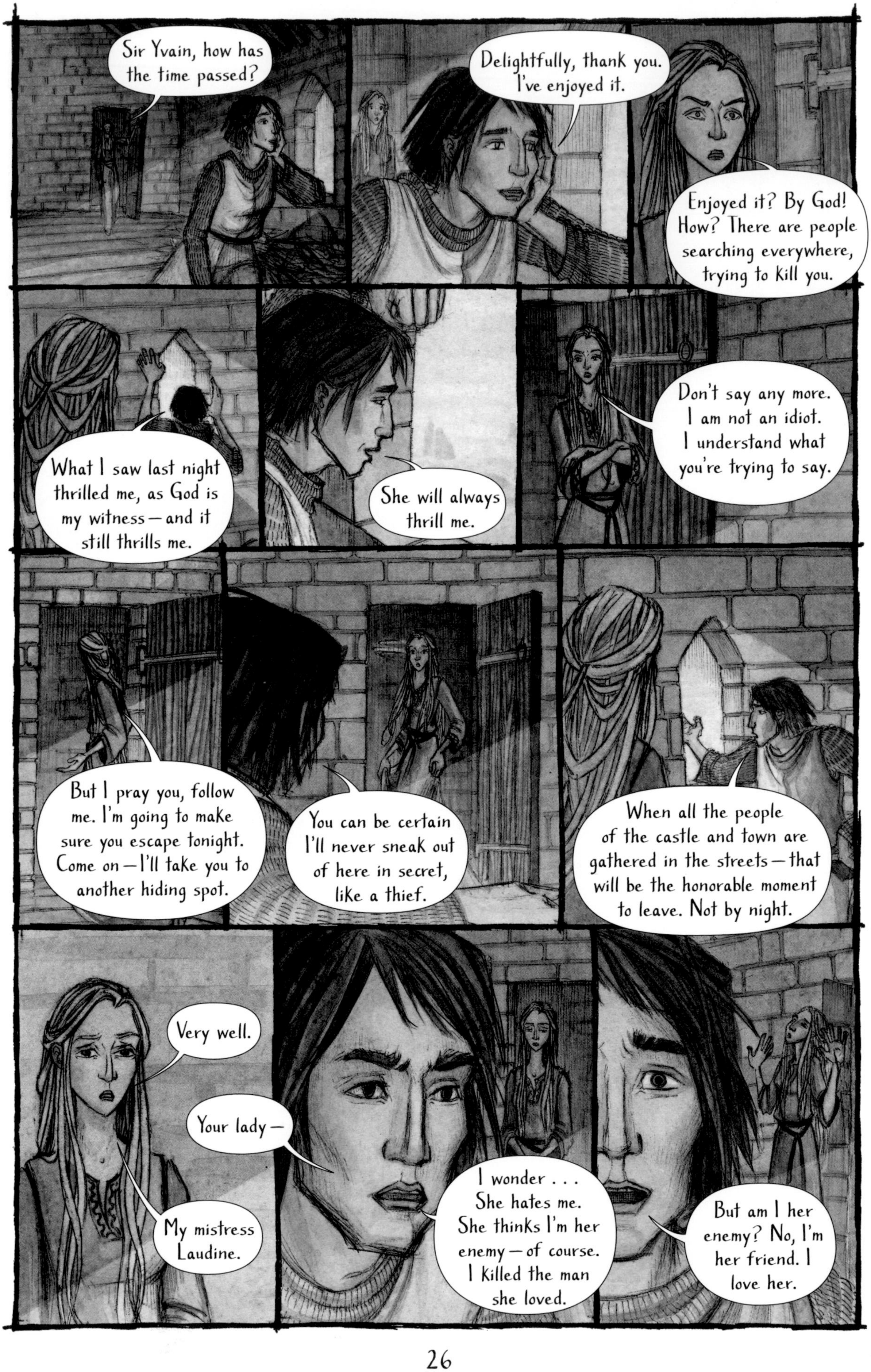
Sir Yvain, how has the time passed?
Delightfully, thank you. I've enjoyed it.
Enjoyed it? By God! How? There are people searching everywhere, trying to kill you.
What I saw last night thrilled me, as God is my witness—and it still thrills me.
She will always thrill me.
Don't say any more. I am not an idiot. I understand what you're trying to say.
But I pray you, follow me. I'm going to make sure you escape tonight. Come on—I'll take you to another hiding spot.
You can be certain I'll never sneak out of here in secret, like a thief.
When all the people of the castle and town are gathered in the streets—that will be the honorable moment to leave. Not by night.
Very well.
Your lady—
My mistress Laudine.
I wonder . . . She hates me. She thinks I'm her enemy—of course. I killed the man she loved.
But am I her enemy? No, I'm her friend. I love her.

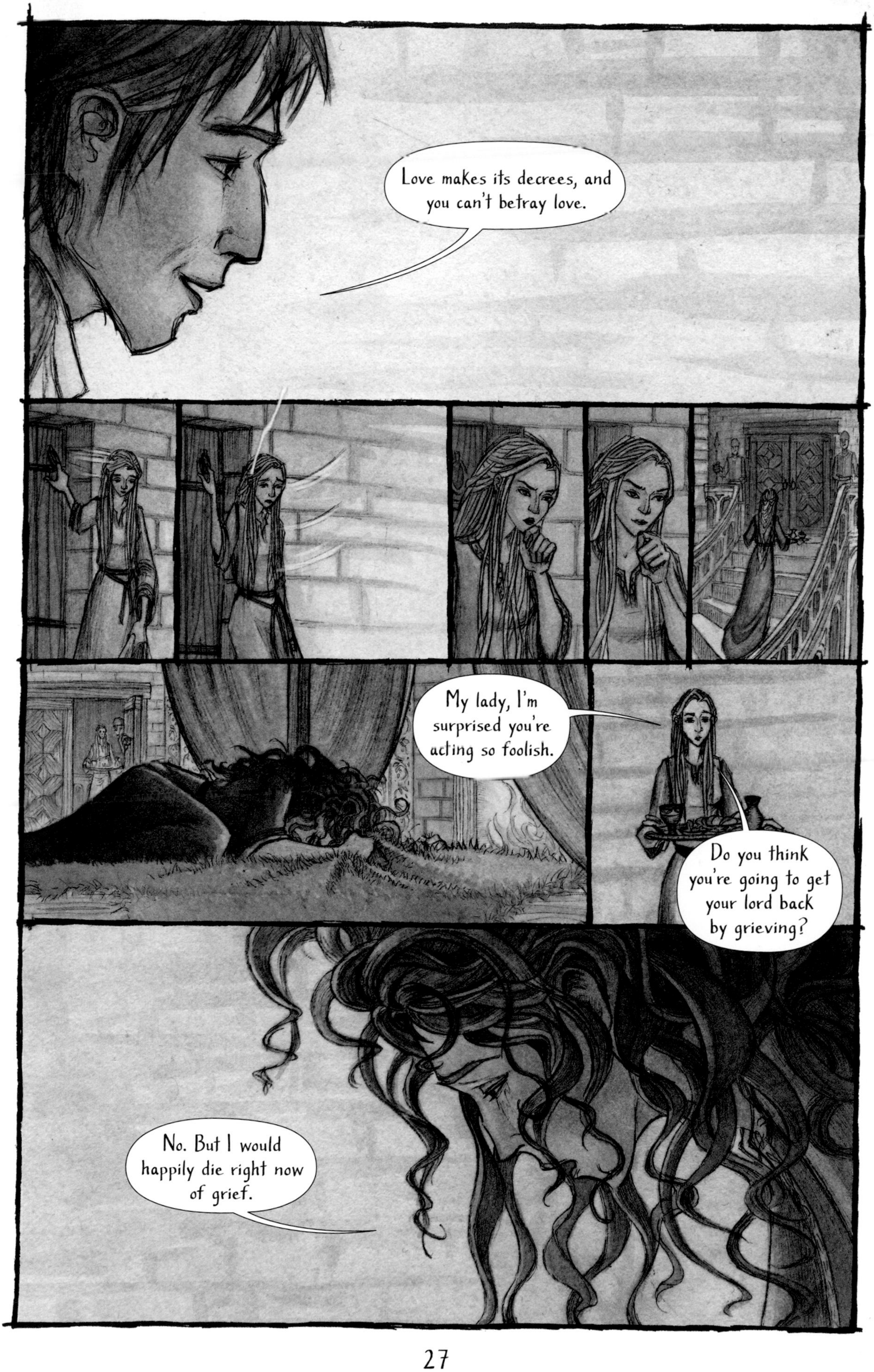
Love makes its decrees, and you can't betray love.
My lady, I'm surprised you're acting so foolish.
Do you think you're going to get your lord back by grieving?
No. But I would happily die right now of grief.

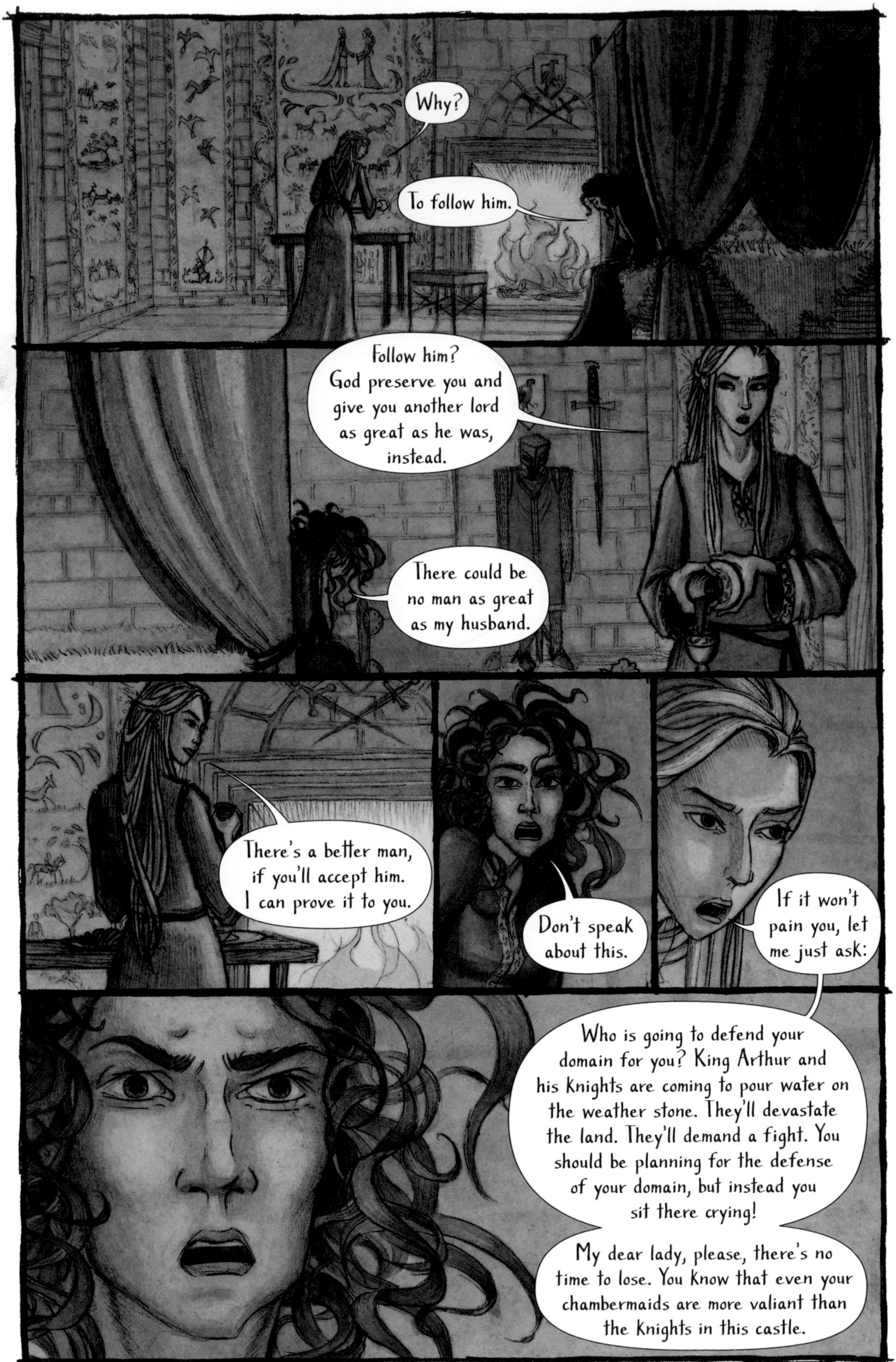
Why?
To follow him.
Follow him? God preserve you and give you another lord as great as he was, instead.
There could be no man as great as my husband.
There's a better man, if you'll accept him. I can prove it to you.
Don't speak about this.
If it won't pain you, let me just ask:
Who is going to defend your domain for you? King Arthur and his Knights are coming to pour water on the weather stone. They'll devastate the land. They'll demand a fight. You should be planning for the defense of your domain, but instead you sit there crying!
My dear lady, please, there's no time to lose. You know that even your chambermaids are more valiant than the knights in this castle.

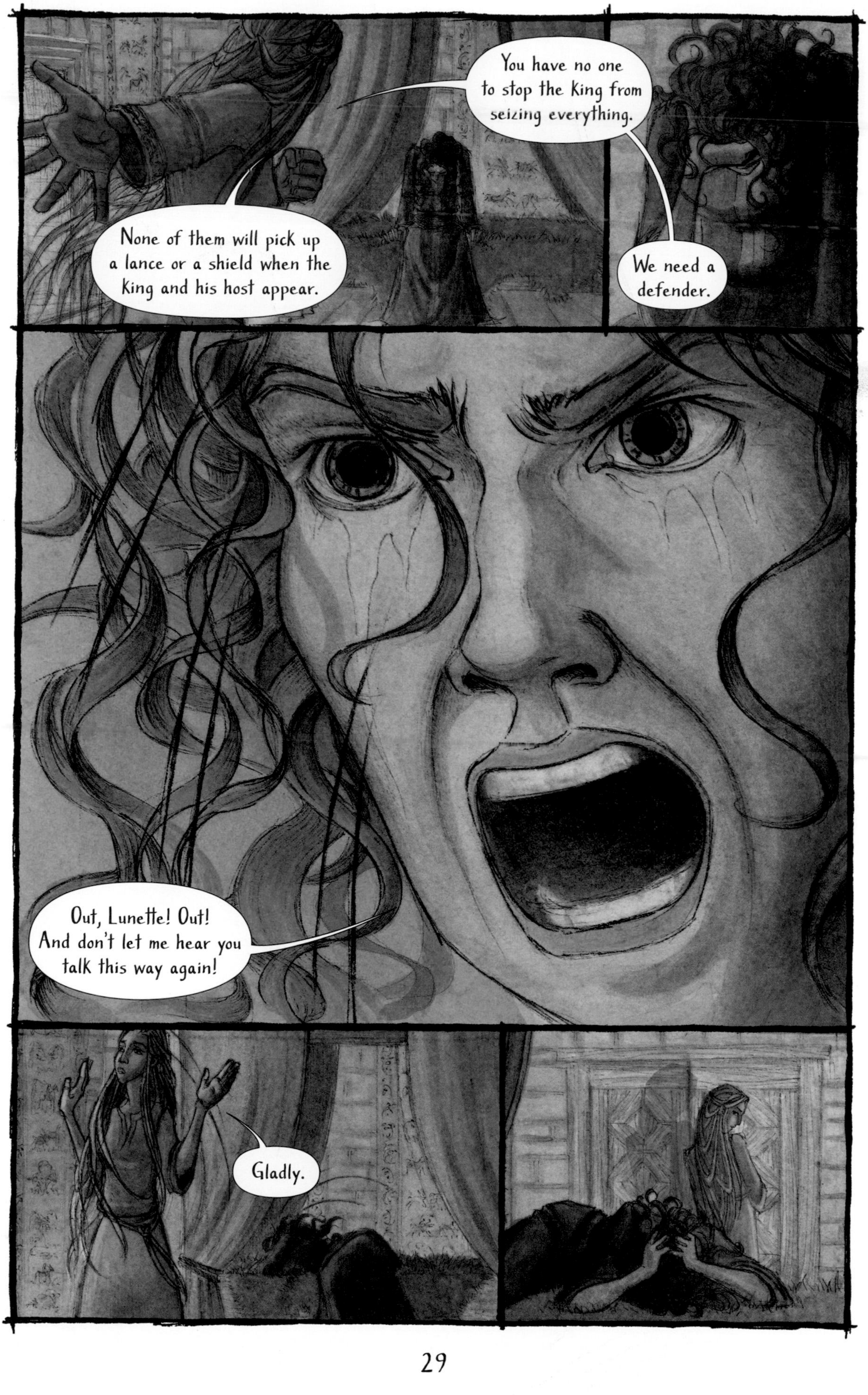
You have no one to stop the King from seizing everything.
None of them will pick up a lance or a shield when the King and his host appear.
We need a defender.
Out, Lunette! Out! And don't let me hear you talk this way again!
Gladly.

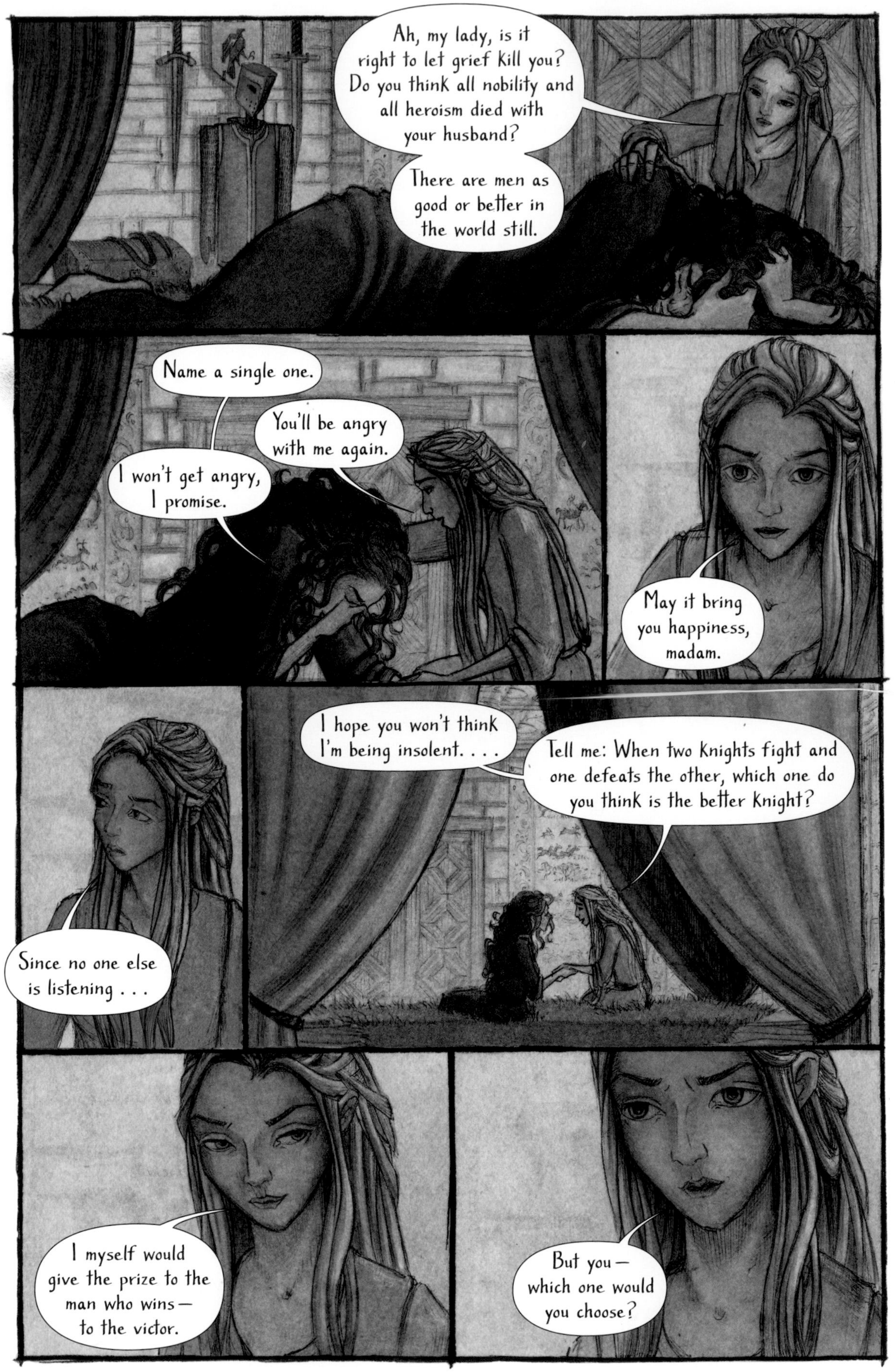
Ah, my lady, is it right to let grief kill you? Do you think all nobility and all heroism died with your husband?
There are men as good or better in the world still.
Name a single one.
You'll be angry with me again.
I won't get angry, I promise.
May it bring you happiness, madam.
Since no one else is listening . . .
I hope you won't think I'm being insolent. . . .
Tell me: When two knights fight and one defeats the other, which one do you think is the better knight?
I myself would give the prize to the man who wins— to the victor.
But you— which one would you choose?

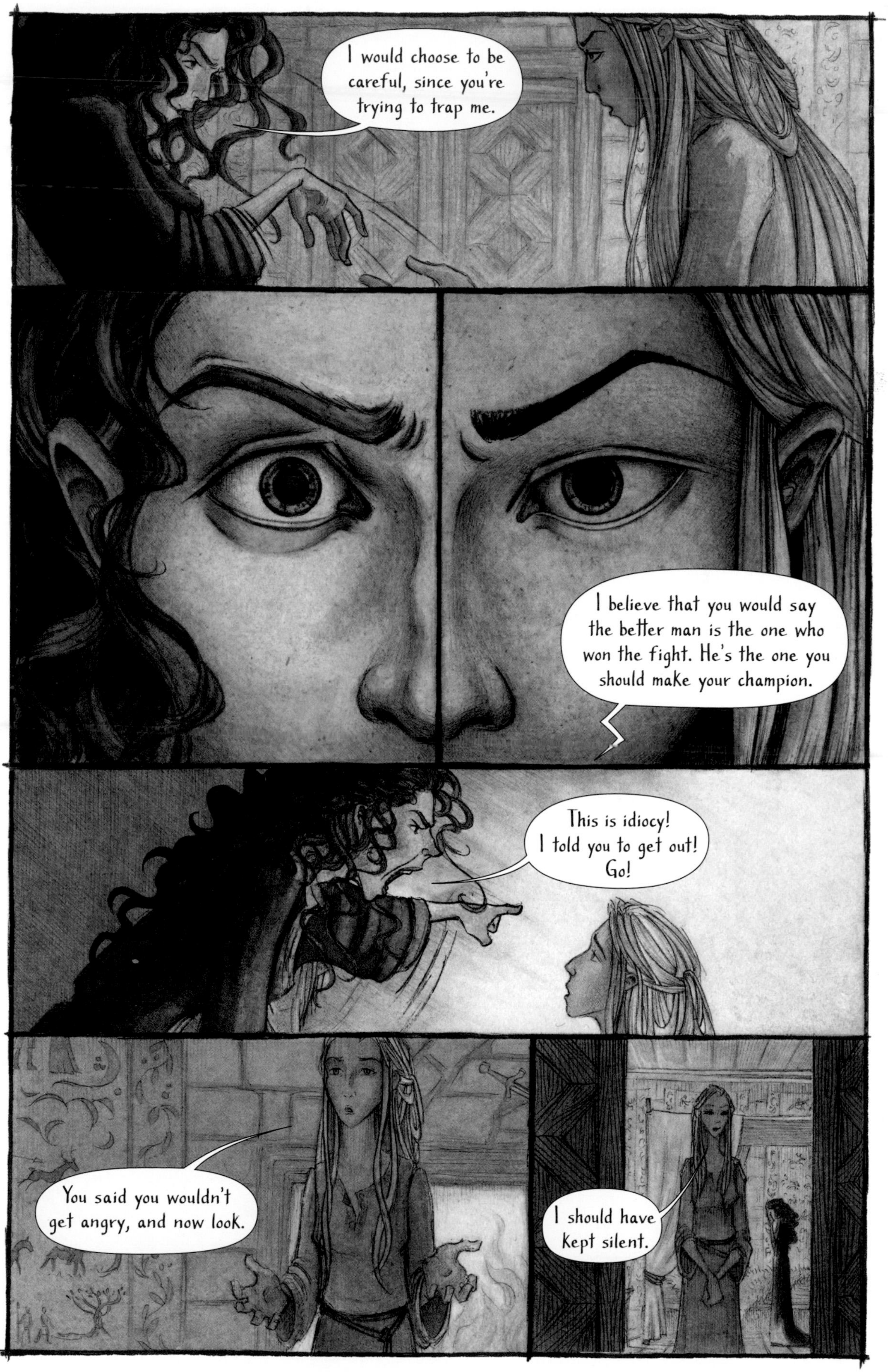
I would choose to be careful, since you're trying to trap me.
I believe that you would say the better man is the one who won the fight. He's the one you should make your champion.
This is idiocy! I told you to get out! Go!
You said you wouldn't get angry, and now look.
I should have kept silent.

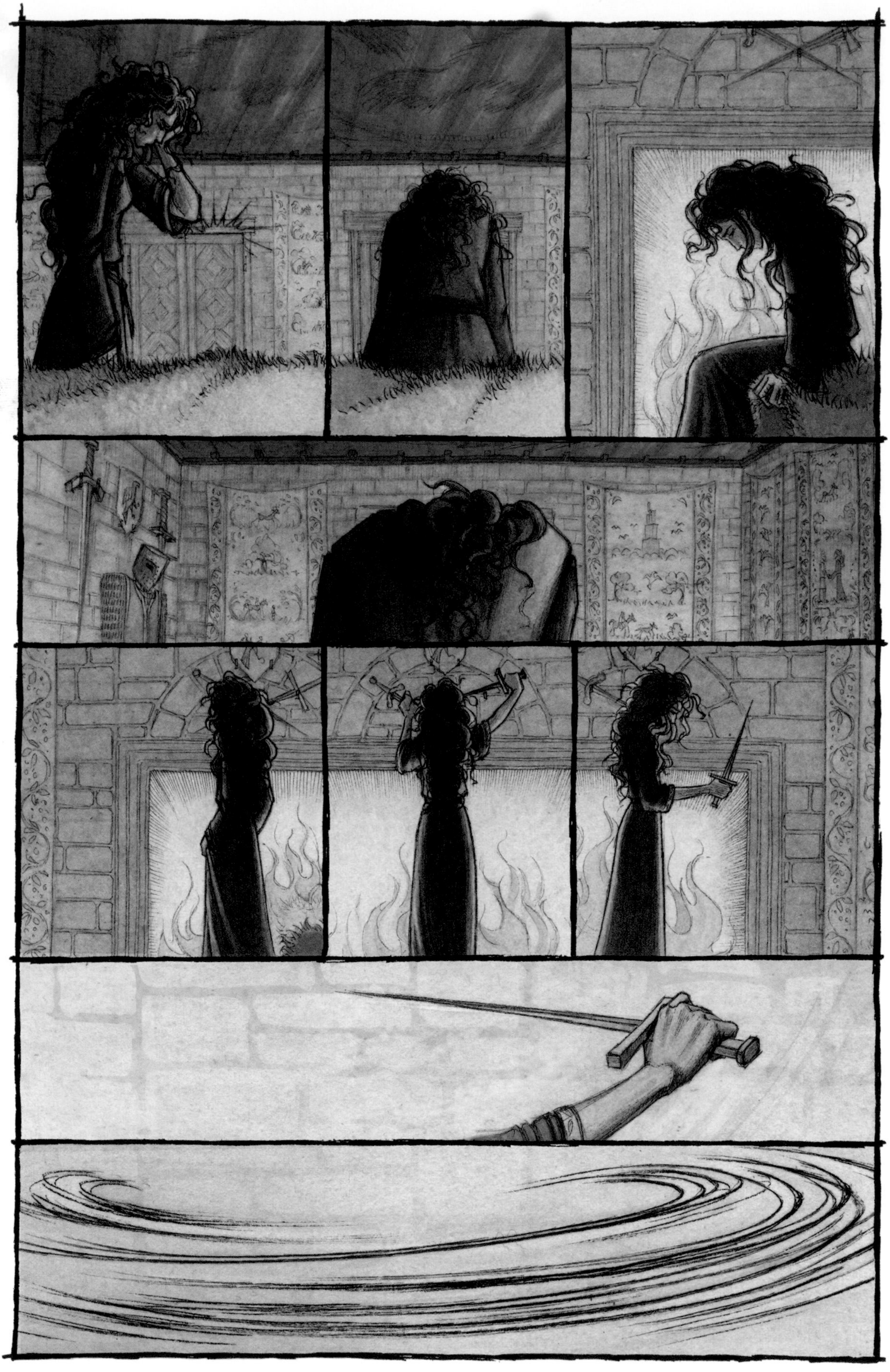

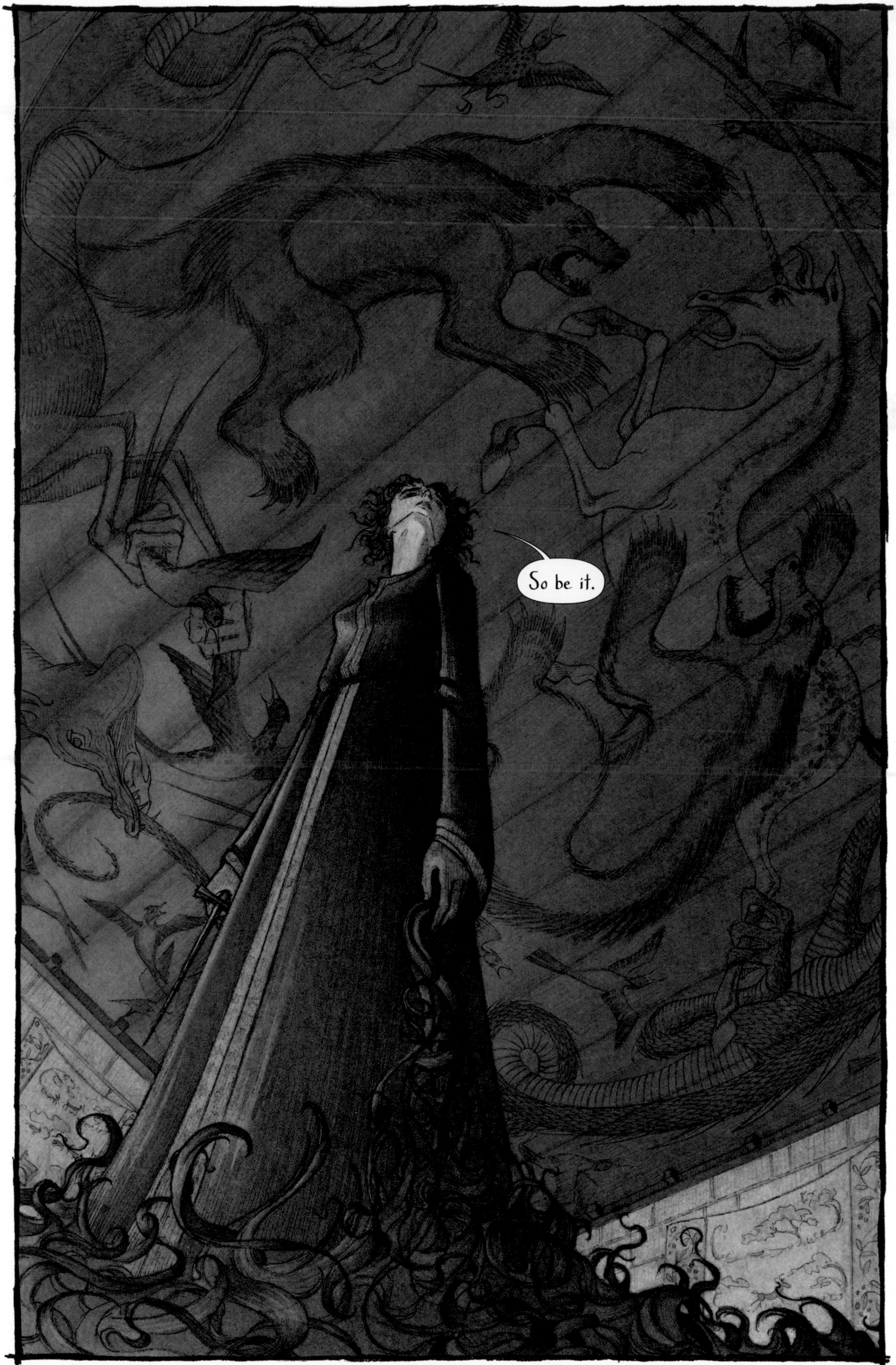
So be it.

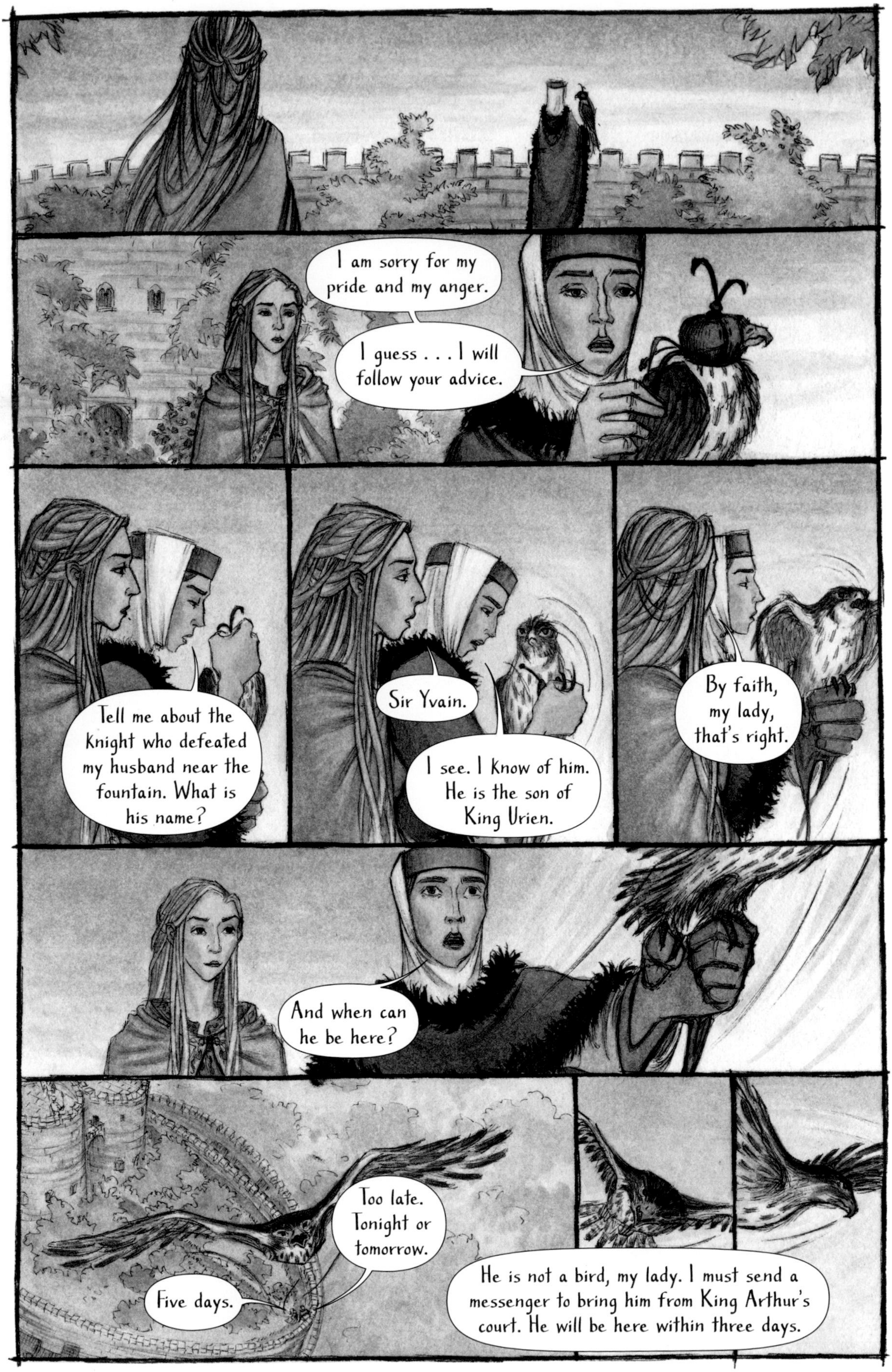
I am sorry for my pride and my anger.
I guess . . . I will follow your advice.
Tell me about the Knight who defeated my husband near the fountain. What is his name?
Sir Yvain.
I see. I know of him. He is the son of King Urien.
By faith, my lady, that's right.
And when can he be here?
He is not a bird, my lady. I must send a messenger to bring him from King Arthur's court. He will be here within three days.
Too late. Tonight or tomorrow.
Five days.

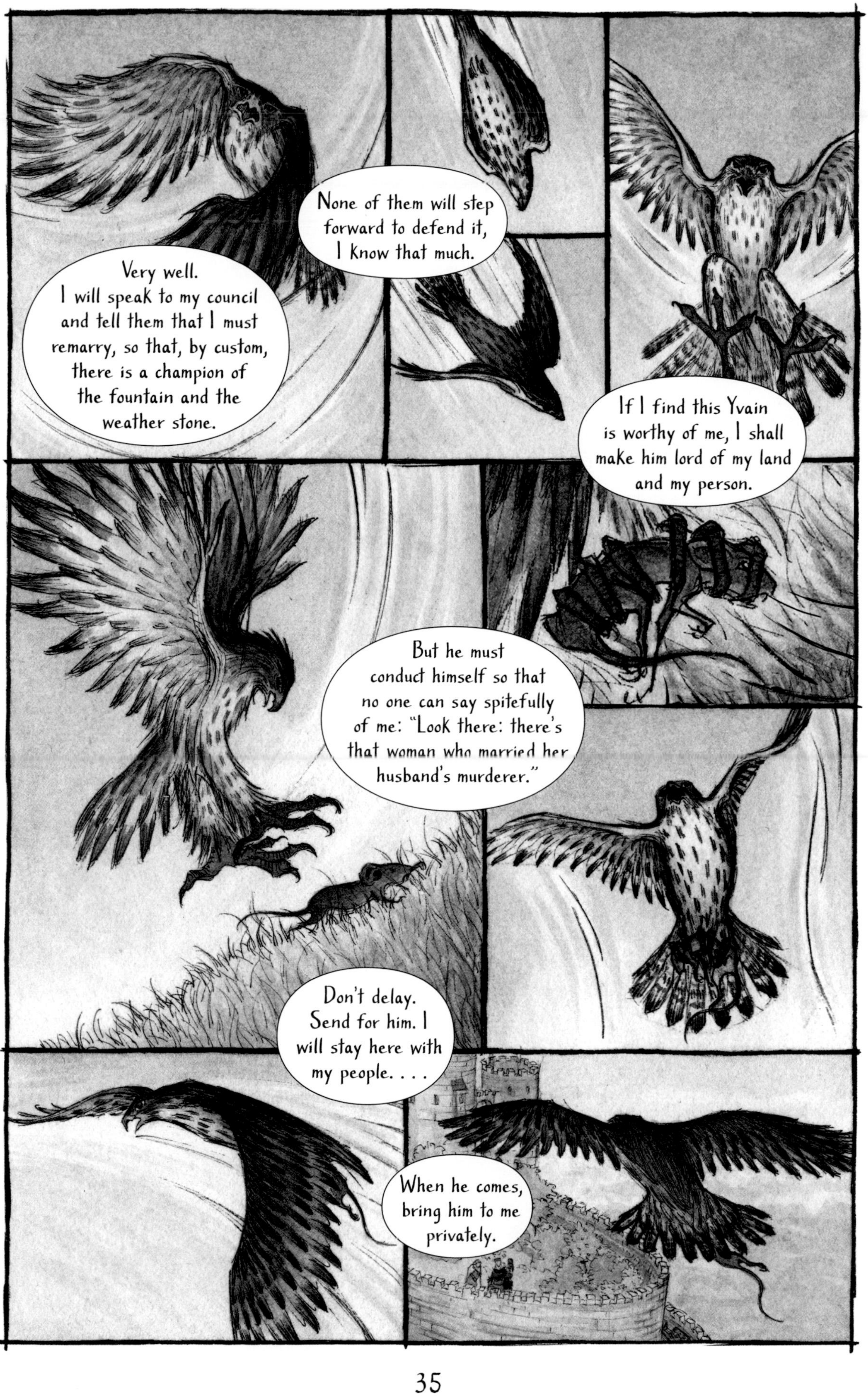
Very well. I will speak to my council and tell them that I must remarry, so that, by custom, there is a champion of the fountain and the weather stone.
None of them will step forward to defend it, I know that much.
If I find this Yvain is worthy of me, I shall make him lord of my land and my person.
But he must conduct himself so that no one can say spitefully of me: "Look there: there's that woman who married her husband's murderer."
Don't delay. Send for him. I will stay here with my people. . . .
When he comes, bring him to me privately.

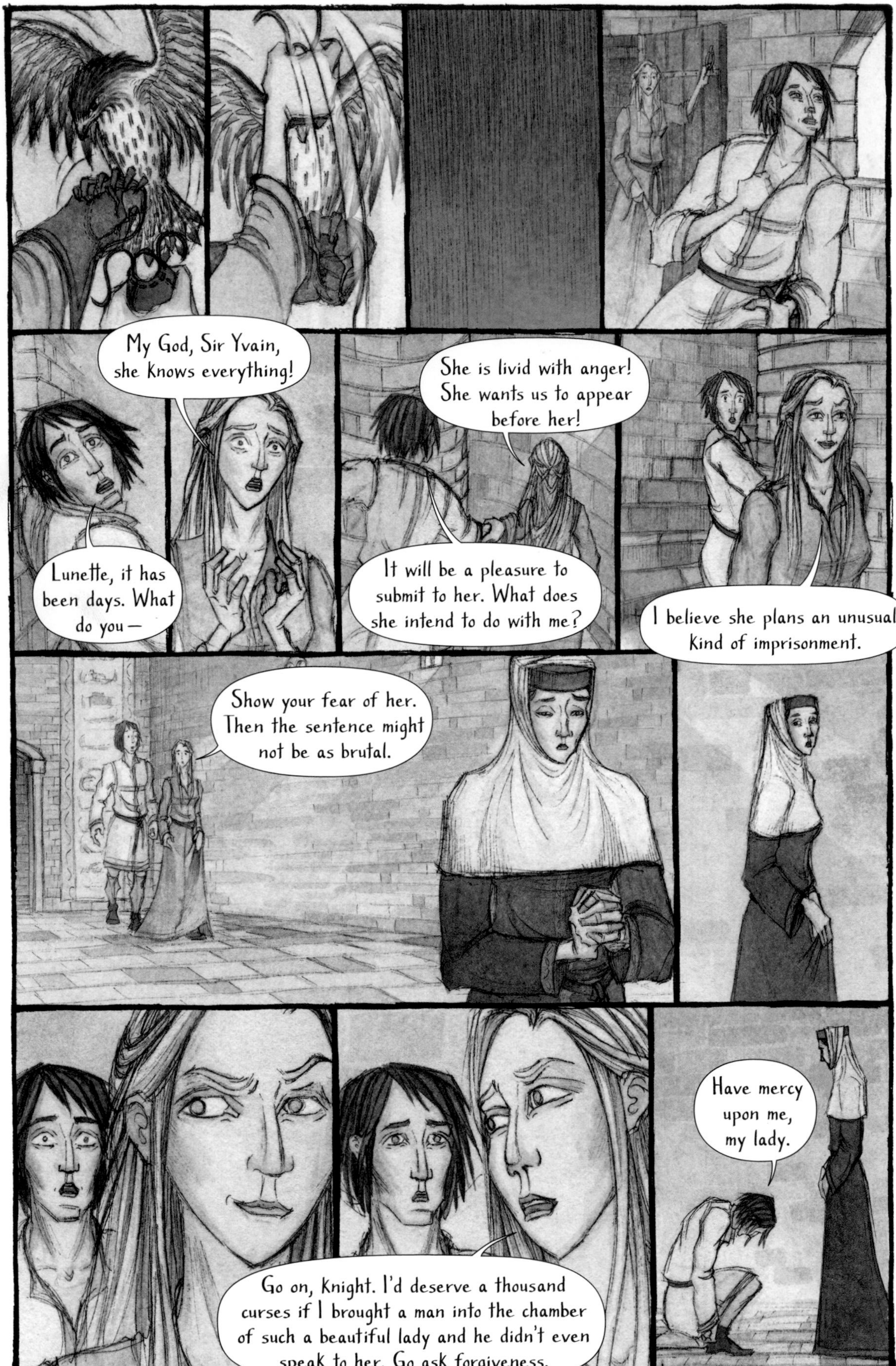
My God, Sir Yvain, she knows everything!
Lunette, it has been days. What do you—
She is livid with anger! She wants us to appear before her!
It will be a pleasure to submit to her. What does she intend to do with me?
I believe she plans an unusual kind of imprisonment.
Show your fear of her. Then the sentence might not be as brutal.
Go on, knight. I'd deserve a thousand curses if I brought a man into the chamber of such a beautiful lady and he didn't even speak to her. Go ask forgiveness.
Have mercy upon me, my lady.

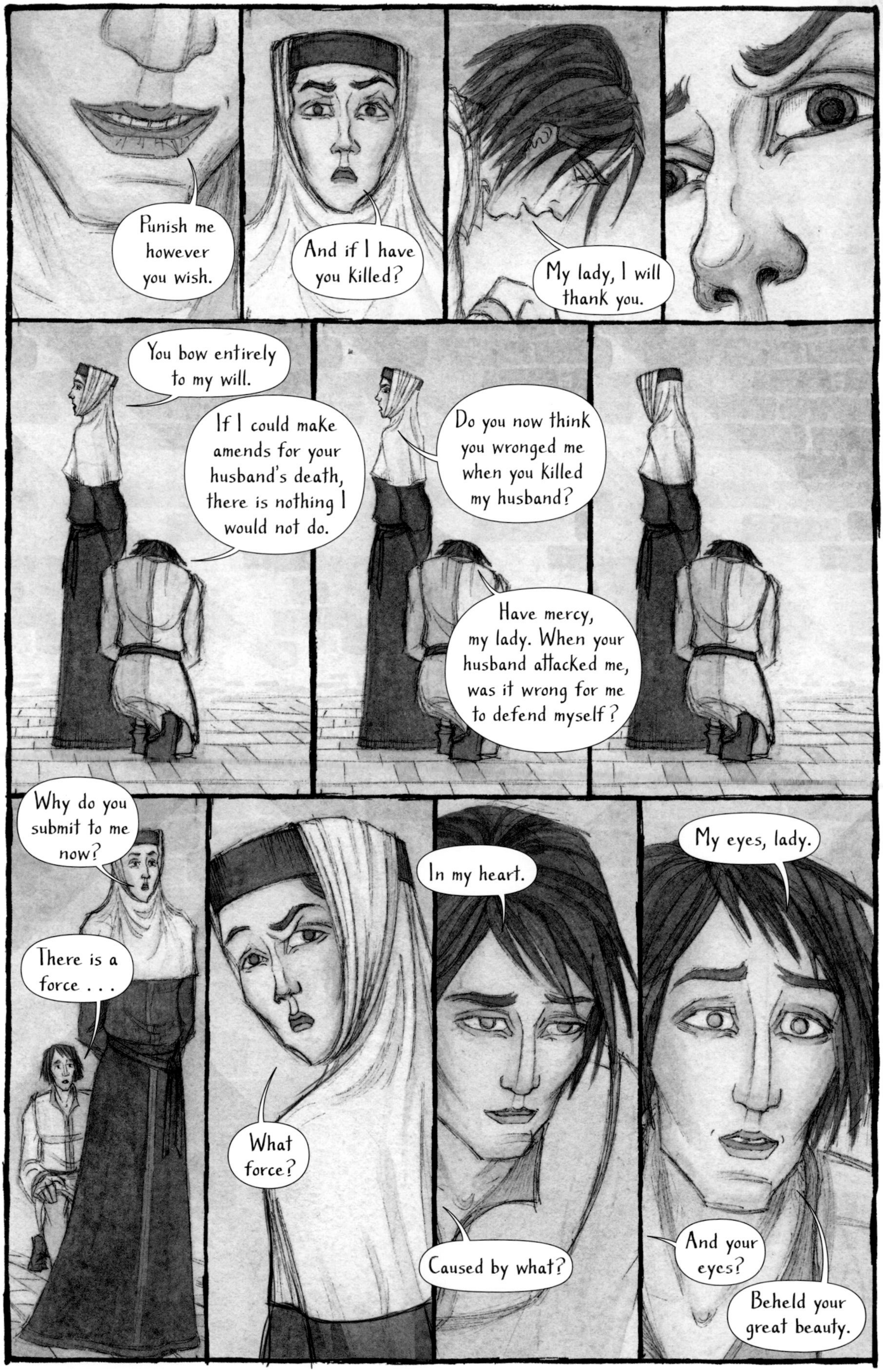
Punish me however you wish.
And if I have you killed?
My lady, I will thank you.
You bow entirely to my will.
If I could make amends for your husband's death, there is nothing I would not do.
Do you now think you wronged me when you killed my husband?
Have mercy, my lady. When your husband attacked me, was it wrong for me to defend myself?
Why do you submit to me now?
There is a force . . .
What force?
In my heart.
Caused by what?
My eyes, lady.
And your eyes?
Beheld your great beauty.

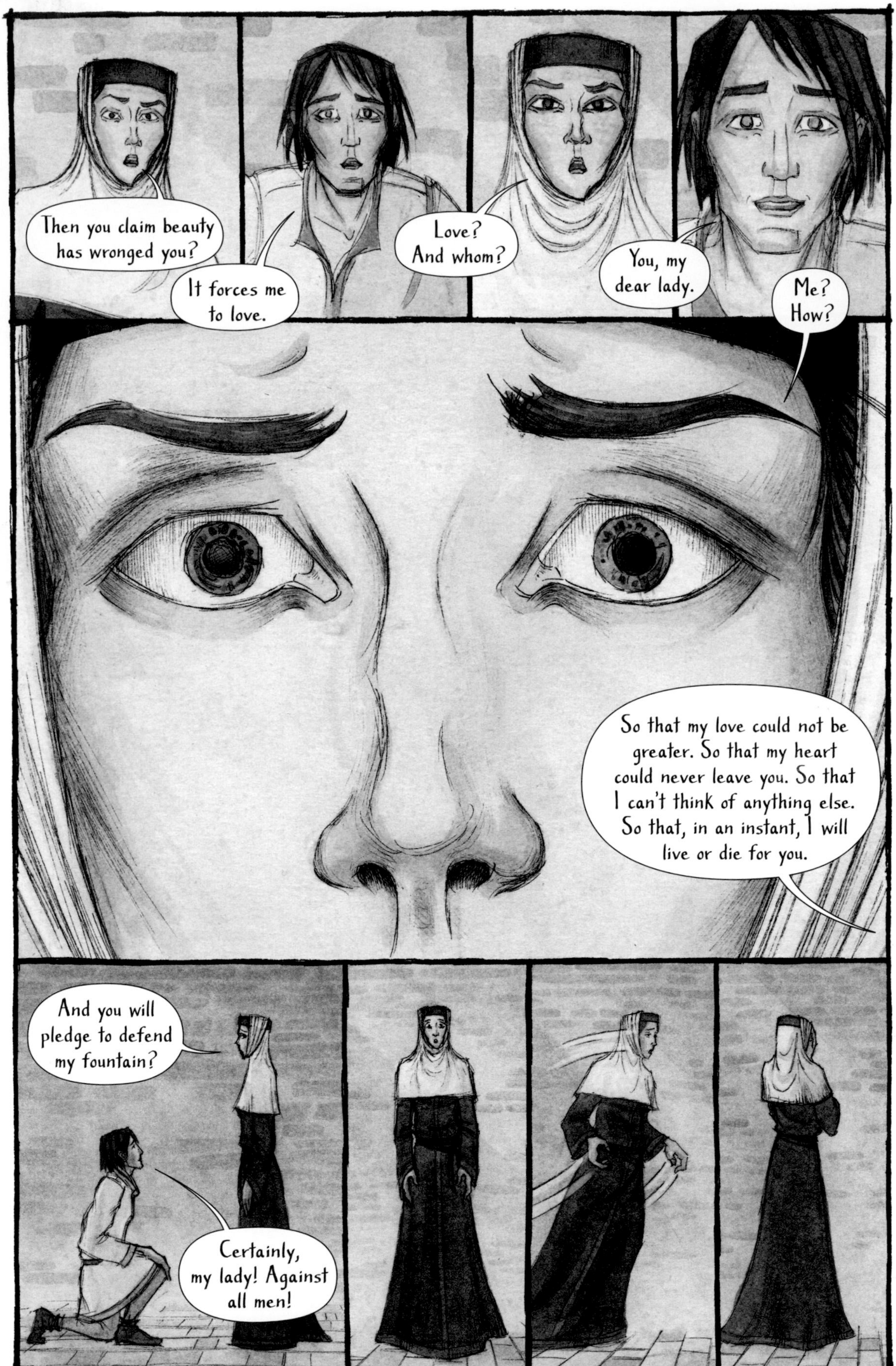
Then you claim beauty has wronged you?
It forces me to love.
Love? And whom?
You, my dear lady.
Me? How?
So that my love could not be greater. So that my heart could never leave you. So that I can't think of anything else. So that, in an instant, I will live or die for you.
And you will pledge to defend my fountain?
Certainly, my lady! Against all men!

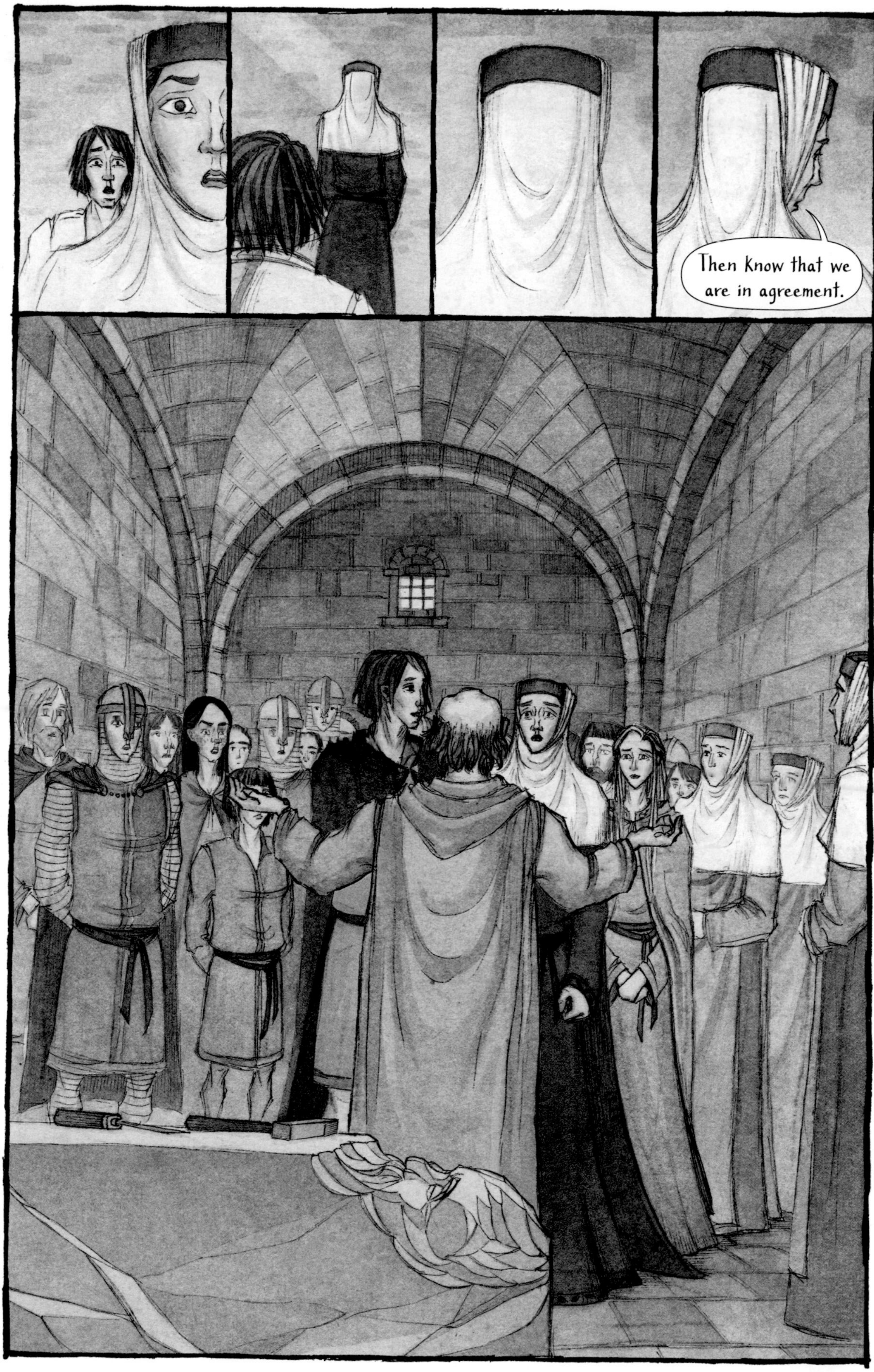
Then know that we are in agreement.

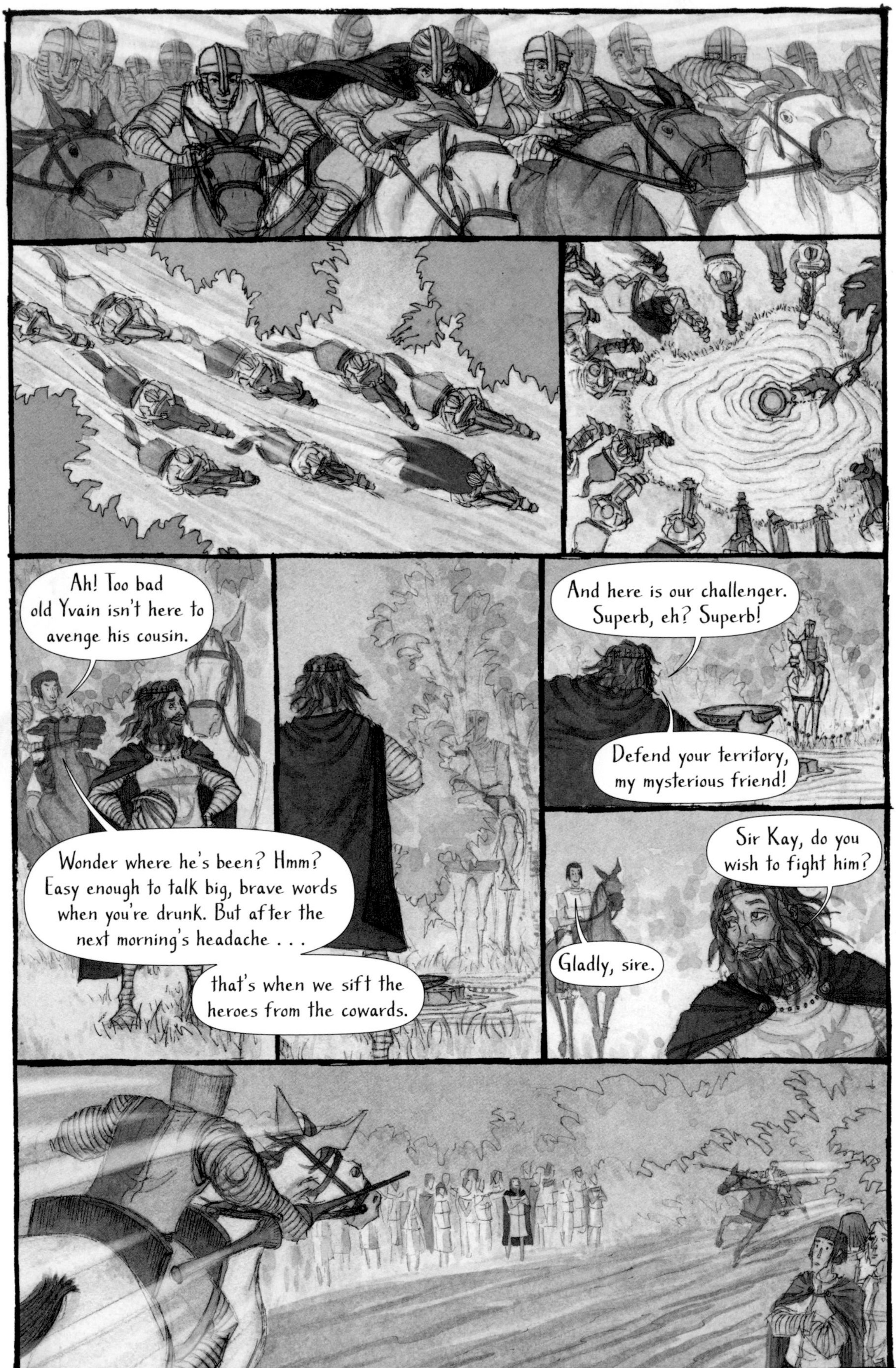
Ah! Too bad old Yvain isn't here to avenge his cousin.
Wonder where he's been? Hmm? Easy enough to talk big, brave words when you're drunk. But after the next morning's headache . . .
that's when we sift the heroes from the cowards.
And here is our challenger. Superb, eh? Superb!
Defend your territory, my mysterious friend!
Sir Kay, do you wish to fight him?
Gladly, sire.

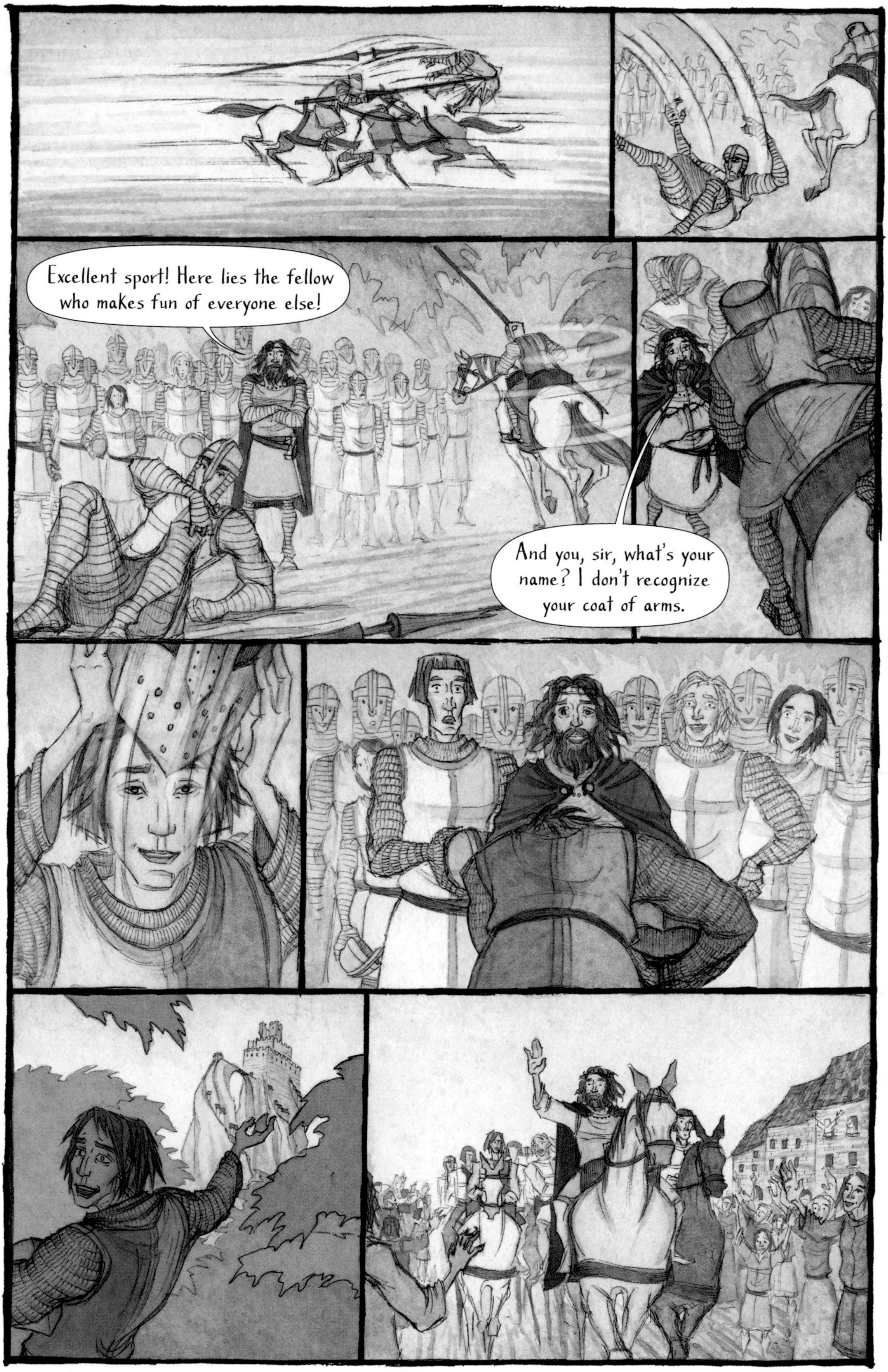
Excellent sport! Here lies the fellow who makes fun of everyone else!
And you, sir, what's your name? I don't recognize your coat of arms.

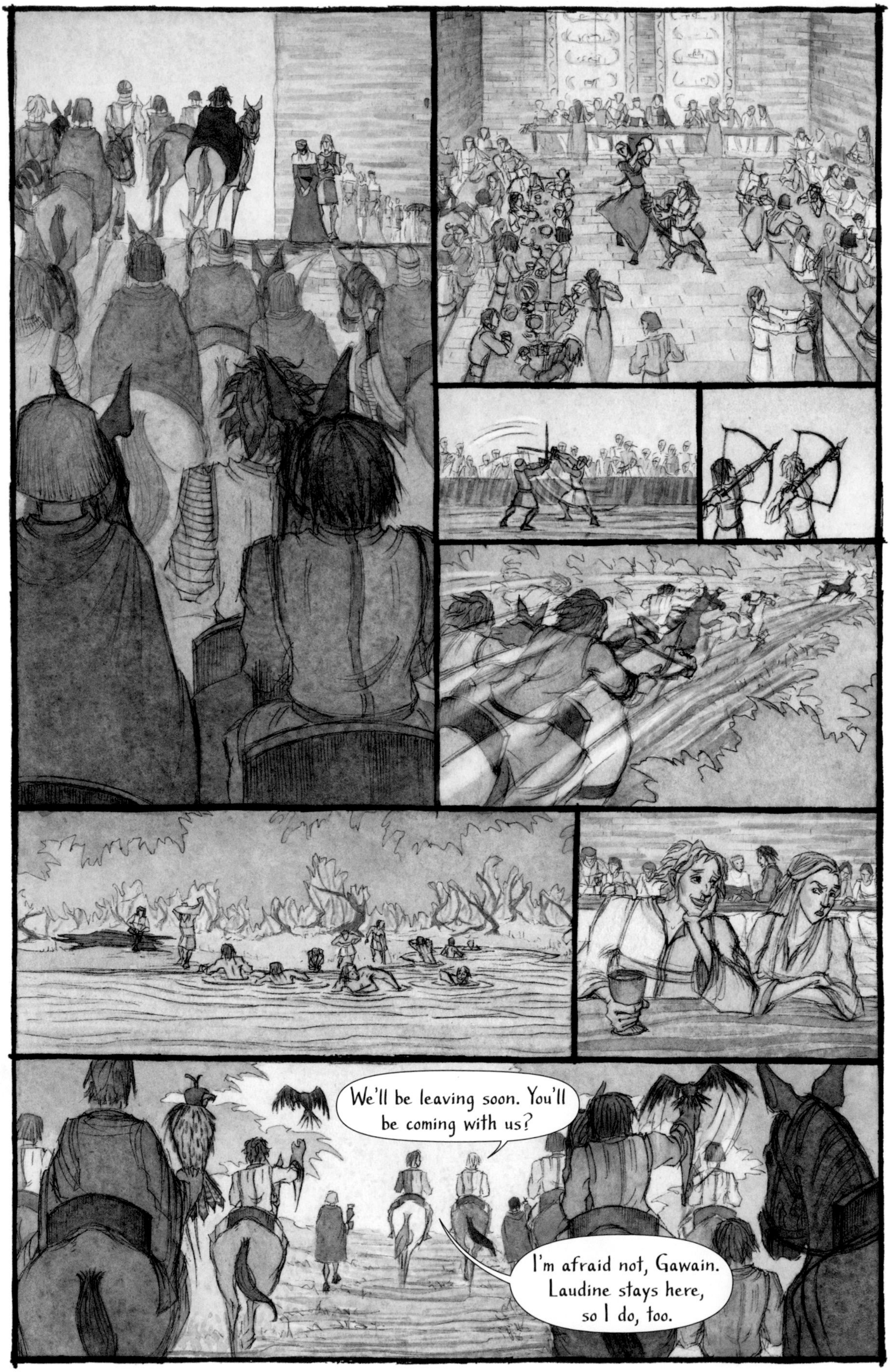
We'll be leaving soon. You'll be coming with us?
I'm afraid not, Gawain. Laudine stays here, so I do, too.

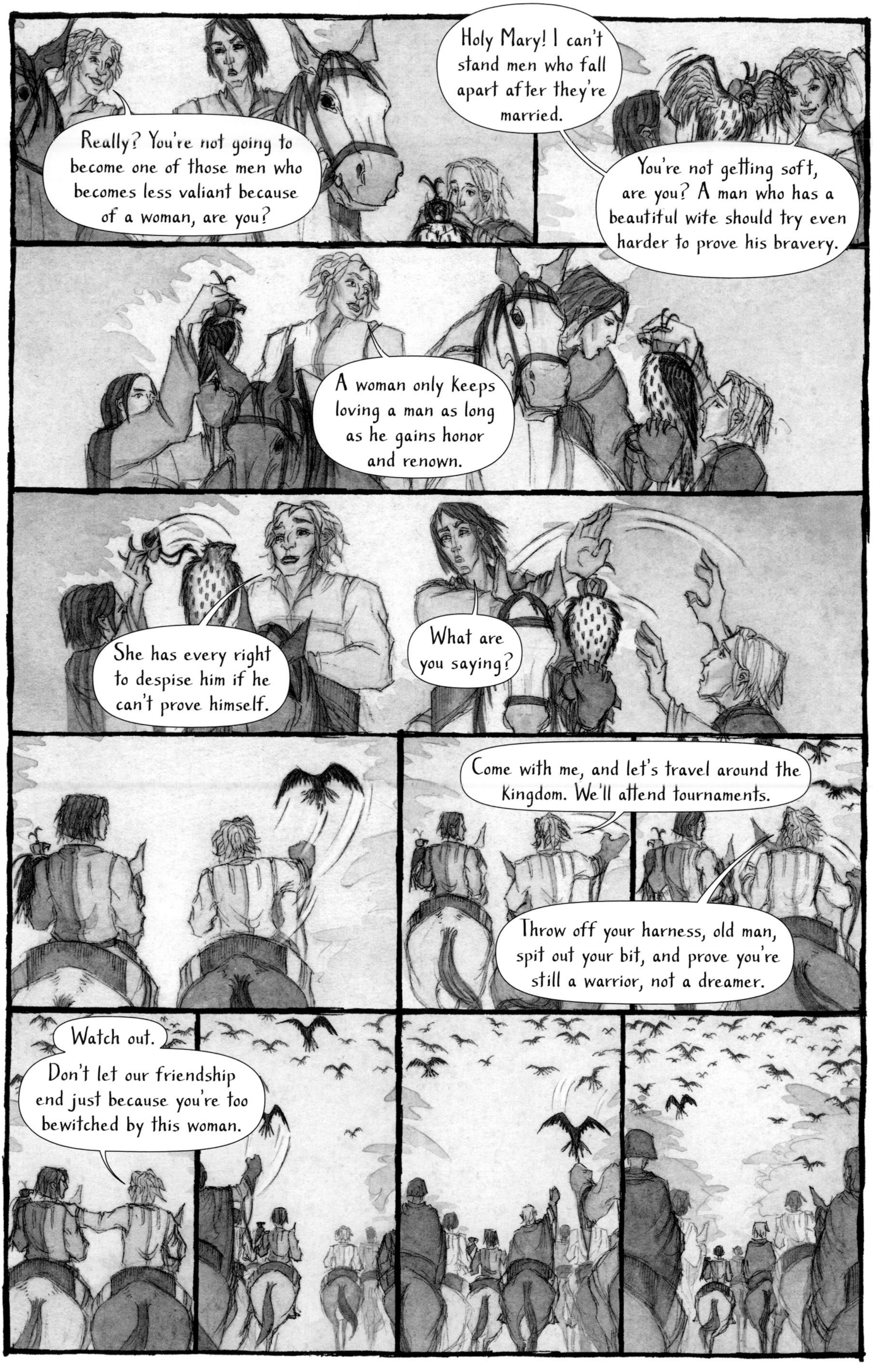
Really? You're not going to become one of those men who becomes less valiant because of a woman, are you?
Holy Mary! I can't stand men who fall apart after they're married.
You're not getting soft, are you? A man who has a beautiful wife should try even harder to prove his bravery.
A woman only keeps loving a man as long as he gains honor and renown.
She has every right to despise him if he can't prove himself.
What are you saying?
Come with me, and let's travel around the Kingdom. We'll attend tournaments.
Throw off your harness, old man, spit out your bit, and prove you're still a warrior, not a dreamer.
Watch out.
Don't let our friendship end just because you're too bewitched by this woman.

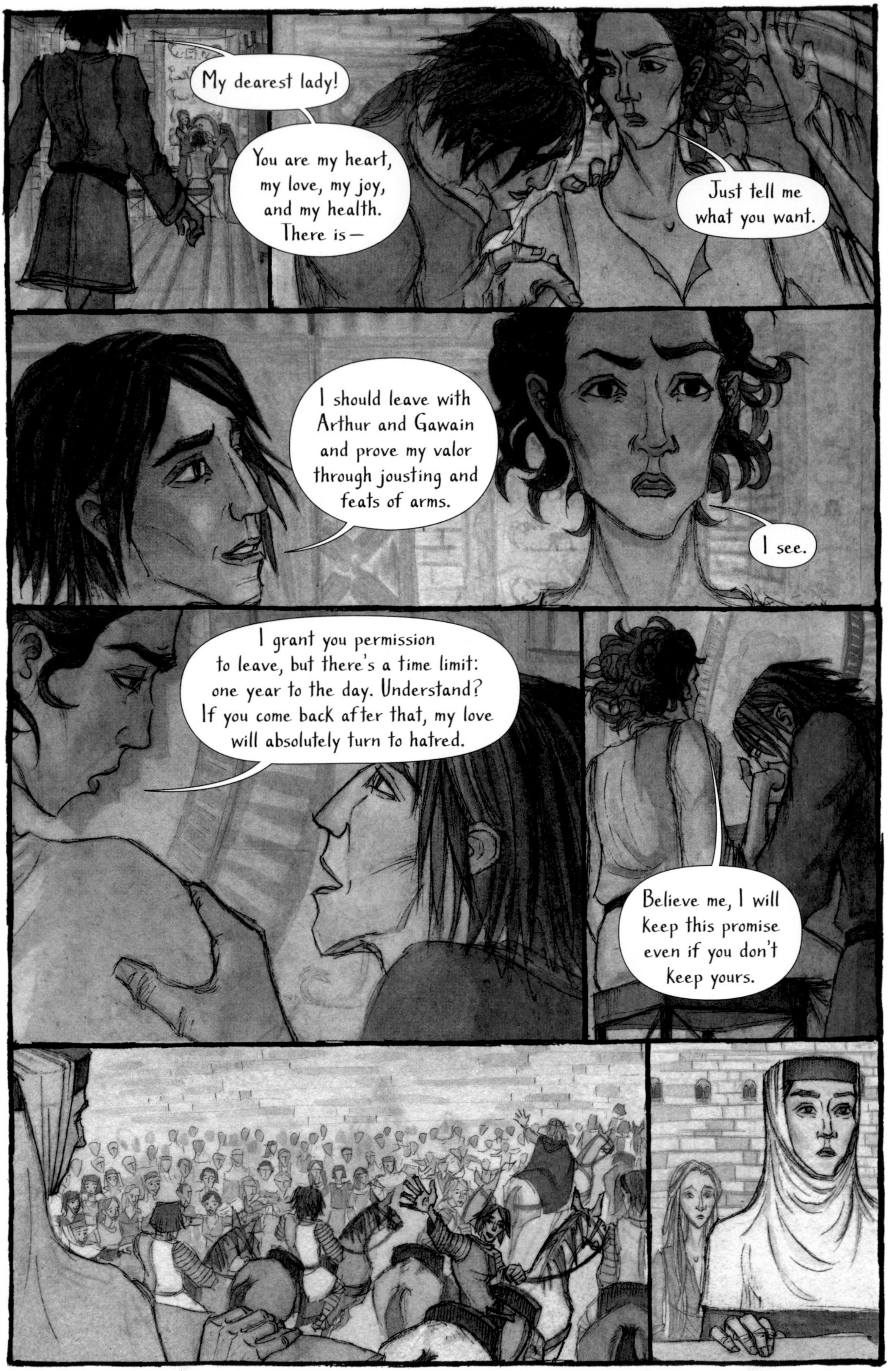

My dearest lady!
You are my heart, my love, my joy, and my health. There is—
Just tell me what you want.
I should leave with Arthur and Gawain and prove my valor through jousting and feats of arms.
I see.
I grant you permission to leave, but there's a time limit: one year to the day. Understand? If you come back after that, my love will absolutely turn to hatred.
Believe me, I will keep this promise even if you don't keep yours.

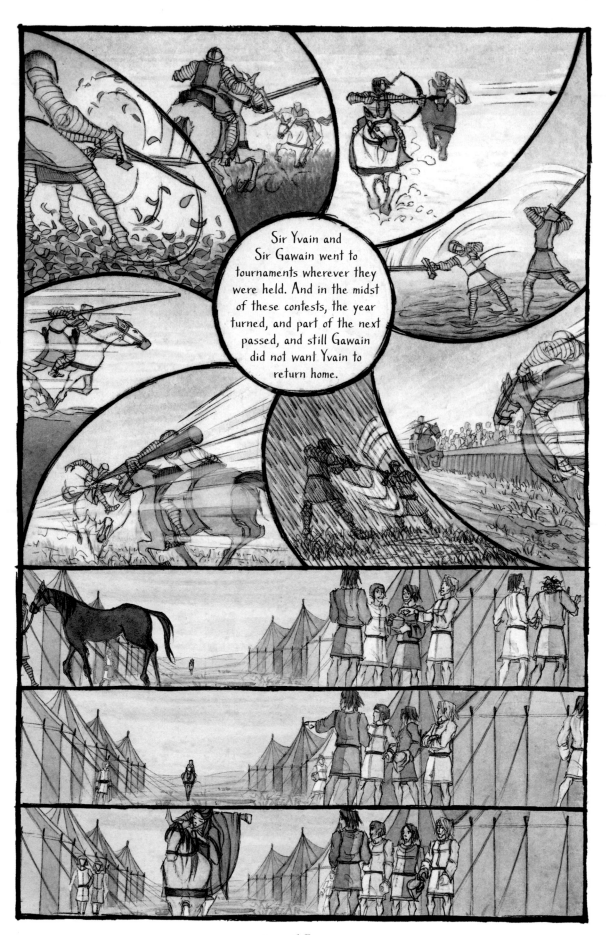

Sir Yvain and Sir Gawain went to tournaments wherever they were held. And in the midst of these contests, the year turned, and part of the next passed, and still Gawain did not want Yvain to return home.

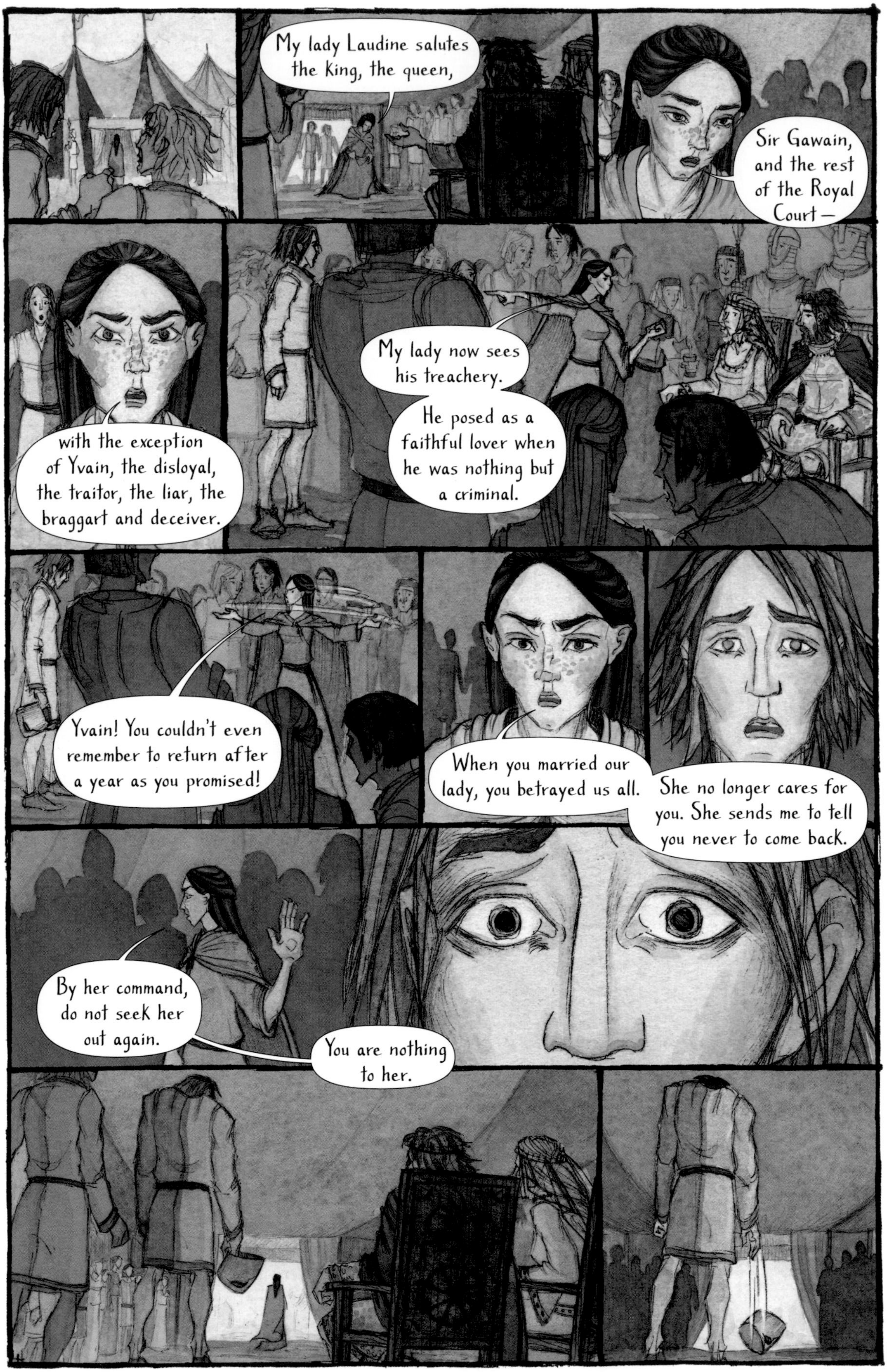
My lady Laudine salutes the King, the queen,
Sir Gawain, and the rest of the Royal Court—
with the exception of Yvain, the disloyal, the traitor, the liar, the braggart and deceiver.
My lady now sees his treachery.
He posed as a faithful lover when he was nothing but a criminal.
Yvain! You couldn't even remember to return after a year as you promised!
When you married our lady, you betrayed us all.
She no longer cares for you. She sends me to tell you never to come back.
By her command, do not seek her out again.
You are nothing to her.

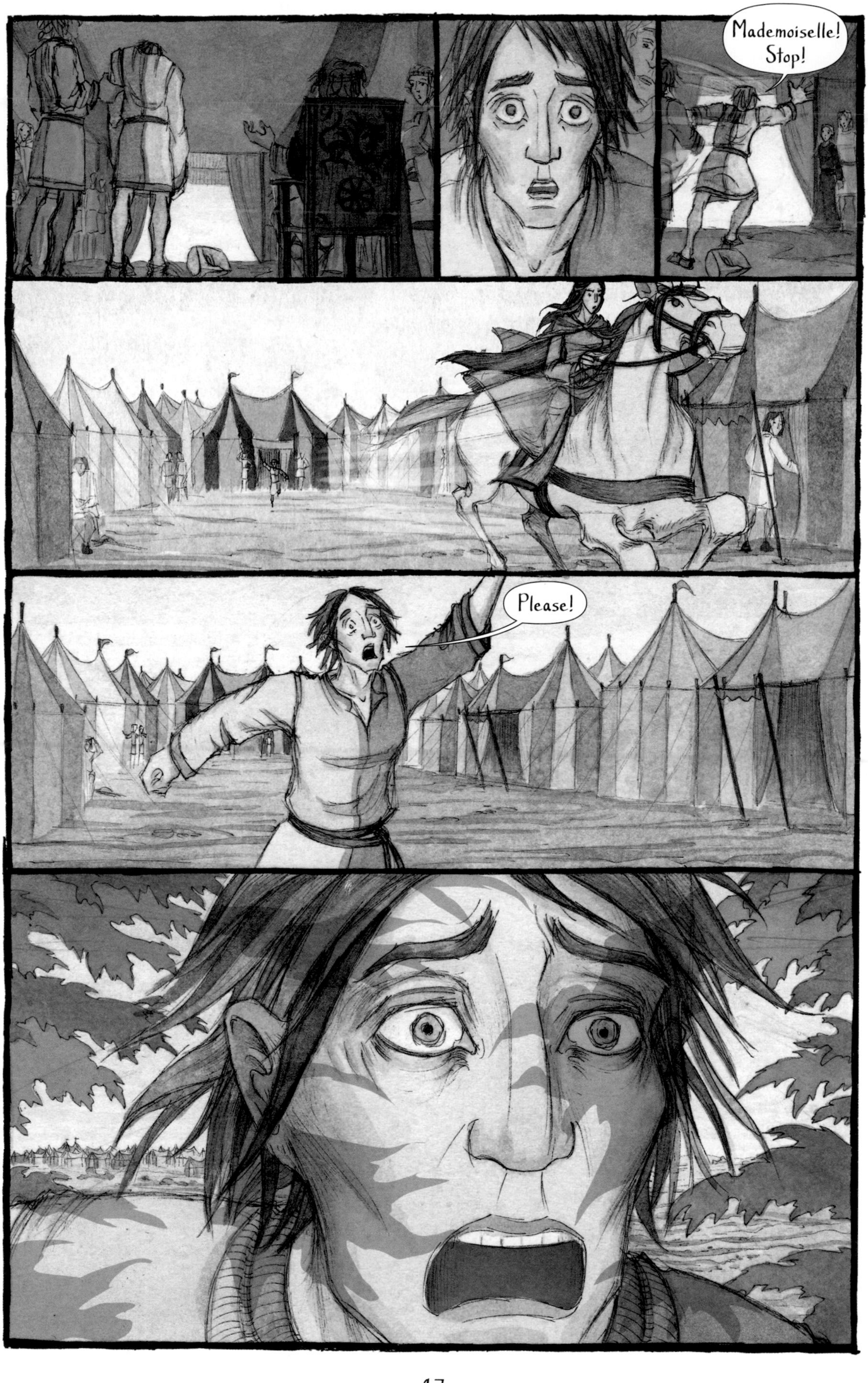
Mademoiselle! Stop!
Please!

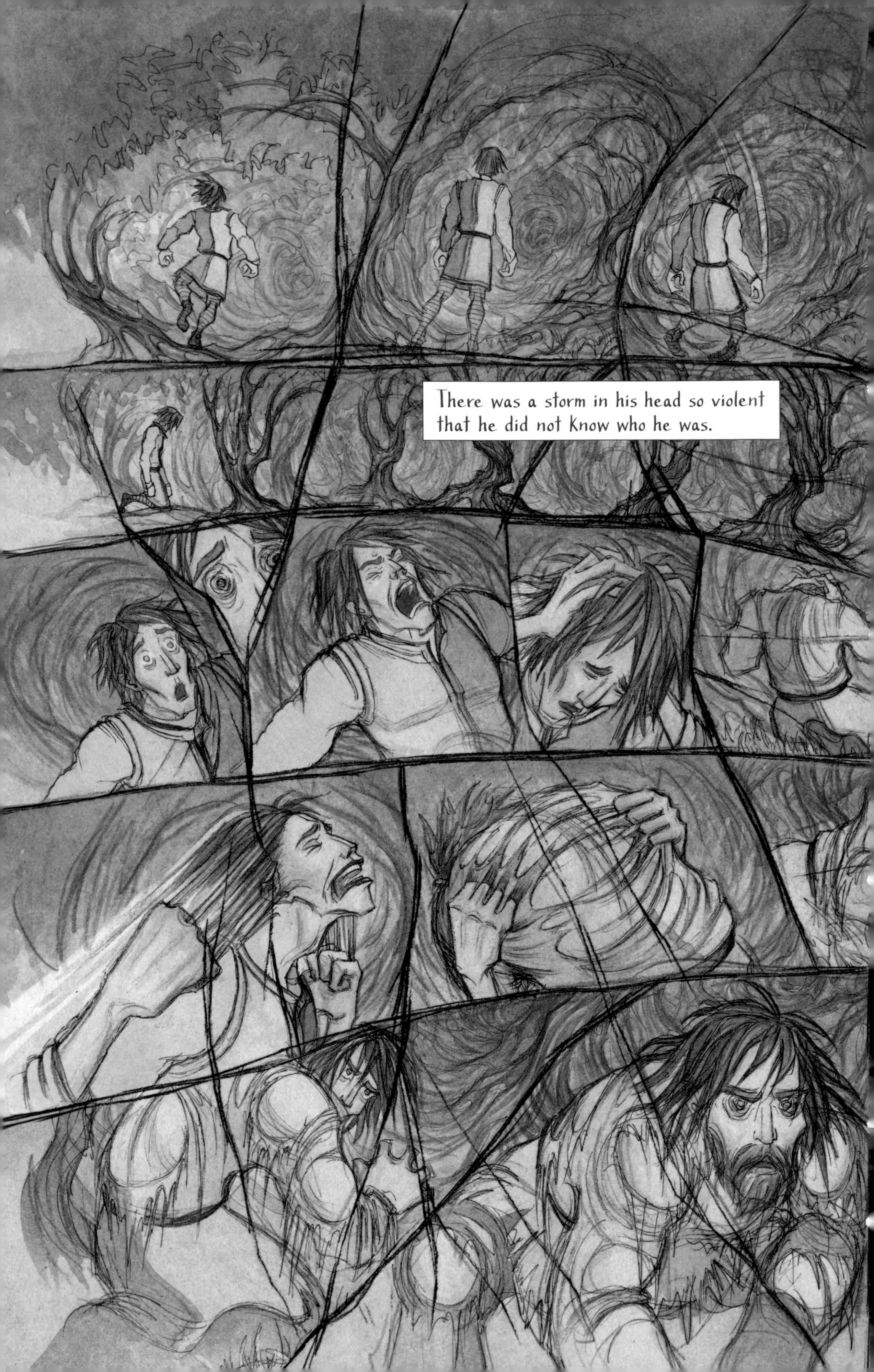
There was a storm in his head so violent that he did not know who he was.

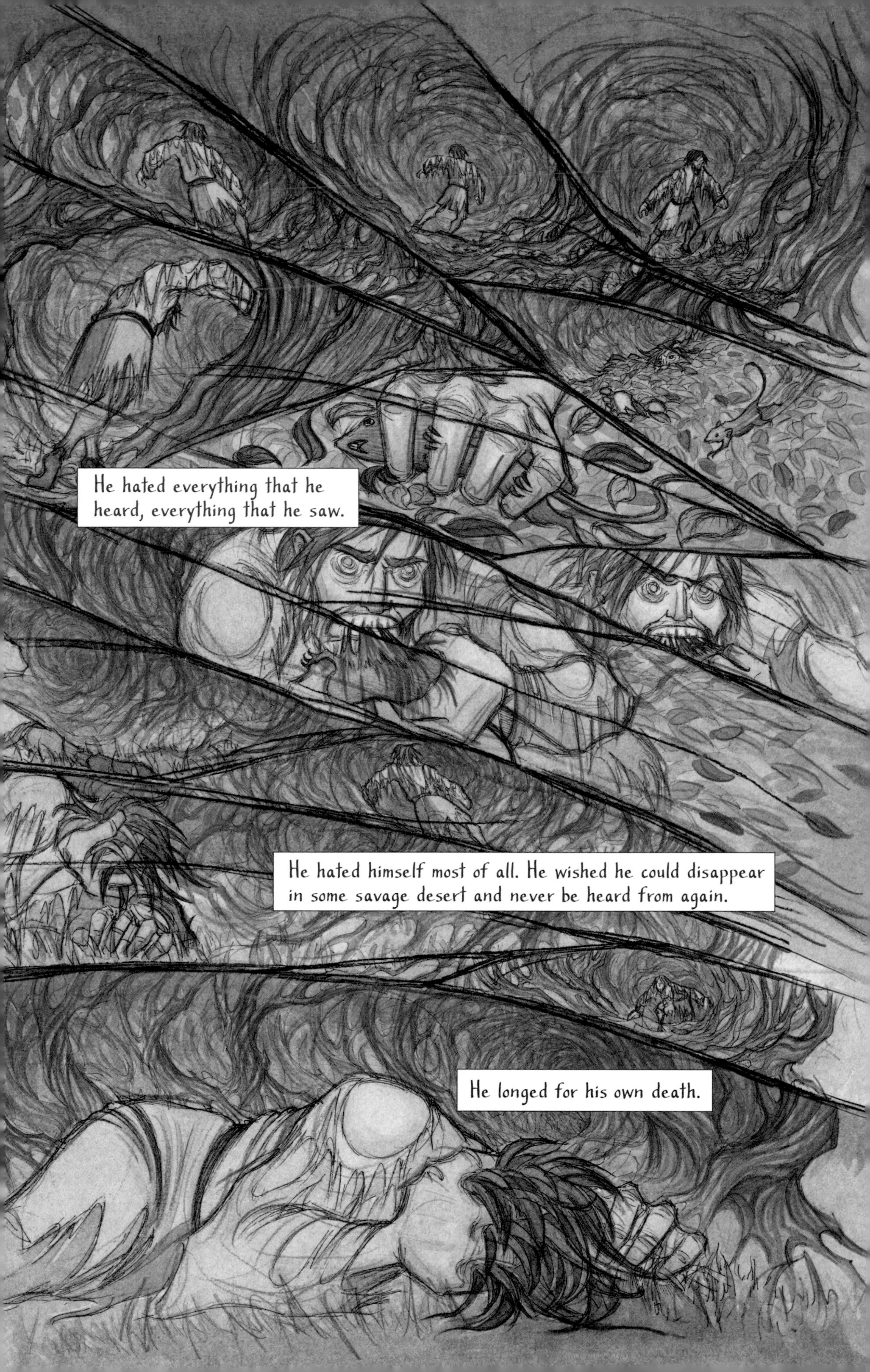
He hated everything that he heard, everything that he saw.
He hated himself most of all. He wished he could disappear in some savage desert and never be heard from again.
He longed for his own death.

PART II

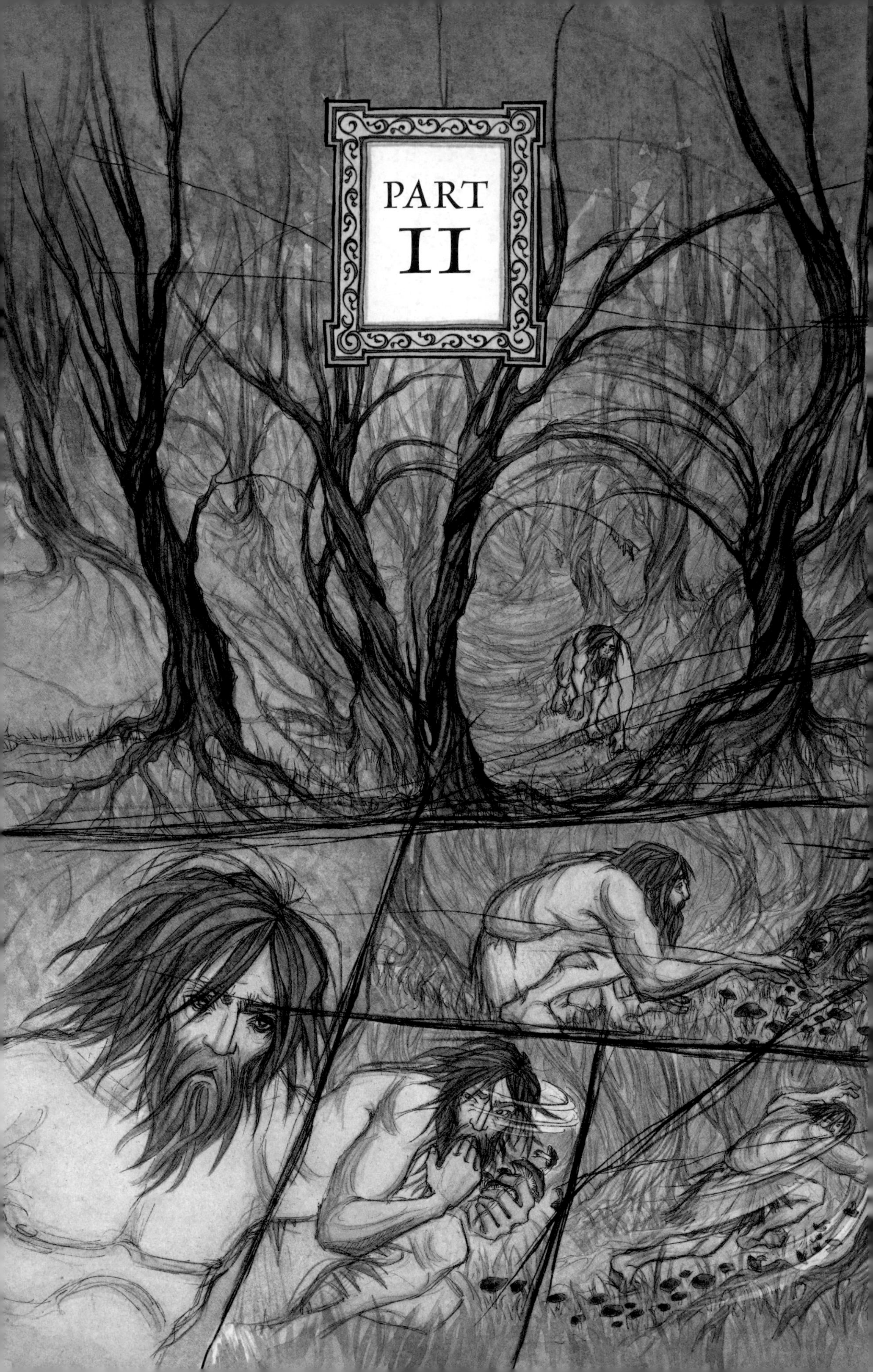

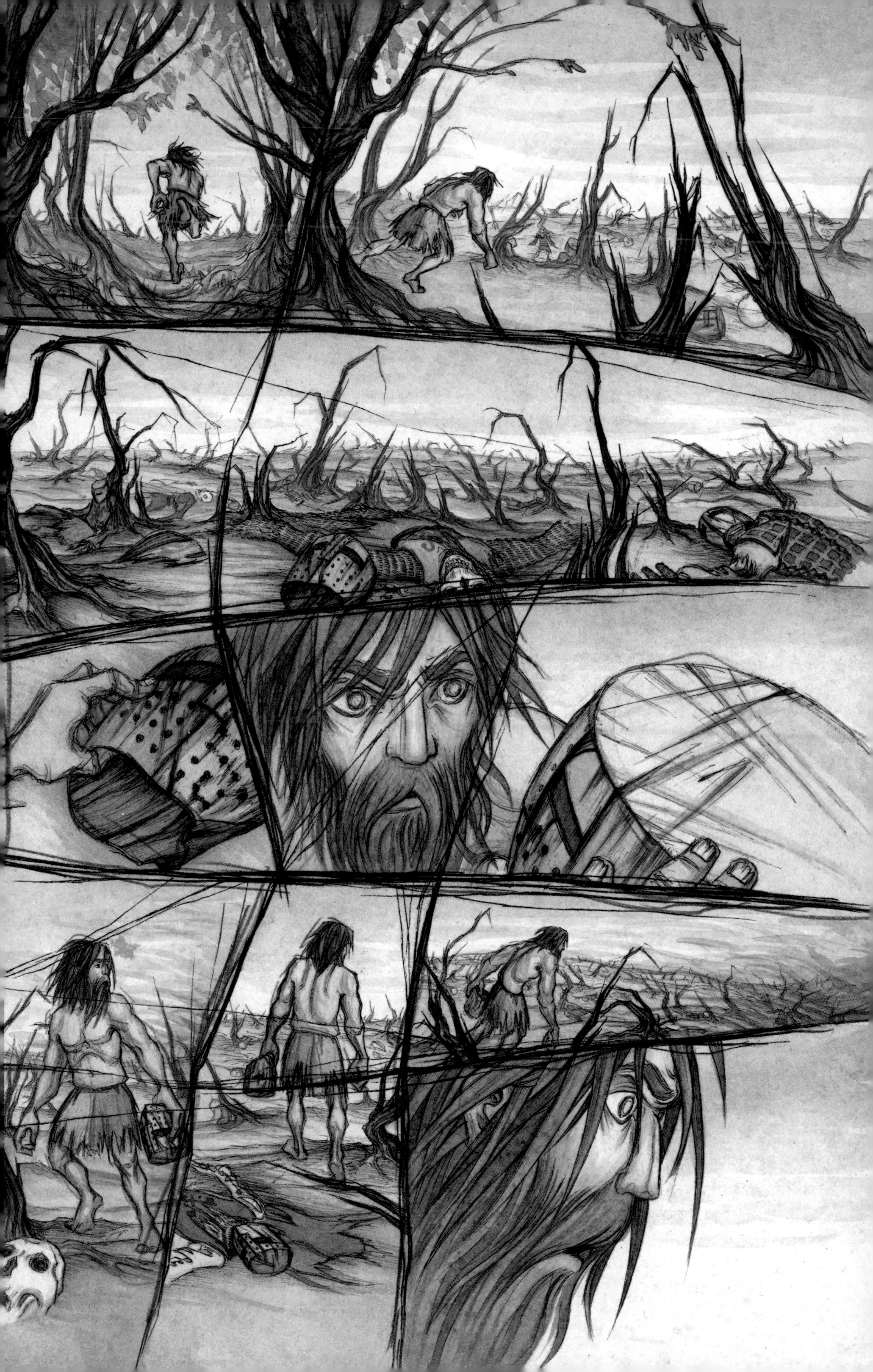

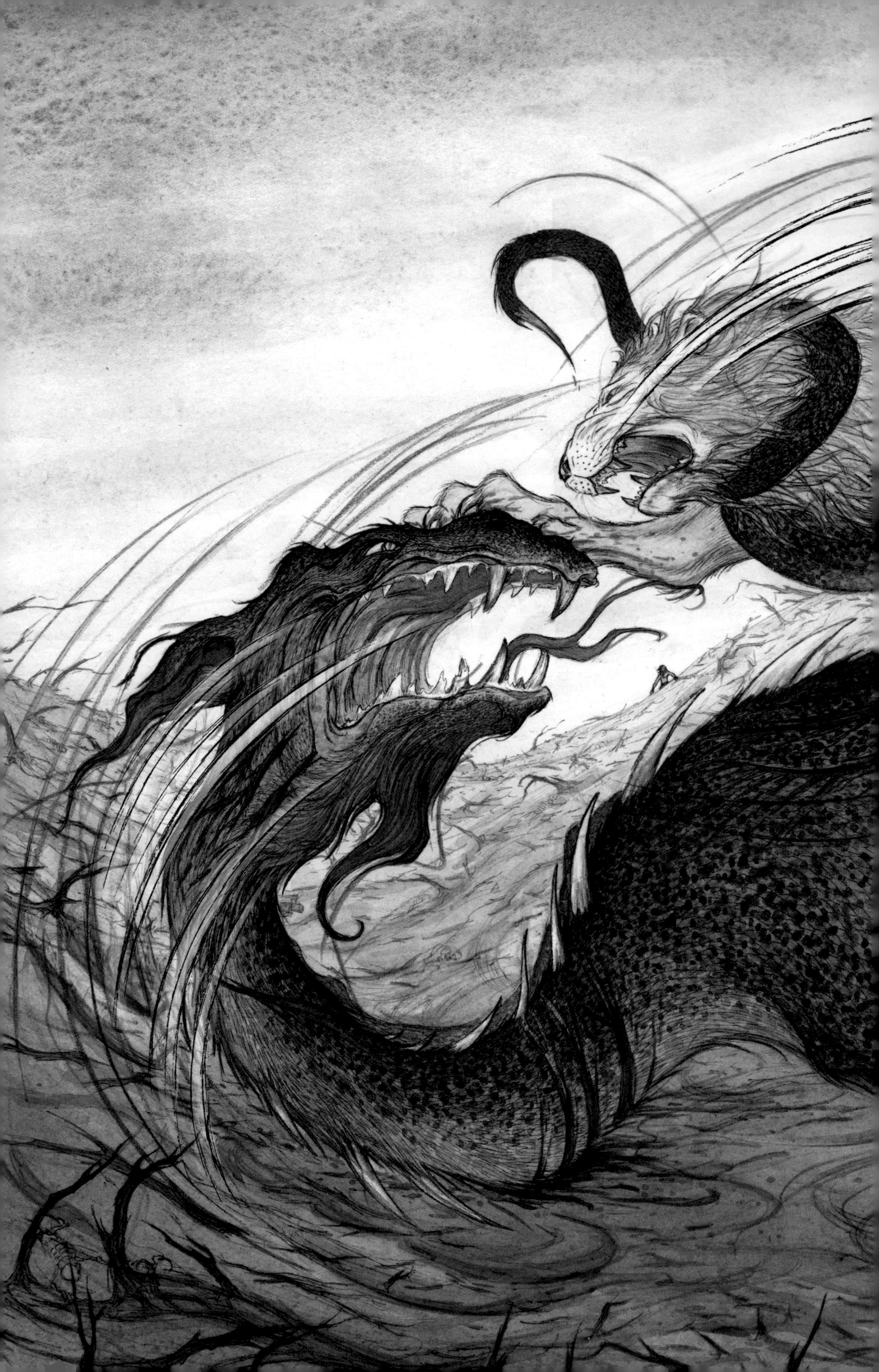

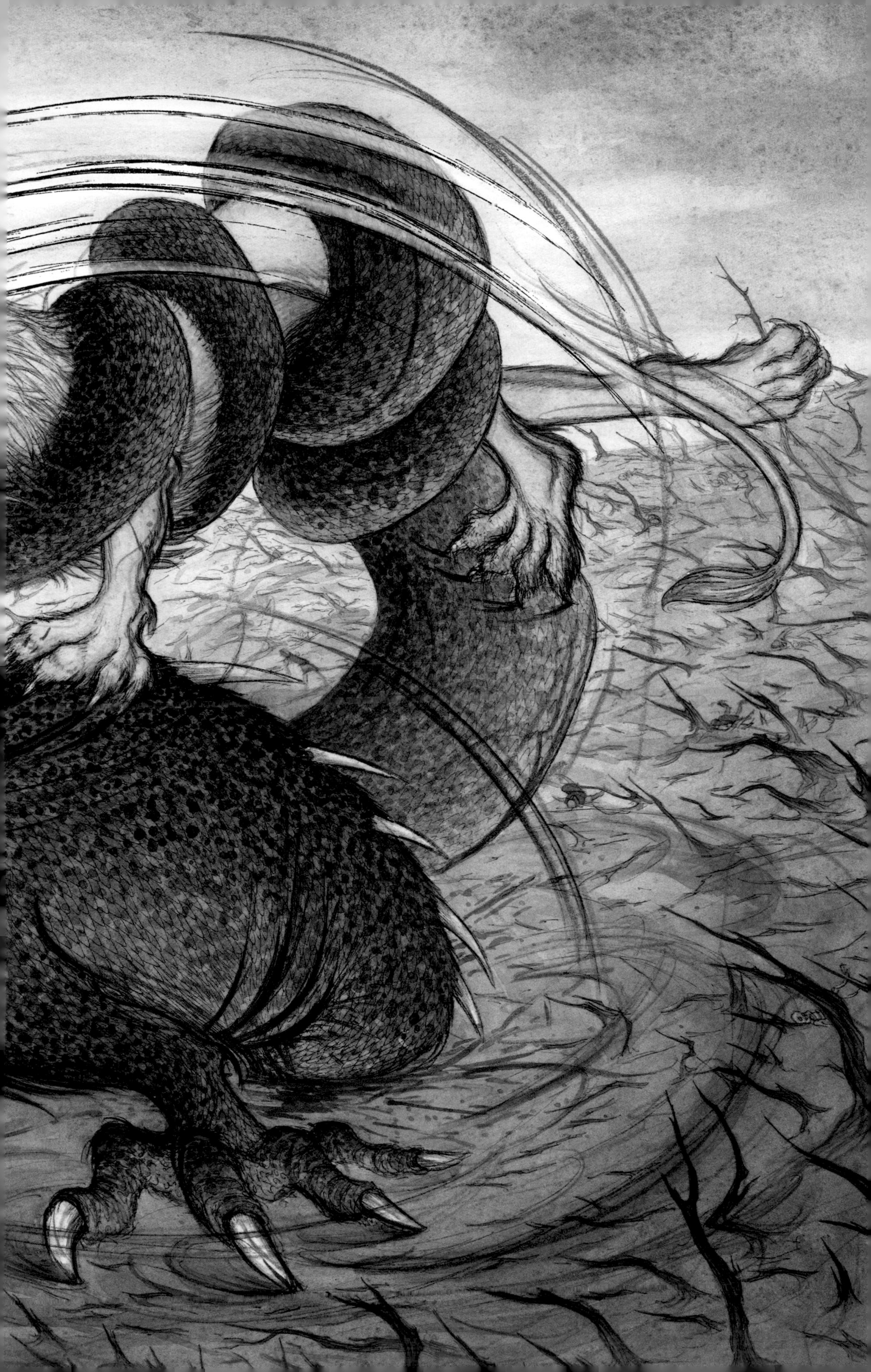

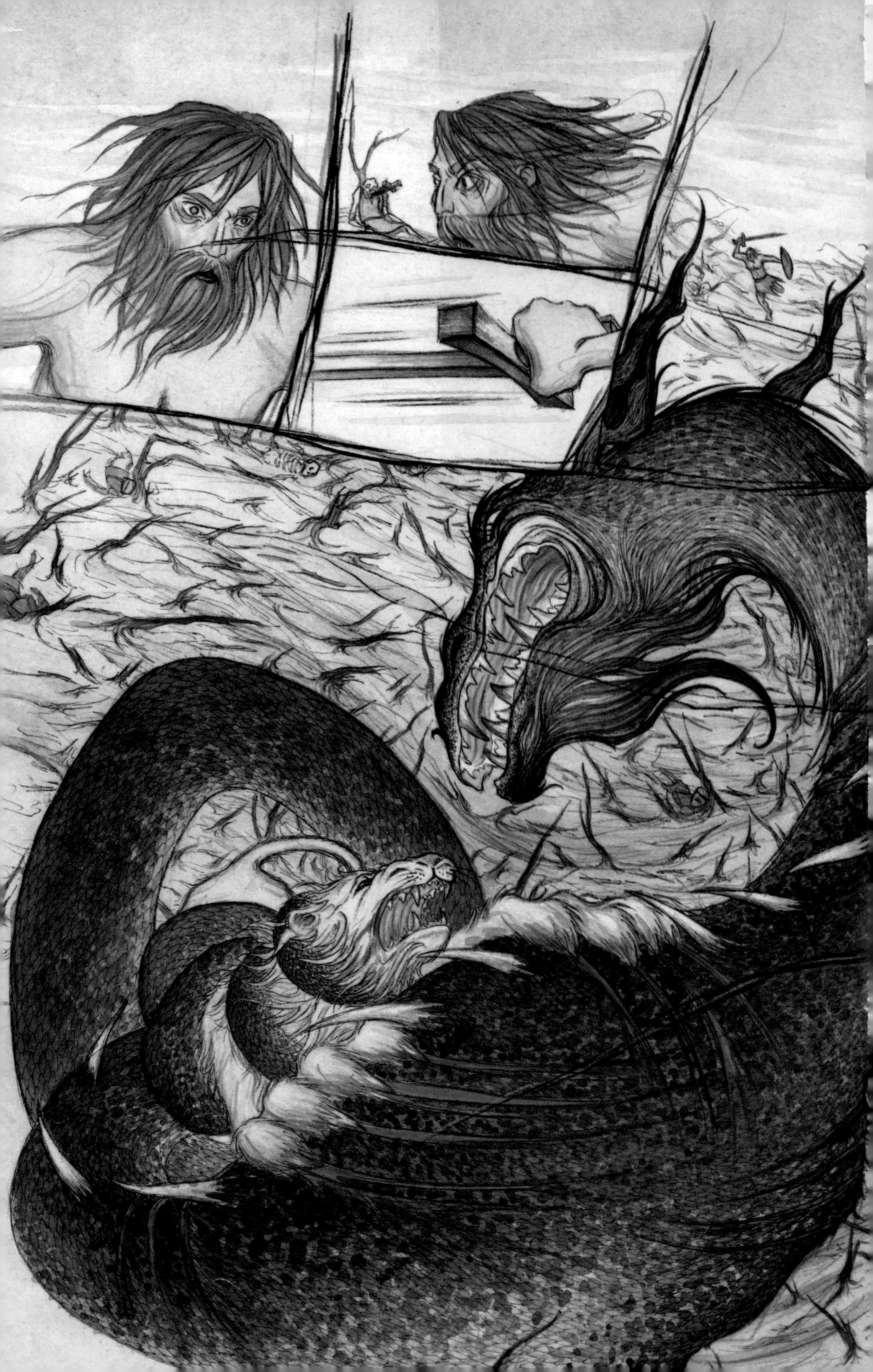

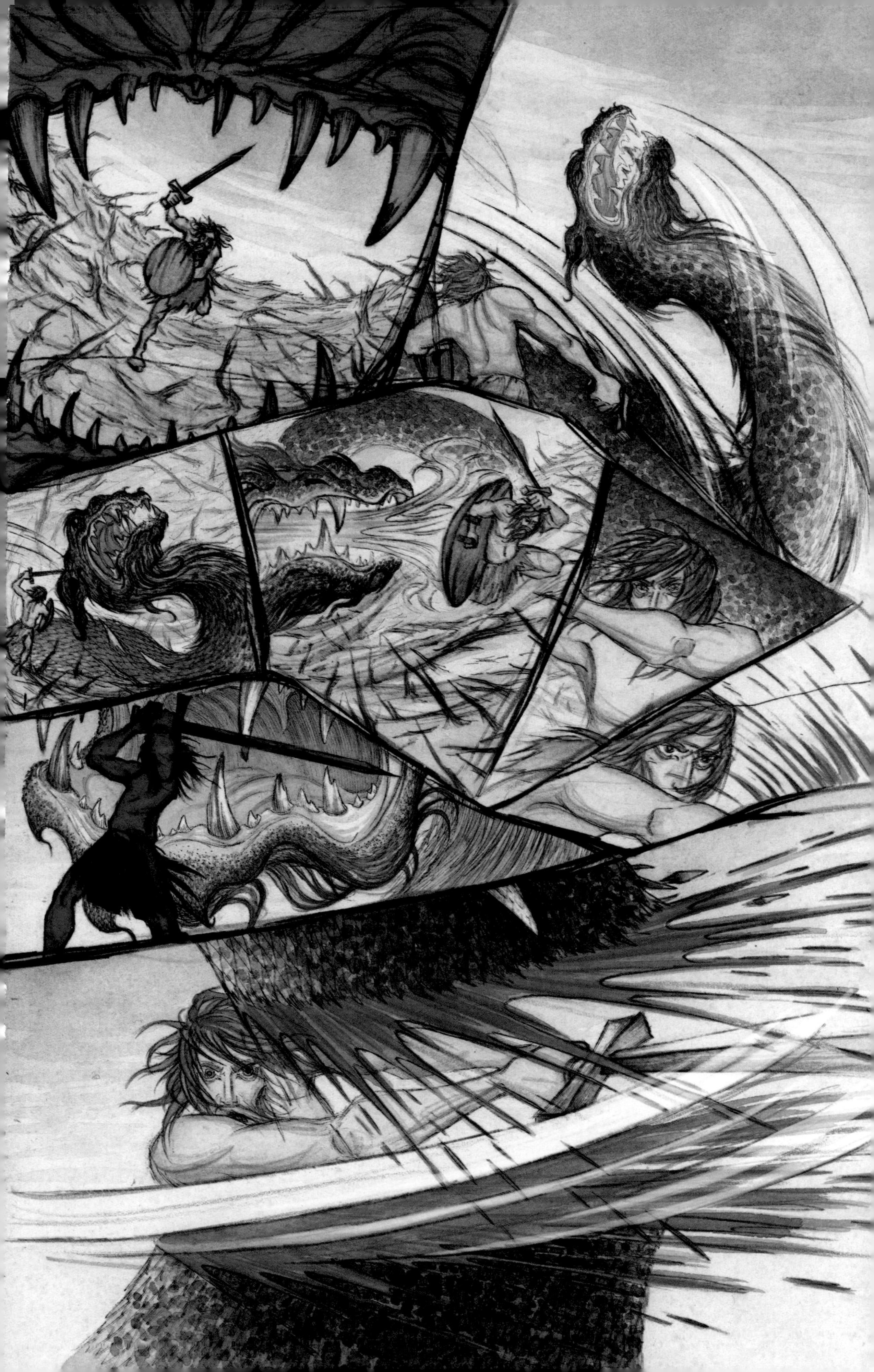

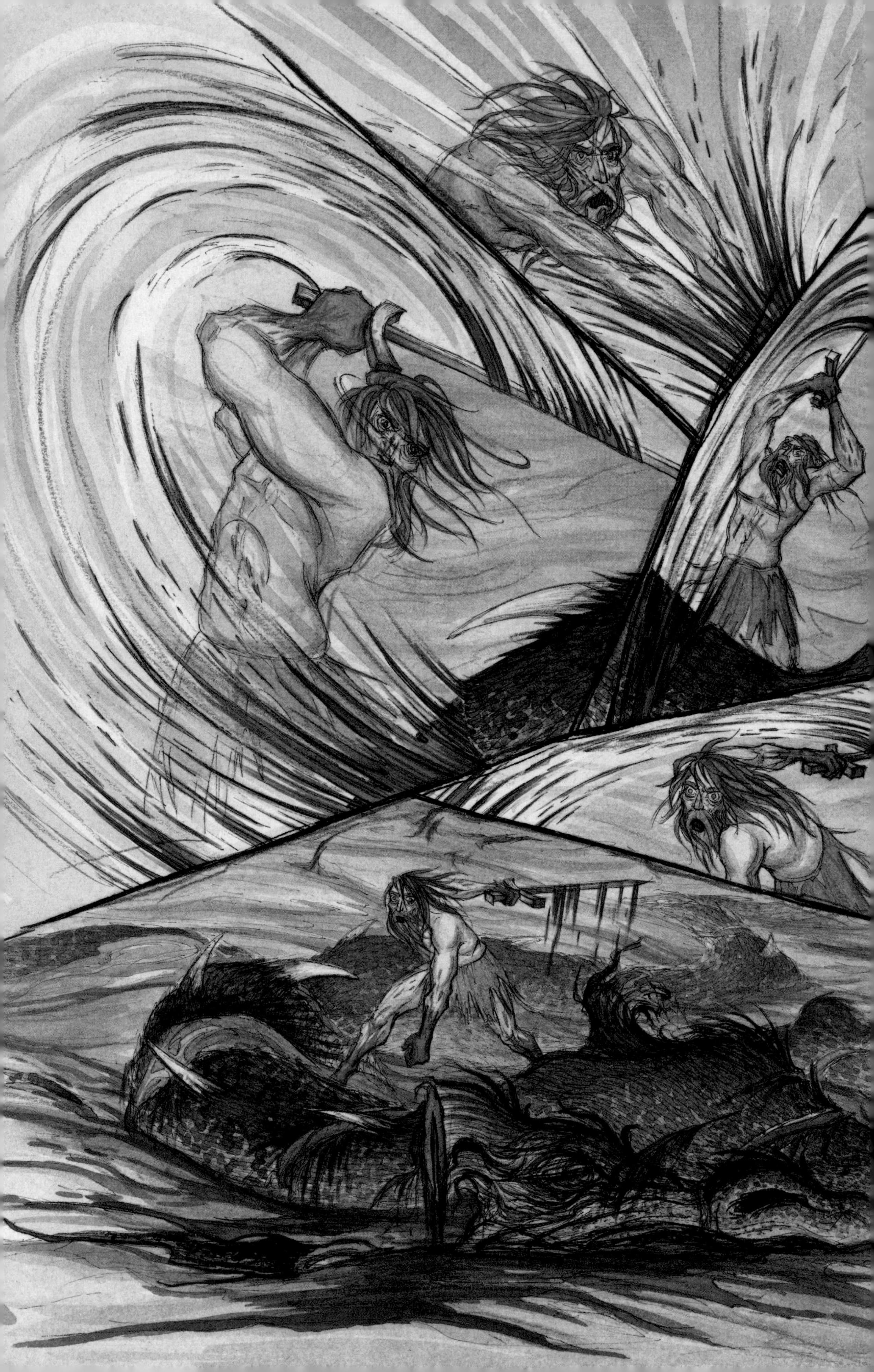

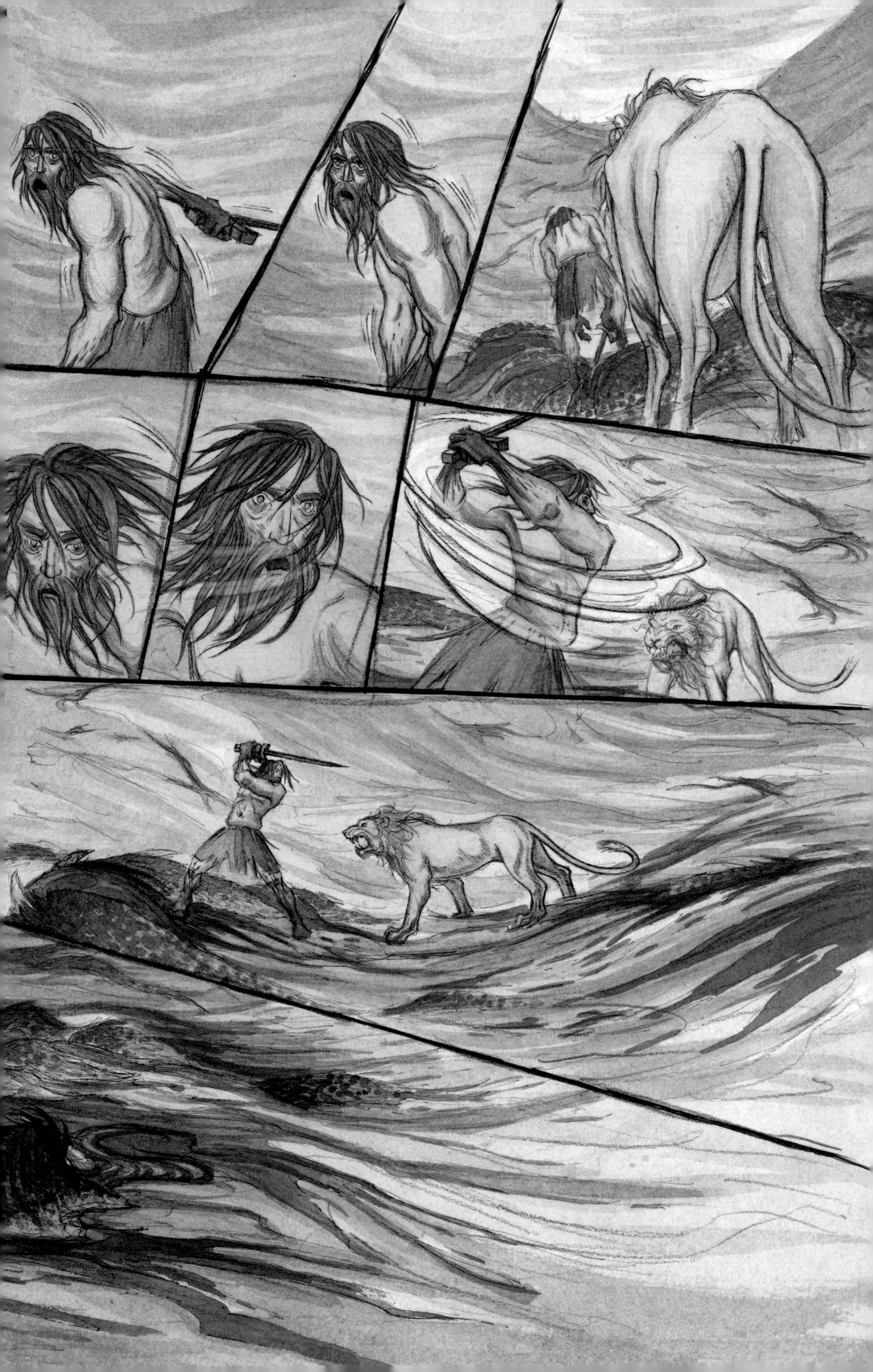

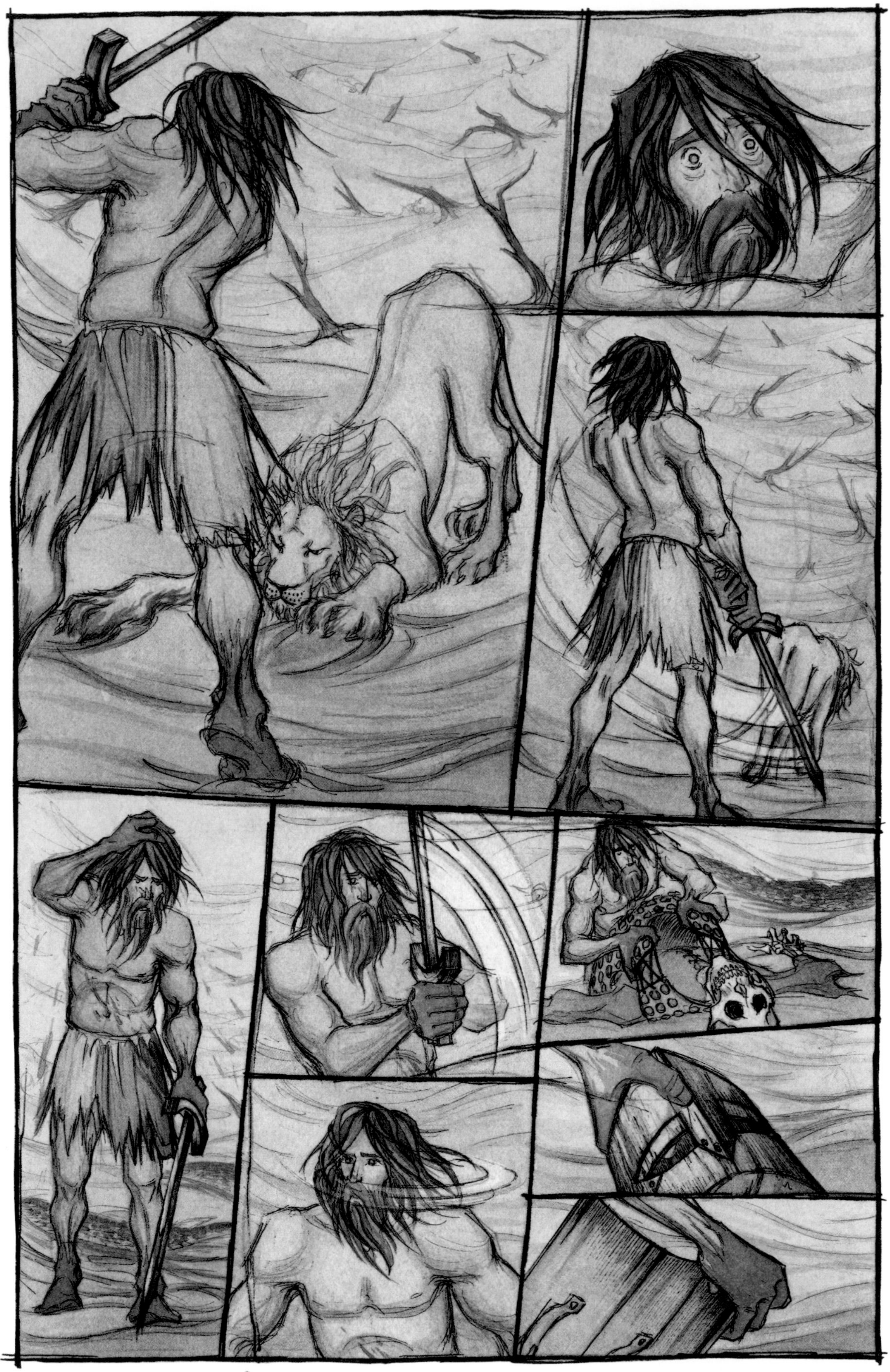

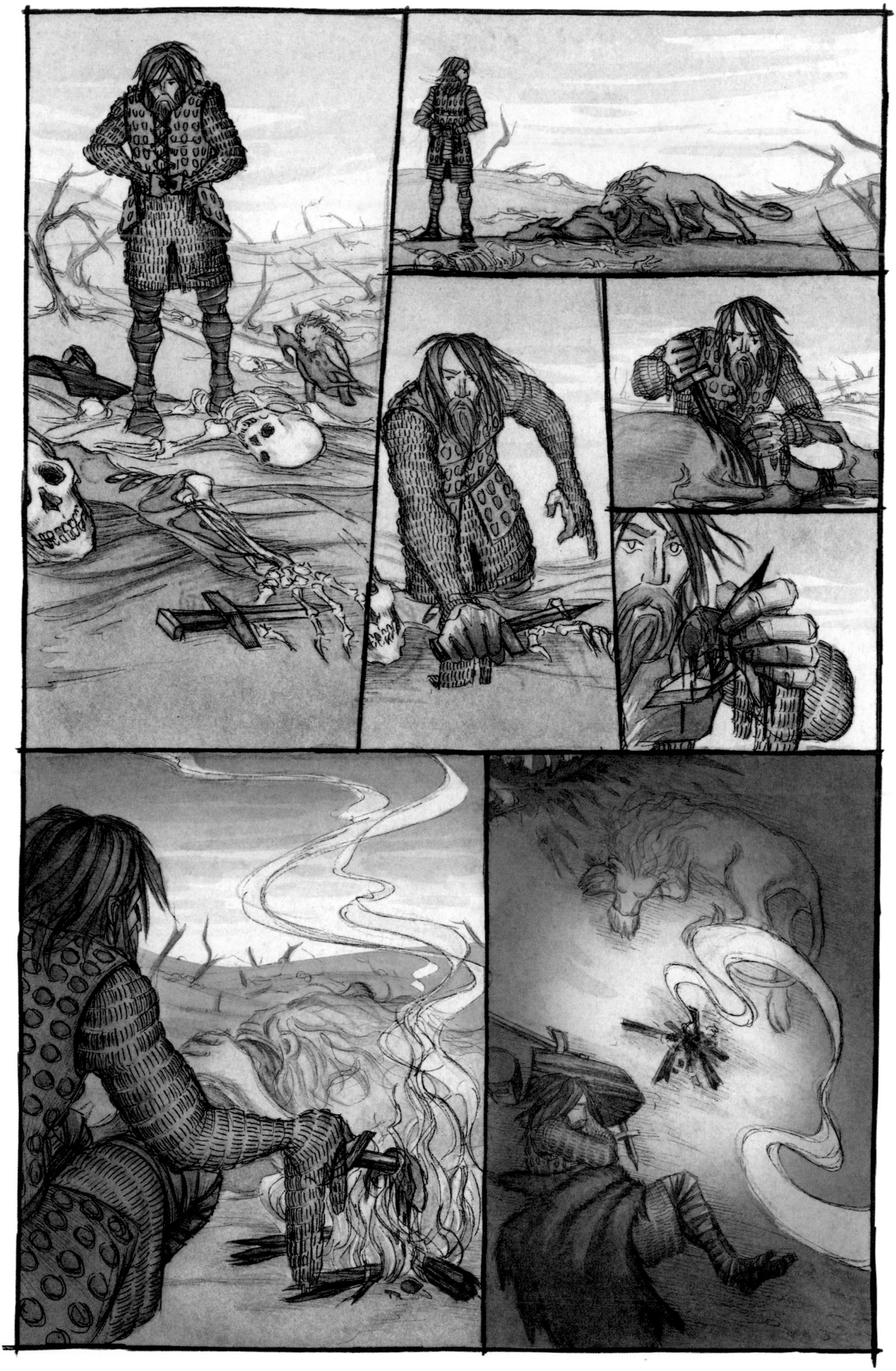

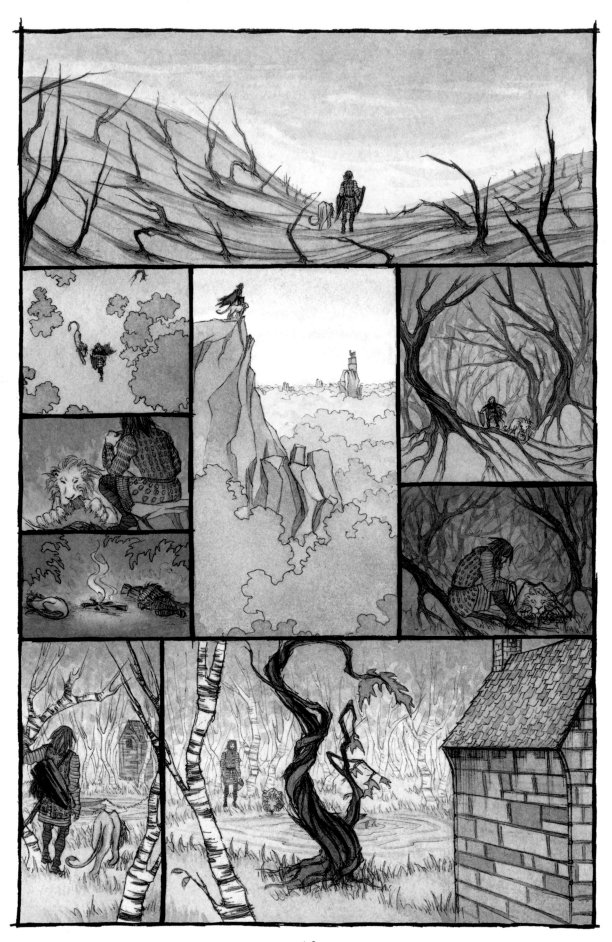

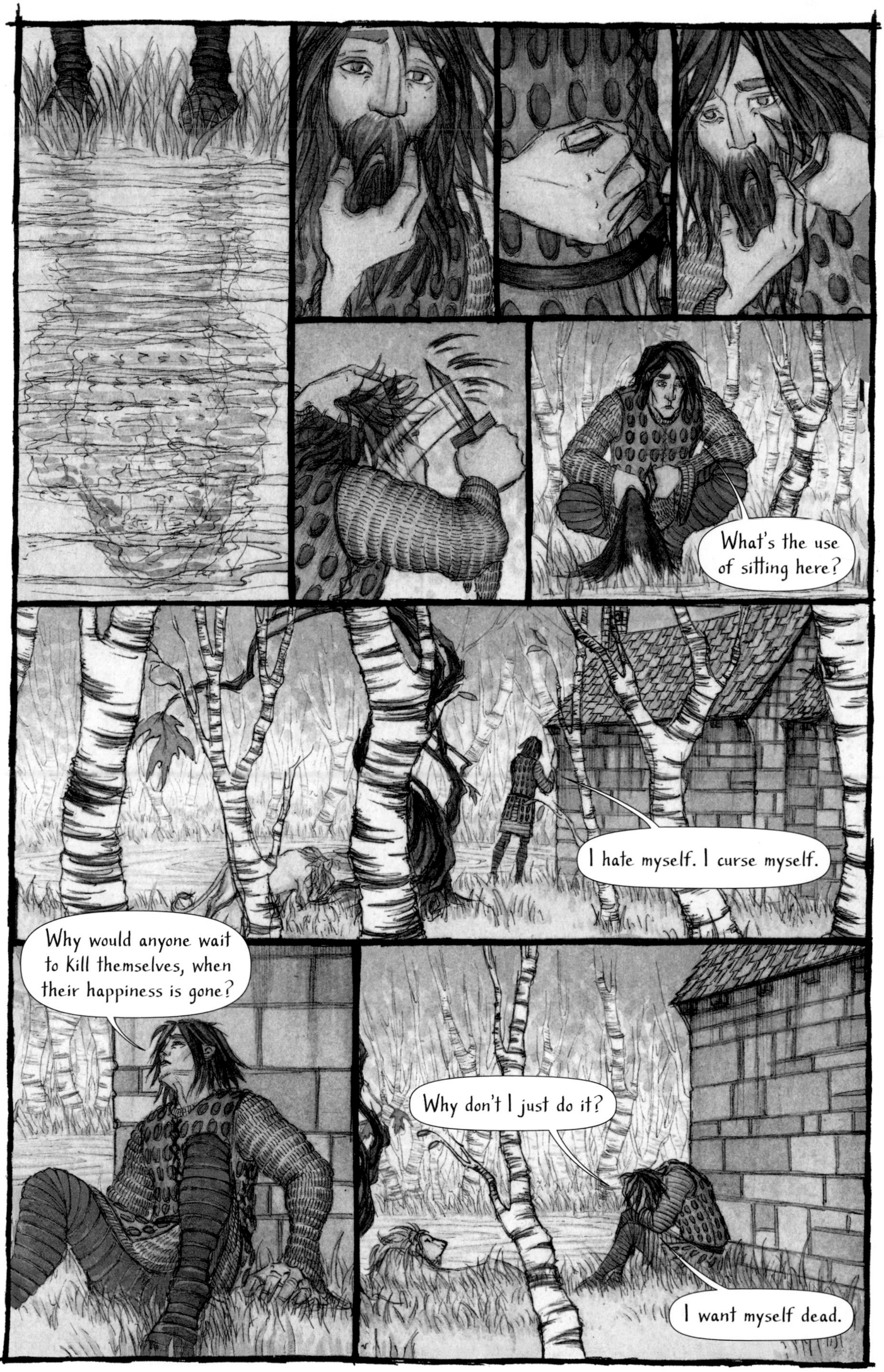
What's the use of sitting here?
I hate myself. I curse myself.
Why would anyone wait to kill themselves, when their happiness is gone?
Why don't I just do it?
I want myself dead.

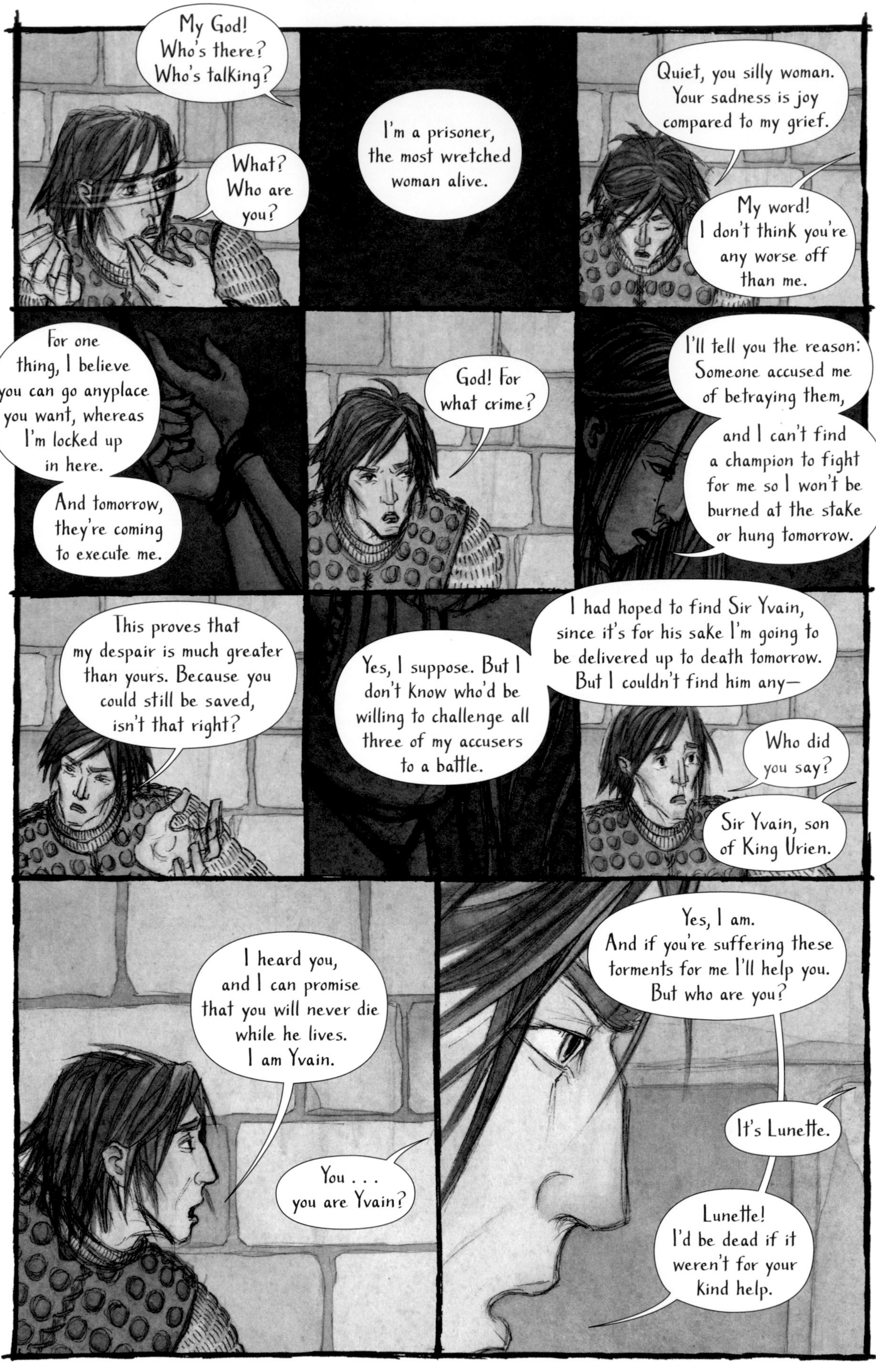
My God! Who's there? Who's talking?
What? Who are you?
I'm a prisoner, the most wretched woman alive.
Quiet, you silly woman. Your sadness is joy compared to my grief.
My word! I don't think you're any worse off than me.
For one thing, I believe you can go anyplace you want, whereas I'm locked up in here.
And tomorrow, they're coming to execute me.
God! For what crime?
I'll tell you the reason: Someone accused me of betraying them,
and I can't find a champion to fight for me so I won't be burned at the stake or hung tomorrow.
This proves that my despair is much greater than yours. Because you could still be saved, isn't that right?
Yes, I suppose. But I don't know who'd be willing to challenge all three of my accusers to a battle.
I had hoped to find Sir Yvain, since it's for his sake I'm going to be delivered up to death tomorrow. But I couldn't find him any—
Who did you say?
Sir Yvain, son of King Urien.
I heard you, and I can promise that you will never die while he lives. I am Yvain.
You . . . you are Yvain?
Yes, I am. And if you're suffering these torments for me I'll help you. But who are you?
It's Lunette.
Lunette! I'd be dead if it weren't for your kind help.

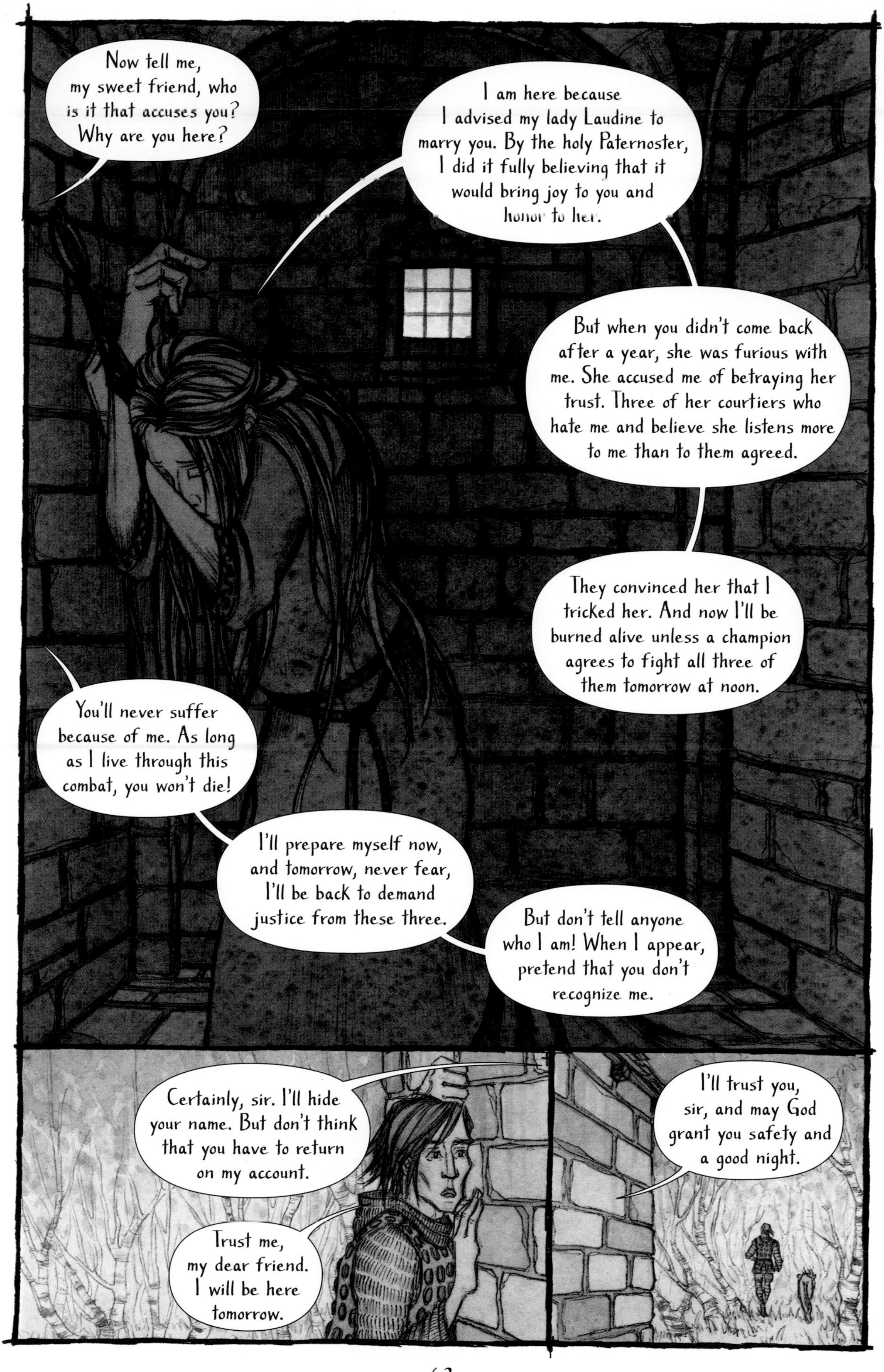
Now tell me, my sweet friend, who is it that accuses you? Why are you here?
I am here because I advised my lady Laudine to marry you. By the holy Paternoster, I did it fully believing that it would bring joy to you and honor to her.
But when you didn't come back after a year, she was furious with me. She accused me of betraying her trust. Three of her courtiers who hate me and believe she listens more to me than to them agreed.
They convinced her that I tricked her. And now I'll be burned alive unless a champion agrees to fight all three of them tomorrow at noon.
You'll never suffer because of me. As long as I live through this combat, you won't die!
I'll prepare myself now, and tomorrow, never fear, I'll be back to demand justice from these three.
But don't tell anyone who I am! When I appear, pretend that you don't recognize me.
Certainly, sir. I'll hide your name. But don't think that you have to return on my account.
Trust me, my dear friend. I will be here tomorrow.
I'll trust you, sir, and may God grant you safety and a good night.

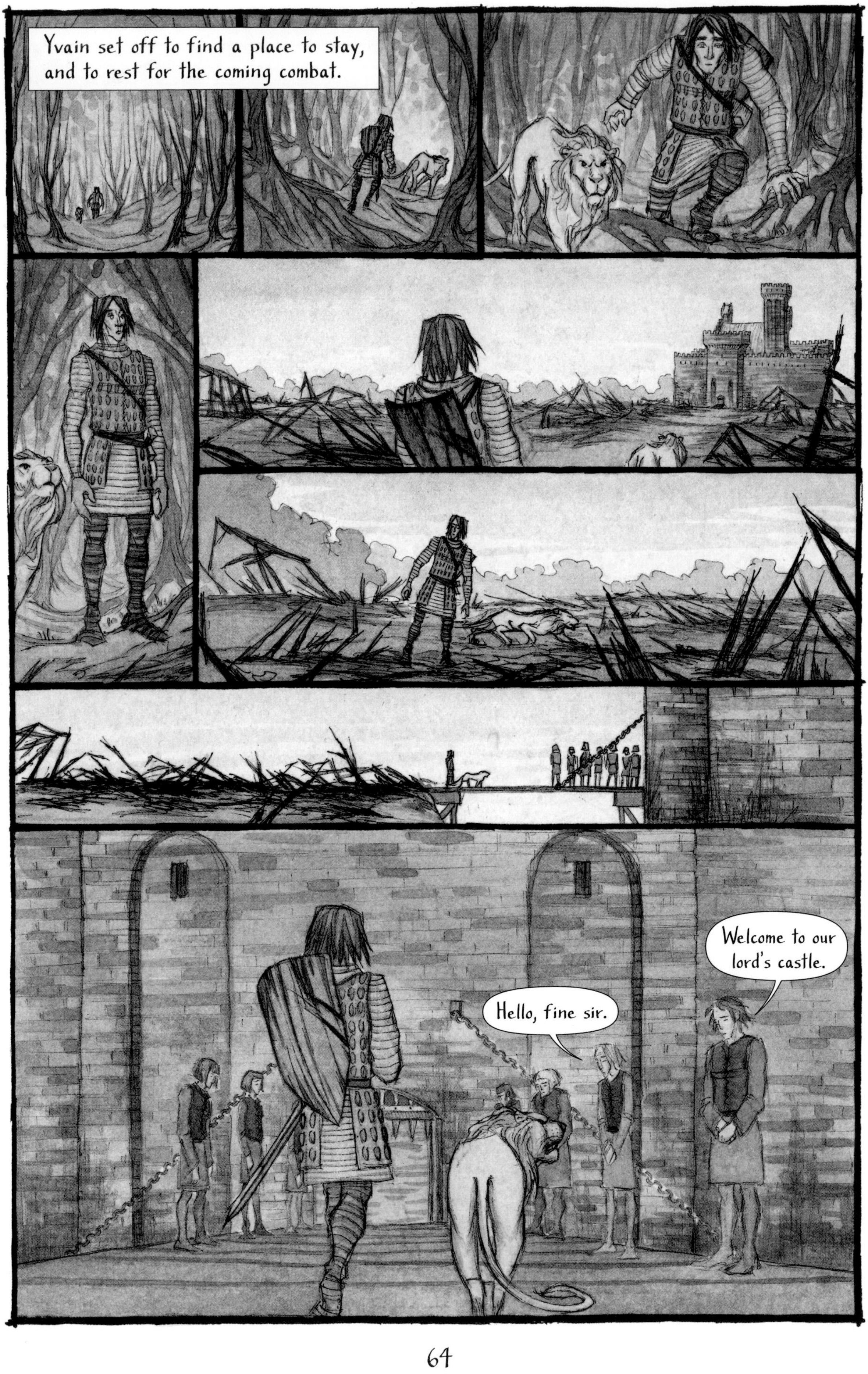
Yvain set off to find a place to stay, and to rest for the coming combat.
Hello, fine sir.
Welcome to our lord's castle.

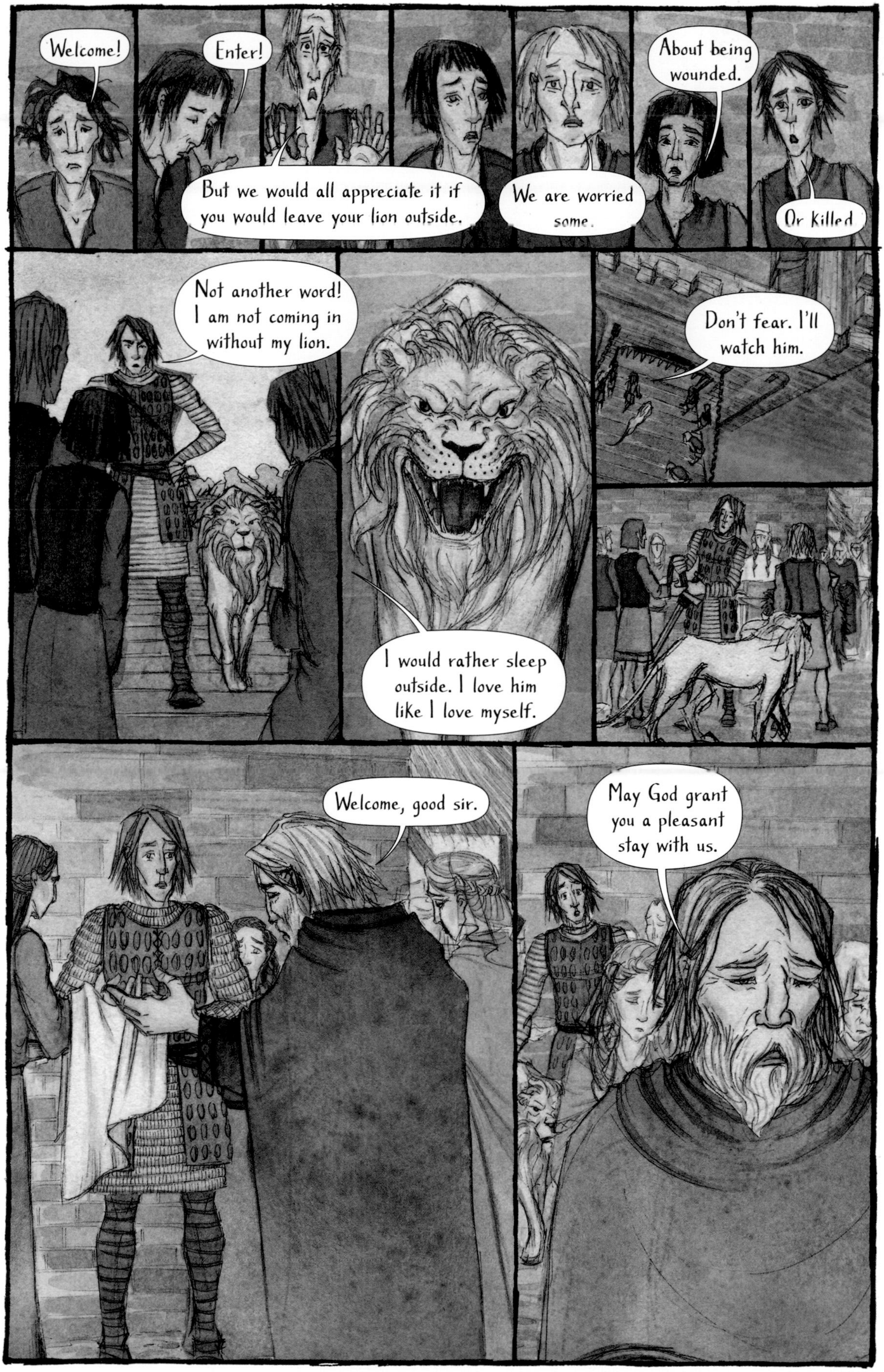

Welcome!
Enter!
But we would all appreciate it if you would leave your lion outside.
We are worried some.
About being wounded.
Or killed
Not another word! I am not coming in without my lion.
I would rather sleep outside. I love him like I love myself.
Don't fear. I'll watch him.
Welcome, good sir.
May God grant you a pleasant stay with us.

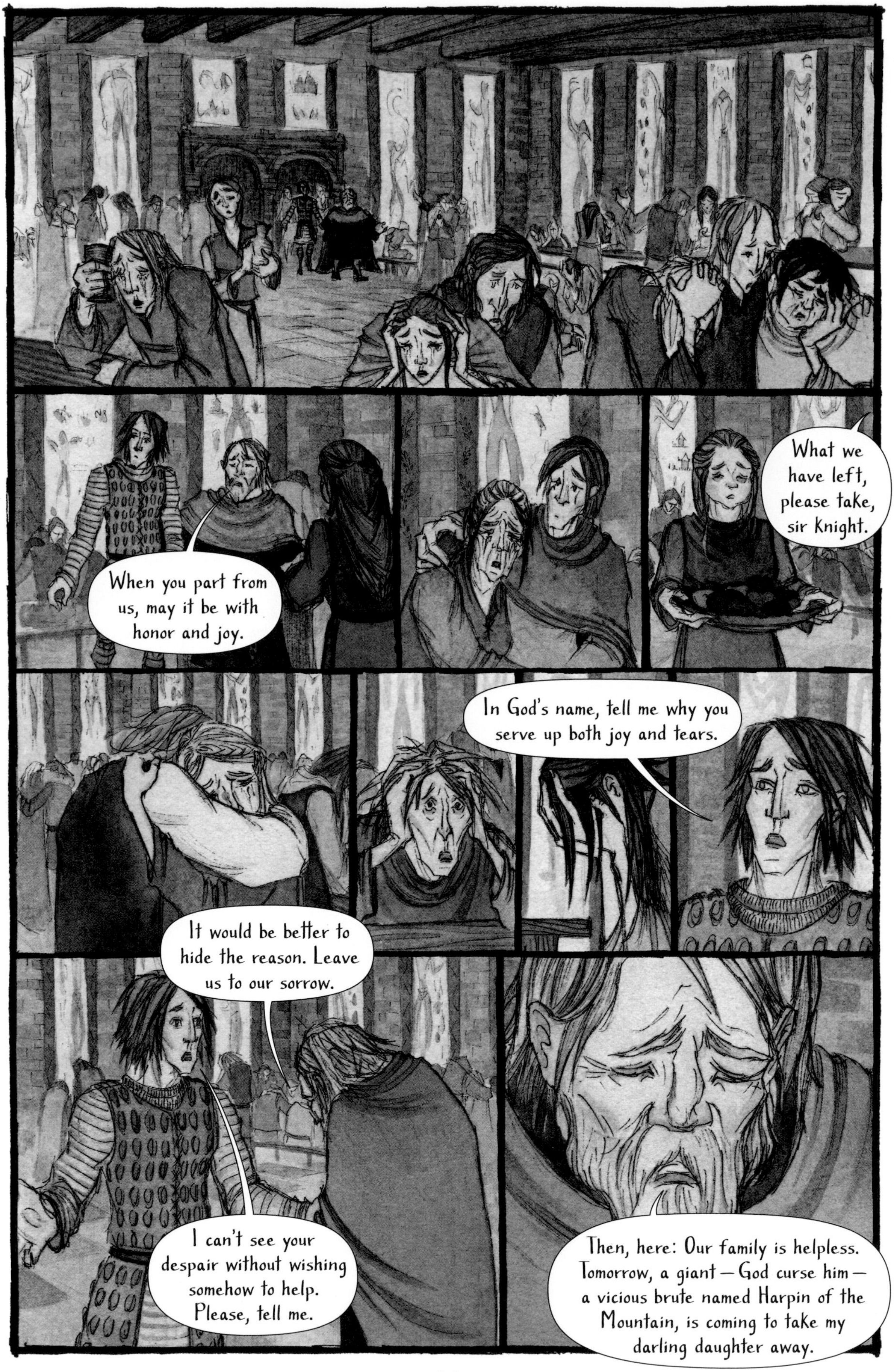
When you part from us, may it be with honor and joy.
What we have left, please take, sir Knight.
In God's name, tell me why you serve up both joy and tears.
It would be better to hide the reason. Leave us to our sorrow.
I can't see your despair without wishing somehow to help. Please, tell me.
Then, here: Our family is helpless. Tomorrow, a giant — God curse him — a vicious brute named Harpin of the Mountain, is coming to take my darling daughter away.

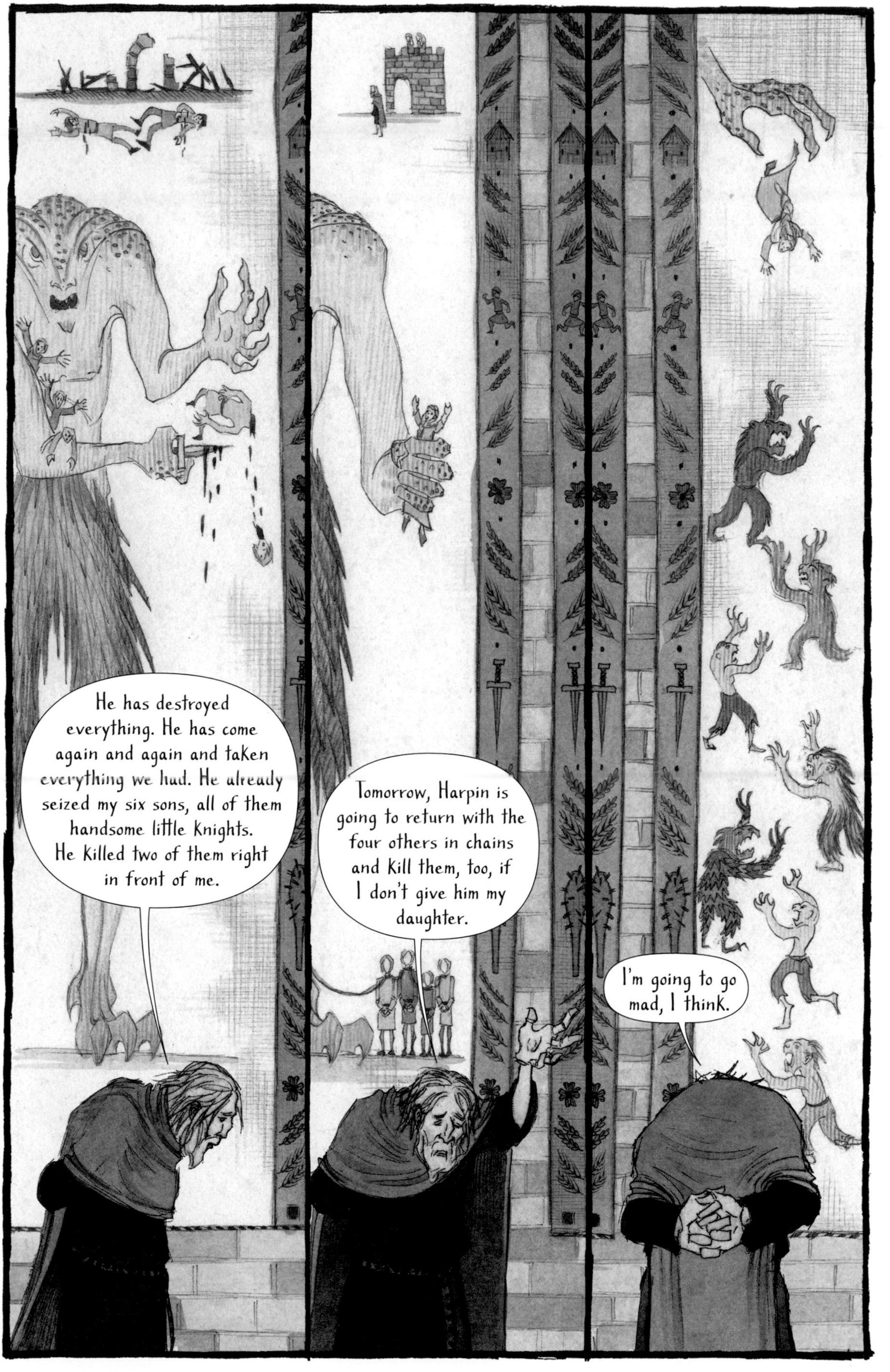
He has destroyed everything. He has come again and again and taken everything we had. He already seized my six sons, all of them handsome little knights. He killed two of them right in front of me.
Tomorrow, Harpin is going to return with the four others in chains and kill them, too, if I don't give him my daughter.
I'm going to go mad, I think.

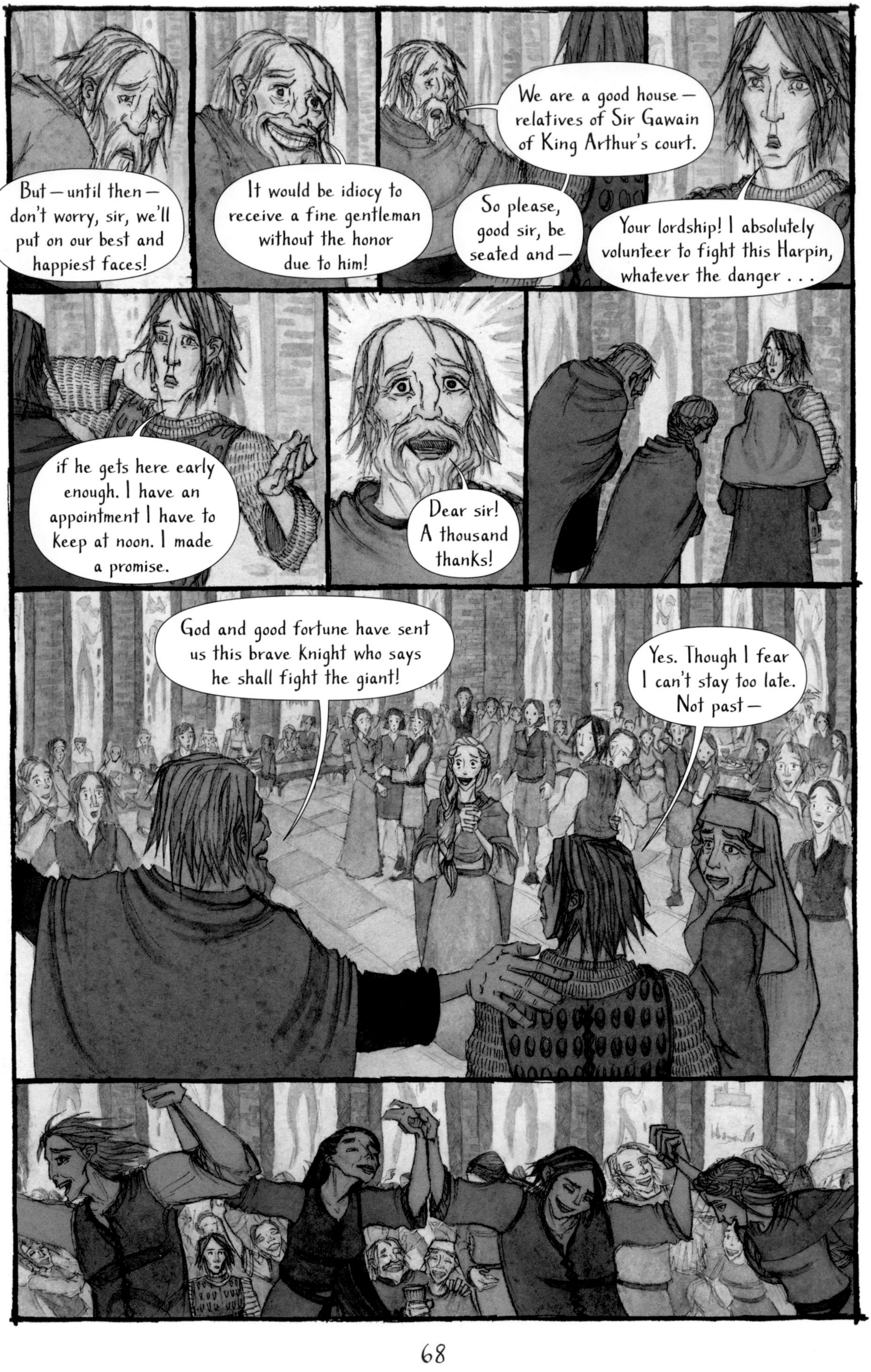
But—until then—don't worry, sir, we'll put on our best and happiest faces!
It would be idiocy to receive a fine gentleman without the honor due to him!
We are a good house—relatives of Sir Gawain of King Arthur's court.
So please, good sir, be seated and—
Your lordship! I absolutely volunteer to fight this Harpin, whatever the danger . . .
if he gets here early enough. I have an appointment I have to keep at noon. I made a promise.
Dear sir! A thousand thanks!
God and good fortune have sent us this brave knight who says he shall fight the giant!
Yes. Though I fear I can't stay too late. Not past—

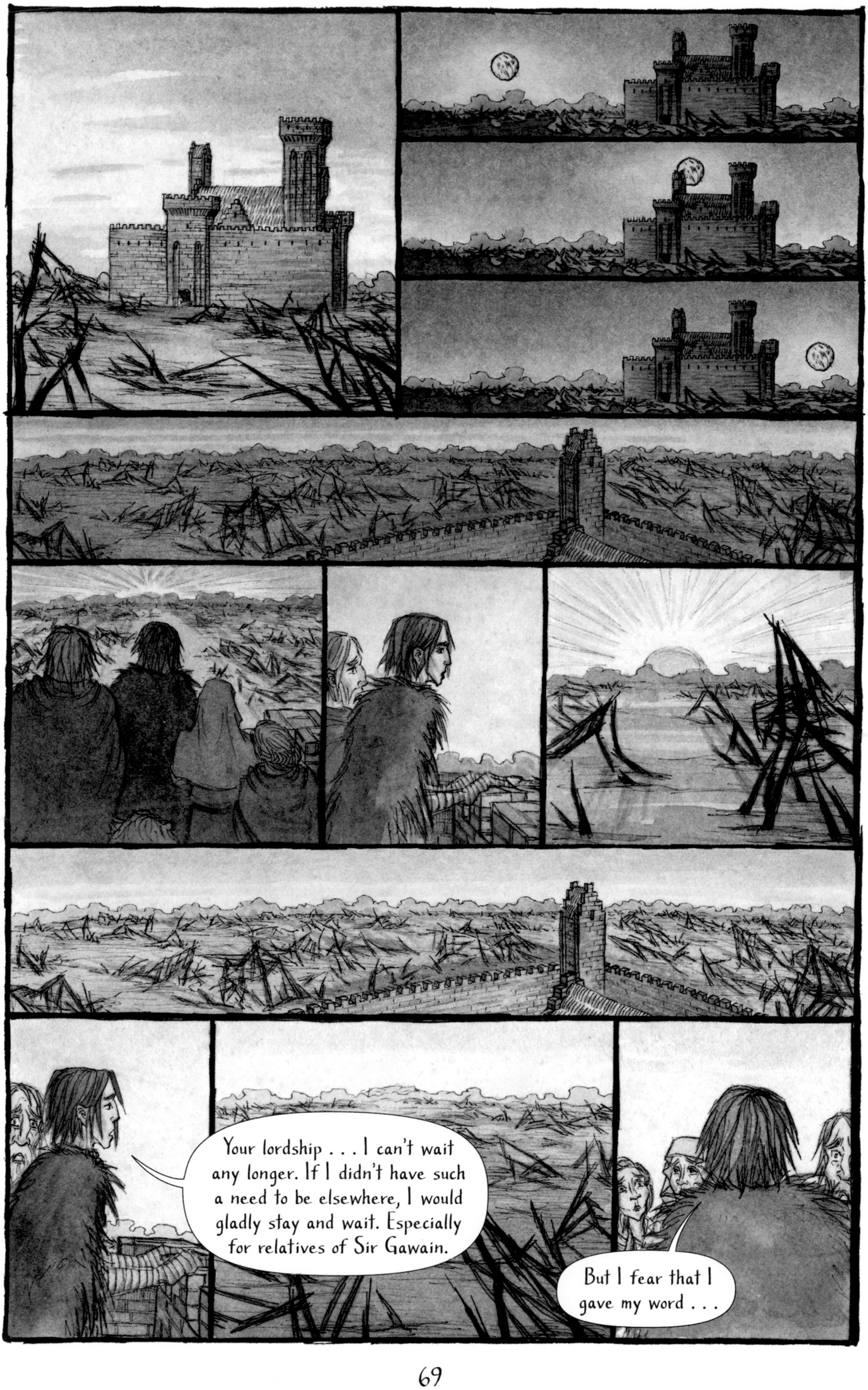
Your lordship . . . I can't wait any longer. If I didn't have such a need to be elsewhere, I would gladly stay and wait. Especially for relatives of Sir Gawain.
But I fear that I gave my word . . .

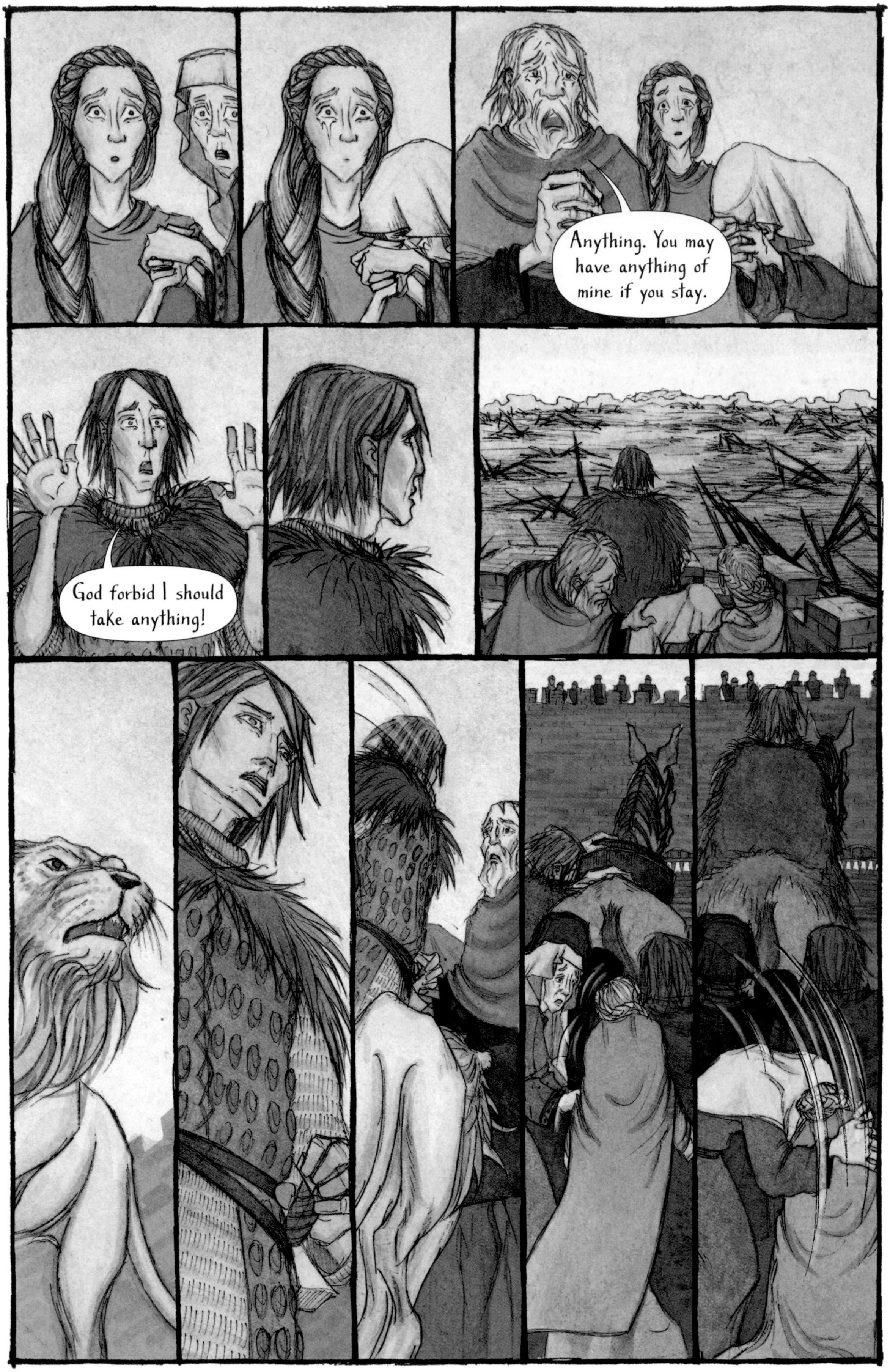
Anything. You may have anything of mine if you stay.
God forbid I should take anything!

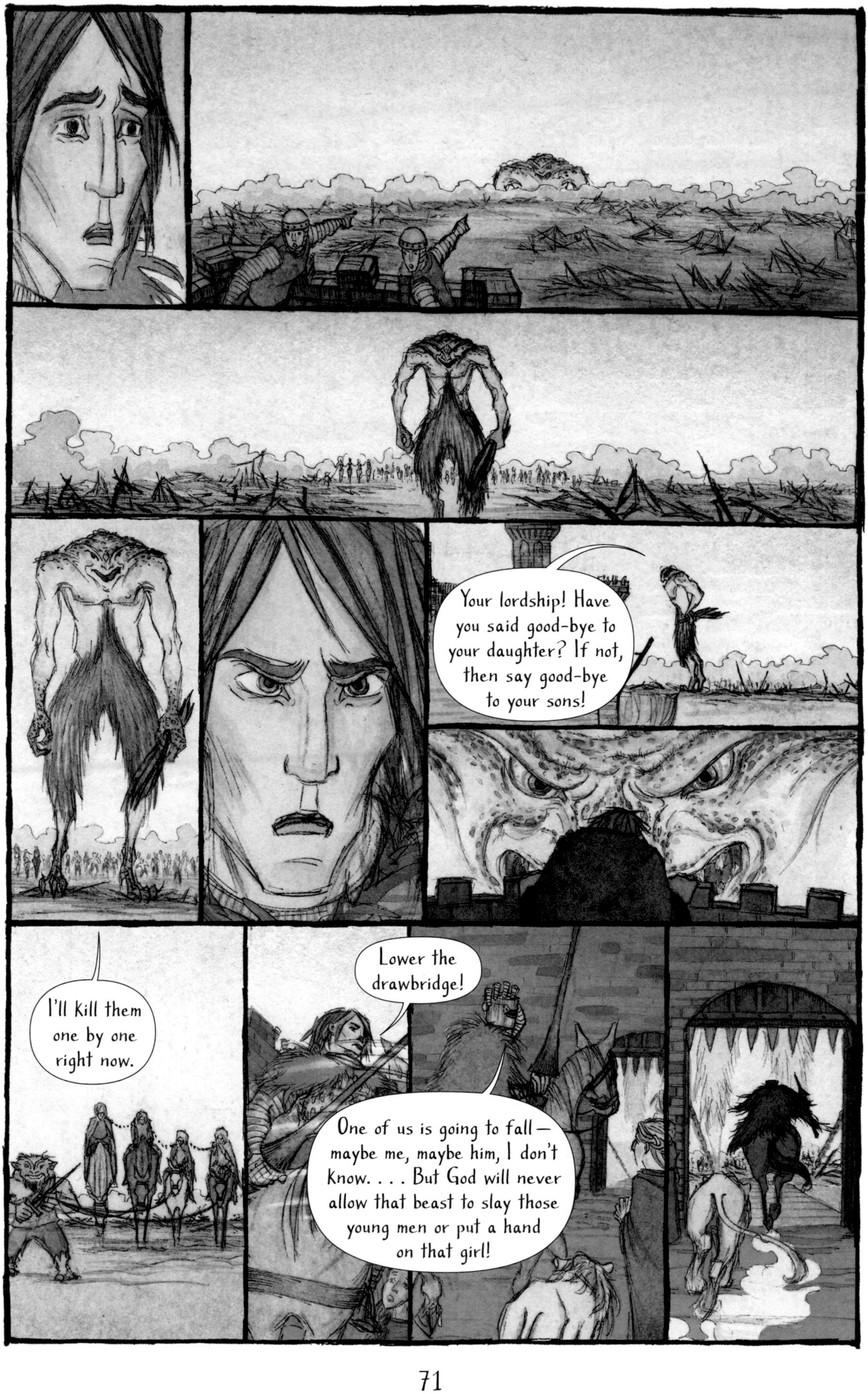
Your lordship! Have you said good-bye to your daughter? If not, then say good-bye to your sons!
I'll kill them one by one right now.
Lower the drawbridge!
One of us is going to fall— maybe me, maybe him, I don't know. . . . But God will never allow that beast to slay those young men or put a hand on that girl!

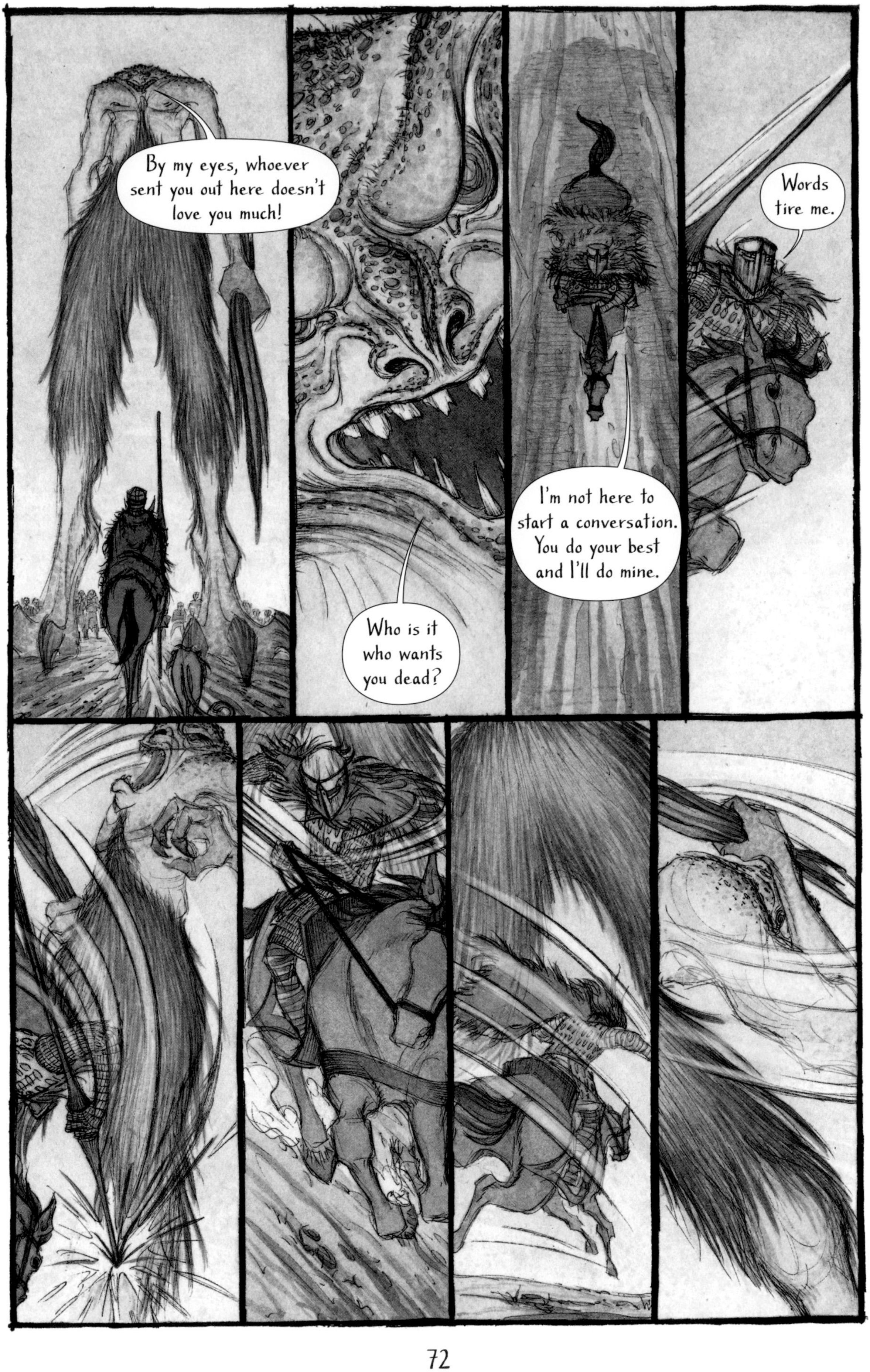
By my eyes, whoever sent you out here doesn't love you much!
Who is it who wants you dead?
I'm not here to start a conversation. You do your best and I'll do mine.
Words tire me.

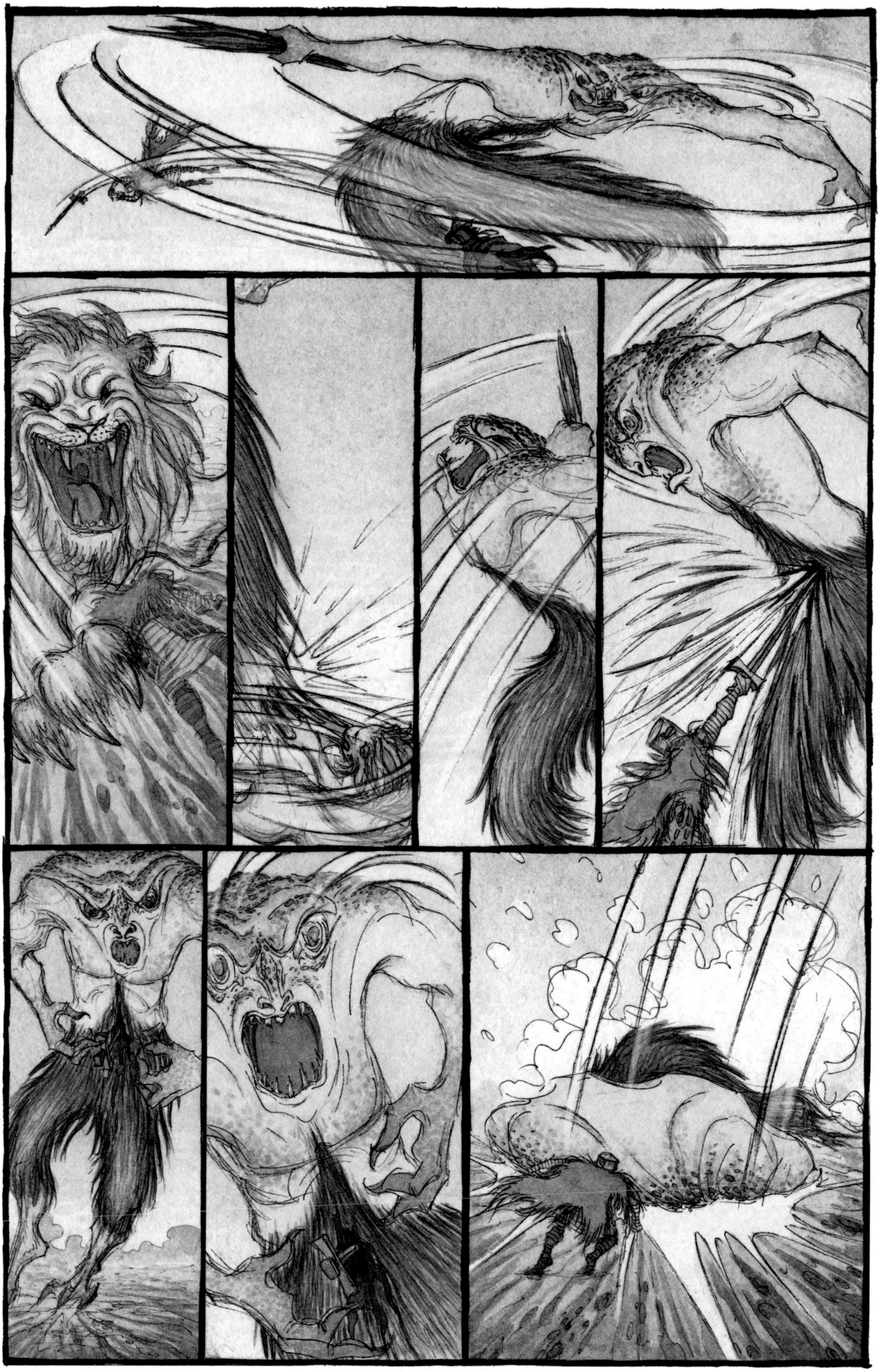

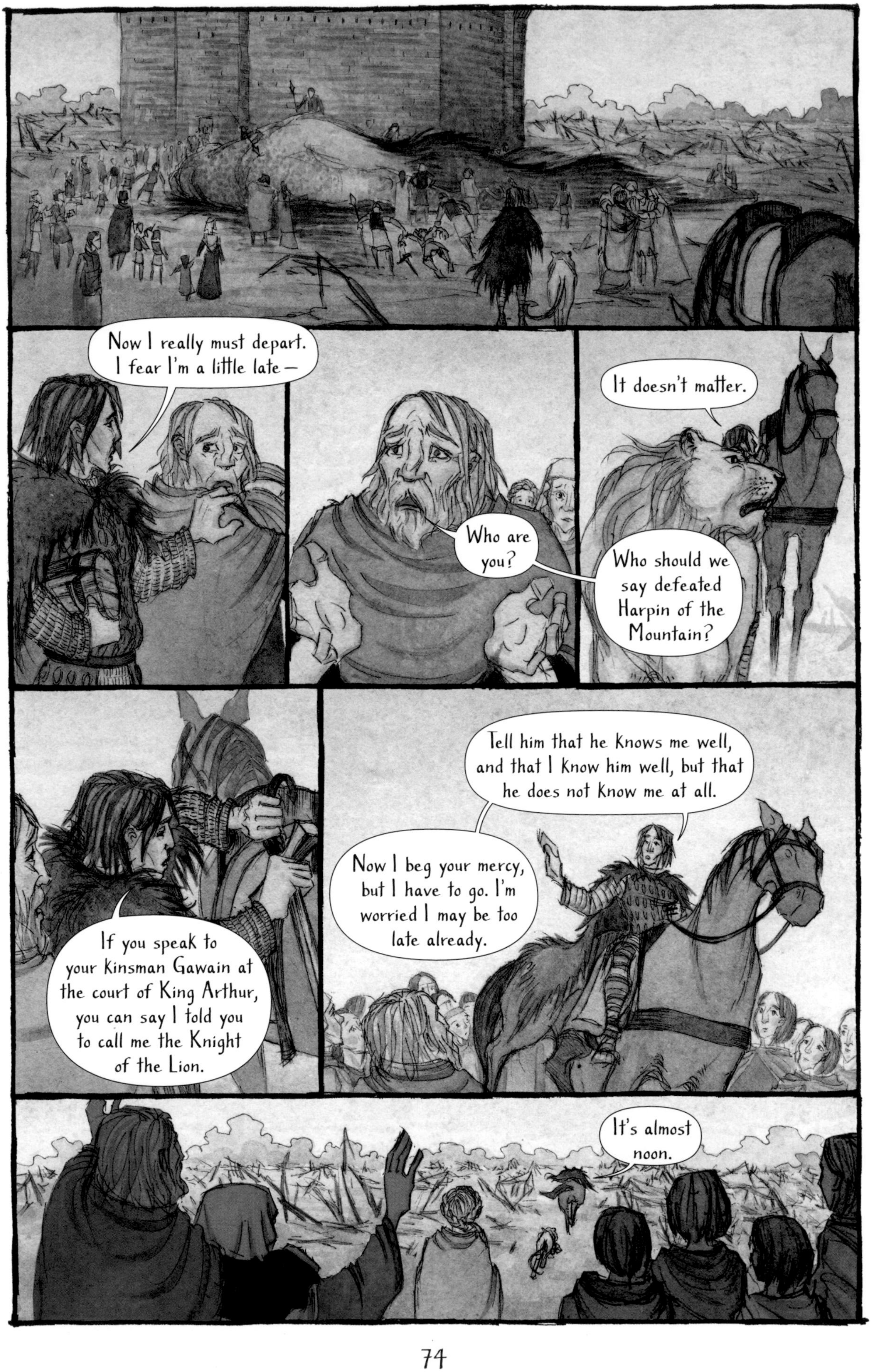

Now I really must depart. I fear I'm a little late —
Who are you?
It doesn't matter.
Who should we say defeated Harpin of the Mountain?
If you speak to your kinsman Gawain at the court of King Arthur, you can say I told you to call me the Knight of the Lion.
Tell him that he knows me well, and that I know him well, but that he does not know me at all.
Now I beg your mercy, but I have to go. I'm worried I may be too late already.
It's almost noon.

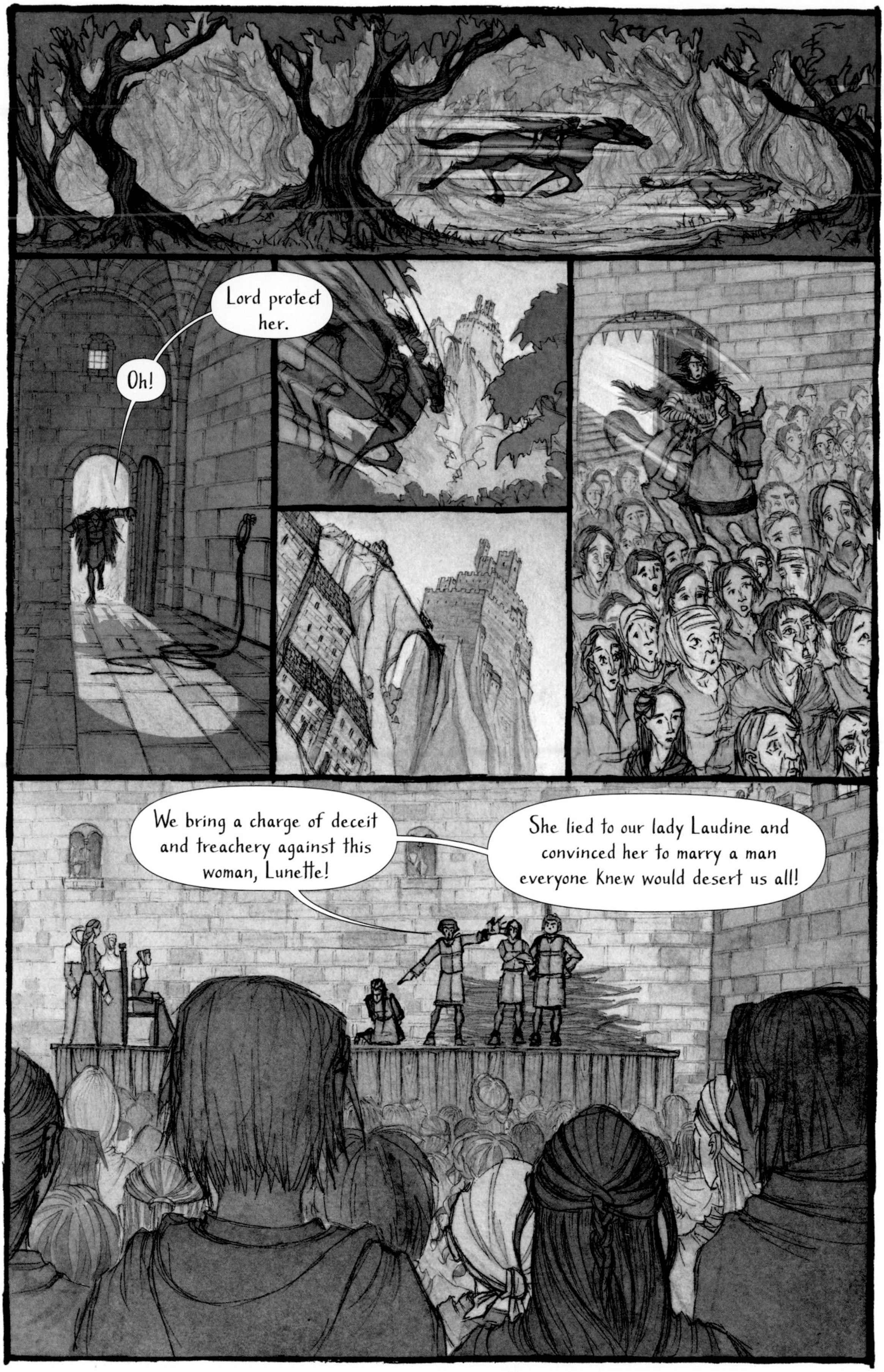
Oh!
Lord protect her.
We bring a charge of deceit and treachery against this woman, Lunette!
She lied to our lady Laudine and convinced her to marry a man everyone knew would desert us all!

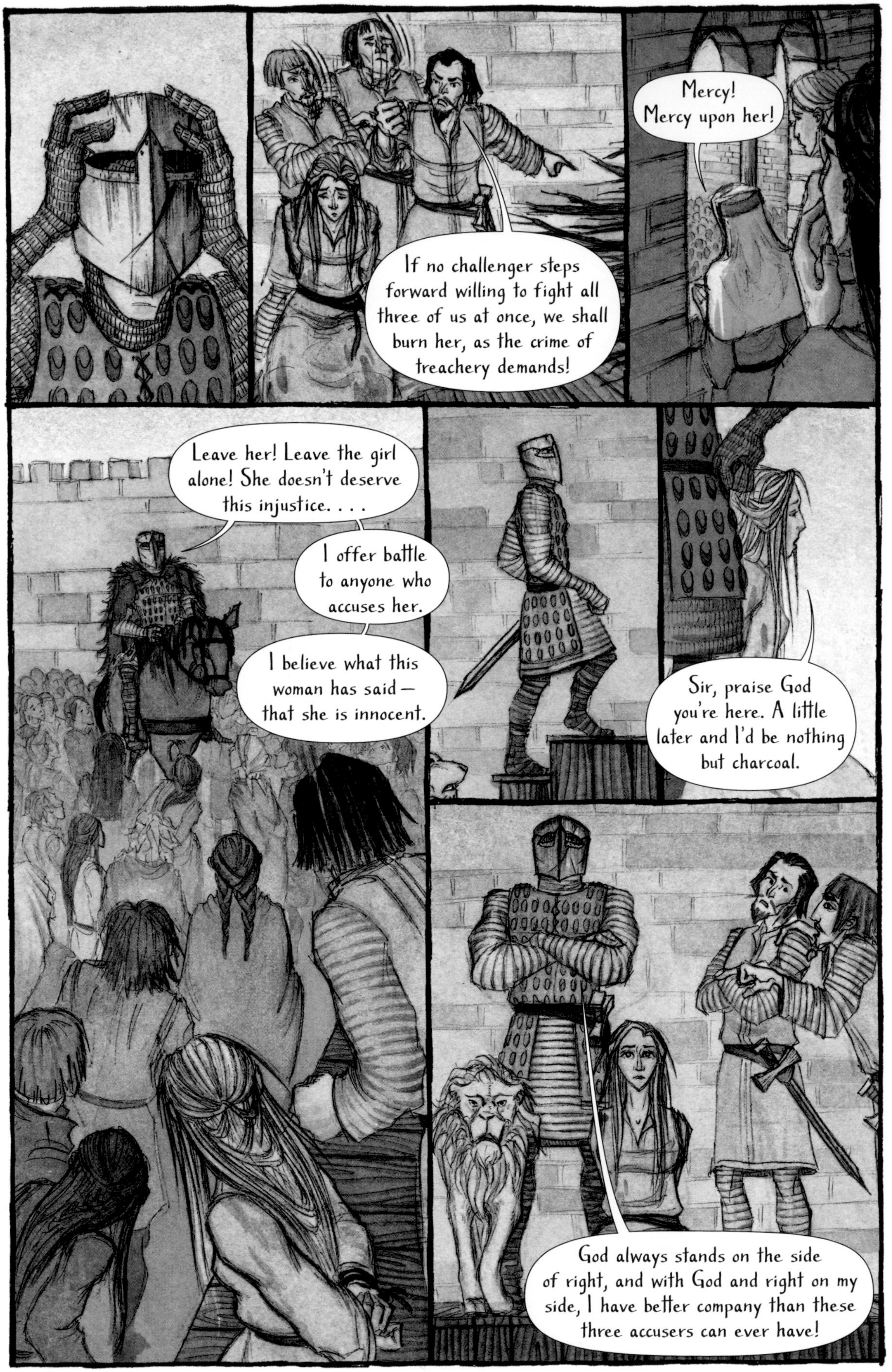
If no challenger steps forward willing to fight all three of us at once, we shall burn her, as the crime of treachery demands!
Mercy! Mercy upon her!
Leave her! Leave the girl alone! She doesn't deserve this injustice. . . .
I offer battle to anyone who accuses her.
I believe what this woman has said— that she is innocent.
Sir, praise God you're here. A little later and I'd be nothing but charcoal.
God always stands on the side of right, and with God and right on my side, I have better company than these three accusers can ever have!

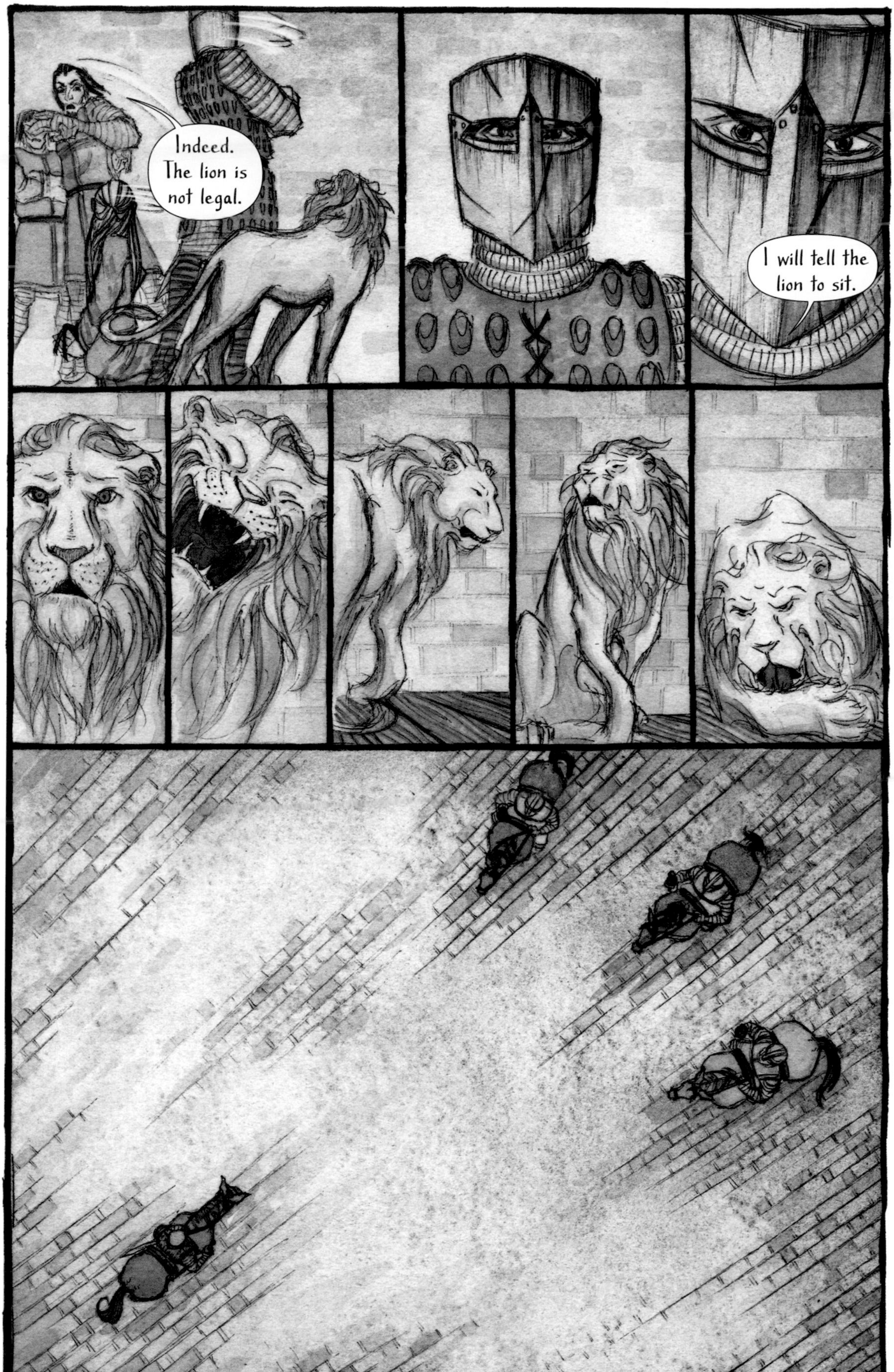
Indeed. The lion is not legal.
I will tell the lion to sit.

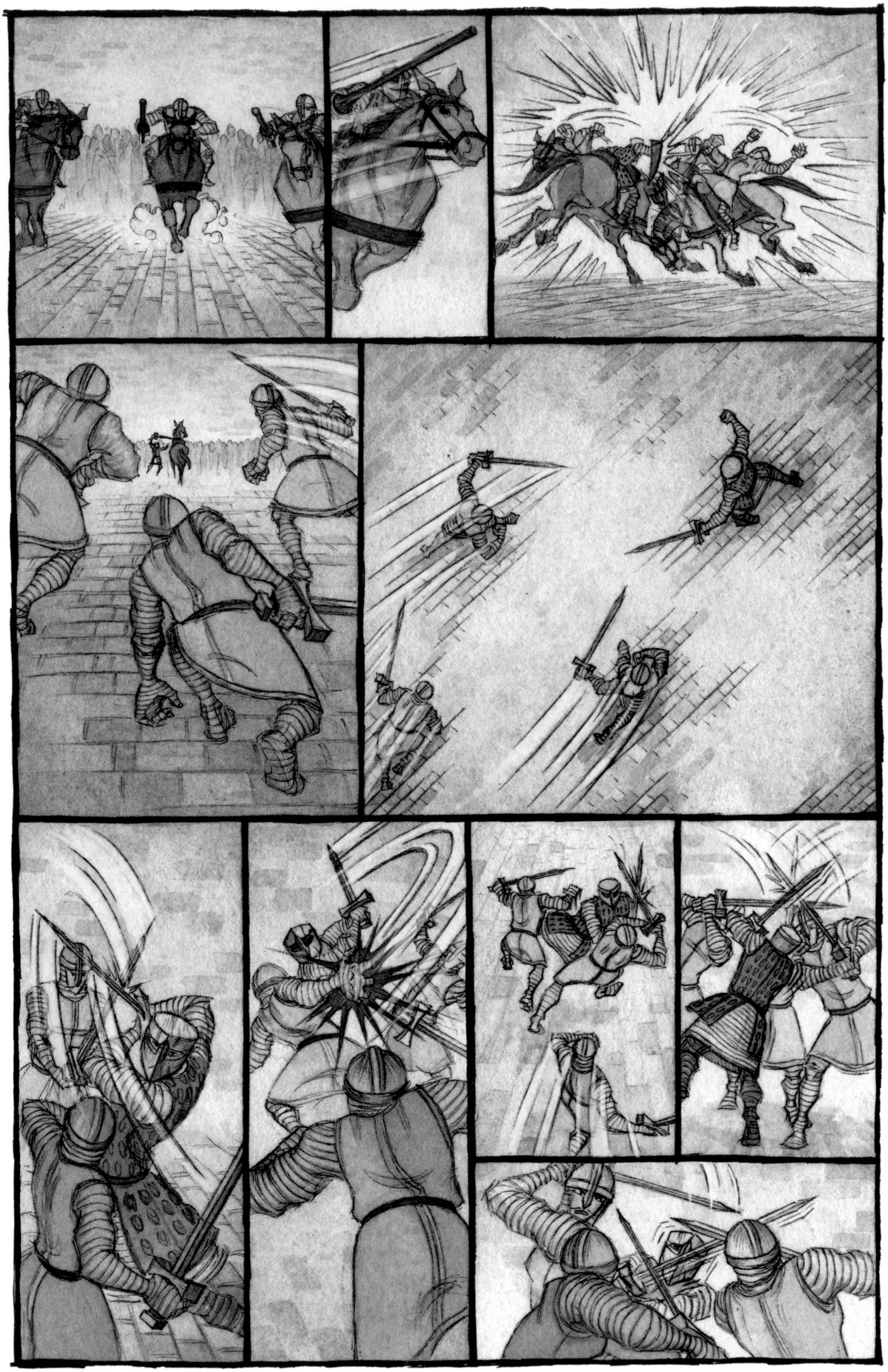

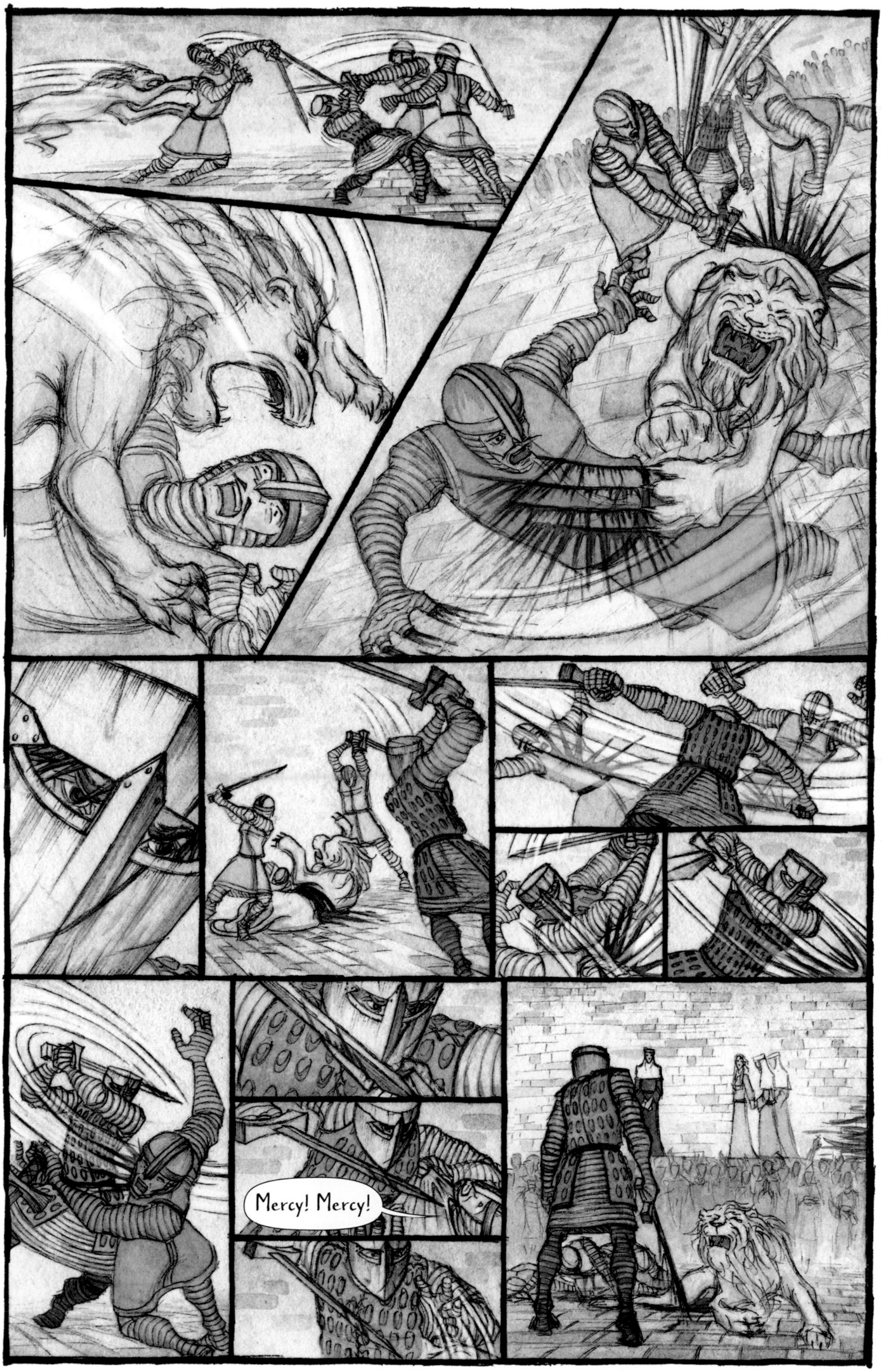
Mercy! Mercy!

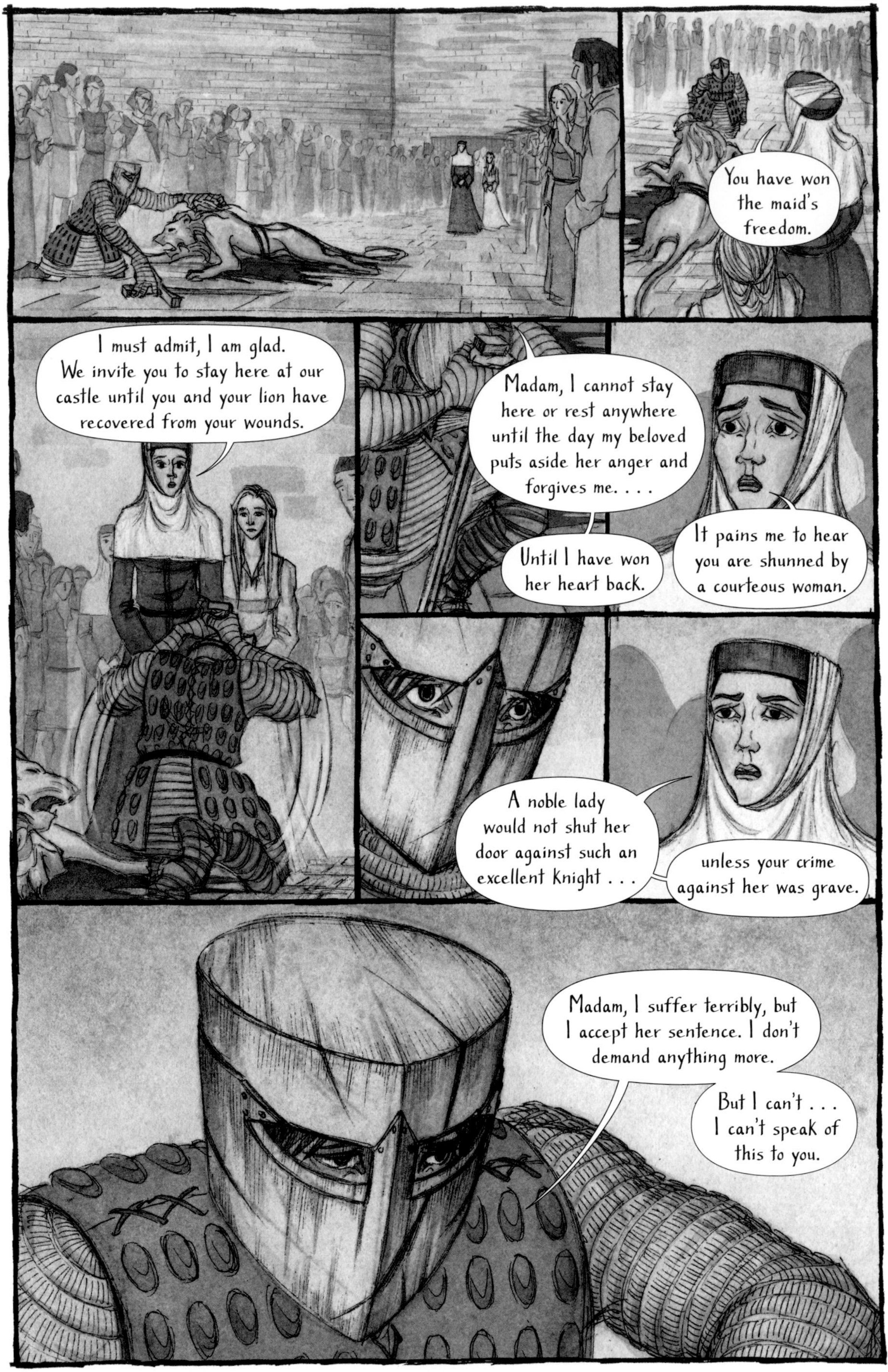
You have won the maid's freedom.
I must admit, I am glad. We invite you to stay here at our castle until you and your lion have recovered from your wounds.
Madam, I cannot stay here or rest anywhere until the day my beloved puts aside her anger and forgives me. . . .
Until I have won her heart back.
It pains me to hear you are shunned by a courteous woman.
A noble lady would not shut her door against such an excellent knight . . .
unless your crime against her was grave.
Madam, I suffer terribly, but I accept her sentence. I don't demand anything more.
But I can't . . . I can't speak of this to you.

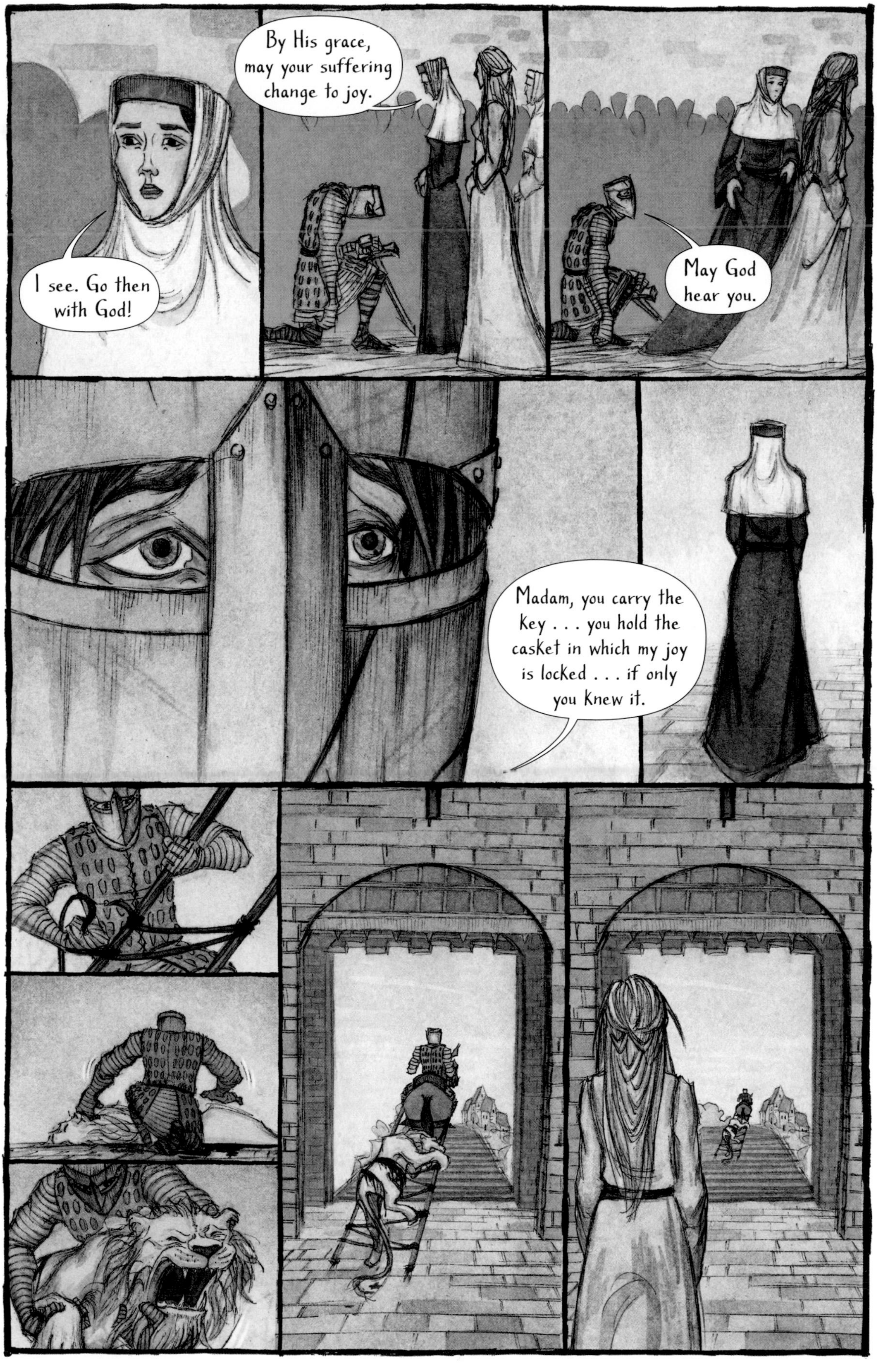
I see. Go then with God!
By His grace, may your suffering change to joy.
May God hear you.
Madam, you carry the key . . . you hold the casket in which my joy is locked . . . if only you knew it.

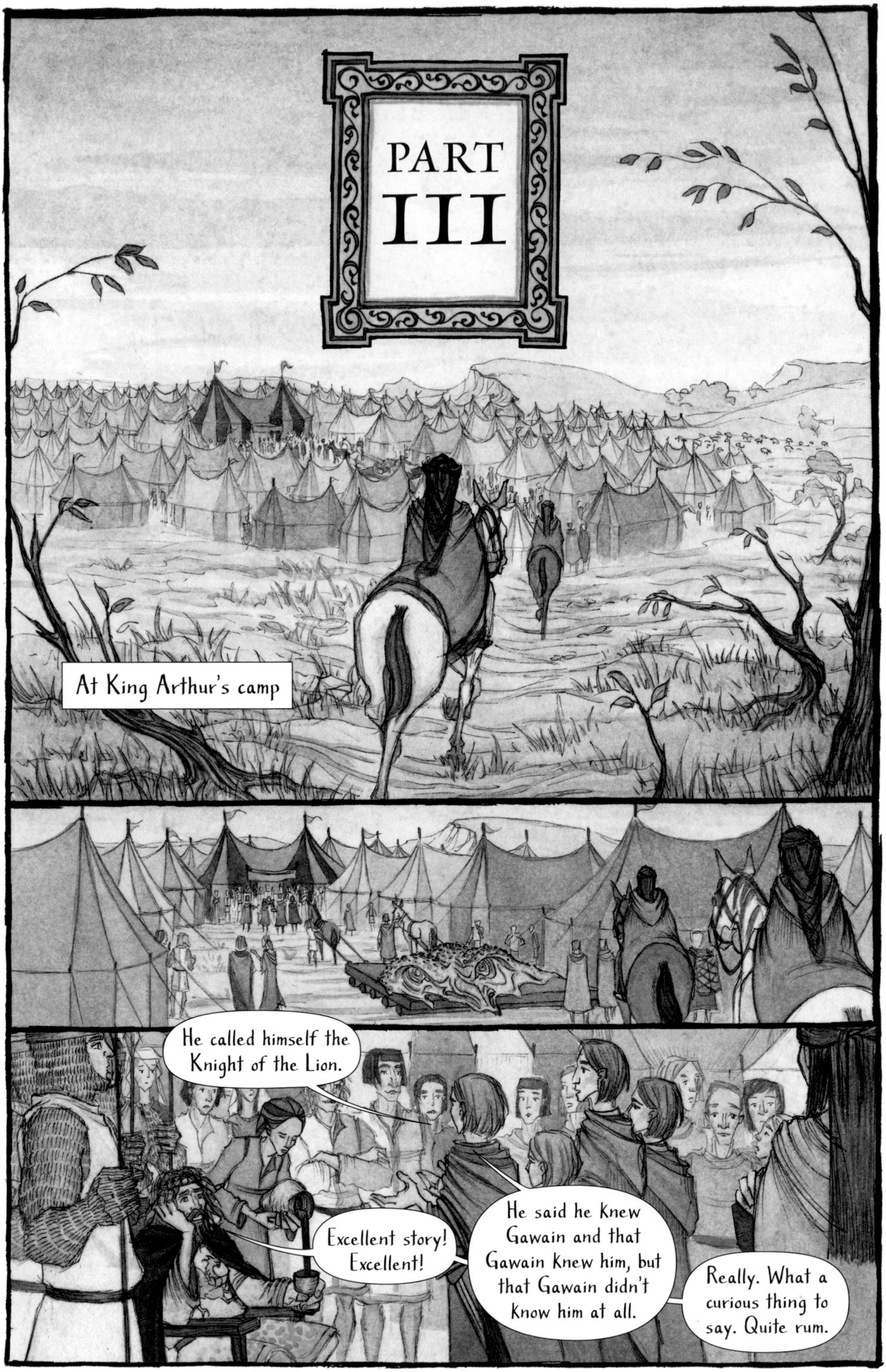
PART III
At King Arthur's camp
He called himself the Knight of the Lion.
Excellent story! Excellent!
He said he knew Gawain and that Gawain knew him, but that Gawain didn't know him at all.
Really. What a curious thing to say. Quite rum.

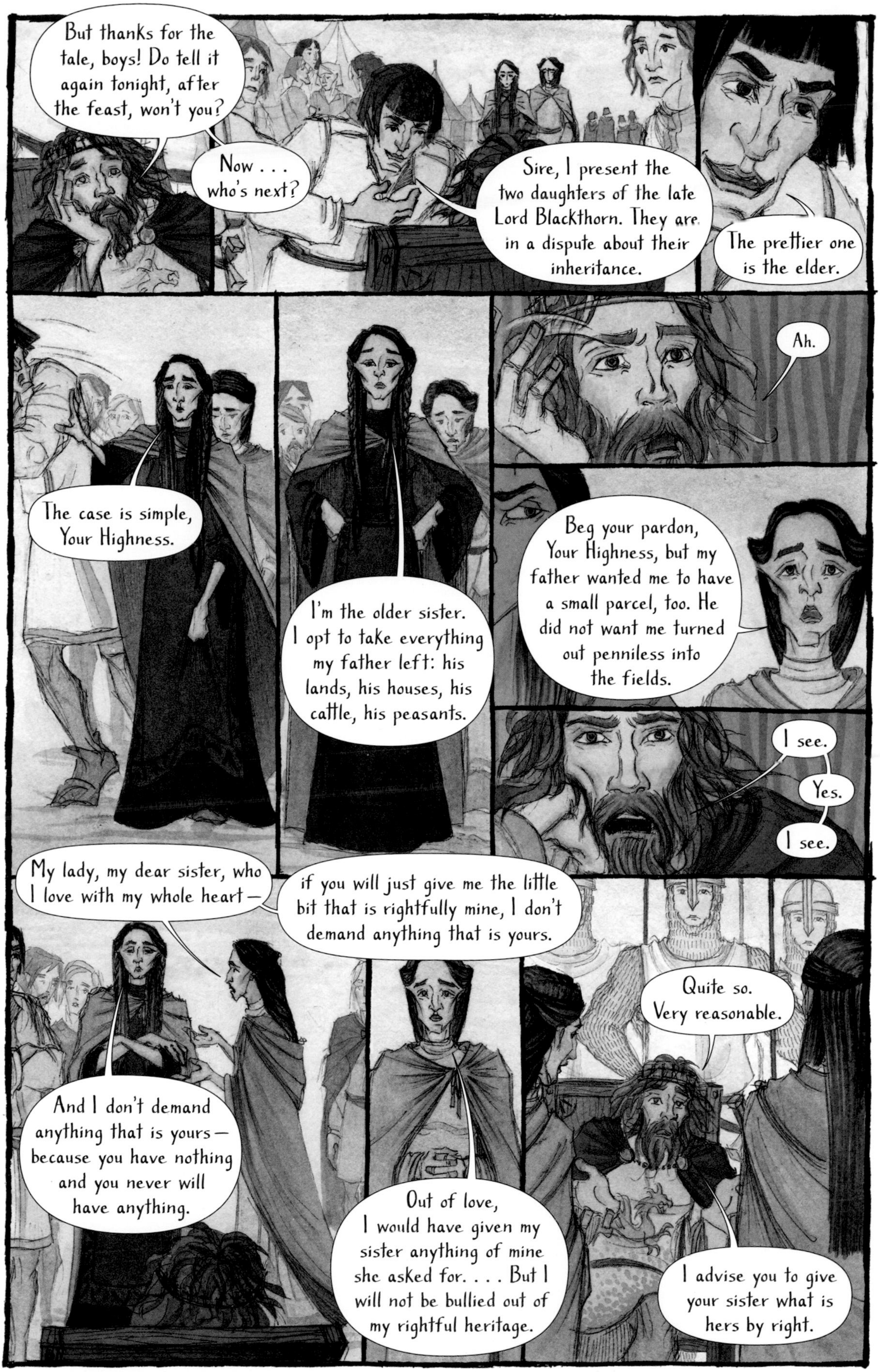
But thanks for the tale, boys! Do tell it again tonight, after the feast, won't you?
Now . . . who's next?
Sire, I present the two daughters of the late Lord Blackthorn. They are in a dispute about their inheritance.
The prettier one is the elder.
The case is simple, Your Highness.
I'm the older sister. I opt to take everything my father left: his lands, his houses, his cattle, his peasants.
Ah.
Beg your pardon, Your Highness, but my father wanted me to have a small parcel, too. He did not want me turned out penniless into the fields.
I see.
Yes.
I see.
My lady, my dear sister, who I love with my whole heart—
if you will just give me the little bit that is rightfully mine, I don't demand anything that is yours.
And I don't demand anything that is yours—because you have nothing and you never will have anything.
Out of love, I would have given my sister anything of mine she asked for. . . . But I will not be bullied out of my rightful heritage.
Quite so. Very reasonable.
I advise you to give your sister what is hers by right.

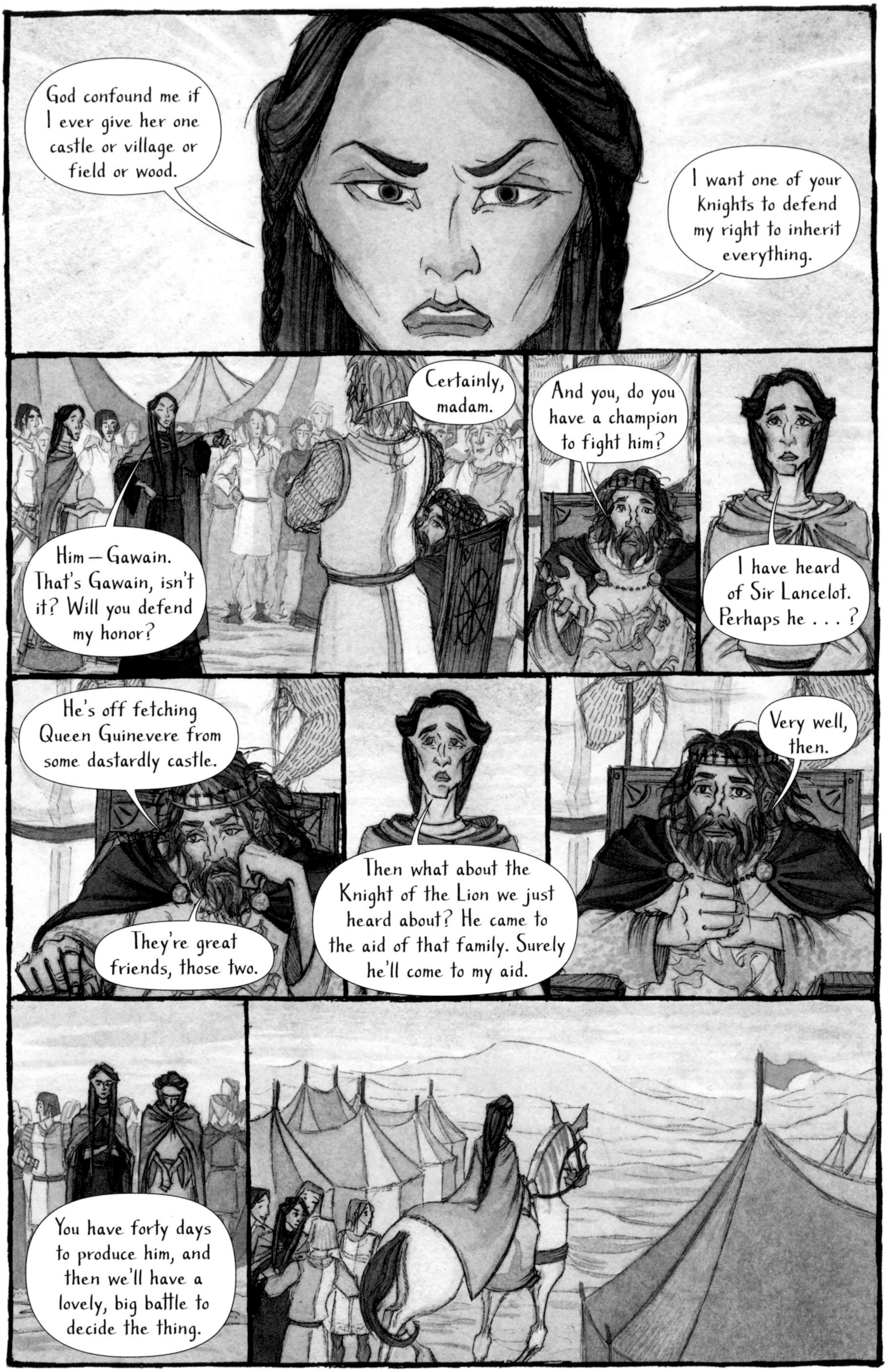

God confound me if I ever give her one castle or village or field or wood.
I want one of your Knights to defend my right to inherit everything.
Certainly, madam.
Him — Gawain. That's Gawain, isn't it? Will you defend my honor?
And you, do you have a champion to fight him?
I have heard of Sir Lancelot. Perhaps he . . . ?
He's off fetching Queen Guinevere from some dastardly castle.
They're great friends, those two.
Then what about the Knight of the Lion we just heard about? He came to the aid of that family. Surely he'll come to my aid.
Very well, then.
You have forty days to produce him, and then we'll have a lovely, big battle to decide the thing.

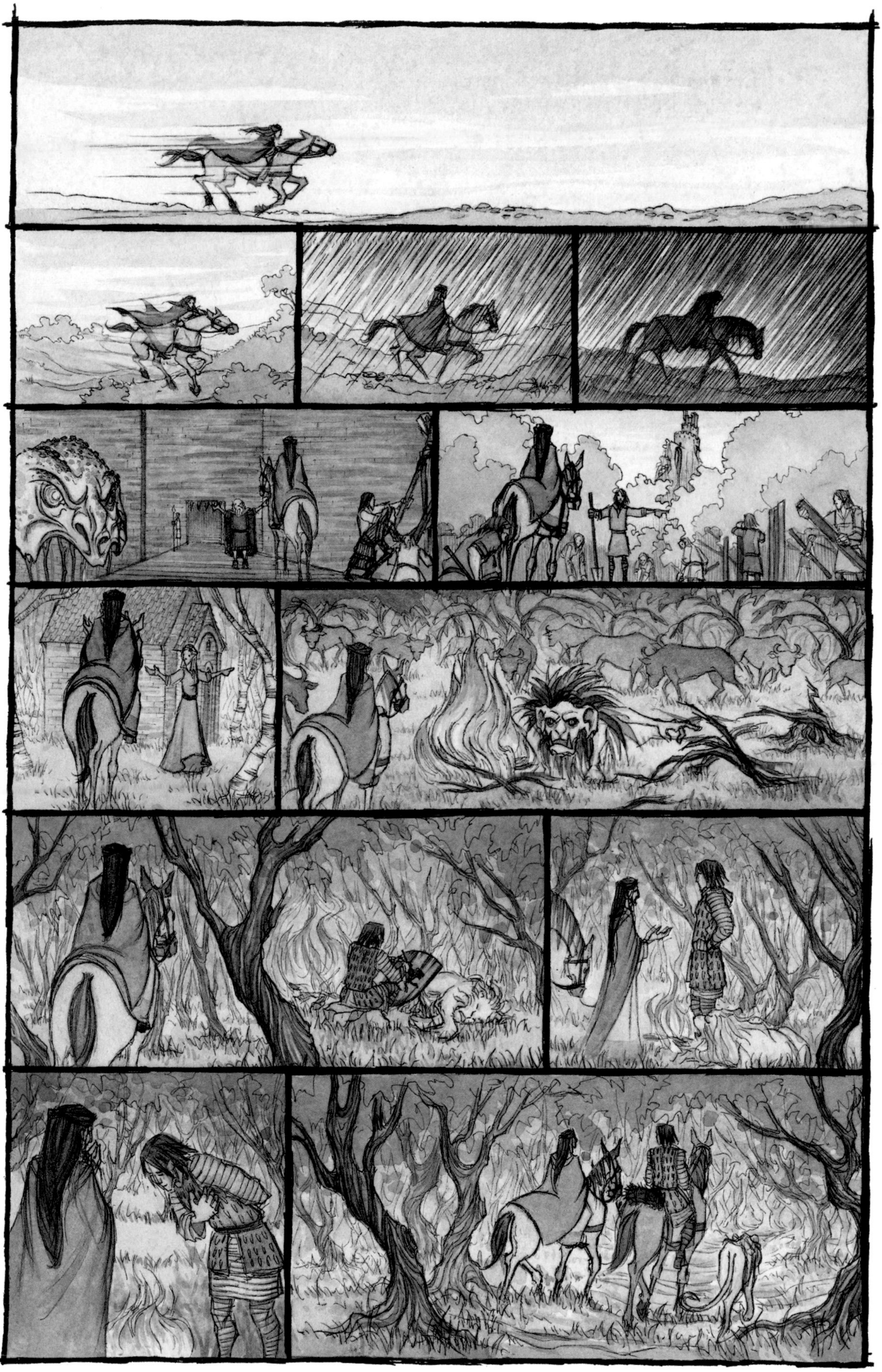

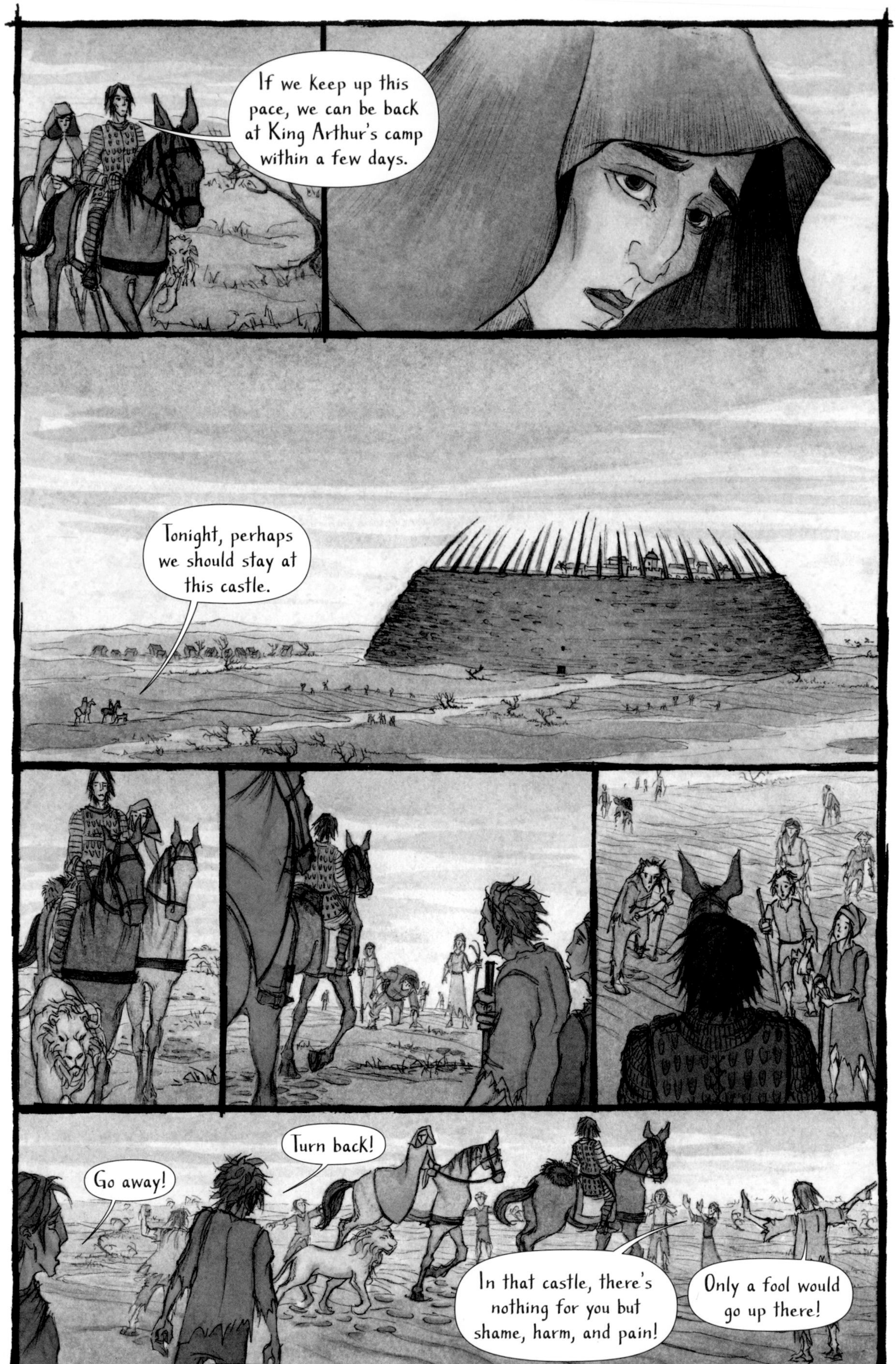
If we keep up this pace, we can be back at King Arthur's camp within a few days.
Tonight, perhaps we should stay at this castle.
Go away!
Turn back!
In that castle, there's nothing for you but shame, harm, and pain!
Only a fool would go up there!

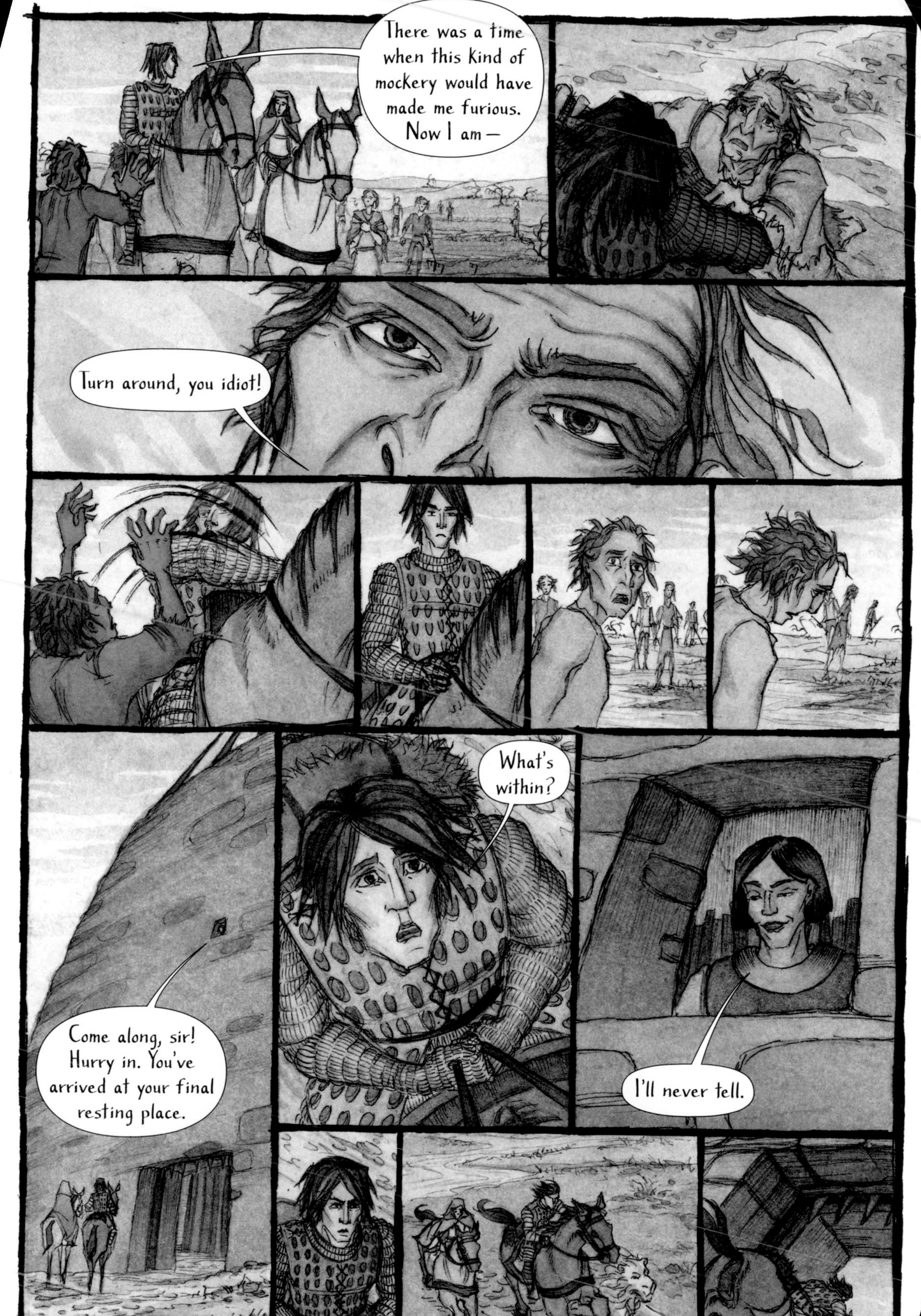
There was a time when this kind of mockery would have made me furious. Now I am —
Turn around, you idiot!
What's within?
Come along, sir! Hurry in. You've arrived at your final resting place.
I'll never tell.

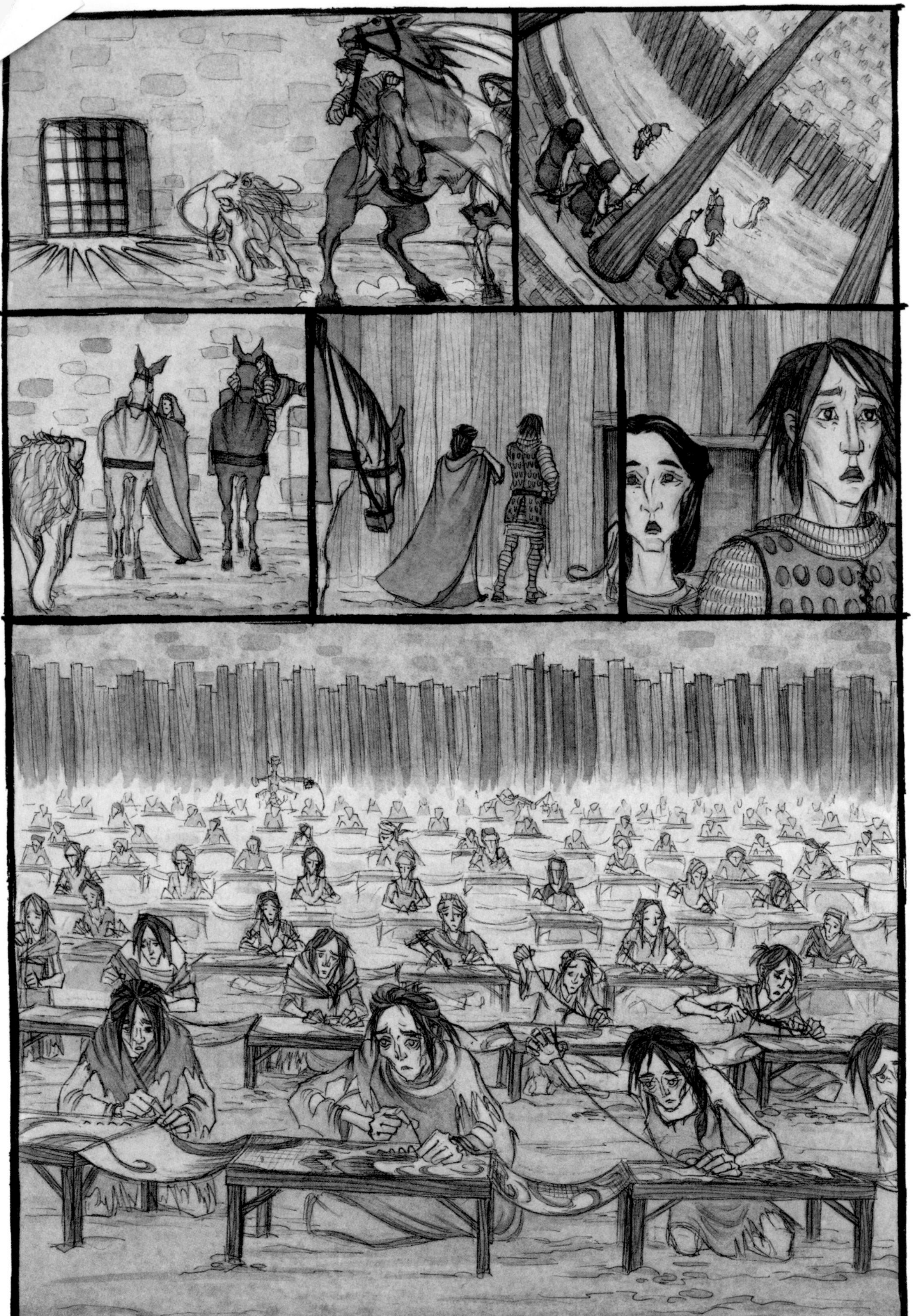

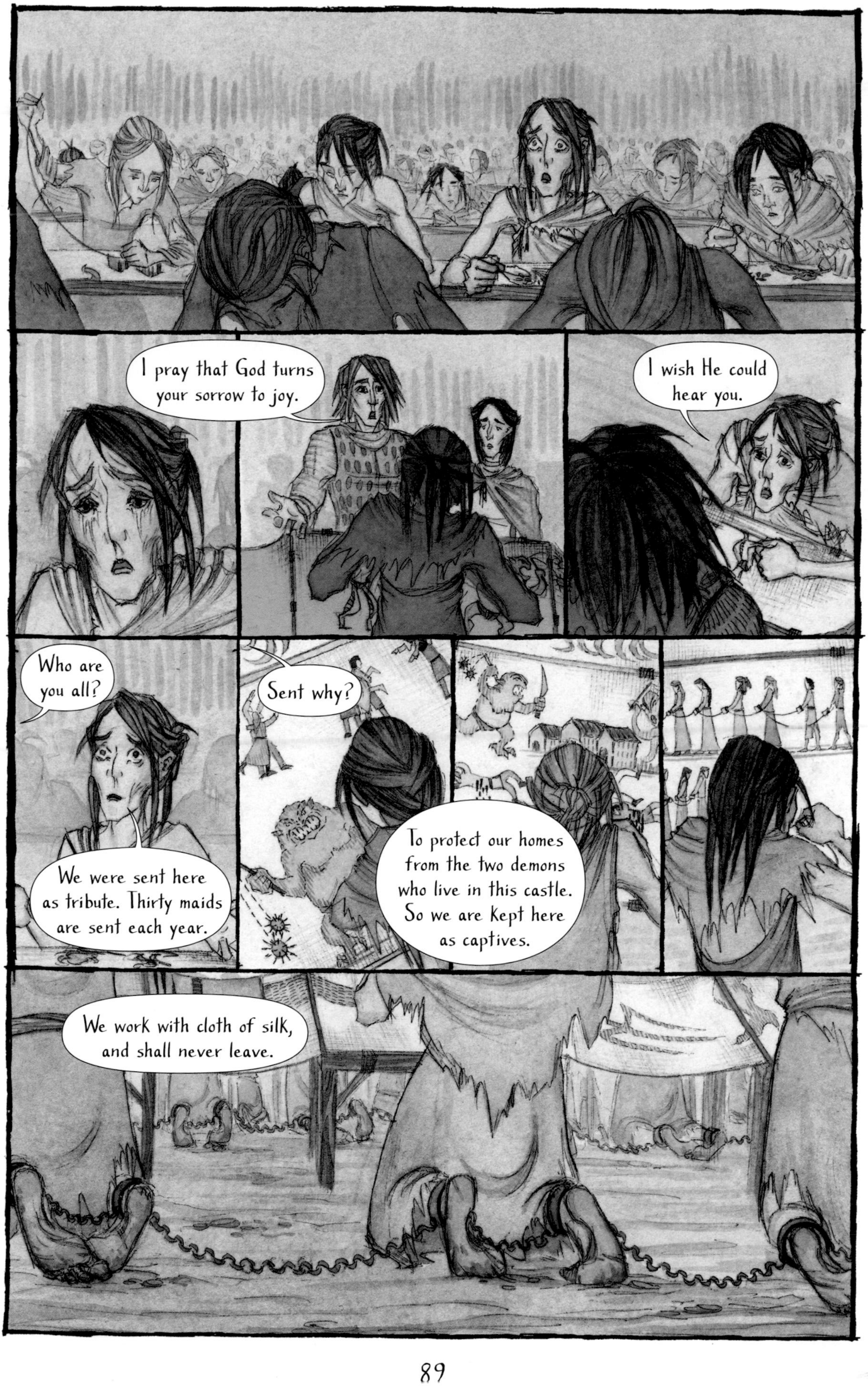
I pray that God turns your sorrow to joy.
I wish He could hear you.
Who are you all?
We were sent here as tribute. Thirty maids are sent each year.
Sent why?
To protect our homes from the two demons who live in this castle. So we are kept here as captives.
We work with cloth of silk, and shall never leave.

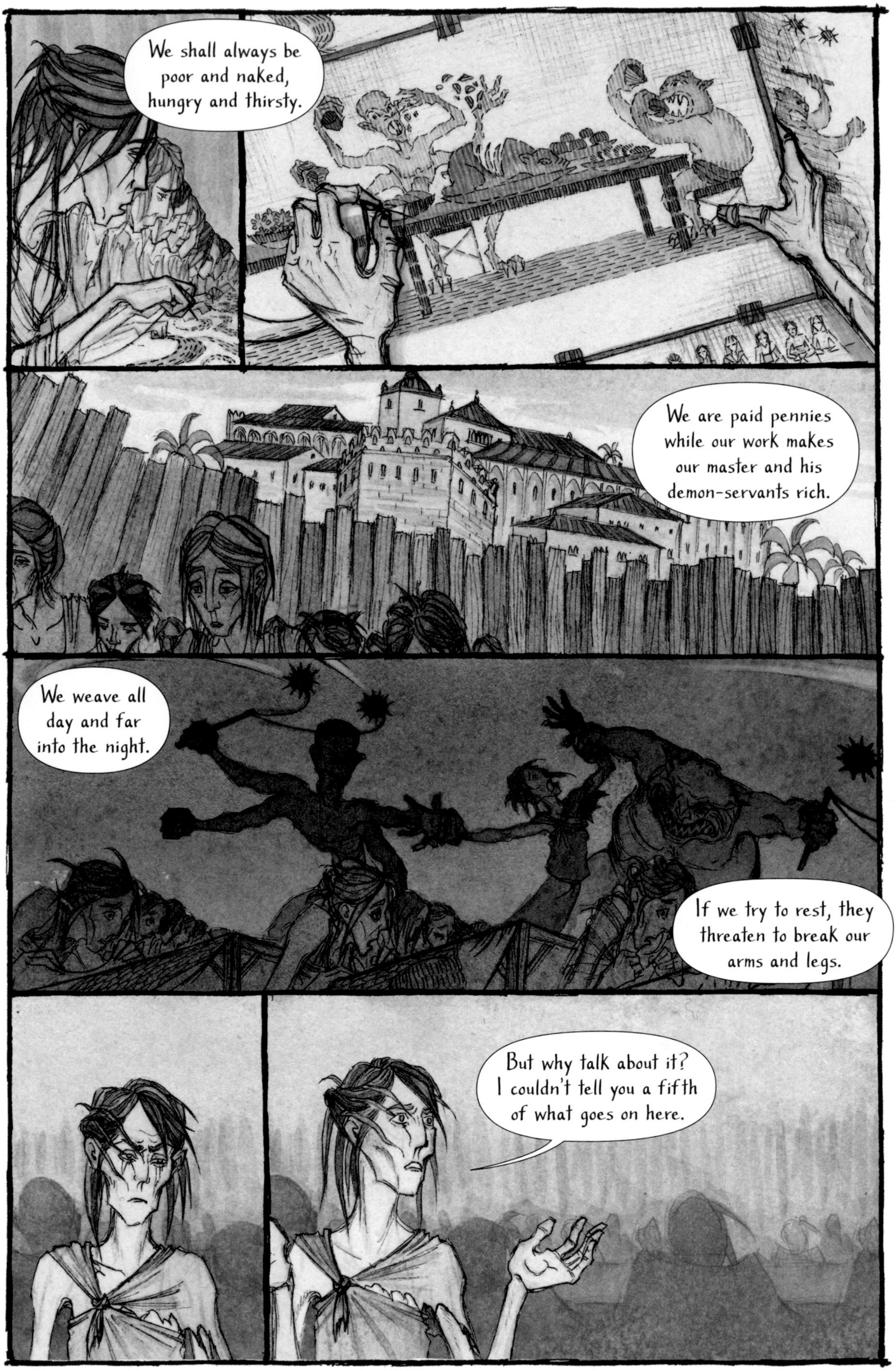
We shall always be poor and naked, hungry and thirsty.
We are paid pennies while our work makes our master and his demon-servants rich.
We weave all day and far into the night.
If we try to rest, they threaten to break our arms and legs.
But why talk about it? I couldn't tell you a fifth of what goes on here.

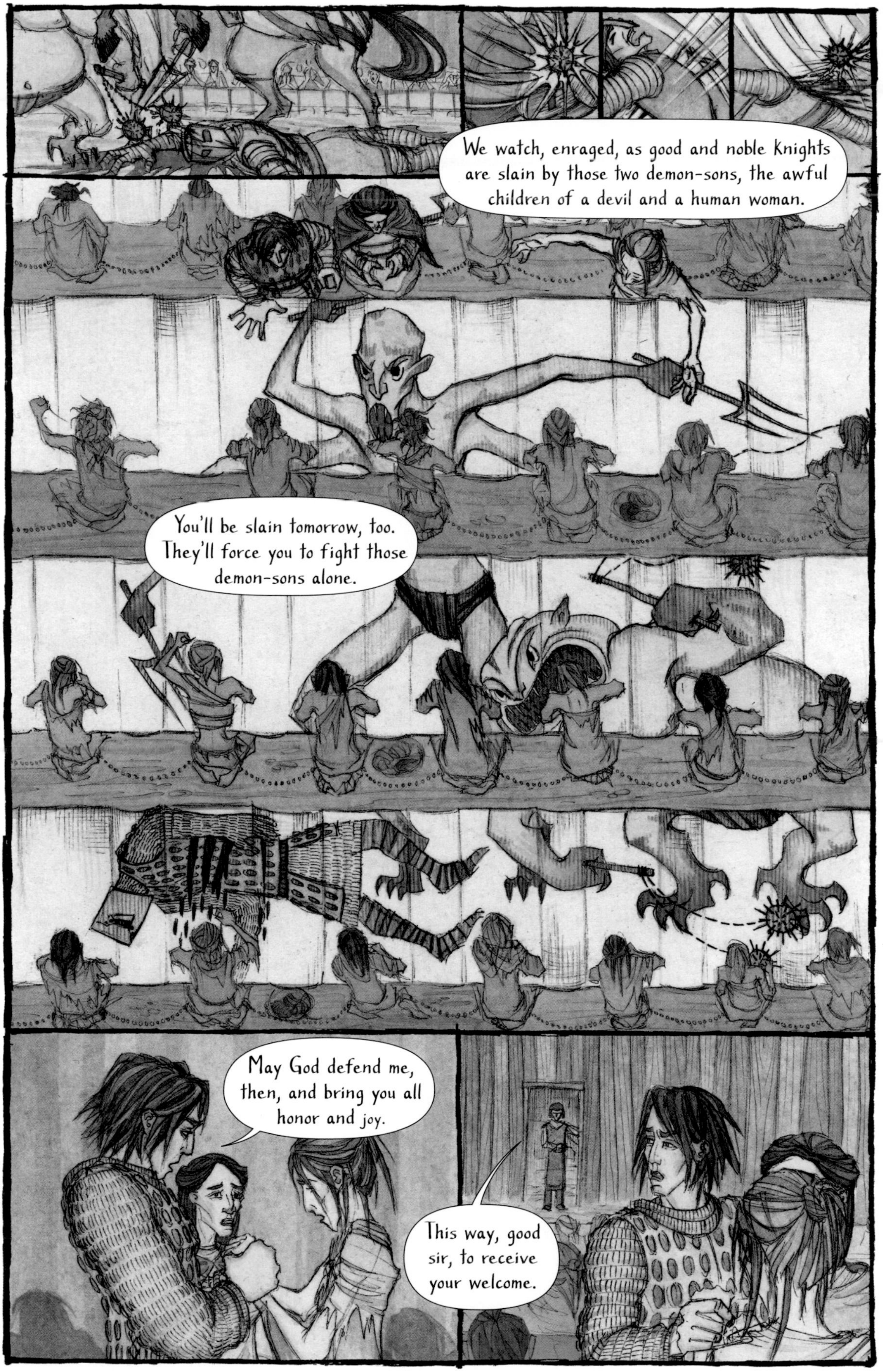
We watch, enraged, as good and noble Knights are slain by those two demon-sons, the awful children of a devil and a human woman.
You'll be slain tomorrow, too. They'll force you to fight those demon-sons alone.
May God defend me, then, and bring you all honor and joy.
This way, good sir, to receive your welcome.

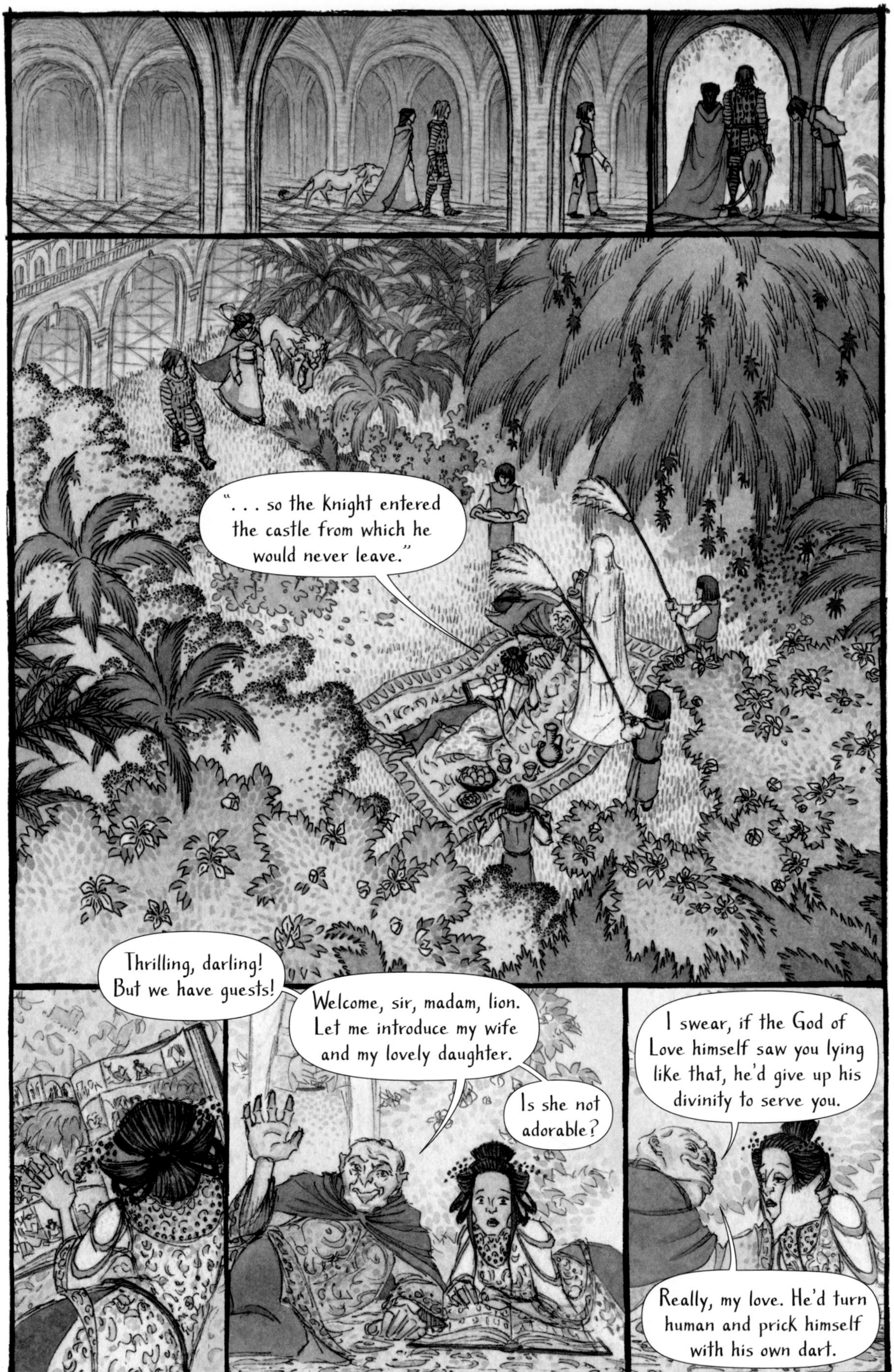
". . . so the Knight entered the castle from which he would never leave."
Thrilling, darling! But we have guests!
Welcome, sir, madam, lion. Let me introduce my wife and my lovely daughter.
Is she not adorable?
I swear, if the God of Love himself saw you lying like that, he'd give up his divinity to serve you.
Really, my love. He'd turn human and prick himself with his own dart.

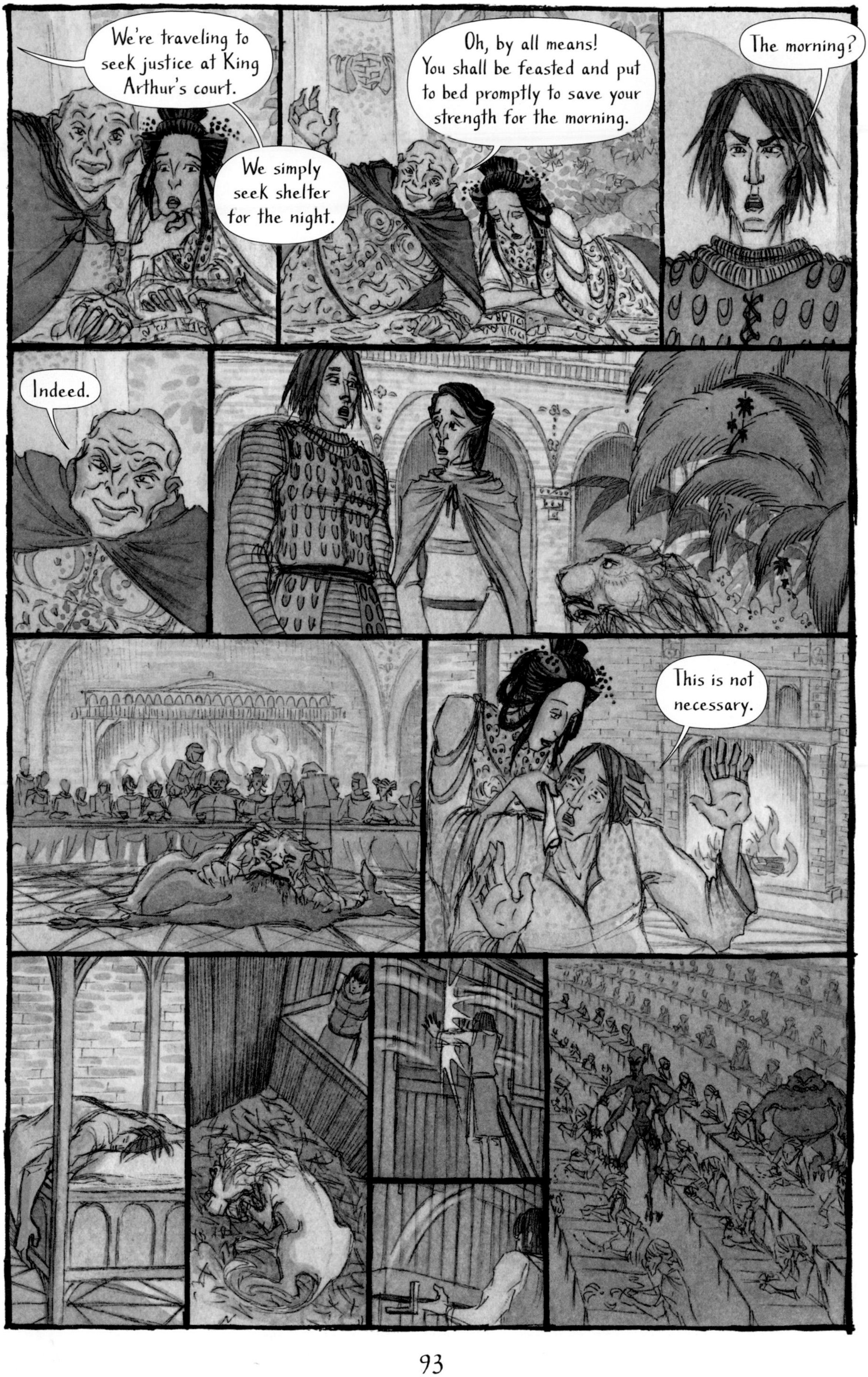
We're traveling to seek justice at King Arthur's court.
We simply seek shelter for the night.
Oh, by all means! You shall be feasted and put to bed promptly to save your strength for the morning.
The morning?
Indeed.
This is not necessary.

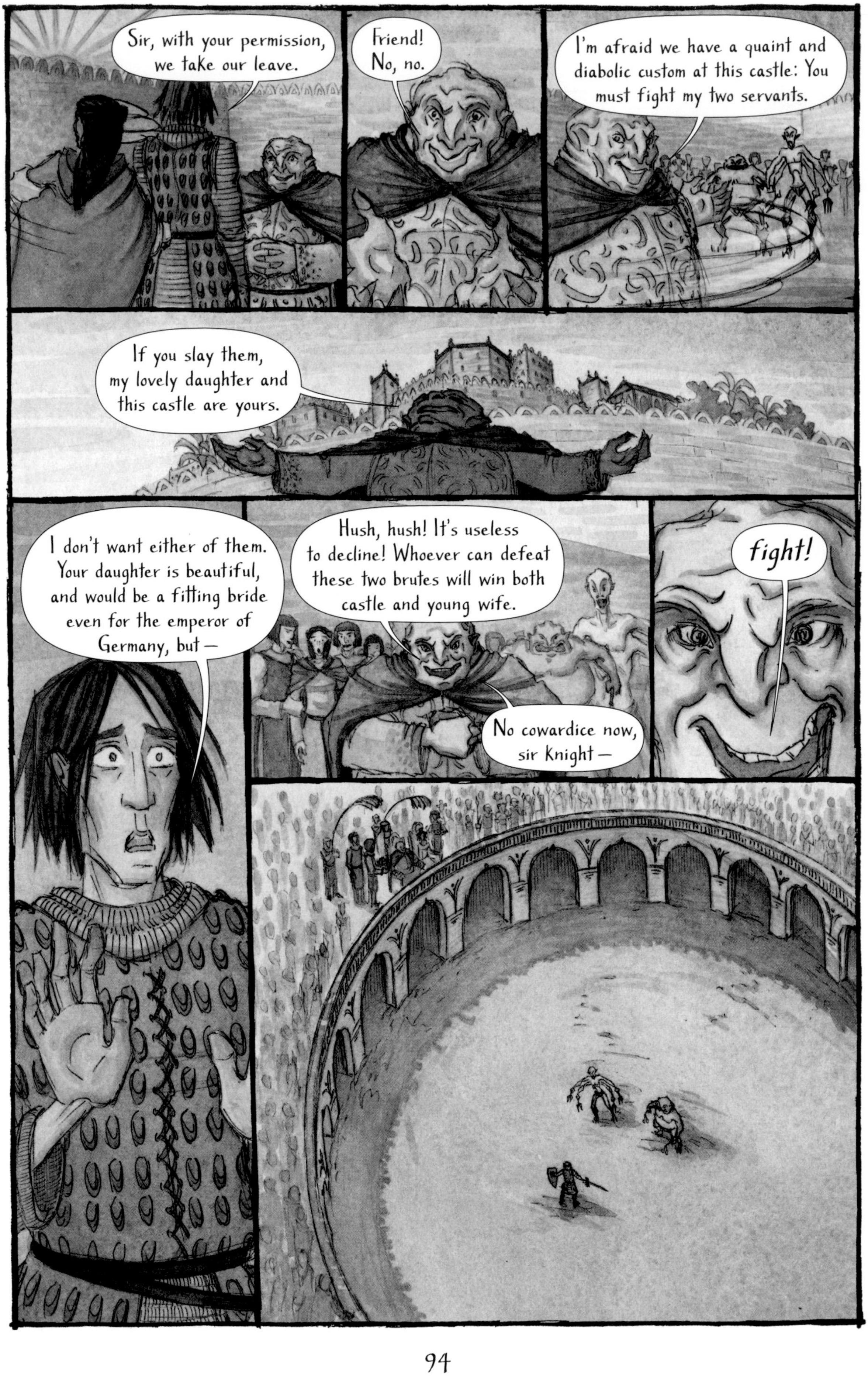
Sir, with your permission, we take our leave.
Friend! No, no.
I'm afraid we have a quaint and diabolic custom at this castle: You must fight my two servants.
If you slay them, my lovely daughter and this castle are yours.
I don't want either of them. Your daughter is beautiful, and would be a fitting bride even for the emperor of Germany, but—
Hush, hush! It's useless to decline! Whoever can defeat these two brutes will win both castle and young wife.
No cowardice now, sir Knight—
fight!

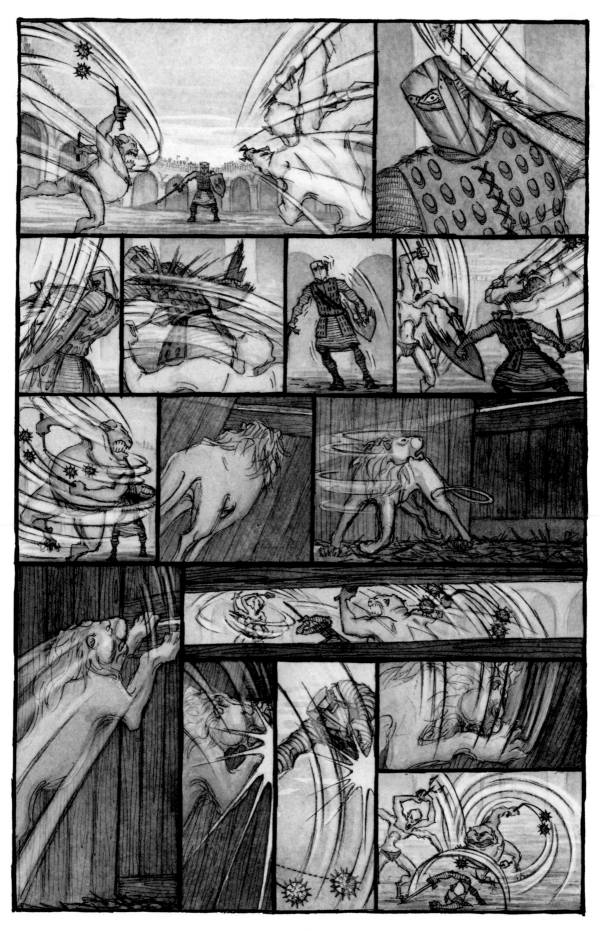

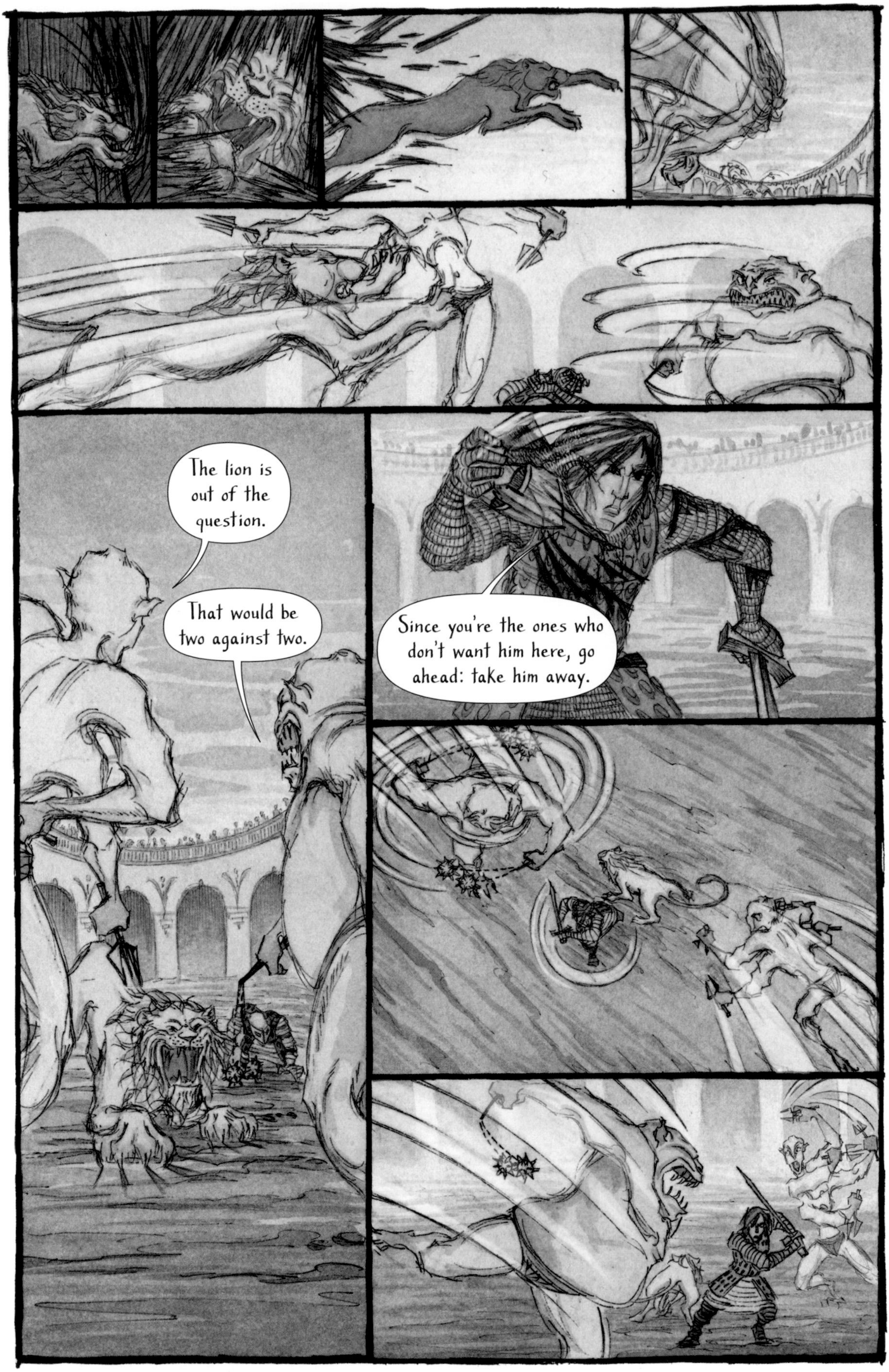
The lion is out of the question.
That would be two against two.
Since you're the ones who don't want him here, go ahead: take him away.

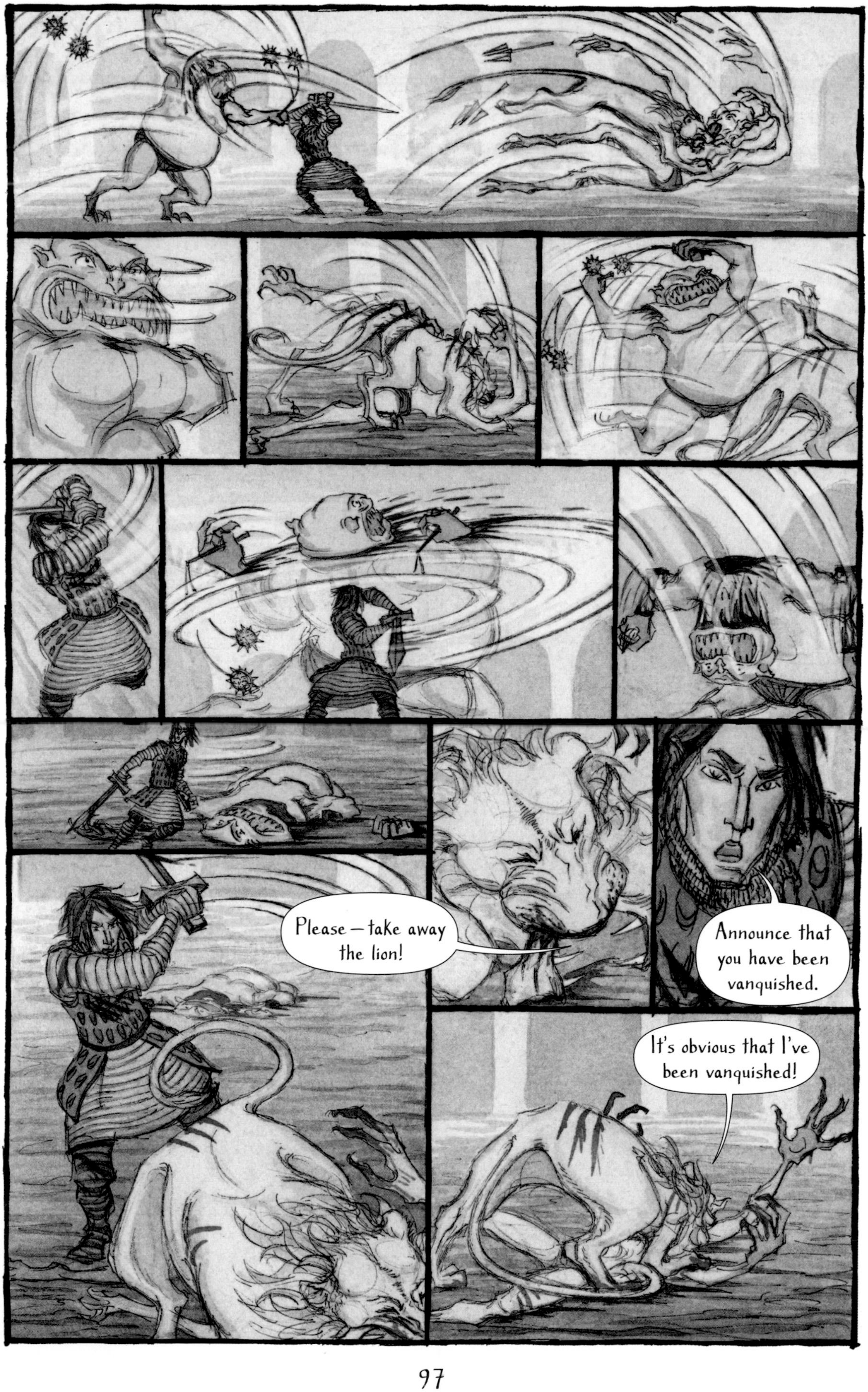
Please—take away the lion!
Announce that you have been vanquished.
It's obvious that I've been vanquished!

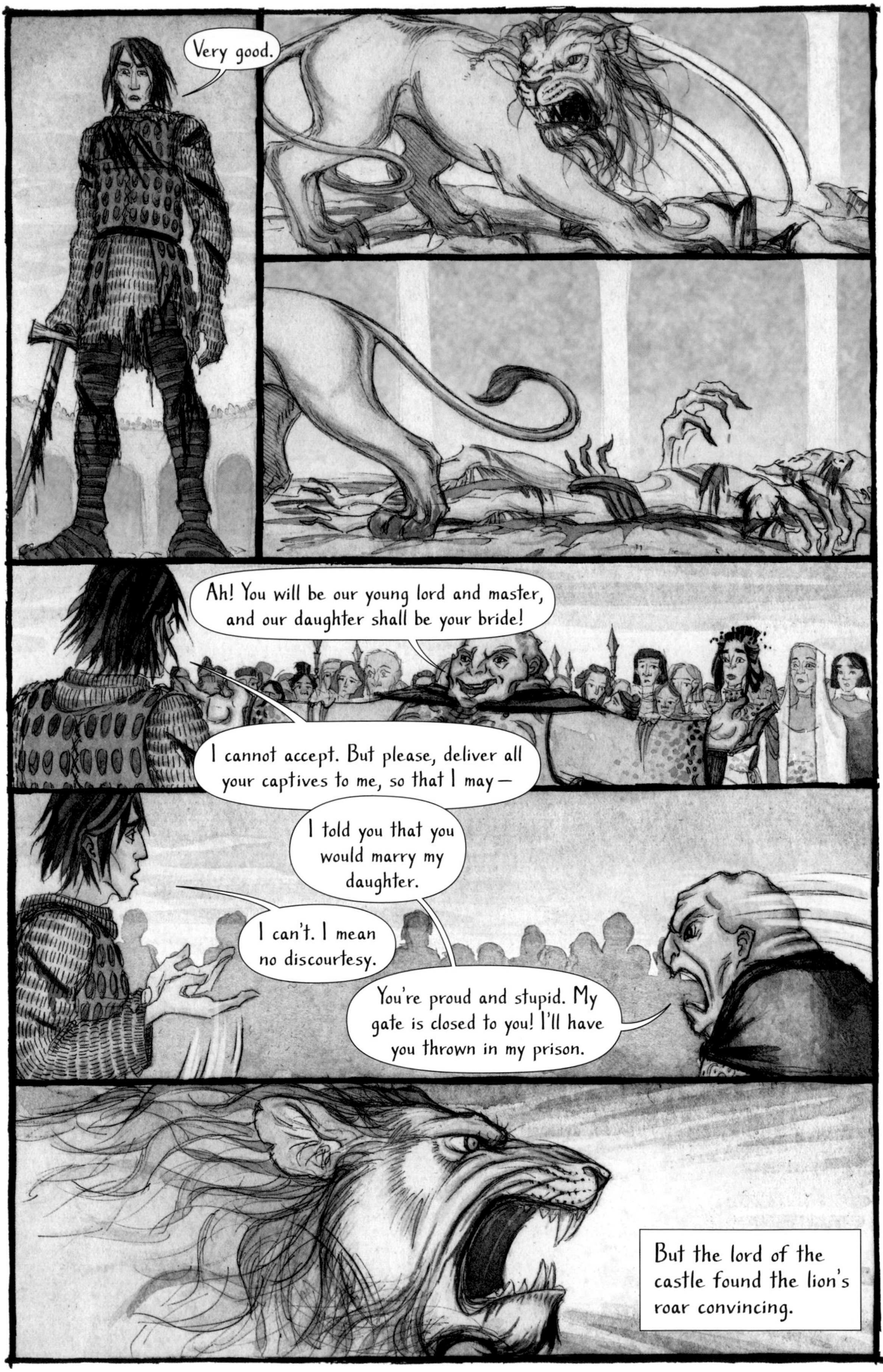
Very good.
Ah! You will be our young lord and master, and our daughter shall be your bride!
I cannot accept. But please, deliver all your captives to me, so that I may—
I told you that you would marry my daughter.
I can't. I mean no discourtesy.
You're proud and stupid. My gate is closed to you! I'll have you thrown in my prison.
But the lord of the castle found the lion's roar convincing.

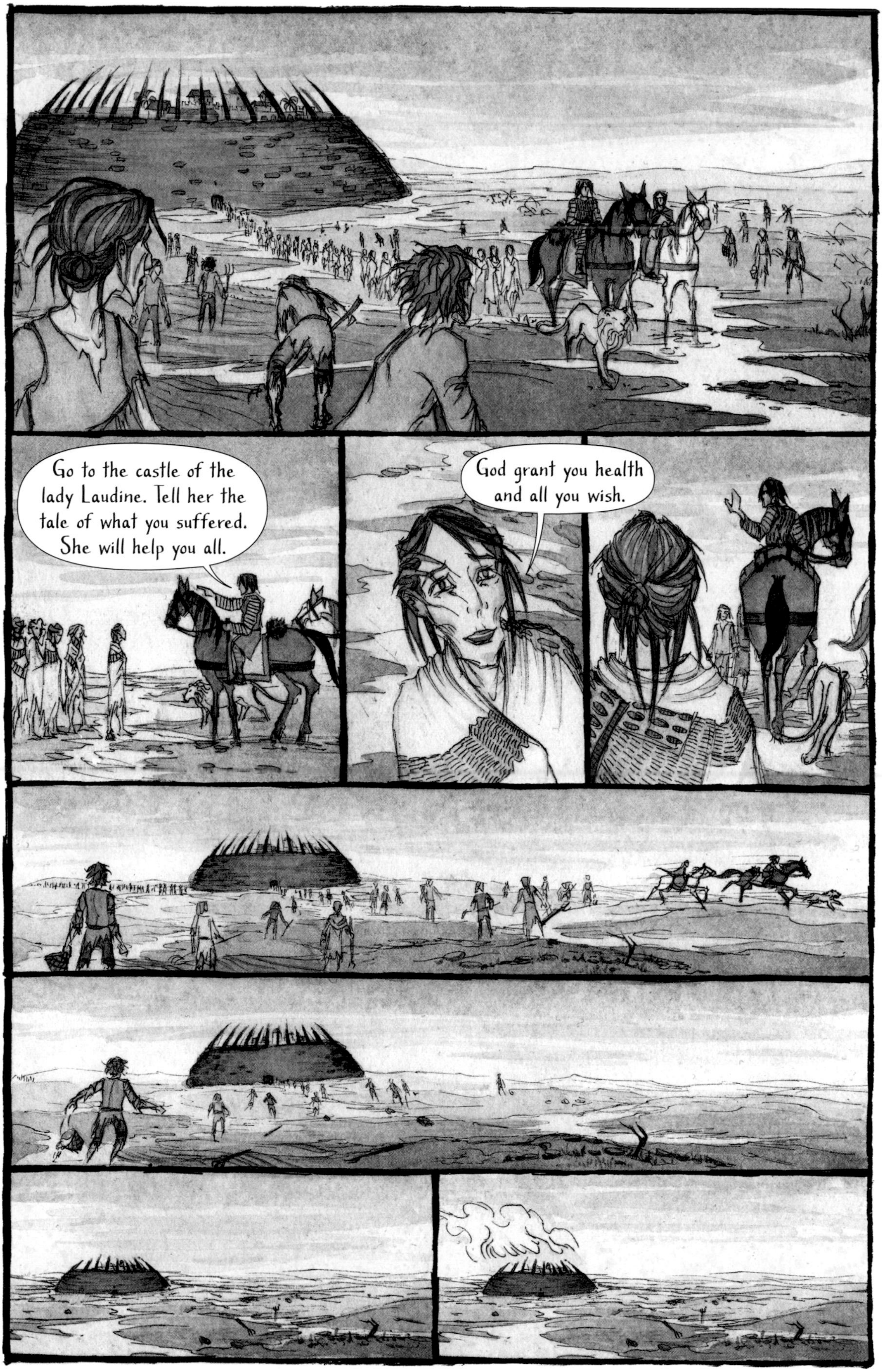
Go to the castle of the lady Laudine. Tell her the tale of what you suffered. She will help you all.
God grant you health and all you wish.

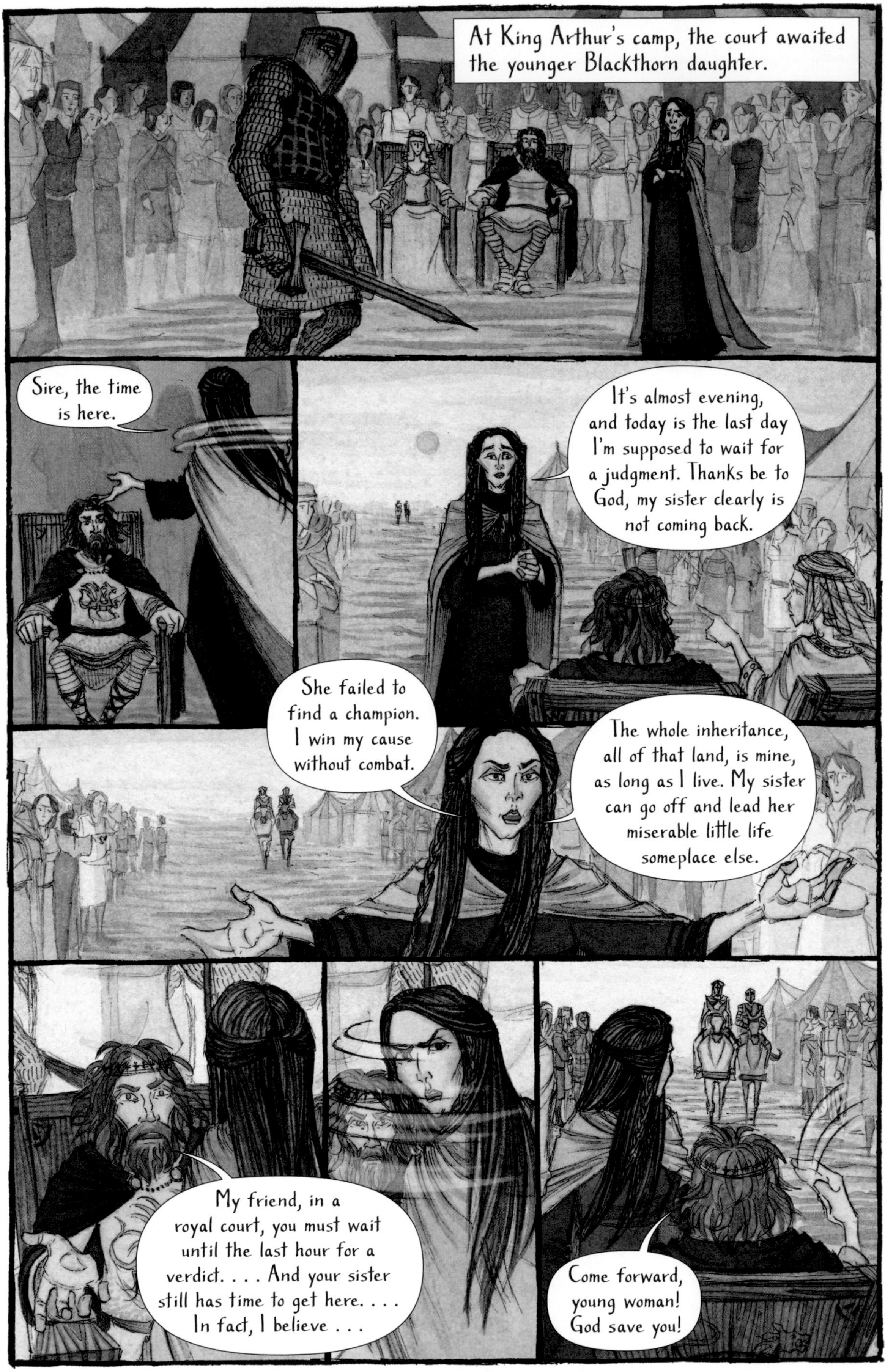
At King Arthur's camp, the court awaited the younger Blackthorn daughter.
Sire, the time is here.
It's almost evening, and today is the last day I'm supposed to wait for a judgment. Thanks be to God, my sister clearly is not coming back.
She failed to find a champion. I win my cause without combat.
The whole inheritance, all of that land, is mine, as long as I live. My sister can go off and lead her miserable little life someplace else.
My friend, in a royal court, you must wait until the last hour for a verdict. . . . And your sister still has time to get here. . . . In fact, I believe . . .
Come forward, young woman! God save you!

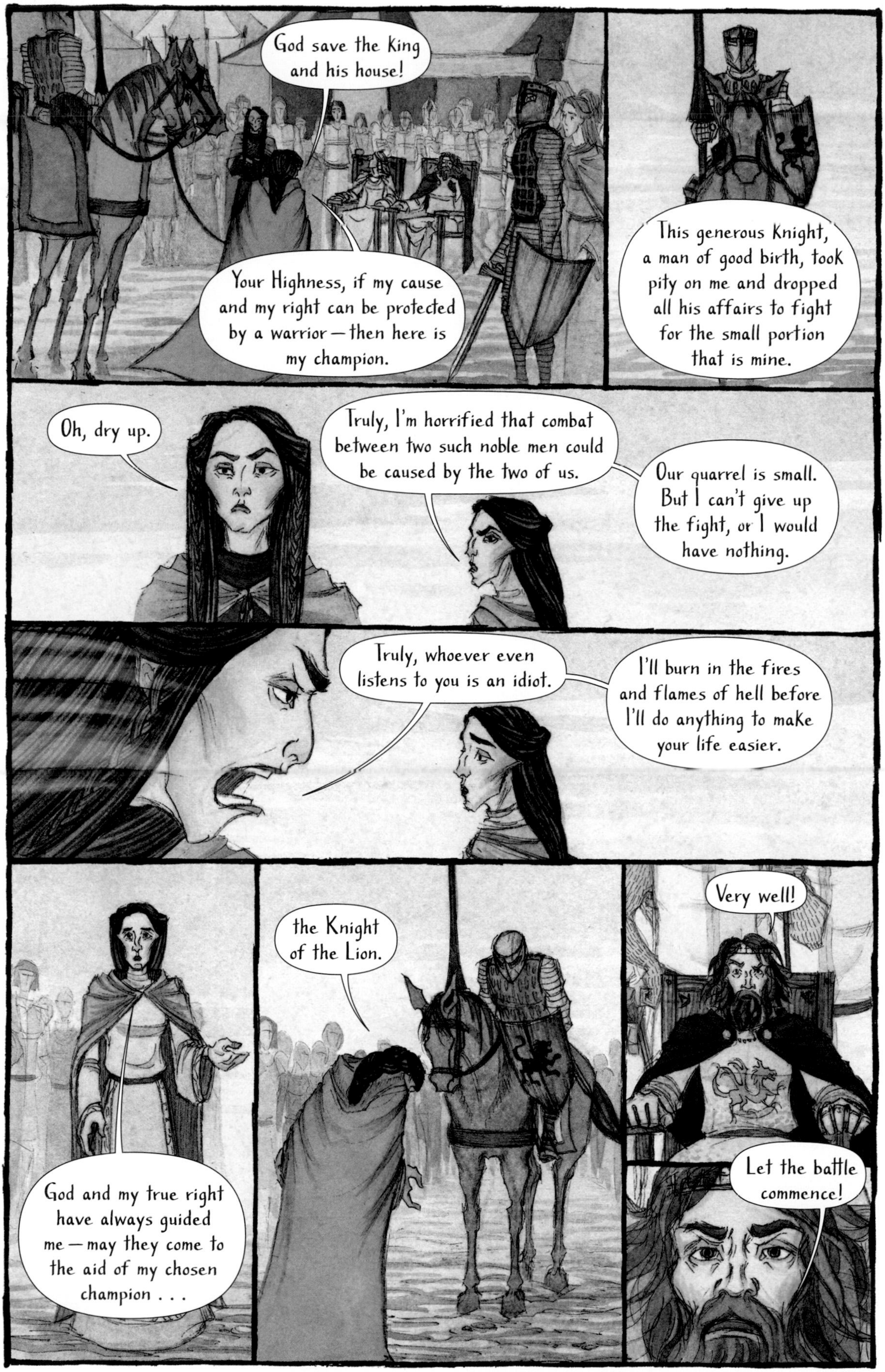
God save the King and his house!
Your Highness, if my cause and my right can be protected by a warrior — then here is my champion.
This generous Knight, a man of good birth, took pity on me and dropped all his affairs to fight for the small portion that is mine.
Oh, dry up.
Truly, I'm horrified that combat between two such noble men could be caused by the two of us.
Our quarrel is small. But I can't give up the fight, or I would have nothing.
Truly, whoever even listens to you is an idiot.
I'll burn in the fires and flames of hell before I'll do anything to make your life easier.
God and my true right have always guided me — may they come to the aid of my chosen champion . . .
the Knight of the Lion.
Very well!
Let the battle commence!

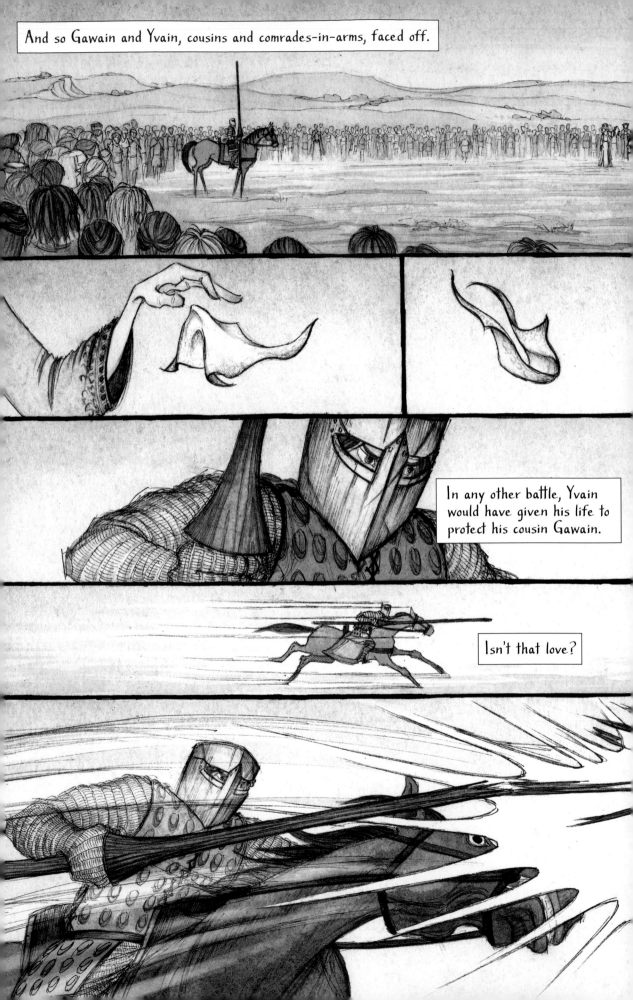

And so Gawain and Yvain, cousins and comrades-in-arms, faced off.

In any other battle, Yvain would have given his life to protect his cousin Gawain.

Isn't that love?

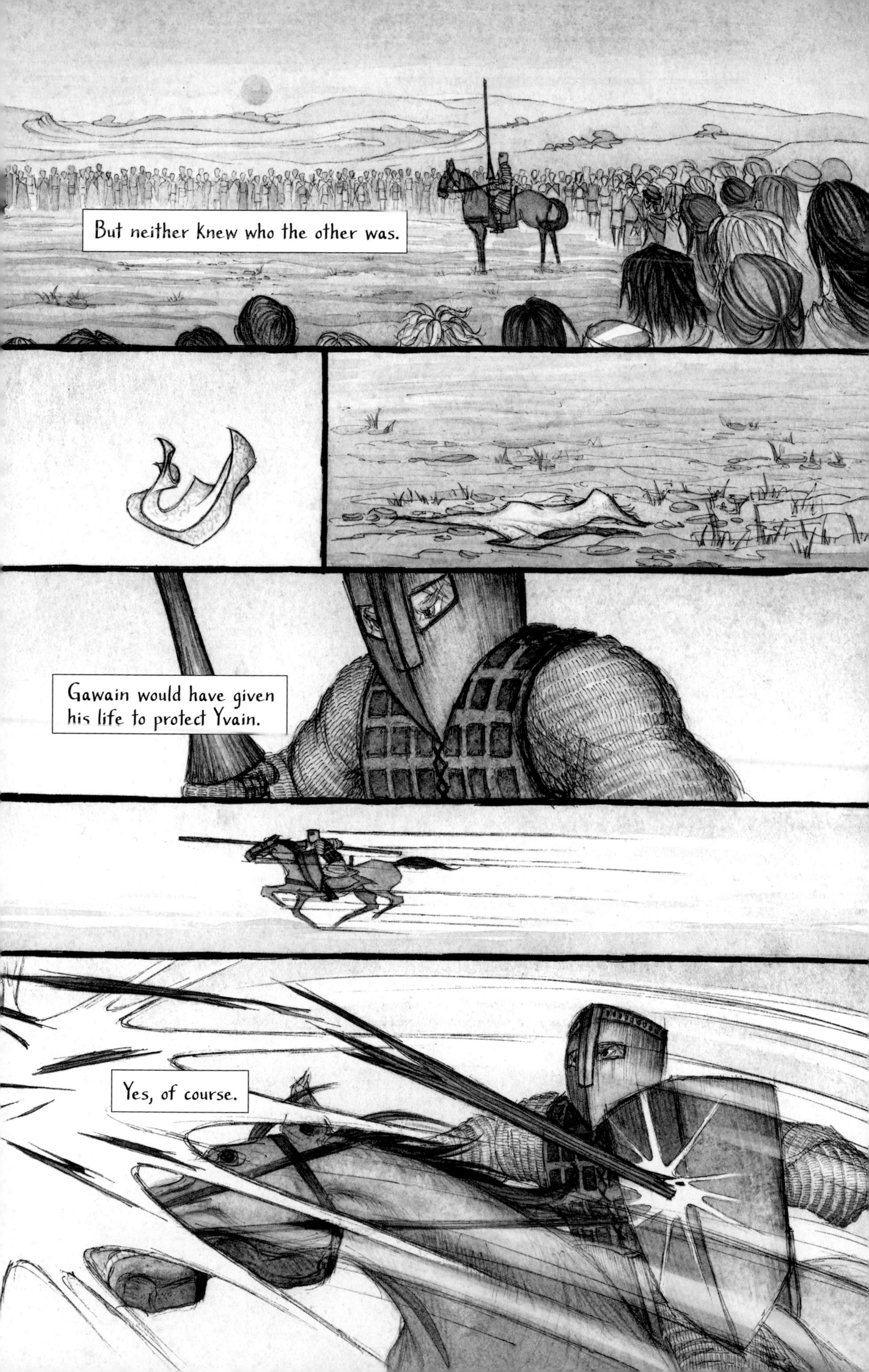
But neither knew who the other was.
Gawain would have given his life to protect Yvain.
Yes, of course.

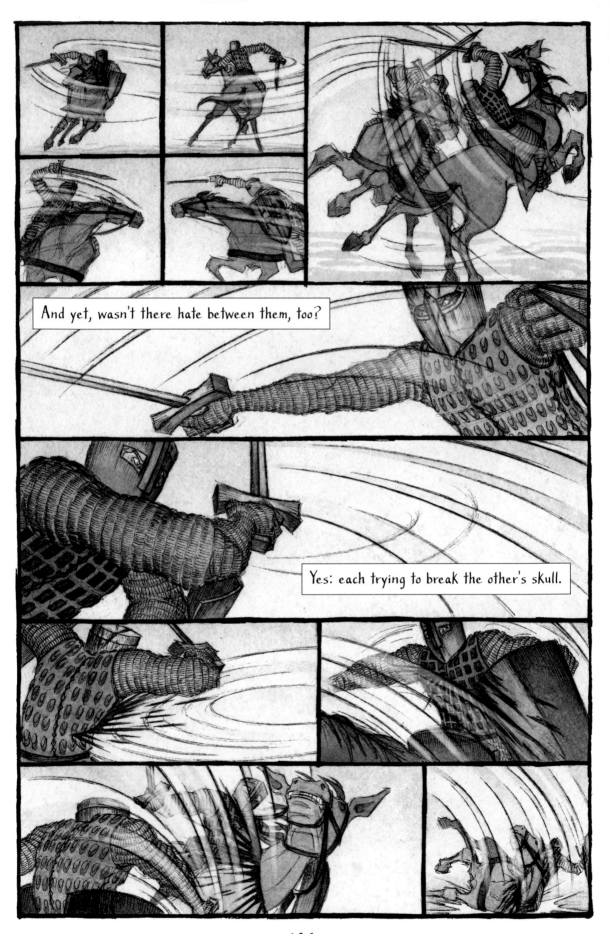

And yet, wasn't there hate between them, too?

Yes: each trying to break the other's skull.

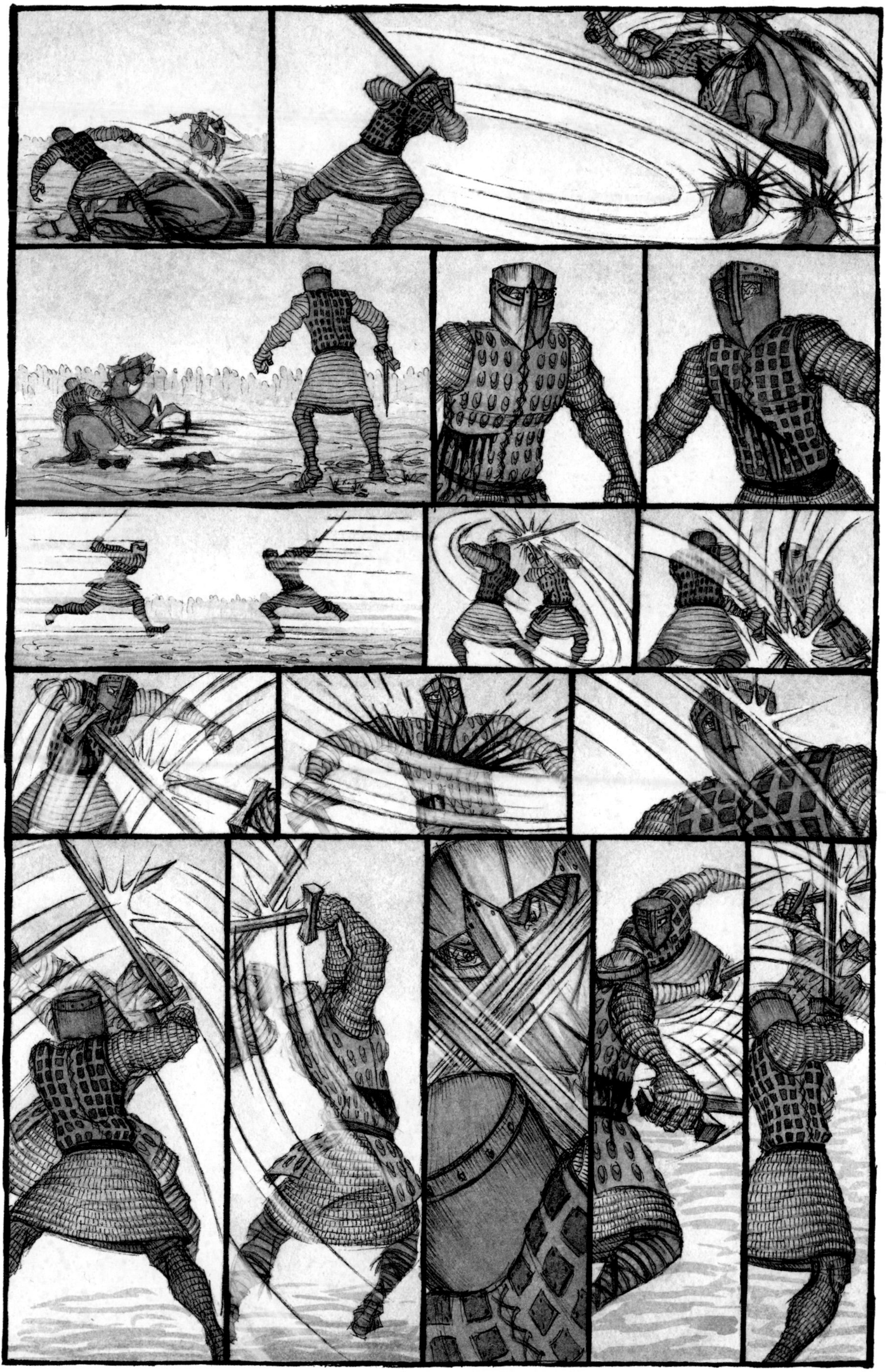

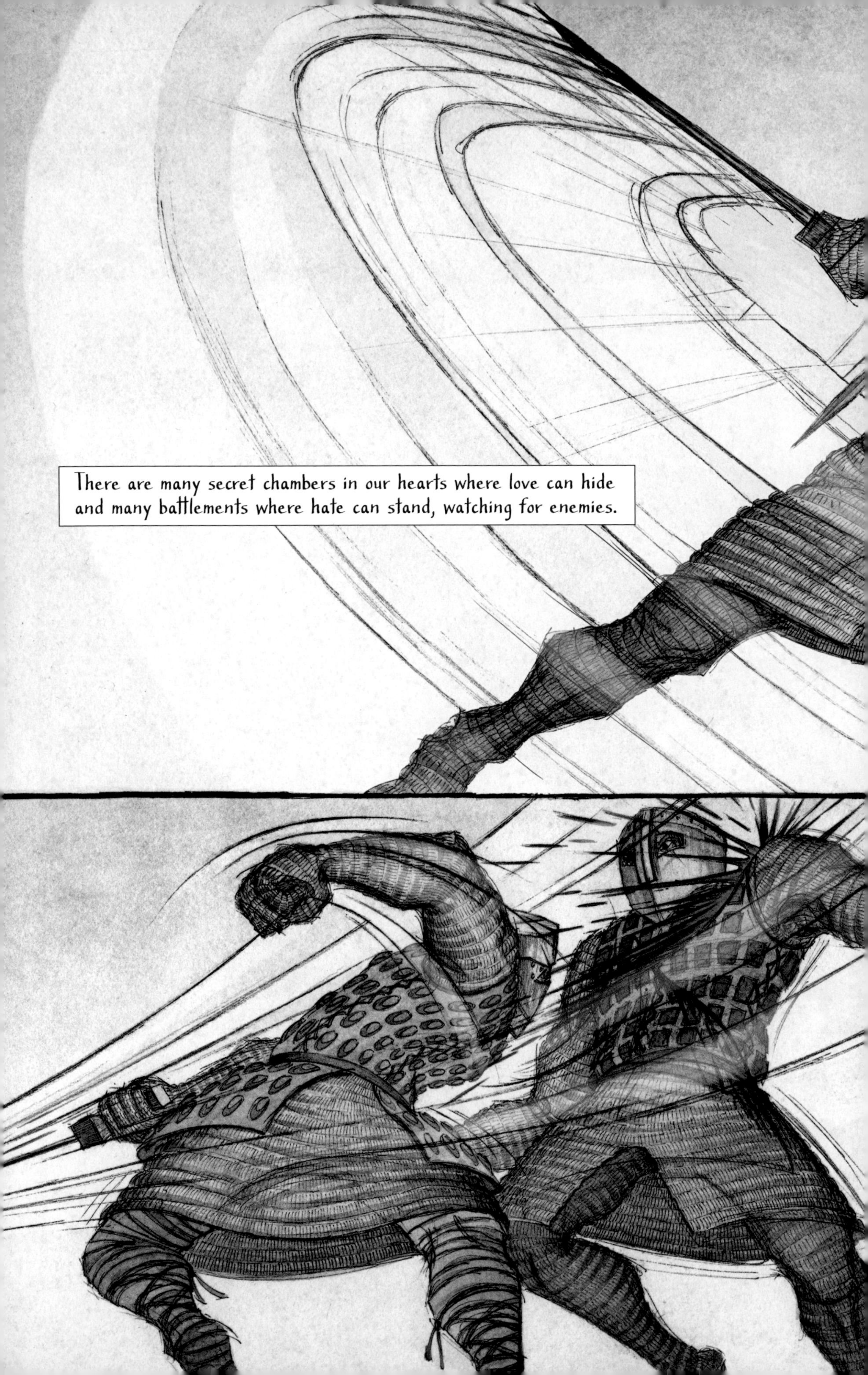
There are many secret chambers in our hearts where love can hide and many battlements where hate can stand, watching for enemies.

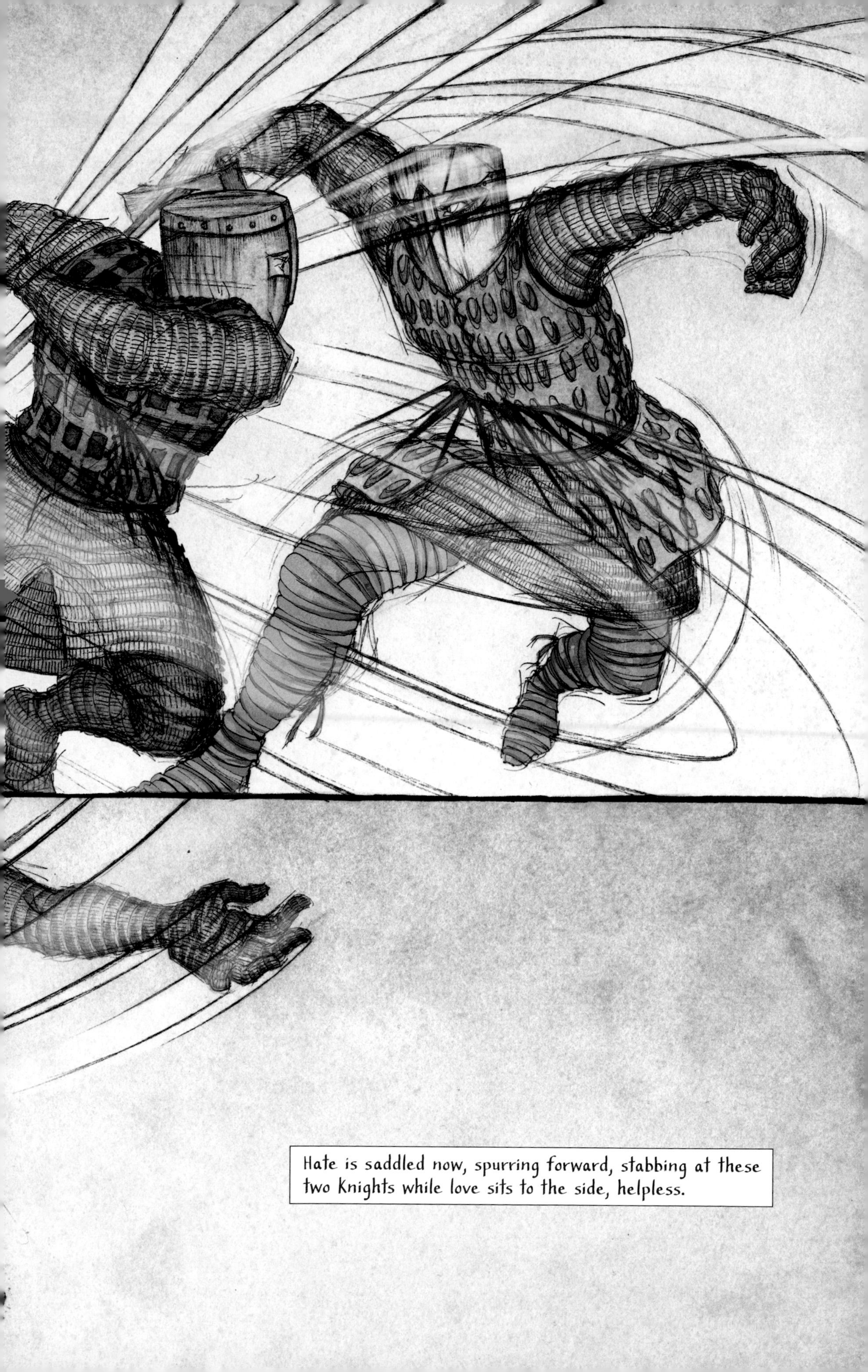
Hate is saddled now, spurring forward, stabbing at these two Knights while love sits to the side, helpless.

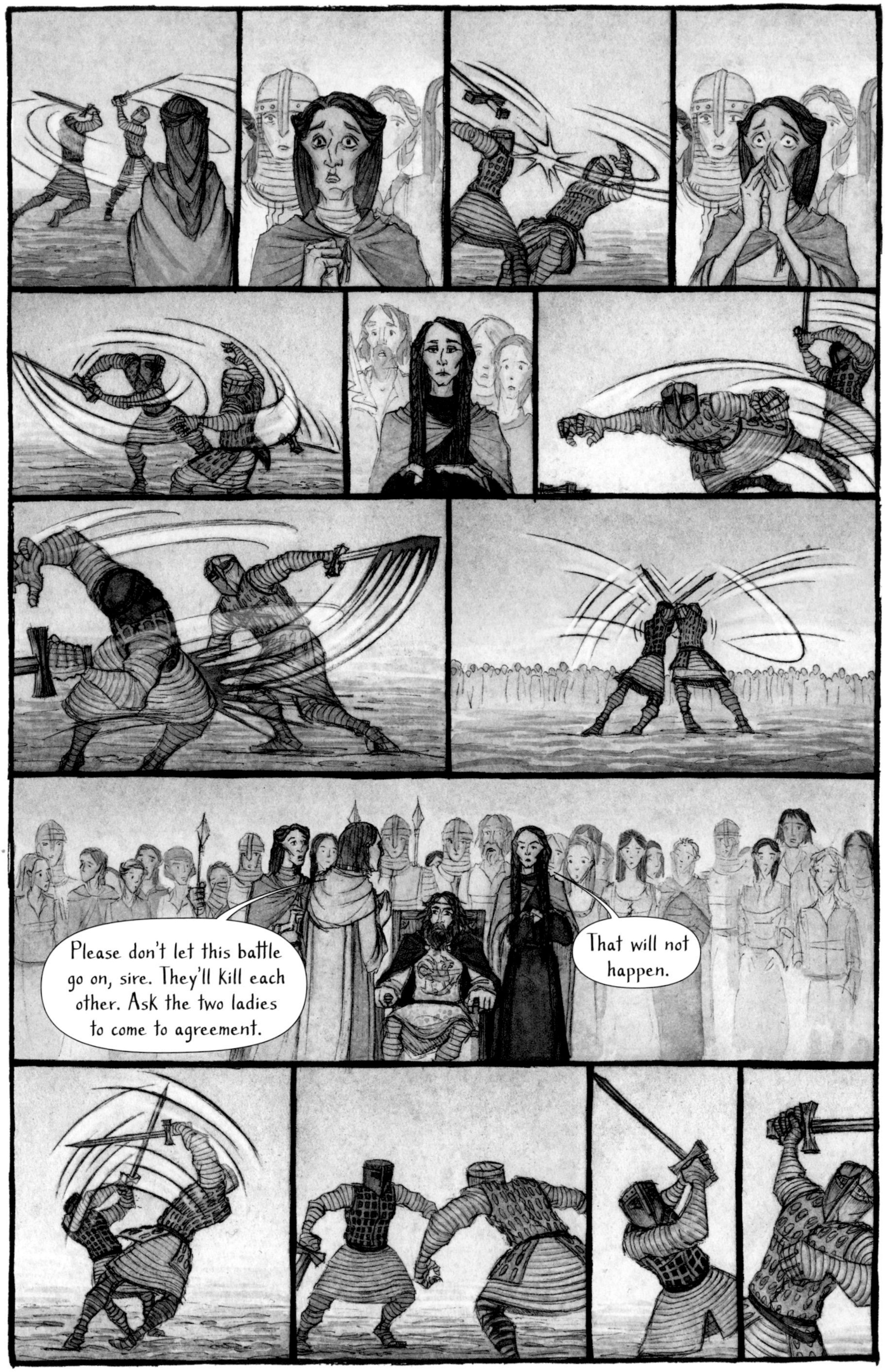
Please don't let this battle go on, sire. They'll kill each other. Ask the two ladies to come to agreement.
That will not happen.

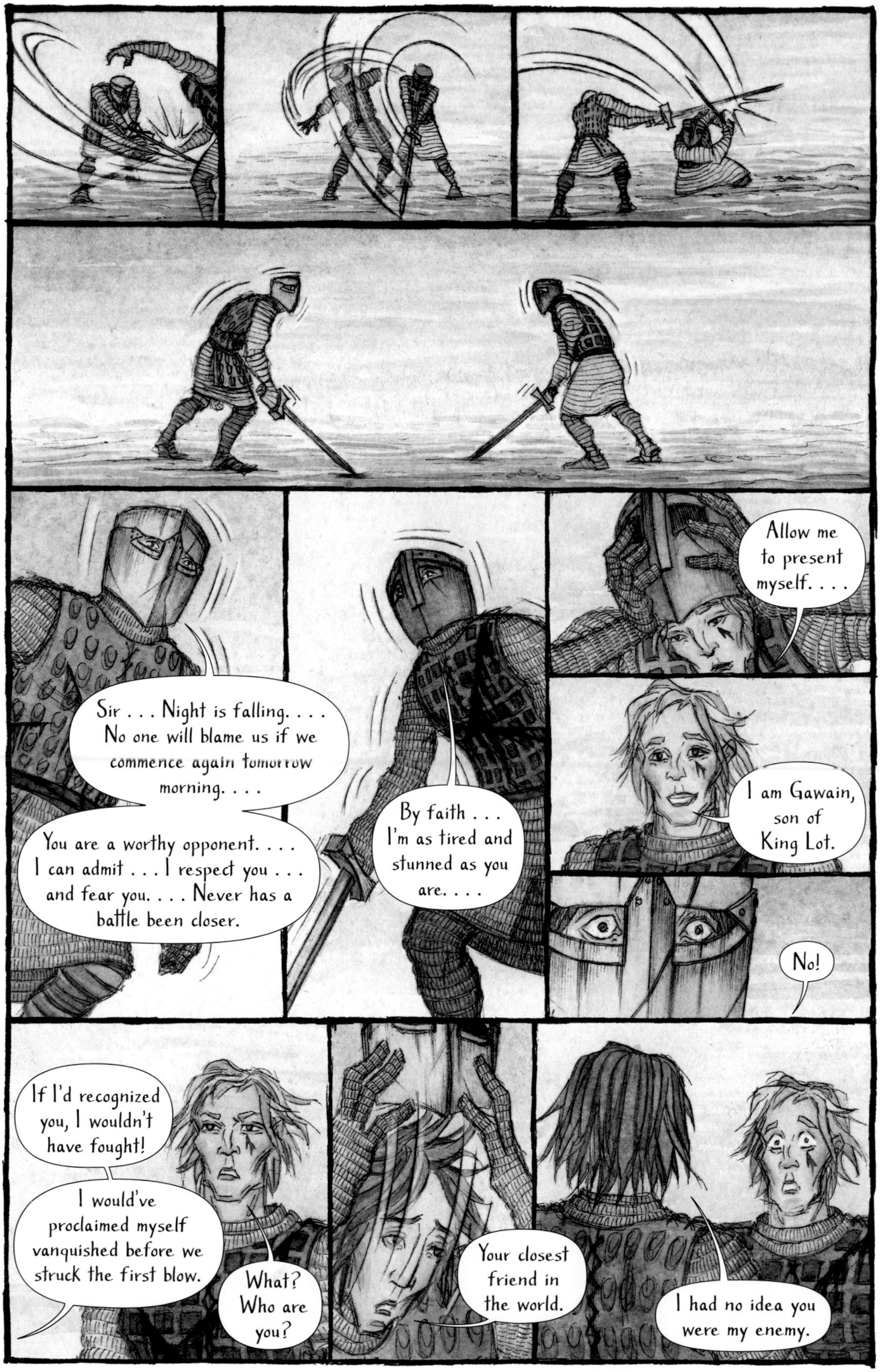

Allow me to present myself. . . .
Sir . . . Night is falling. . . . No one will blame us if we commence again tomorrow morning. . . .
You are a worthy opponent. . . . I can admit . . . I respect you . . . and fear you. . . . Never has a battle been closer.
By faith . . . I'm as tired and stunned as you are. . . .
I am Gawain, son of King Lot.
No!
If I'd recognized you, I wouldn't have fought!
I would've proclaimed myself vanquished before we struck the first blow.
What? Who are you?
Your closest friend in the world.
I had no idea you were my enemy.

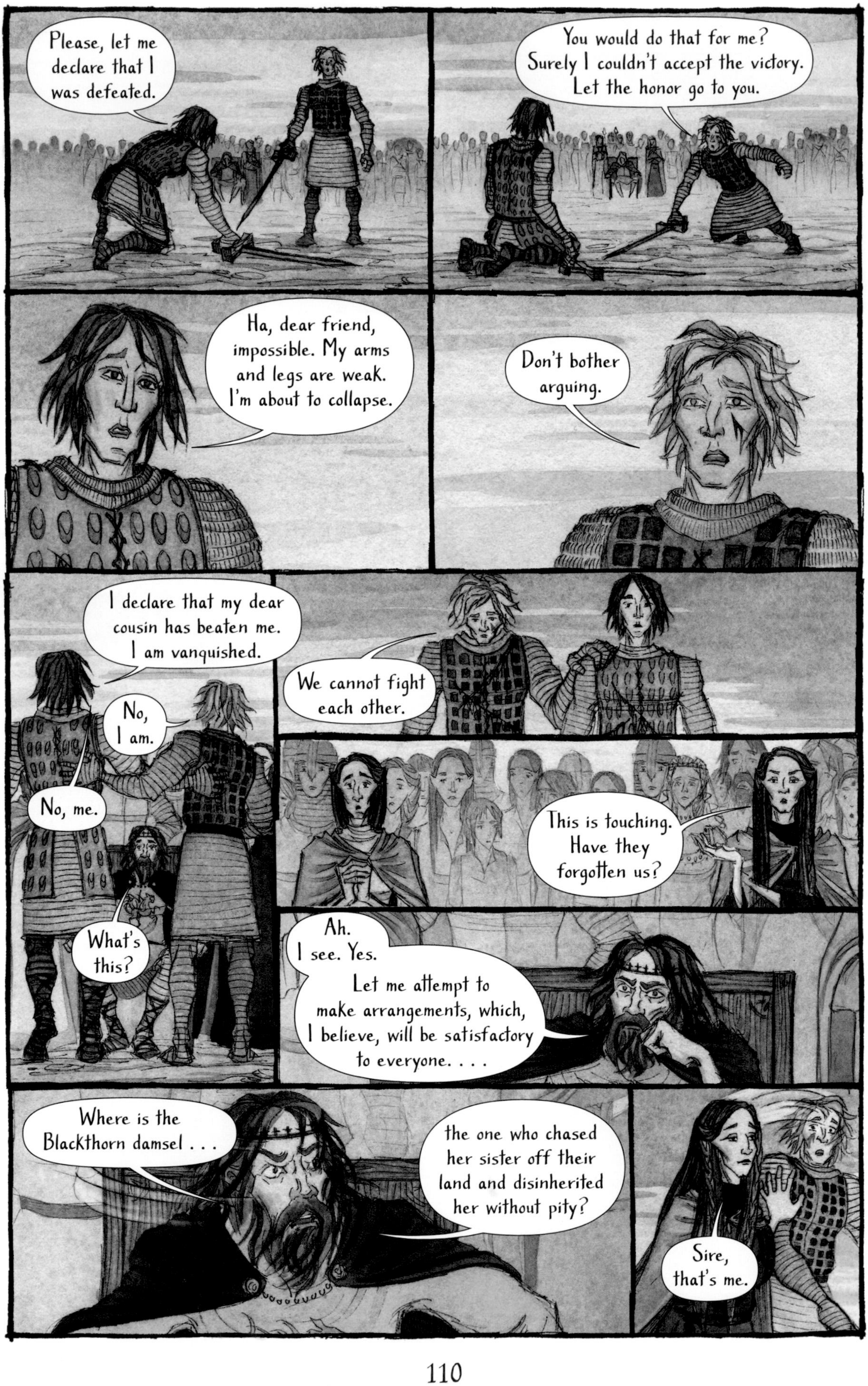
Please, let me declare that I was defeated.
You would do that for me? Surely I couldn't accept the victory. Let the honor go to you.
Ha, dear friend, impossible. My arms and legs are weak. I'm about to collapse.
Don't bother arguing.
I declare that my dear cousin has beaten me. I am vanquished.
No, I am.
No, me.
What's this?
We cannot fight each other.
This is touching. Have they forgotten us?
Ah. I see. Yes.
Let me attempt to make arrangements, which, I believe, will be satisfactory to everyone. . . .
Where is the Blackthorn damsel . . .
the one who chased her sister off their land and disinherited her without pity?
Sire, that's me.

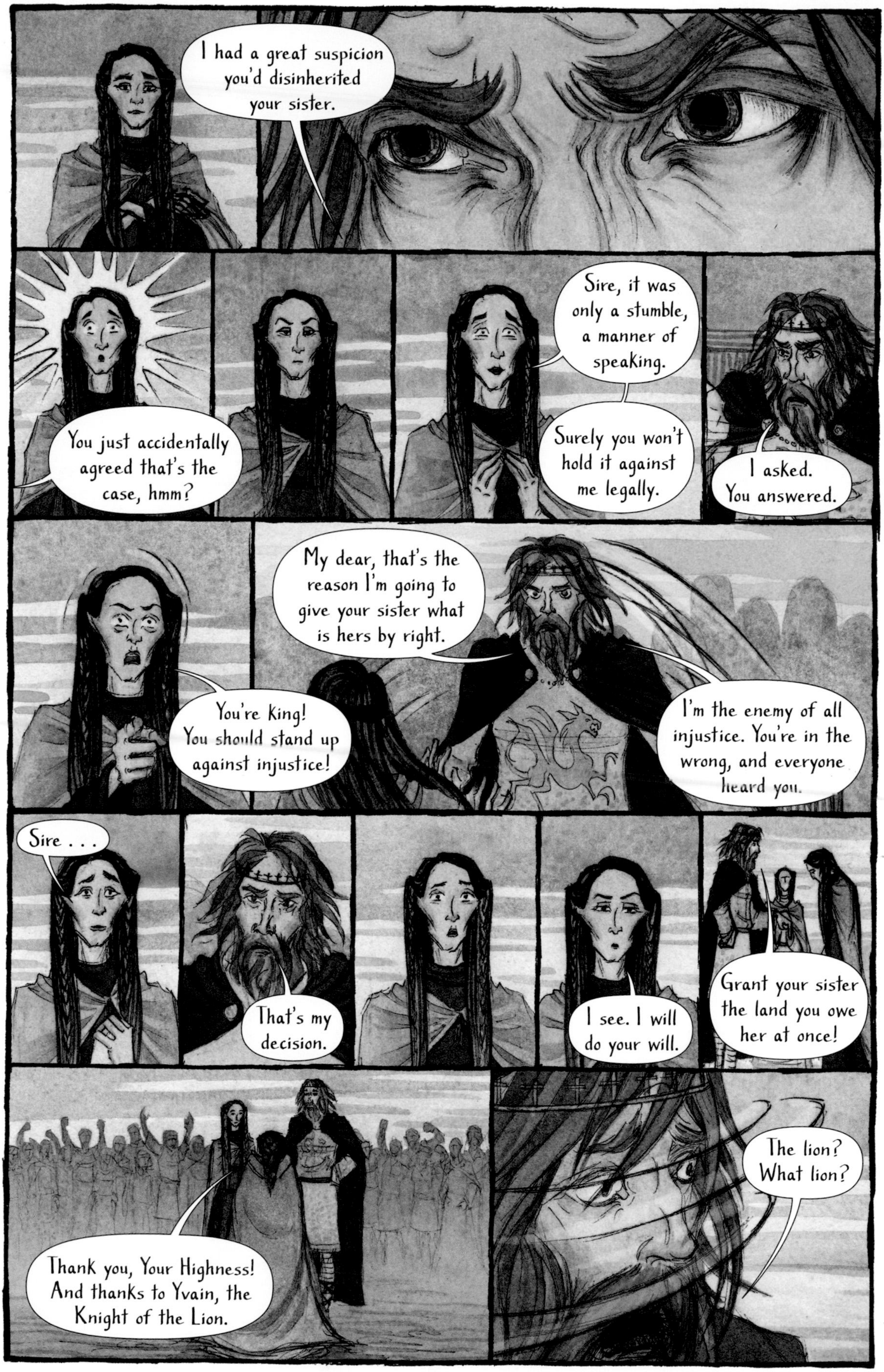
I had a great suspicion you'd disinherited your sister.
You just accidentally agreed that's the case, hmm?
Sire, it was only a stumble, a manner of speaking.
Surely you won't hold it against me legally.
I asked. You answered.
You're King! You should stand up against injustice!
My dear, that's the reason I'm going to give your sister what is hers by right.
I'm the enemy of all injustice. You're in the wrong, and everyone heard you.
Sire . . .
That's my decision.
I see. I will do your will.
Grant your sister the land you owe her at once!
Thank you, Your Highness! And thanks to Yvain, the Knight of the Lion.
The lion? What lion?

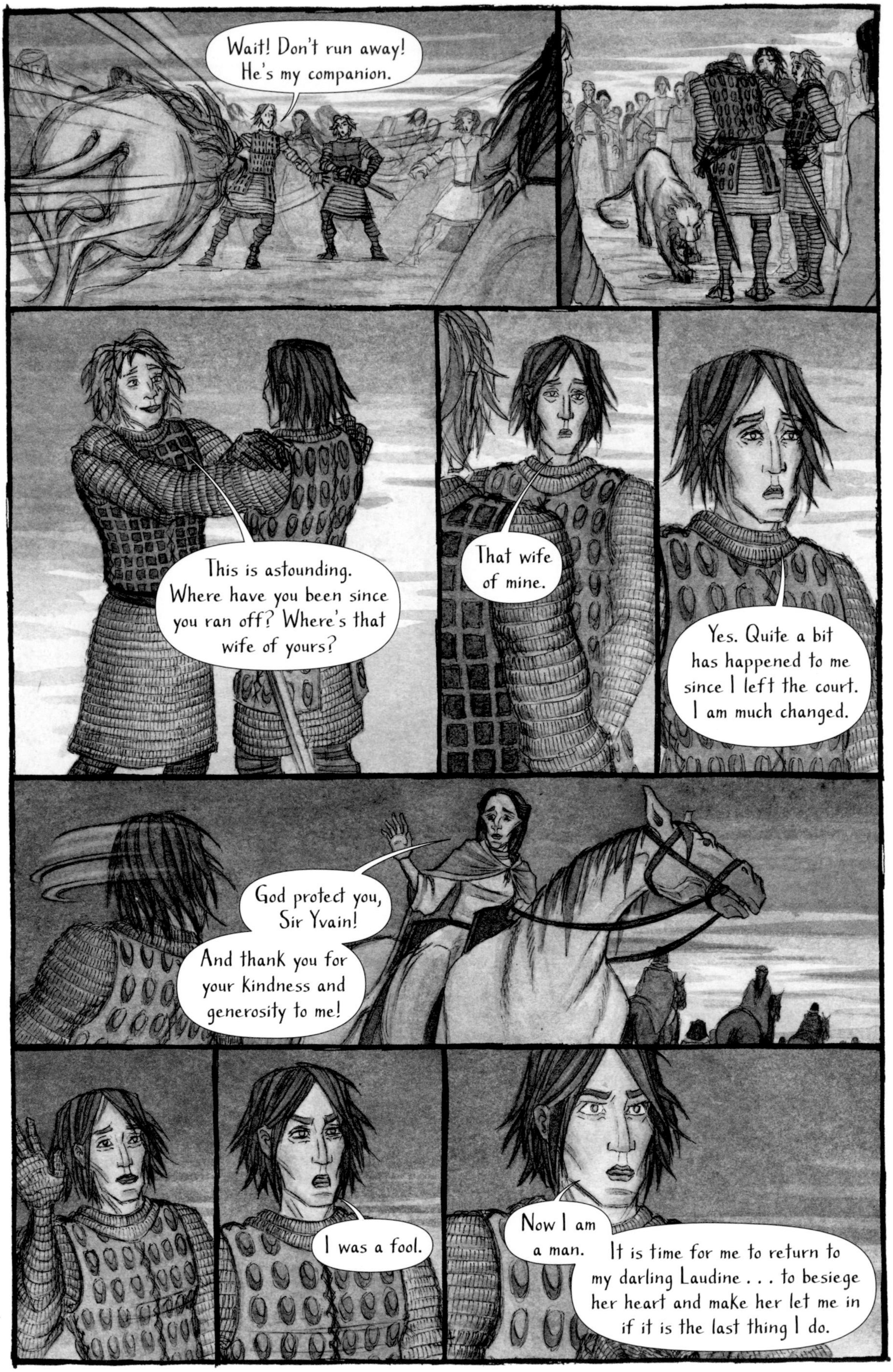
Wait! Don't run away! He's my companion.
This is astounding. Where have you been since you ran off? Where's that wife of yours?
That wife of mine.
Yes. Quite a bit has happened to me since I left the court. I am much changed.
God protect you, Sir Yvain!
And thank you for your kindness and generosity to me!
I was a fool.
Now I am a man.
It is time for me to return to my darling Laudine . . . to besiege her heart and make her let me in if it is the last thing I do.

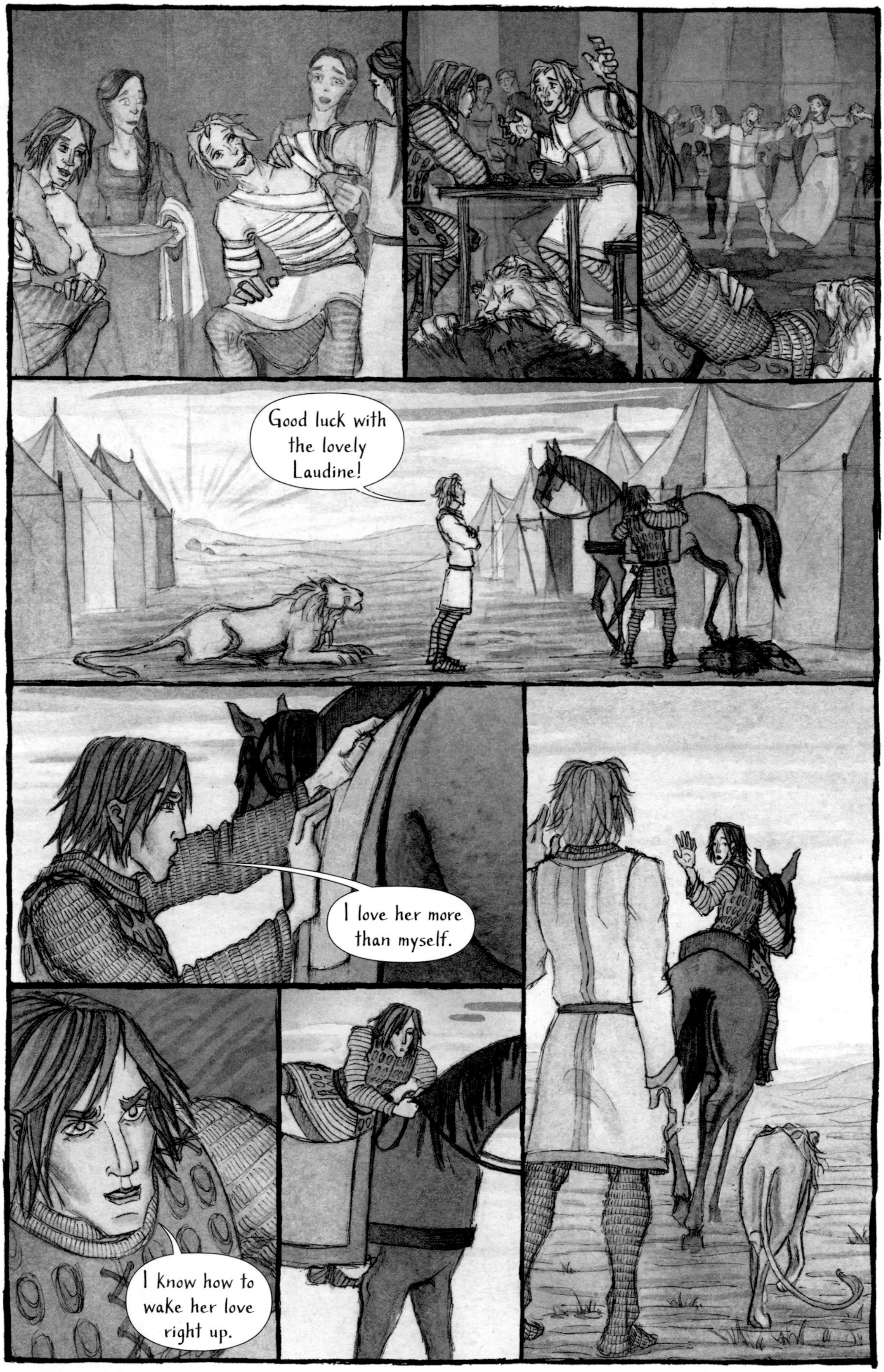
Good luck with the lovely Laudine!
I love her more than myself.
I know how to wake her love right up.

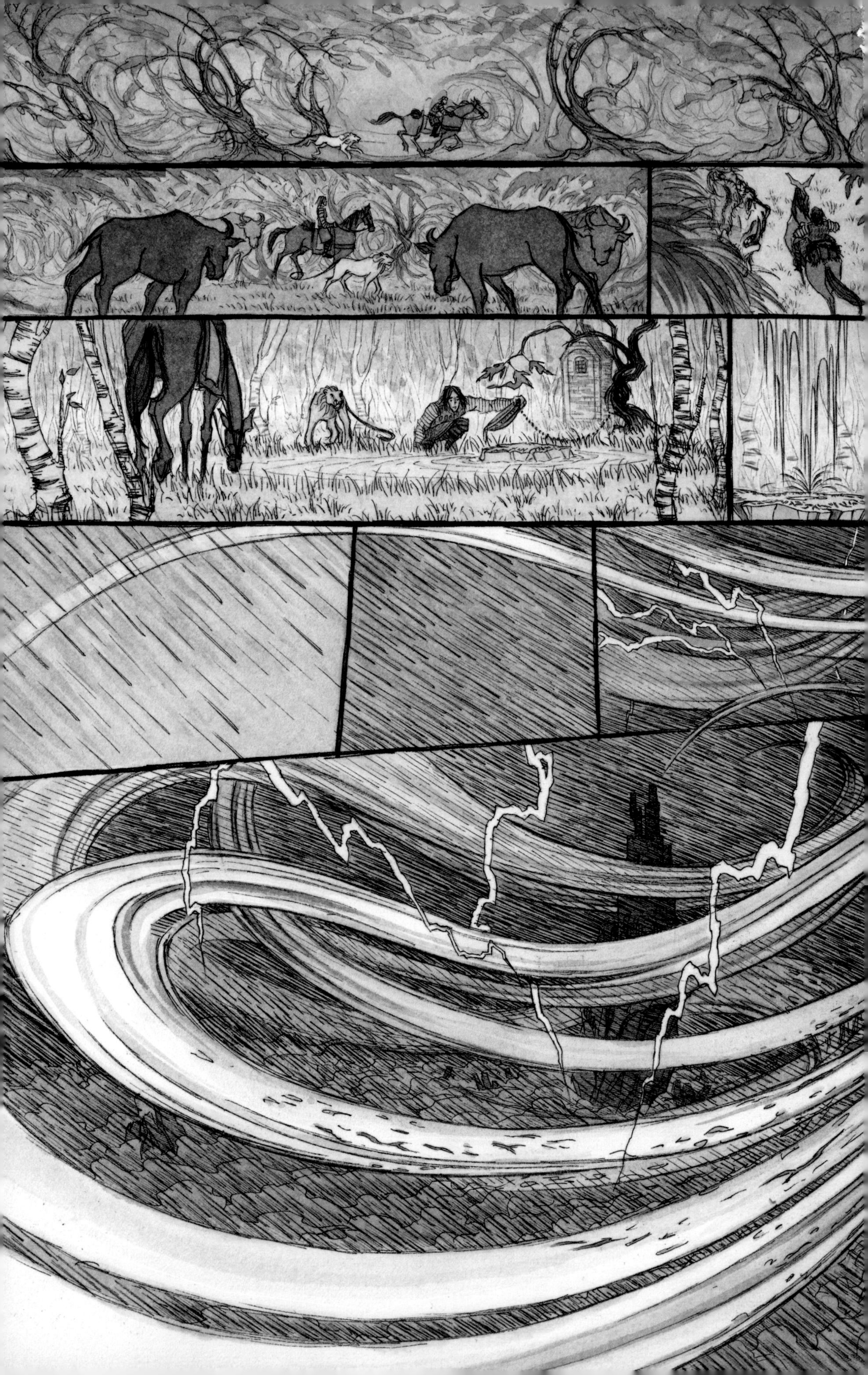

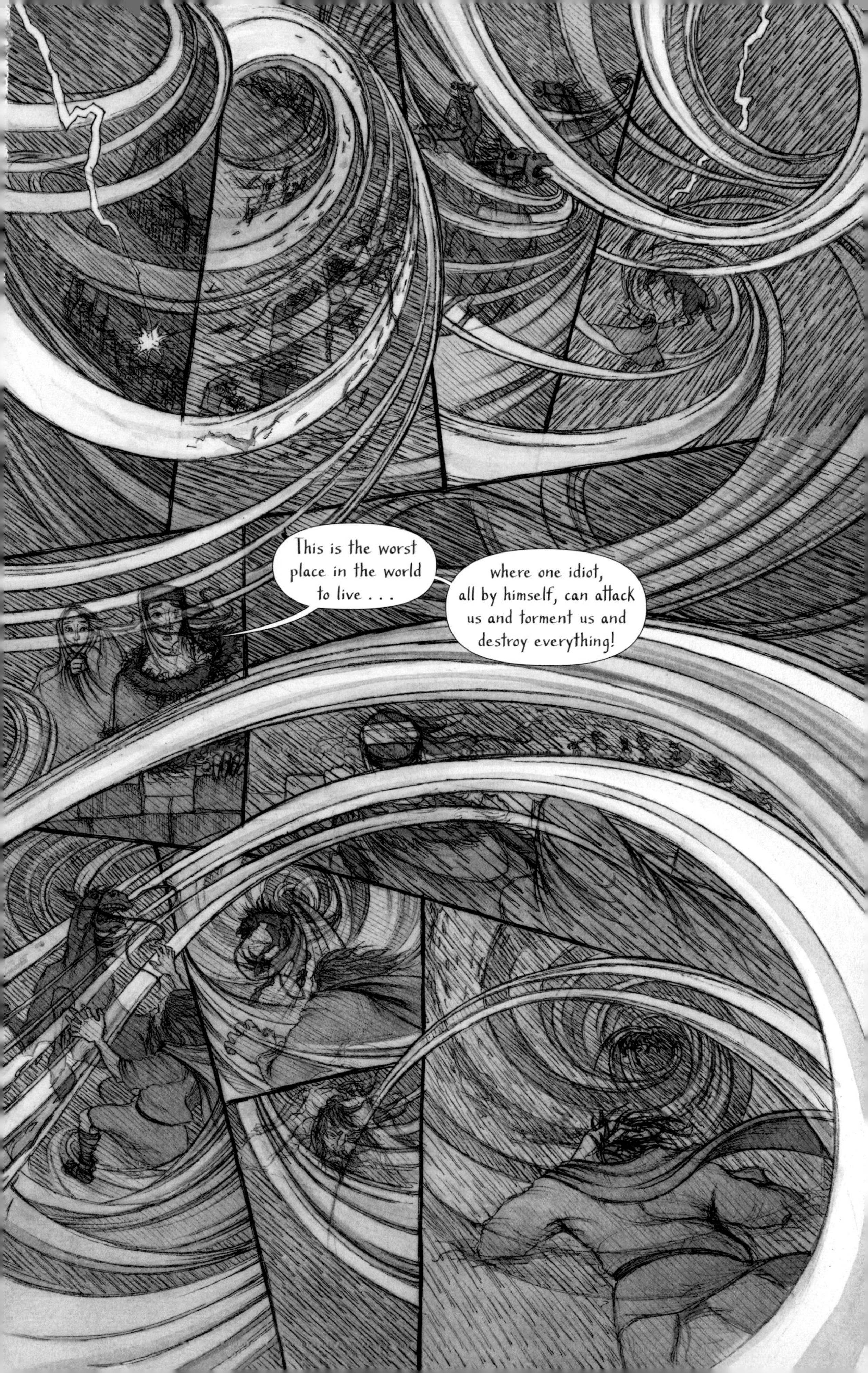
This is the worst place in the world to live . . .
where one idiot, all by himself, can attack us and torment us and destroy everything!

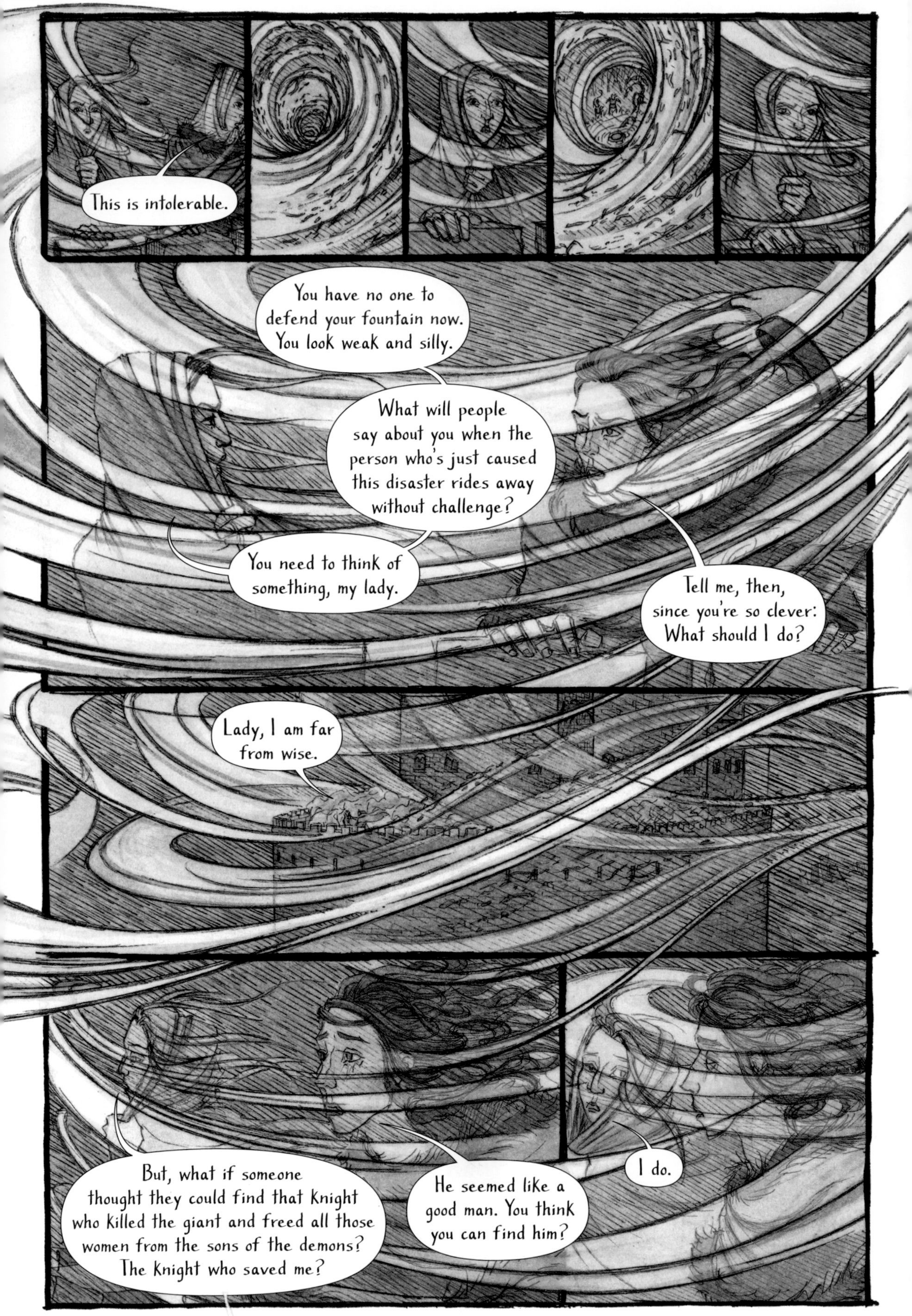
This is intolerable.
You have no one to defend your fountain now. You look weak and silly.
What will people say about you when the person who's just caused this disaster rides away without challenge?
You need to think of something, my lady.
Tell me, then, since you're so clever: What should I do?
Lady, I am far from wise.
But, what if someone thought they could find that knight who killed the giant and freed all those women from the sons of the demons? The knight who saved me?
He seemed like a good man. You think you can find him?
I do.

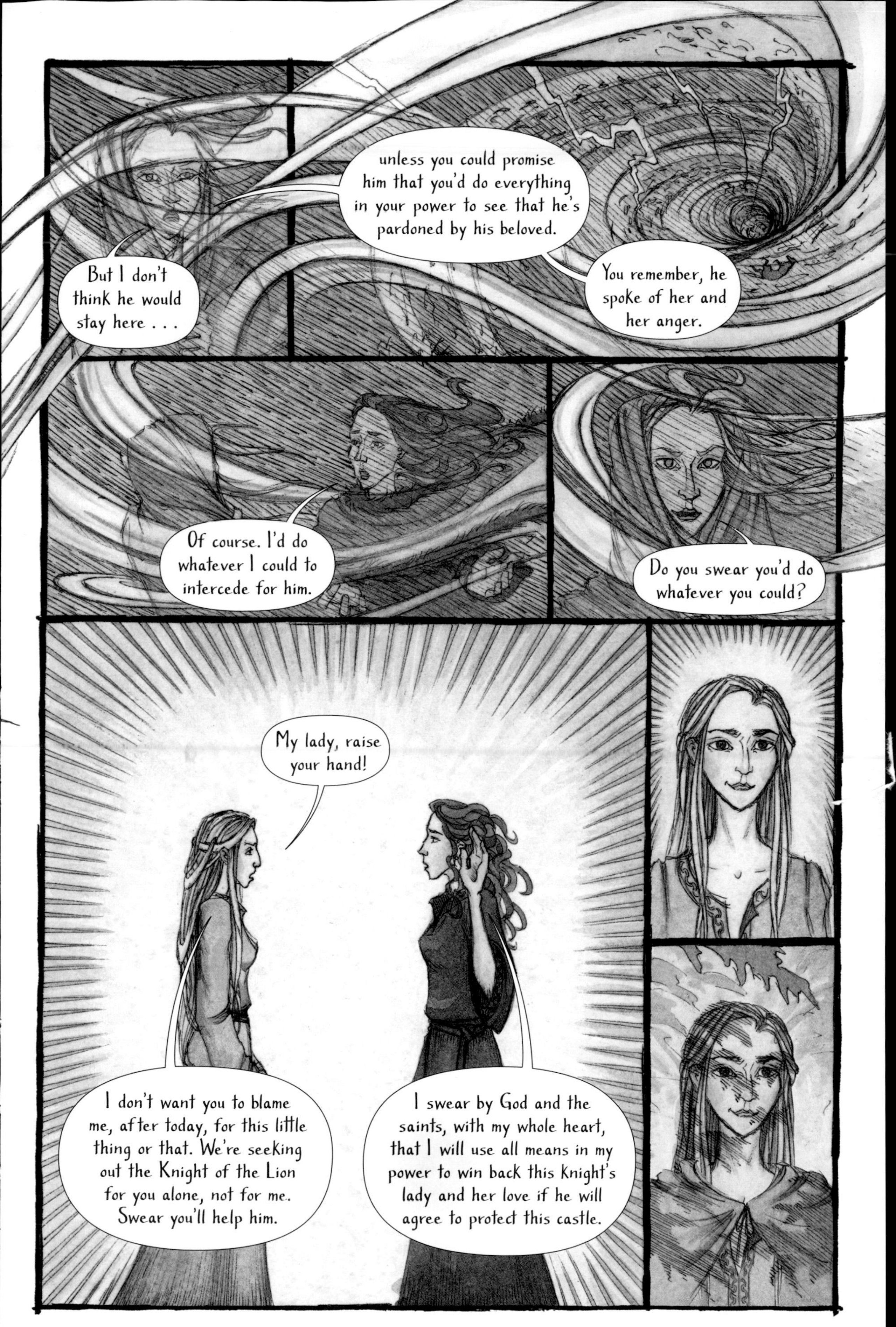
But I don't think he would stay here . . .
unless you could promise him that you'd do everything in your power to see that he's pardoned by his beloved.
You remember, he spoke of her and her anger.
Of course. I'd do whatever I could to intercede for him.
Do you swear you'd do whatever you could?
My lady, raise your hand!
I don't want you to blame me, after today, for this little thing or that. We're seeking out the Knight of the Lion for you alone, not for me. Swear you'll help him.
I swear by God and the saints, with my whole heart, that I will use all means in my power to win back this Knight's lady and her love if he will agree to protect this castle.

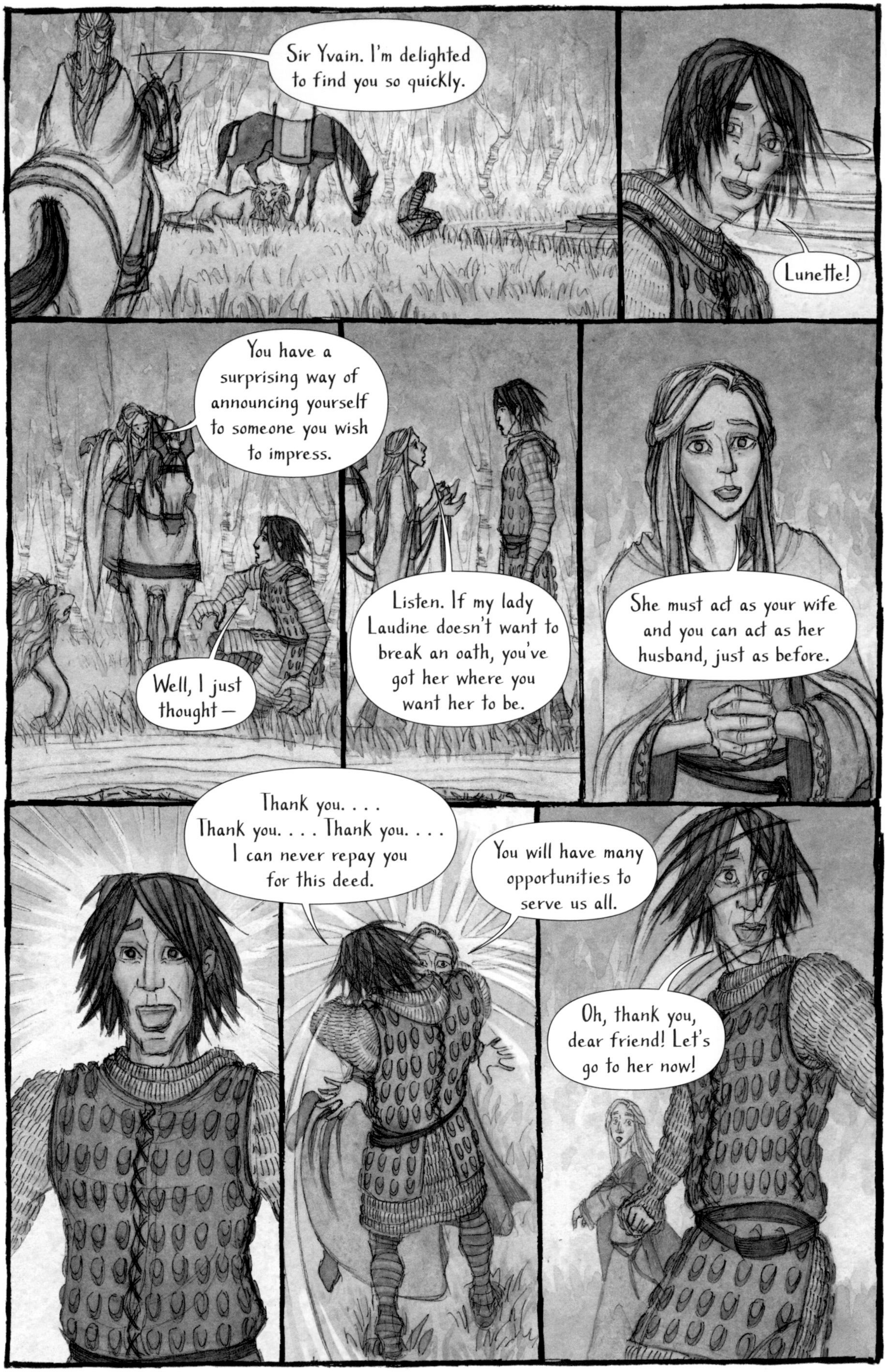
Sir Yvain. I'm delighted to find you so quickly.
Lunette!
You have a surprising way of announcing yourself to someone you wish to impress.
Well, I just thought—
Listen. If my lady Laudine doesn't want to break an oath, you've got her where you want her to be.
She must act as your wife and you can act as her husband, just as before.
Thank you. . . . Thank you. . . . Thank you. . . . I can never repay you for this deed.
You will have many opportunities to serve us all.
Oh, thank you, dear friend! Let's go to her now!

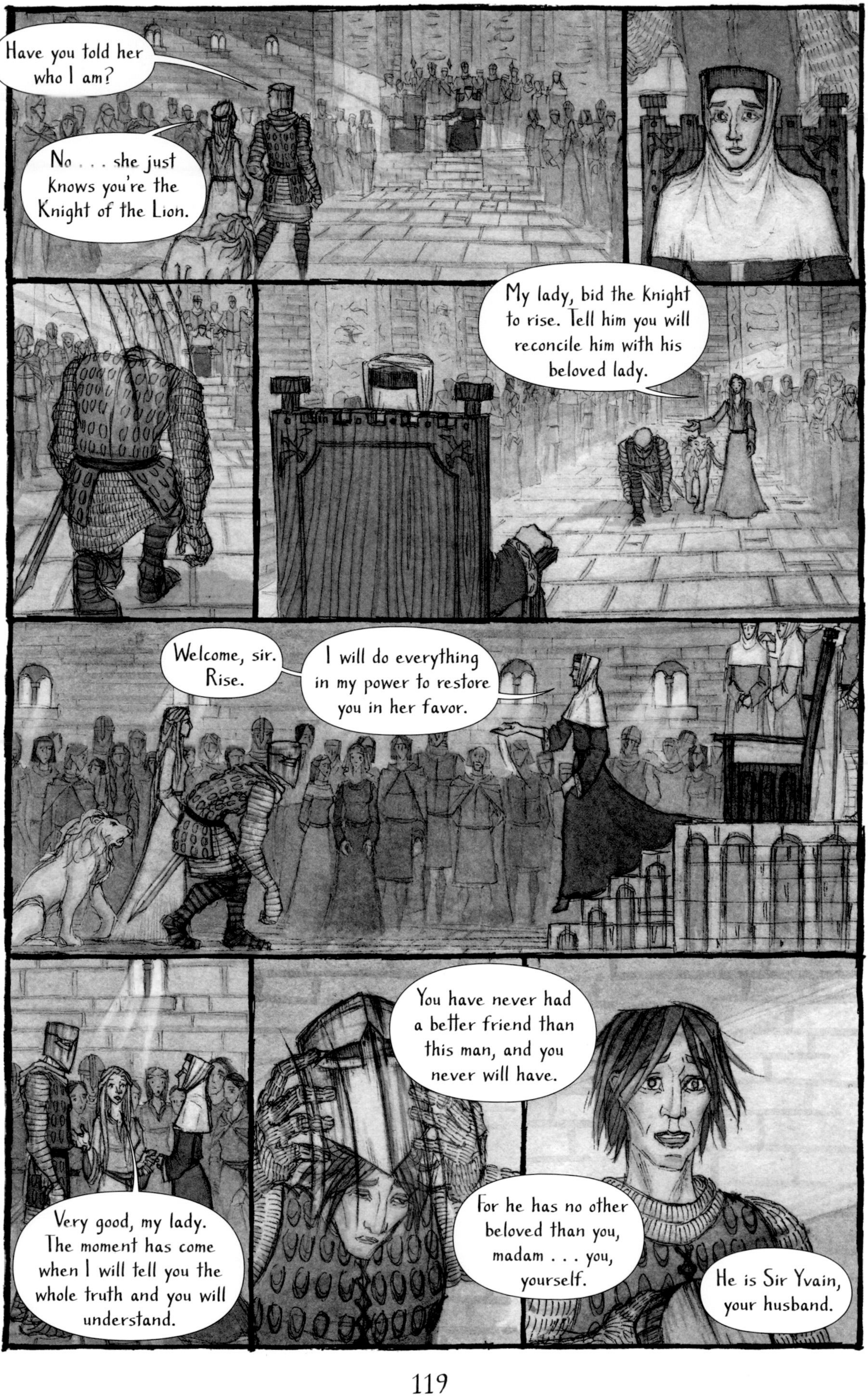
Have you told her who I am?
No . . . she just knows you're the Knight of the Lion.
My lady, bid the knight to rise. Tell him you will reconcile him with his beloved lady.
Welcome, sir. Rise.
I will do everything in my power to restore you in her favor.
Very good, my lady. The moment has come when I will tell you the whole truth and you will understand.
You have never had a better friend than this man, and you never will have.
For he has no other beloved than you, madam . . . you, yourself.
He is Sir Yvain, your husband.

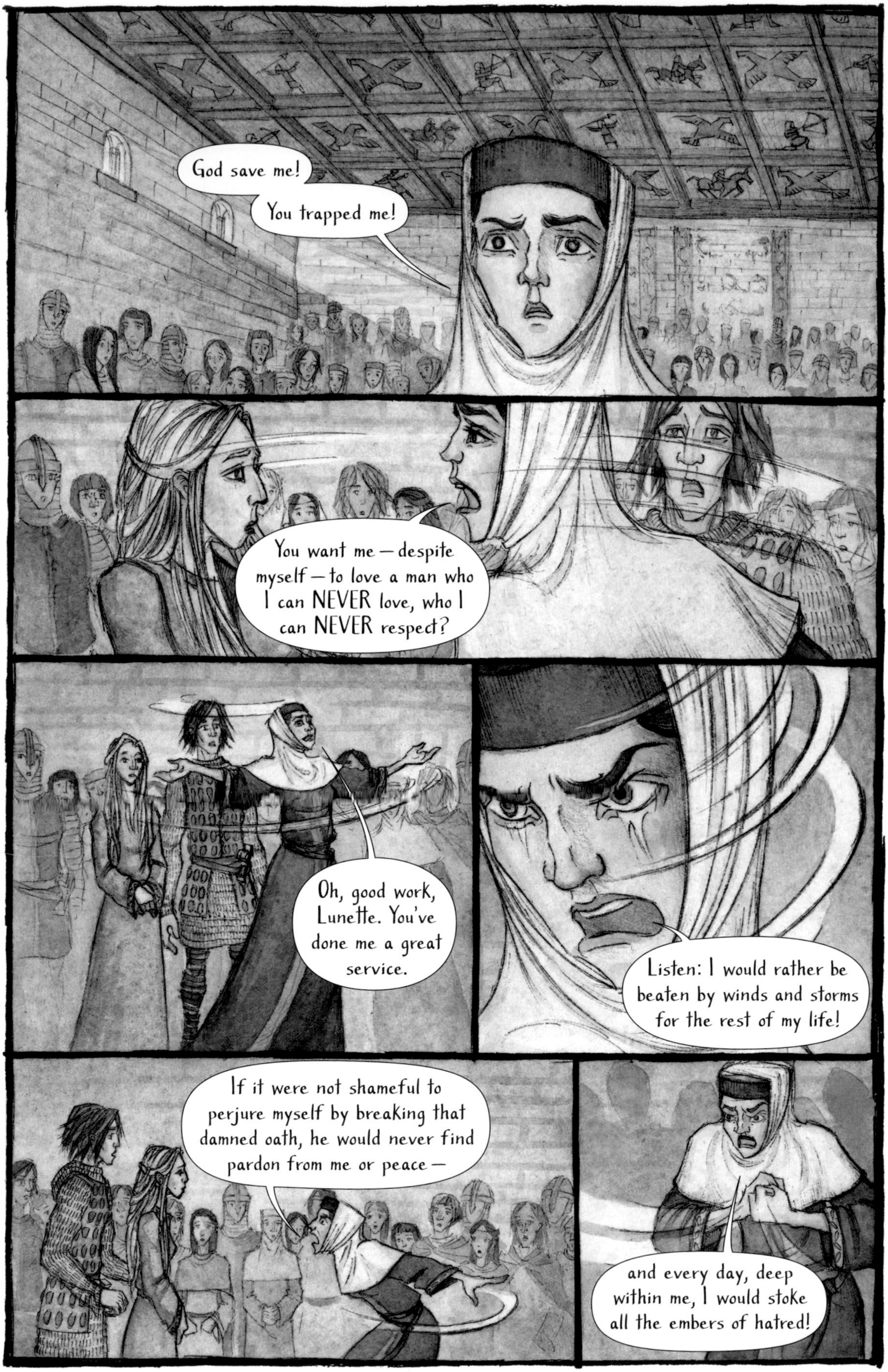
God save me!
You trapped me!
You want me — despite myself — to love a man who I can NEVER love, who I can NEVER respect?
Oh, good work, Lunette. You've done me a great service.
Listen: I would rather be beaten by winds and storms for the rest of my life!
If it were not shameful to perjure myself by breaking that damned oath, he would never find pardon from me or peace —
and every day, deep within me, I would stoke all the embers of hatred!

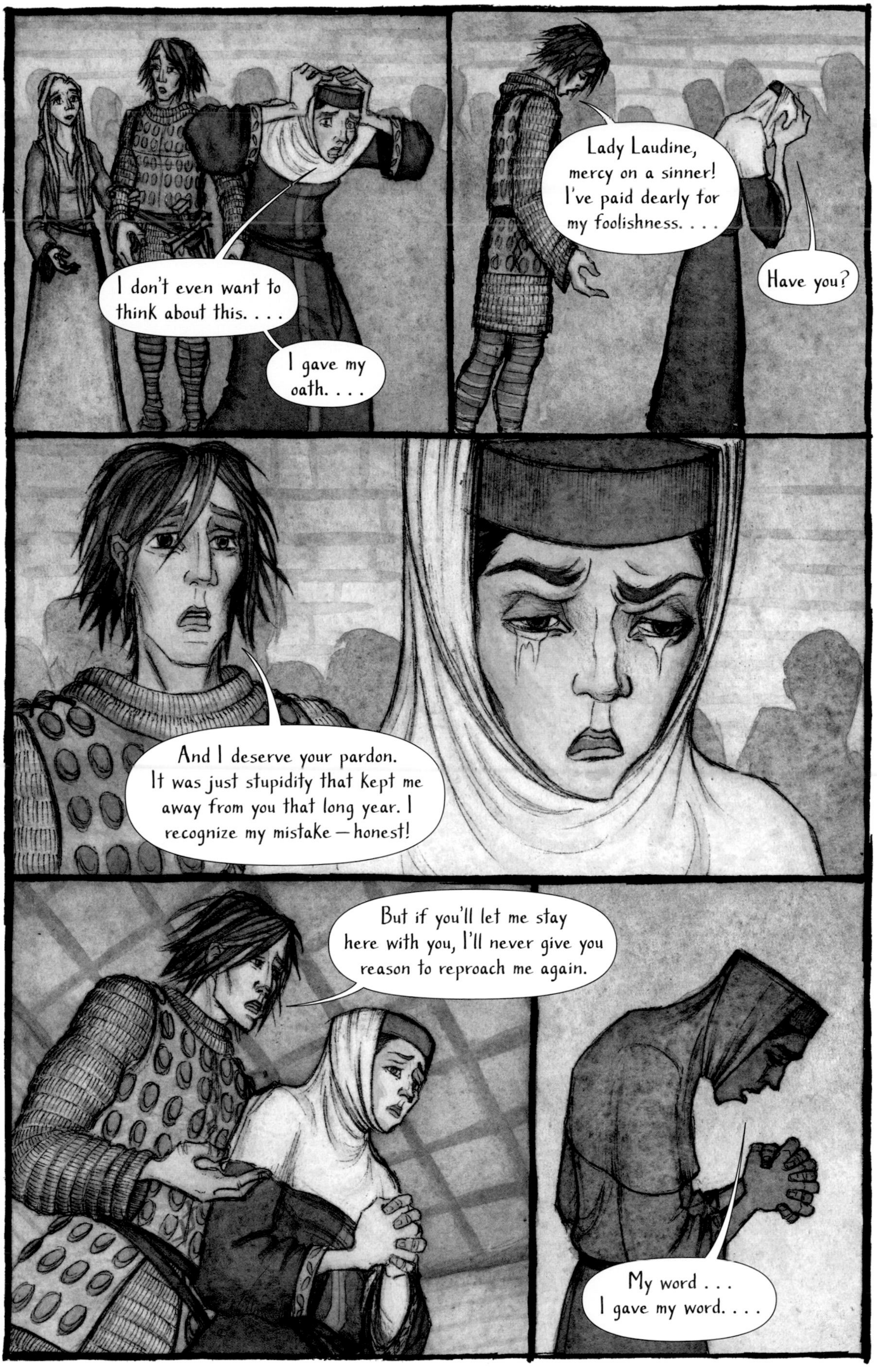
I don't even want to think about this. . . .
I gave my oath. . . .
Lady Laudine, mercy on a sinner! I've paid dearly for my foolishness. . . .
Have you?
And I deserve your pardon. It was just stupidity that kept me away from you that long year. I recognize my mistake — honest!
But if you'll let me stay here with you, I'll never give you reason to reproach me again.
My word . . . I gave my word. . . .

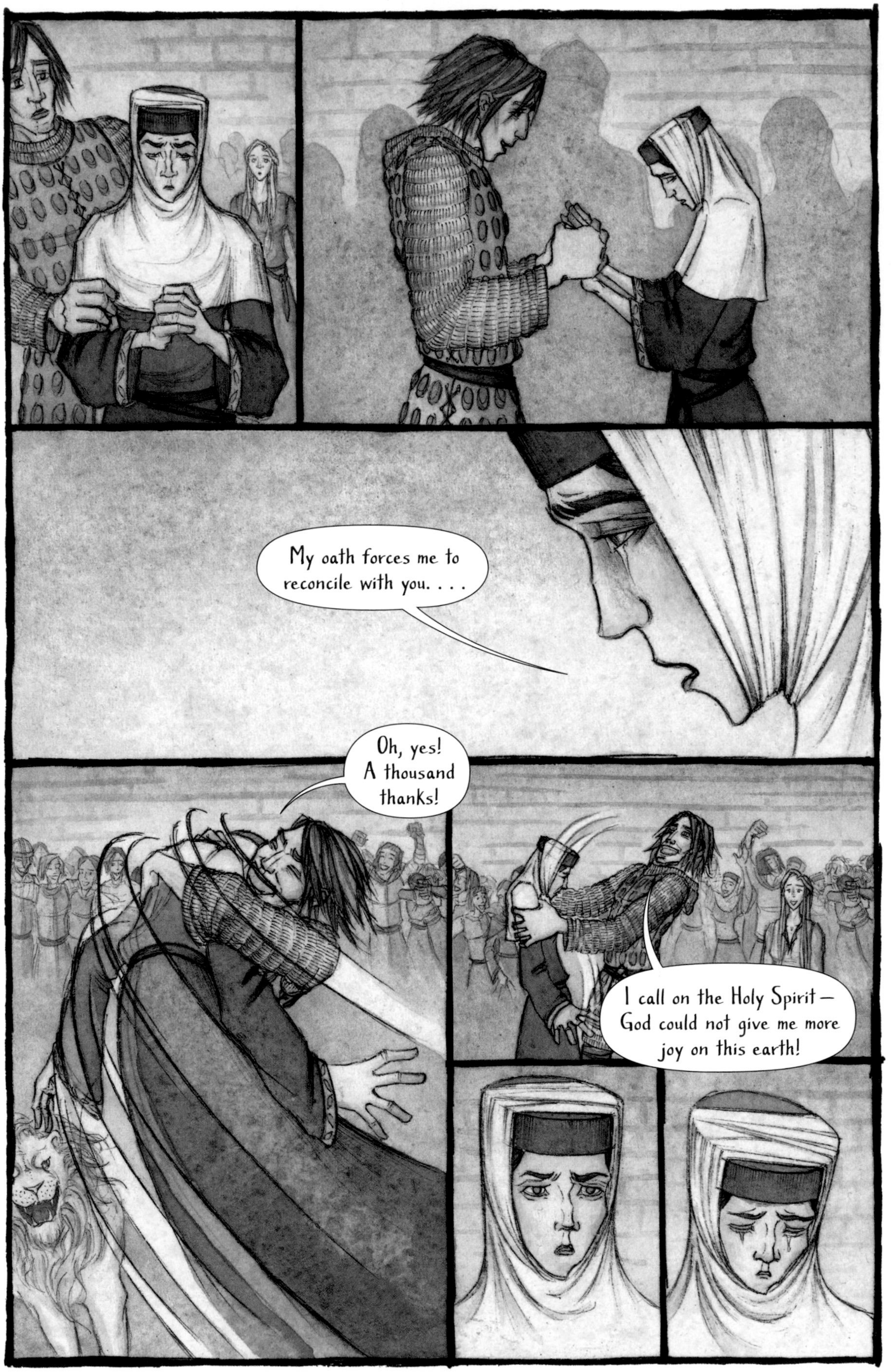
My oath forces me to reconcile with you. . . .
Oh, yes! A thousand thanks!
I call on the Holy Spirit— God could not give me more joy on this earth!

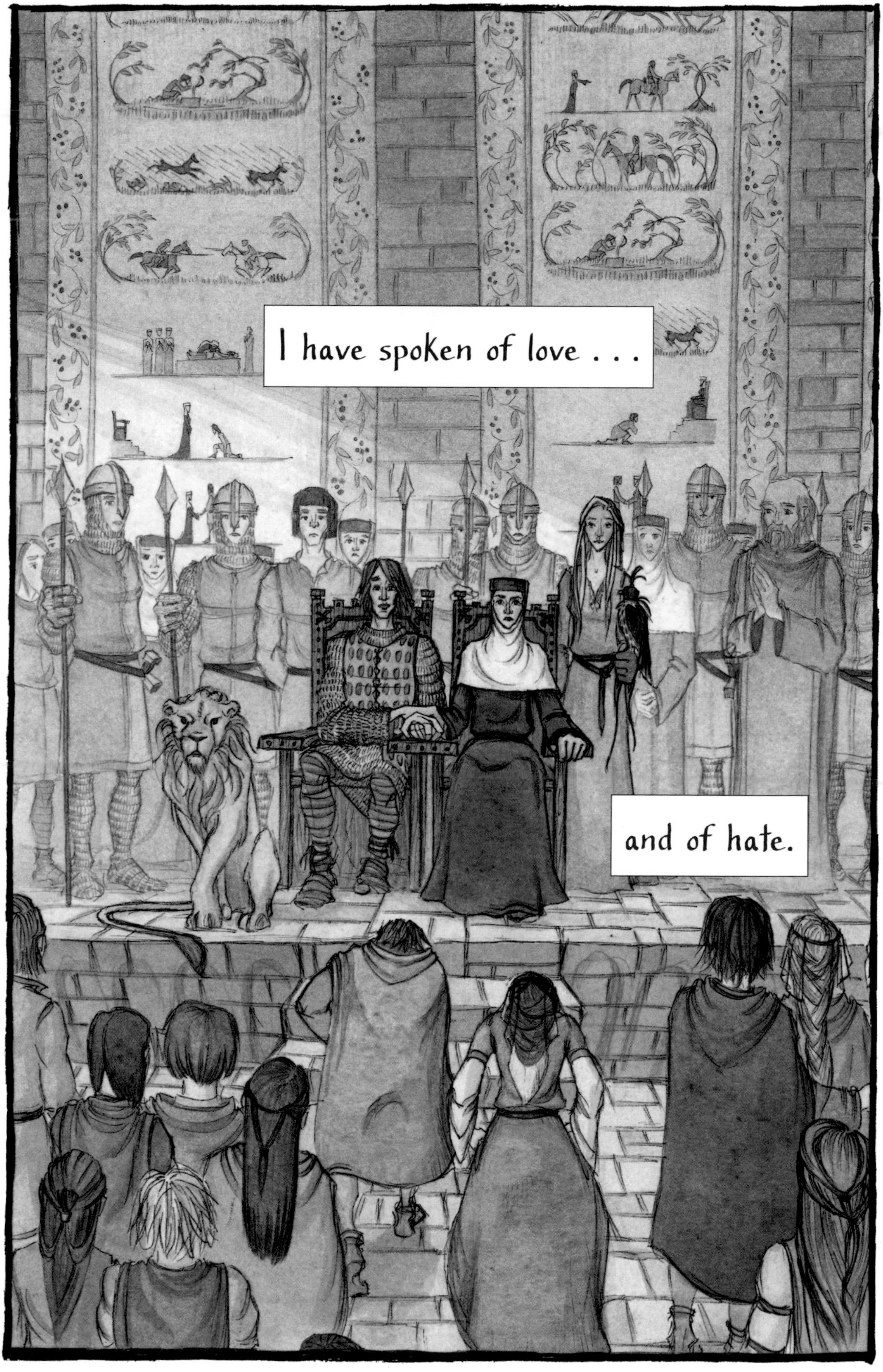
I have spoken of love . . .
and of hate.

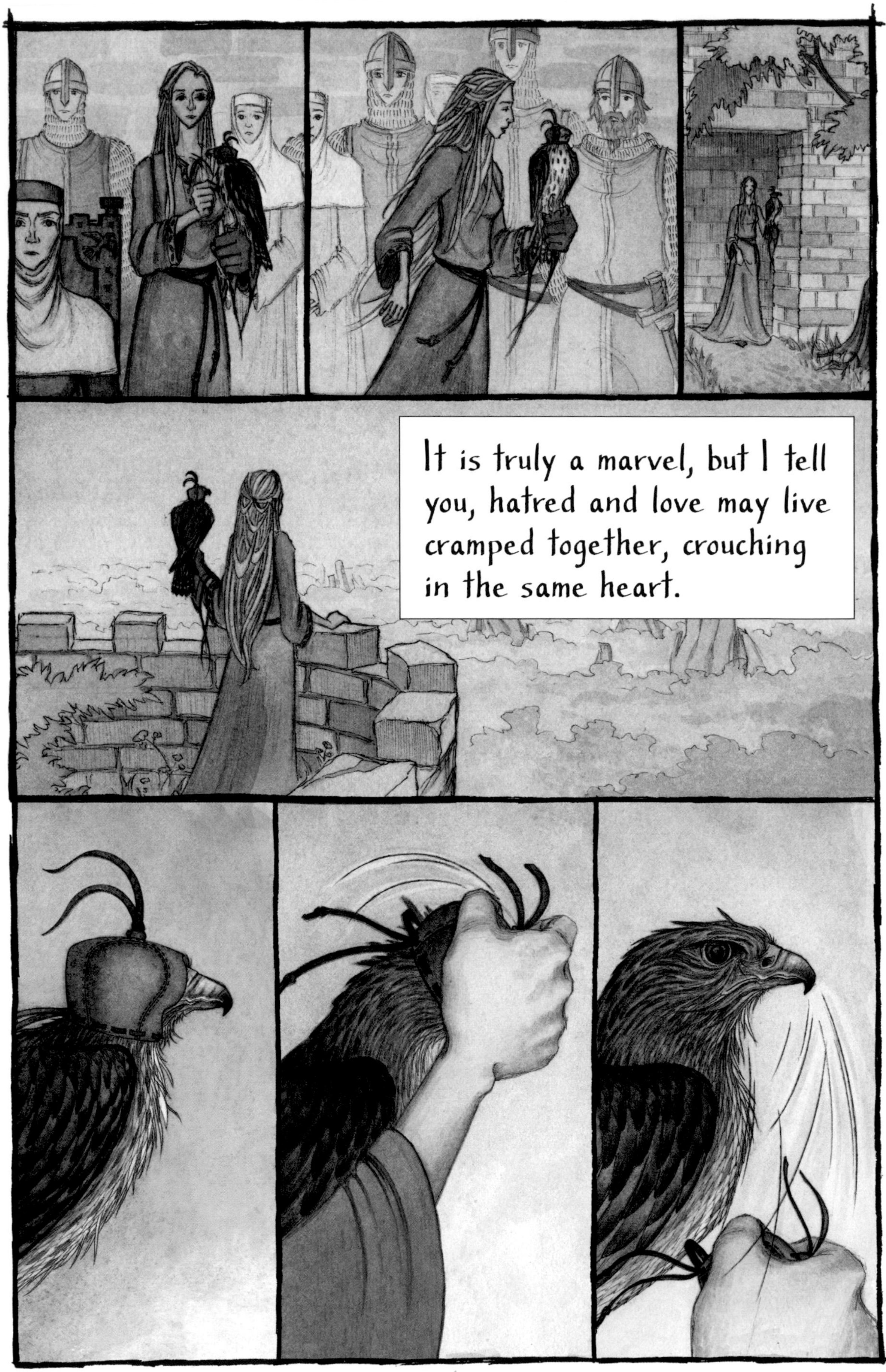
It is truly a marvel, but I tell you, hatred and love may live cramped together, crouching in the same heart.

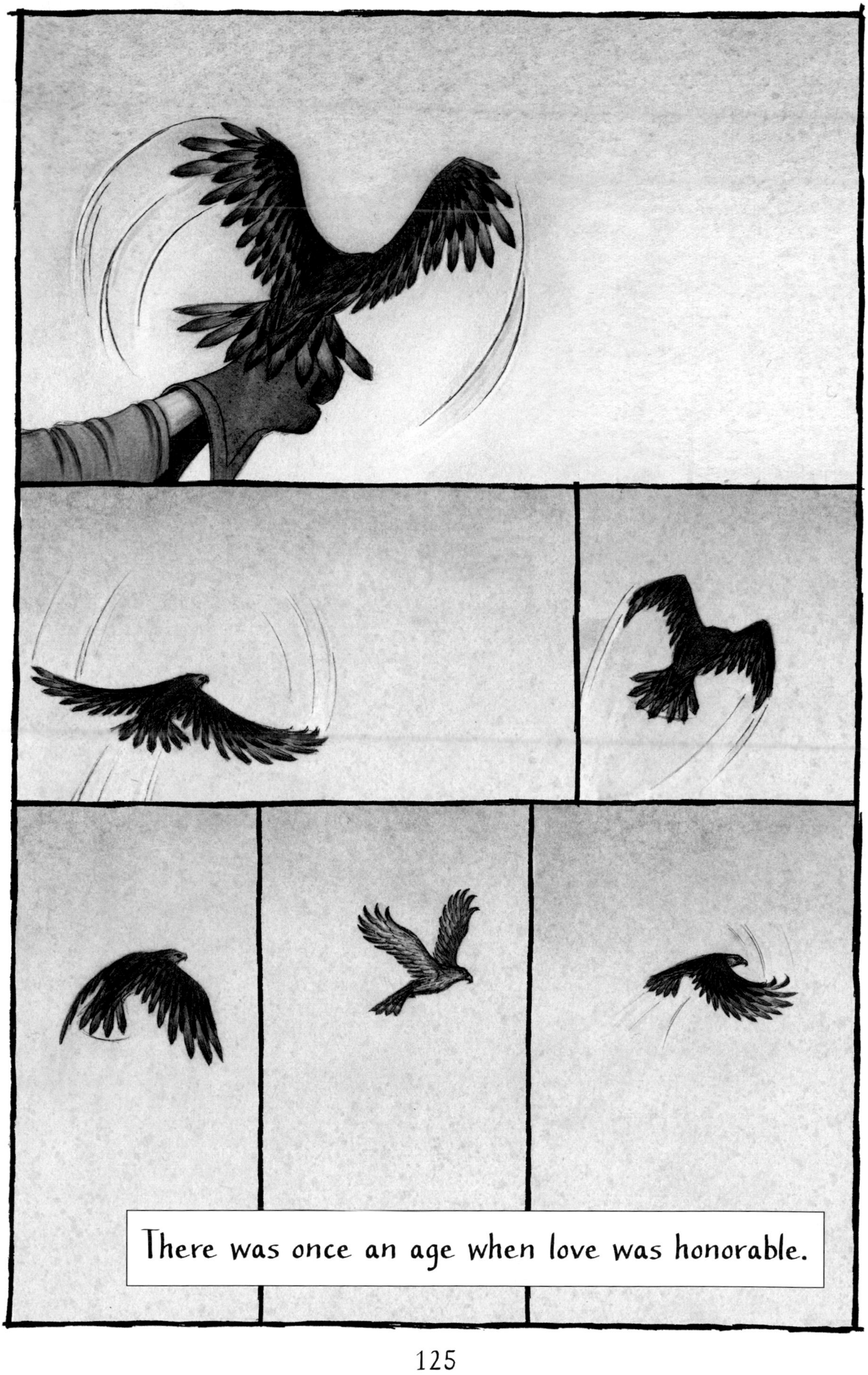
There was once an age when love was honorable.

Or so I've heard.

For Chrétien de Troyes
M. T. A.

For David
A. O.

First edition 2017

Library of Congress Catalog Card Number 2015943546
ISBN 978-0-7636-5939-4

16 17 18 19 20 21 CCP 10 9 8 7 6 5 4 3 2 1

Printed in Shenzhen, Guangdong, China

MIX
Paper from responsible sources
FSC www.fsc.org FSC® C008047

This book was typeset in WPG Southern Belle.
The illustrations were done in ink and watercolor and finished digitally.

Candlewick Press
99 Dover Street
Somerville, Massachusetts 02144

visit us at www.candlewick.com

This chain had to be constantly held with one hand; otherwise it would all slide down. An example of this can be seen in the sculptures at the west portal of Angers Cathedral in France, which hold the chains of their coats with one hand. The result was that you couldn't do much other than stand and pose. This attire did not seem fitting for the very strong and active noblewomen in this story. I therefore made the clothes a bit more practical and easier to move around in, to allow Laudine and Lunette especially the acting space their characters suggest.

Most of the clothing and armor I designed is similar for all characters to support the idea that they are part of the same world; they all have the same rules to abide by and very similar roles to play. However, I used color to reflect the individual characters and to clearly connect each figure with the location they belong to. When Yvain returns from his time in the forest, he is wearing a different set of armor to show that his understanding of his role as knight has changed. Lunette stands a little apart in dress and in color to reflect her enigmatic role.

Tapestries were widely used in castles for several reasons. They were both a status symbol and very practical: they could be rolled up and taken everywhere and would instantly transform an uninhabited place into a sort of home, adding familiarity through the well-known images and warmth through insulation. They were an important story-telling device at a time when books were rare and expensive and few people could read. Everybody could follow the images, if not the text woven on them. However, there still needed to be a storyteller to tie the images together into a narration. Therefore it seemed fitting to use tapestries in places where a character is telling a story within the story (for example, see pages 8–9 and 67) and as background elements that hint at past or upcoming events in the narrative. The tapestries also allowed me to tie the different locations together, so that despite their differences, they are all clearly part of the world Yvain moves in. Lastly, I like that tapestries are early forerunners of comics, and thus I could pay homage to the storytelling medium I love so much.

The original ballad by Chrétien de Troyes is written in verse, developing from the oral tradition where stories were told or sung to an audience. I wanted to reference the rhythm in the original text by picking up certain rhythmic elements in the placement of panels on the page (see the dialogue of Yvain and Laudine on pages 36–39 or the fight scenes on pages 95–97 and 102–109). The fight scenes especially allowed me to play with choreography, timing, and viewpoints that enhance the story's rhythmic quality and create a melodious sequence of images to honor the origins of Chrétien's story.

This graphic novel has been a great challenge and a wonderful project to work on. I would like to thank Jens R. Nielsen for his advice and resources on medieval text, art, and all things graphic novel, and Daria Fernandez Dagach for her support and critical eye. Thank you to Sherry Fatla and everybody at Candlewick Press for always striving to make this book even more beautiful and extraordinary. And most important, thank you to my family, David and Elsa Ainhoa, for going on this adventure with me.

ILLUSTRATOR'S NOTE

It might seem surprising that this "illumination" of *Yvain: The Knight of the Lion* starts and ends with a falcon. Medieval readers would have made a direct connection between these images and the words on the pages because, at the time, the falcon symbolized love and the soul. However, a modern reader would see the falcon as representing power, freedom, and victory. This contradiction creates a tension that establishes the irony and ambiguity with which Chrétien de Troyes describes his tale from the start.

When creating the artwork for this graphic novel, I focused on imagery, like the falcon, which symbolically captures both the real and imaginary of Chrétien's world. The character and circumstances of the bird itself are also significant: a complicated, proud, wild creature is tamed and trained, its natural hunting behavior curbed for the artifice of sport. At the time, noble men and women lived lives bound by obligations and decorum. They were often forced to suppress their true character and check their passions. In his introduction, Chrétien uses the term "honorable love," and then moves on to unveil the absurd and contradictory actions the figures have to take in his story to fulfill the rules of honorable behavior. It seems to me that quite a few of Chrétien's characters would have related to the image of the falcon.

Castles in medieval tales served as a safe place in which the story could move forward, as opposed to the outside world, where danger lurked around every corner and no complicated interaction between characters could unfold. My designs for the castles in this story are all based on existing buildings: the sweatshop castle is modeled in part after the beautiful Alhambra, in Spain; the castle in the woods was inspired by Guédelon, in France, among other castles; and parts of Laudine's castle and its surrounding forest were influenced by those in Saxon Switzerland.

In the twelfth century, castles were rather simple in layout, built mostly from wood with one strong stone building or tower, which housed the main hall. The castles I designed for *Yvain* are much more elaborate. They reflect the characters living there and the scenes taking place. Laudine's castle is a labyrinth of stairs and rooms; it is impossible to figure out the layout of the place. Yet the building sits high on a rock overlooking her land. Despite her complicated emotions, Laudine (with the help of Lunette) can clearly see the actions she has to take in order to protect herself and her people. In contrast, the sweatshop castle is divided into the part where the slaves are kept and the part where the family lives, symbolizing the clear division of good and evil Chrétien describes at this place. Both parts are enclosed by a thick wall to show how detached they are from the real world outside. Once Yvain enters the castle, it is as if he had stepped into a dream — or rather, a nightmare.

To design clothes and armor, I referenced church sculptures, illuminated scripts such as the Codex Manesse, and tapestries such as the famous Bayeux tapestry. Courtly attire at Chrétien's time was rather complicated, especially for noblewomen. There was lots and lots of fabric held loosely together, topped by a coat that was fastened by a chain.

he creates two wonderfully outspoken women, both clever and politically astute: the lady Laudine and her sorcerous servant, Lunette. They are trapped in a world of Old Boy adventurism, forced to manipulate bumptious menfolk — and each other — in order to secure what they need. Chrétien wrote the poem while in the employ of just such a woman: Marie de Champagne, daughter of the powerful Eleanor of Aquitaine. (Eleanor was once married to the king of France, and decided he was too dull; she divorced him and married the king of England instead.) Perhaps this accounts for the fact that Chrétien allows Laudine, for example, to express fury at the "happy" outcome of the romance, as she submits to Yvain's will out of political and military necessity, rather than out of love.

Yvain himself comes off looking surprisingly obtuse and unaware of his true love's hatred for him. As commentators have pointed out, on one level, there's a pat, moralizing structure to the story: Yvain moves from being a self-involved seeker after his own fame and glory to being an anonymous knight who fights for the good of others. But Yvain's transformation is strangely contradicted at the last minute by his decision to woo his lost Laudine by wrecking her castle again. She's not so much convinced as blackmailed. And Chrétien does nothing to hide this. It's likely that in Chrétien's world, in which noble marriage was often political and had nothing to do with affection, readers found this conclusion a bit less surprising than we do now — but Chrétien still gives voice to Laudine's white-hot anger, the anger, we might imagine, of many women of the period. In many ways the poem is about a confrontation between the world of women and the world of men (the friendship of Yvain and his cousin Gawain) — a chivalric contest, as it were, between romance and bromance.

This irony and deft characterization is what makes Chrétien's epic romances worth reading, something more than musty books from a long-lost age: not just the giants, the dragons, the bridges of knives, the perilous beds that spit darts — but the ambiguities of how people act, how they try to be moral, how they fail, and how they carry on regardless.

When I visited the Fountain of Barenton, I of course, being a man, couldn't resist pouring water on the weather stone. About four minutes later, it started softly to rain. Maybe the wood and the spring retain some of their ancient magic. But the skies were often overcast, and in Brittany, rain never seems that far away.

Sources: For this translation/adaptation, I used Michel Rousse's edition of the Old French original (Paris: GF-Flammarion, 1990). Almost all of the text in this graphic novel is drawn directly from Chrétien's original. For clarifications, I consulted the following English translations: Ruth Harwood Cline (Athens, Georgia: University of Georgia Press, 1975); David Staines (Bloomington: Indiana University Press, 1990); and an anonymous medieval translation, "Ywain and Gawain," in Medieval English Romances, Part 2, *ed. by A.V.C. Schmidt (London: Hodder & Stoughton, 1980).*

AUTHOR'S NOTE

The magical pool deep in the wood of Brocéliande is real; I have visited it. It is a natural spring, the Fountain of Barenton, which lies deep within what is now known as the forest of Paimpont in Brittany, the westernmost part of France. This fountain boils even when cold (as a result of nitrogen bubbles) and supposedly summons rain when rituals are performed over the stone at its head. It is also said that the Lady of the Lake dwelled in a pond a few miles away, and that Merlin was trapped by his lover in a tomb nearby. The enchantress Morgan le Fay was believed to imprison unfaithful lovers in a local valley. It's a mystical landscape, even today. The moors and woodlands of Brittany are studded with standing stones, castles, and ancient chapels erected to dragon-slaying saints. Unfortunately, much of the forest of Paimpont was cleared in the nineteenth century as fuel for iron-smelting furnaces. No one has performed the ritual to summon rain since a delegation sent during a drought in 1954.

Chrétien de Troyes, the author of *Yvain, le chevalier au lion,* wrote his tale almost eight centuries ago. He took fragments of Celtic stories that were even older, things half remembered from the age of British paganism; he wove them together and embroidered them, lacing them with golden threads of the sophisticated court life of his own day. They became some of the most influential stories in Europe. Almost all the tales we tell of King Arthur and his court are derived from Chrétien's epic poems.

Chrétien was the first author we know of to describe Sir Lancelot's adulterous passion for Queen Guinevere; the first to narrate the quest for a Holy Grail; the first to mention the castle of Camelot (though for him, it was no special place). We don't know how much Chrétien invented and how much he borrowed. We do know that his work was quickly imitated all over Europe, and seems to have started a vogue for depicting Arthur's reign as an era of mythic heroism, rather than as the muddy and hardscrabble rule of a warrior-chieftain on a Viking-sacked isle.

What's surprising, therefore, is the irony and subtlety of Chrétien's depiction. Arthur himself is no hero. He's a little dense and occasionally even incompetent. Like the kings of Chrétien's era, he spends most of his time roaming from one side of his realm to the other, holding feasts to secure the support of his barons — but it is his Knights of the Round Table who actually sally forth and who have all the adventures.

In Chrétien's day, the king of England ruled more of France than the king of France did. This is reflected in the shape of Arthur's realm in *Yvain:* The story starts at a castle on the border of England and Wales. The knights ride off on their horses to Brocéliande, the mythical wood in Brittany, in what is now France. There is, apparently, no need for a boat to cross the English Channel. The two countries are one. This is a geography of legend.

One of the things that drew me to this story is Chrétien's searing, ironic treatment of the role of women in this highly masculine, honor-based, chivalric society. In *Yvain,*

♦

POSTSCRIPT

Here I, Chrétien, end the romance of
the Knight of the Lion. There is nothing
more to know of the story; and if you
hear more, it is lies. So the story closes.
It was copied by Guiot, whose shop lies
beside the church of Our Lady of the
Valley. It was translated into the
vulgar tongue of the English by
Tobin of Vermont, and
illuminations were drawn by
Andrea of Hamburg.
God have mercy upon them all.

♦